small miracles

EDWARD M. LERNER

small miracles

A TOM DOHERTY ASSOCIATES BOOK
NEW YORK

This is a work of fiction. All of the characters, organizations, and events portrayed in this novel are either products of the author's imagination or are used fictitiously.

SMALL MIRACLES

A Tor Book
Published by Tom Doherty Associates, LLC
175 Fifth Avenue
New York, NY 10010

www.tor-forge.com

Tor® is a registered trademark of Tom Doherty Associates, LLC.

Design by Greg Collins

Library of Congress Cataloging-in-Publication Data

Lerner, Edward M.
    Small miracles / Edward M. Lerner.—1st ed.
        p.   cm.
    "A Tom Doherty Associates book."
    ISBN 978-0-7653-2094-0
    1. Nanotechnology—Fiction.   I. Title.
    PS3562.E726S63   2009
    813'.54—dc22

                                     2009019455

First Edition: October 2009

Printed in the United States of America

0 9 8 7 6 5 4 3 2 1

preface and acknowledgments

Small Miracles is a novel of medical nanotechnology.

Nanotech deals with science and engineering at a very small scale (one nanometer = one billionth of a meter), but "small" fails to do the subject justice. Traditional manufacturing, even of the tiniest microchips, manipulates matter in bulk. We are not as far removed as we might like to believe from chipping our tools out of chunks of flint. Nanotech, in contrast, involves the arrangement of matter with atom-by-atom precision. At least nanotech *will* do that; this is a technology very much in its infancy.

But the baby is growing up quickly. . . .

And medical nanotech? In the near future, complex machines smaller than individual biological cells—and with the potential, therefore, to access, diagnose, and treat any cell in our bodies—will revolutionize medical practice. I defer to the story for examples. And surprises.

Doing research for this novel, I attended the conference Productive Nanosystems: Launching the Technology Roadmap. For two days I immersed myself in the theory, practice, and likely evolution of nanotech, presented by experts from academia, government laboratories, and industry. Emergent technologies often draw upon more established disciplines. Nanotech is no exception, with practitioners schooled in physics, computer science, chemistry, biology, and engineering.

Conference participants graciously shared their time and insights before, between, and after conference sessions. My appreciation and thanks go to everyone involved in this most informative event—too many, alas, to credit individually. That said, I will single out one: Dr. K. Eric Drexler, a pioneer and leader in the field. I especially appreciate his books, which began my interest in nanotech, and his in-depth answers to my questions.

For medical aspects of the story, I had the good fortune to consult experts in biology, biophysics, medicine, neurology, and psychology. I am grateful for their insights, knowledge, and experience, and the patience to share so much with me. Thanks to:

Jeffrey Barth, Ph.D., University of Virginia
Jason Cooper, M.D.
Barbekka Hurtt, Ph.D., Rocky Vista University
Marc Mangel, Ph.D., University of California Santa Cruz
Diane Mayland, M.D.
Richard Robinson, Ph.D., Columbia University
Henry G. Stratmann, M.D.

On the subjects of police and hospital procedure, my thanks go, respectively, to Sgt. Jeff Bowerman of the Frederick County (Virginia) Sheriff's Office and Karen Bowerman, physician assistant at the Martinsburg (West Virginia) Veterans Administration hospital.

Where the novel gets the details right, credit goes to the experts. Responsibility for all extrapolations, errors, simplifications, and fictional license lies with the author.

My appreciation also goes to Bob Gleason, my editor, for encouraging me to take on a near-future nanotech novel, and to Eleanor Wood, my agent, for her support.

Last but certainly not least, I thank my first and favorite reader: my wife, Ruth. As always, she helped me keep the story's focus on the people rather than the technology. (The characters, if they could, would thank her, too.)

EDWARD M. LERNER

contents

sowing

thursday, july 23, 2015

A blue-and-white squad car, number 343, idled near the garage exit at Angleton police headquarters. The driver, its lone occupant, looked pissed.

"You could just shoot me," Brent offered.

"Too much paperwork. Get in the cruiser."

Brent reached through an open window to unlock the front passenger door. He dropped into the bucket seat, its black vinyl cracked. He shut the car door and offered his hand. "Brent Cleary, from Garner Nanotechnology. Call me Brent."

The cop threw the transmission into drive and all the doors locked themselves. His foot remained on the brake. "Sergeant Korn. Call me Sergeant Korn. Buckle up."

Brent withdrew his hand. This was his sixth ride-along, with his fourth police department. He had learned a few things. Don't bring doughnuts. Don't discuss TV cop shows. Don't expect "I'm here to help" to make friends. Don't push too hard, or too fast.

"I *said*, buckle up, Cleary."

Brent latched his seat belt, unnecessary as that was. "Sergeant, I have a signed copy of the ride-along waiver for you."

Flat-panel displays covered the console between the bucket seats. Korn tapped the biggest screen and the image of a form popped up.

Brent leaned over to where he could read the display. He recognized his own photo and the scrawled approval of the captain. The waiver text absolved the department of responsibility for anything that might happen—taken verbatim, even if the sergeant *did* shoot him. Not that it would matter. "You're a step ahead of me."

"Yes, I am." Korn raised the passenger-side window, then tapped his headset once. "Car 343 leaving on patrol." With a throaty V-8 growl, the cruiser turned right onto Main Street and went past headquarters. As though an afterthought, Korn added, "Visitor onboard."

That was another thing Brent had learned. Except maybe on CB, no one used numeric radio codes anymore. After 9/11 first responders got serious about communicating across jurisdictions. It had been easier to switch to English than to standardize on codes. On all but one ride-along, much of the routine comm had been by wireless texting between computers.

"So what's the plan tonight?" Brent asked.

"Working."

It was going to be a long eight hours. Brent looked around the cruiser. Big and roomy: a Crown Vic hybrid. Still, the computer-and-comm console encroached on the passenger and driver spaces. On the dash a metal cylinder reminiscent of a water glass lay on its side: a radar antenna. A second antenna sat on the shelf behind the rear bench seat. The hinged, clear divider between front and backseats was folded down. He leaned forward and to his right to peer behind the rearview mirror and found, as he had expected, a forward-looking camera. All very standard.

Korn paid him no attention.

The sergeant appeared to be in his late thirties. He was pinch faced, with pale skin and thinning, sandy hair. His tan uniform was clean and pressed and a bit snug. His holstered handgun was the only weapon in sight.

An "appearances first" department, then. There was yet another thing Brent had learned, that some departments insisted that the big guns—rifle, shotgun, tear-gas launcher—be hidden in the trunk lest they offend public sensibilities. Other PDs had a term for such sensitivity: "chicken shit." It put cops' lives at risk.

Brent cleared his throat experimentally. Korn ignored it.

Brent had sisters, the first two years older than he and the other two years younger. Growing up, Wendy and Jeanine went through an "eew, boys" phase. He would enter a room where they were playing, and one sister would tell the other, and any friend who might be over, to ignore *it*. Korn's silent treatment? Not a problem. Brent had been shunned by experts.

The street went from working class to needy to seedy. Plastic bags and sheets of newspaper scudded before the wind. Paper cups, fast-food wrappers, and broken glass clogged the gutters. It was an integrated neighborhood, but people clustered by race, eying one another warily. Night was falling and shopkeepers extended sturdy metal fences across sad-looking storefronts.

The cruiser AC was blasting, but outside it was brutal. The ambient temperature registered 98 on the in-dash display. Kids splashed in the water that pulsed and gurgled from open fire hydrants. Youths in baggy shorts and T-shirts or tank tops melted away as the cruiser approached. In Brent's side-view mirror, they regrouped as quickly as they had dispersed. Rush hour was long past and traffic was light, stripped cars at the curb almost outnumbering those moving along the roadway.

Korn muttered under his breath, something about toads. He turned left onto Jefferson, past tired, old clapboard houses whose doors stood open. Broken windows gaped like missing teeth. The last hints of twilight bled away, but most streetlights remained dark.

From time to time one of the cruiser displays lit up. The angle from the passenger side was too oblique to let Brent read incoming messages from Dispatch, and Korn volunteered nothing. He would tap the comm screen to clear it and that would be that. Informational only, apparently.

At Eighth they turned left again. Cars queued for the pumps at a no-brand gas station. Beside the uneven sidewalk, weeds growing through the cracks, a sandwich board listed prices. Unleaded regular was $8.57 a gallon. Ouch. Back home, the highest Brent had seen was $7.99. That was bad enough, and he drove a late-model hybrid that got seventy miles to the gallon.

The cars waiting to gas up were huge, like the cruiser, but far older: relics of a bygone era. Many had mismatched doors or fenders: junk-yard replacements. Only the poorest drove rust-bucket gas guzzlers like those. To buy something newer and more energy efficient took money, or at least credit.

Korn drove in silence, his intentions obvious. Wait for the civilian to plead to be returned to safety. End of unwelcome ride-along.

Sorry, Sergeant. Not going to happen.

Barry Rosen, the marketing VP at Garner Nanotech, had volunteered that half of cops, more or less, resented civilian ride-alongs. Asked for his sources, Barry had only smiled. Korn made it three for six, so Barry was right again. He usually was.

But what choice did they have? Garner's ultimate markets—the FBI, Homeland Security, the DoD—were far more receptive to new tech, *much* easier to deal with . . . right to the point of closing a deal. Then the Federal Acquisition Regulations, umpty-ump gigabytes of them, came into play, slowing the sales process to a crawl. Bureausclerosis was why Americans *still* bought body armor privately to send to their sons and daughters in Iraq, Iran, and the former Pakistan.

So, receptive or not, local PDs were Garner's market of choice, be-cause there were so darn many of them. If only one department in twenty took interest, the people at Garner would make a fortune. Even a lowly sales-support engineer like Brent.

Humming softly, Korn turned right on Railroad. This spur was long abandoned, the rails pulled up for scrap, and the right-of-way resold. Atop the embankment that paralleled the rippled and potholed street, a fat pipe seemed to float above tall weeds.

Brent raised the hood of his jumpsuit and pulled the transparent visor down over his face. Viewed in night mode, the pipe—even the graffiti—looked new. From time to time as they rode, he glimpsed through the weeds one of the stanchions that supported the pipe. Probably this was one of the gasoline pipelines recently extended from the north. Canada, unlike New England, occasionally managed to build a refinery.

Korn sneaked a peek at Brent in his hood, and snickered.

A small comp was sewn into the left forearm of the jumpsuit. Brent fingered in a code string for color selection. The suit turned black: body and hood, boots and gloves. A second code made the visor black, but polarized so he could still see out. Brent pictured himself disappearing into the black seat.

Korn laughed again, this time with a trace of warmth. "Camo. That I see a use for." He pulled the cruiser into the lot of a twenty-four-hour mini-mart and tapped his headset. "Car 343. Out of service, personal." To Brent he added, "Fluid adjustment break. If you're planning to go inside, lose the ninja look."

His hood back down, and the jumpsuit reprogrammed to a denim-like blue, Brent followed Korn into the mini-mart. Unsealing and re-sealing the jumpsuit took time, and Korn was in the cruiser, his mini-mart coffee half-finished, when Brent rejoined him.

"Here's a tip about the wonder suit," Korn said. "It needs a fly."

Brent's sisters both sewed. Jeanine was especially good at it; she had even made suits for her husband. A fly in men's pants was apparently a big deal, although it amused Jeanine when Hubby once described it that way. "Pretty proud of yourself, aren't you?" Jeanine had said.

The jumpsuit was not made of simple fabric. Every seam and seal required careful engineering. Not until the next iteration, a beta-test model potential customers might try, was designing in a fly worth the cost.

"Thanks for the suggestion, Sergeant." Never mind that it was offered sarcastically. It could be construed as an invitation to discuss the suit. "Any other impressions?"

In an uninflected voice: "Excuse me, I have to go. Somewhere there is a crime happening."

"Ah, RoboCop," Brent said. "This jumpsuit is nothing like that." Well, he had a microchip implanted in his arm that was a *bit* like Robo-Cop, but that detail could wait.

"Cruiser 343, back in service." Korn backed the cruiser onto the street. He flipped a toggle on the dashboard and the dark street scene turned green—and as bright as day.

That was interesting. It was Brent's first night ride-along. He hadn't realized any cruisers had a night-vision mode. He looked down to scribble a—

"Christ!" Korn said. He was driving left-handed, shaking his right hand as though it stung. "That's hard."

Had the jumpsuit's left arm stiffened for a moment? Perhaps. "Sergeant, did you hit me?"

"Just testing." Korn flexed his fingers some more. "Don't tell me you didn't feel it."

Brent grinned. "I didn't. That's the point."

They turned onto Sixth. A dozen or more youths congregated around the block's one working streetlight. Korn flicked his flashers and siren. They scattered. "Okay, Cleary. I guess I *am* interested."

Success. "This isn't just any jumpsuit, Sergeant. It's made from nanofabric. That's why, for example, it can change colors."

"Like a mood ring."

"Only programmable." And much more complex and precise than a mood ring. "Many properties of the fabric are controllable at the finest scales, not merely the color."

The comm console came on again. Korn read something, muttered once more about toads, and tapped to acknowledge. "The natives are restless tonight." He turned onto Washington. "So what happened when I slugged your arm?"

"Nanites—sorry, that's geek speak for smaller-than-microscopic machines—in the fabric linked up to distribute the impact. The harder or faster the blow, the more of the fabric stiffens. An instant later, the fabric reverts to normal. I don't feel much of anything."

Korn bit his lower lip, considering. "How much impact can it handle?"

"Knife thrust. Bullet. I wasn't kidding earlier when I said you could shoot me."

They pulled up to the curb. Korn reached over to pinch a fold of the jumpsuit fabric between thumb and forefinger. "Damn, that's lightweight."

"Then I have your attention, Sergeant? I assume you carry body armor."

"Ron. Yeah, there's a bulletproof vest in the trunk."

Ron, now, is it? That was progress. "My jumpsuit weighs less than two pounds. Correct me if I'm mistaken, but that's lighter than your vest." The pause for any correction was pro forma. Brent knew damn well police bulletproof vests generally weighed almost five pounds. "And this jumpsuit will stop a rifle round." Which Korn's vest would not, not without adding heavy and uncomfortable ceramic or metal plates.

"Damn," Korn said respectfully. He put the cruiser back into drive and resumed the patrol. "And it protects you head to toe. And you don't even look hot."

Not hot was a theme. On every ride-along, sooner or later, that always came up. Conventional body armor was hot. "Because I'm *not* hot, Ron. Evaporative cooling. The nanofabric wicks out any sweat."

The comm console lit up again. Korn tapped his headset. "Acknowledged. Be there in two minutes." He flipped on the flashers and siren. An abrupt U-turn, then a tire-squealing left onto Railroad. "Domestic disturbance, Cleary."

They pulled up to a decaying high-rise housing project. In many of the apartments, the only light was the flickering of a TV. Other units were entirely dark, whether vacant or conserving electricity. None of the nearby streetlights worked. A single flickering fluorescent bulb lit the entryway. Korn took the key from the ignition and the cruiser's windows went passive. It was *dark* out there. Korn flung open his door. "I'll be back in a few minutes. Stay in the car."

"But I'll be perfectly safe in—"

"I *said*, stay put." Korn slammed his door. All four doors locked with a click.

Waiting in the dark gave Brent the creeps. The toggle for the cruiser's night-vision mode did nothing without a key in the ignition. He raised and sealed his hood. The visor's night-vision mode revealed people in several apartments, few looking his way. Hip-hop echoed into the night, raps competing, little but throbbing bass distinct. Somewhere above, a man and a woman cursed.

I'm in an invulnerable suit. I'm in an invulnerable suit. I'm in an invulnerable suit.

Not truly invulnerable, but the exceptions were surely academic. He couldn't be stabbed. He couldn't be shot. He couldn't, although he had yet to mention it to Korn, be poisoned or infected. With his hood up and sealed, he was inside the world's most lightweight hazmat suit. Oxygen and nitrogen—and nothing else—could get in. CO_2 and water vapor got out. And if, against all logic and science, he were injured? Why then—

What was that?

Nothing seemed changed in front of the housing project. Something in his peripheral vision, then. He unbuckled, twisting around and staring to left and right. Staring behind. No one was within fifty feet of the cruiser. Just nerves.

He was in an invulnerable suit, damn it.

One of Brent's college professors liked to quote Edward Teller, father of the hydrogen bomb. "There's no system foolproof enough to defeat a sufficiently great fool."

Brent cranked the gain in the hood visor. Now he could see far up and down the street. Loiterers along the sidewalk, up on the old railroad embankment, and in the darker shadows beneath the few scraggly trees. As far as he could tell, no one was paying him any attention. He turned forward in his seat, staring at the project entrance, willing Korn to hurry up.

What the hell was he so nervous about?

Brent looked around again, more slowly this time. Residents in the apartment units, most watching TV. Korn was nowhere to be seen, which probably meant only that he was in a unit on the back of the building. People eying—casing?—a car parked down the block. People up on the embankment, clustered along the pipeline. More graffiti in the works, Brent supposed. People on a street corner, smoking, and he could care less what they smoked. A hooker in short shorts and a boa, strutting for the few passing cars.

The bunch on the embankment seemed awfully animated. Could they be up to something other than spray painting? Gas at $8.57 a gallon must be painful to the people who lived here. Were they tapping the pipeline for free gas?

He cranked the visor gain to max. The activity on the embankment was clearer, but no less enigmatic. He wished Korn would get a move on—

Wishing wasn't good enough. If a spark ignited gasoline vapor or a spill, then . . . well, Brent didn't know what would happen. Only he was certain it would be *bad*.

Should he go inside, hunt for Korn? There had to be at least a hundred apartments. That could take too long. Maybe he could scare them off. He flipped the siren-and-flasher toggle. Nothing happened. Like the cruiser's night-vision mode, it must need a key in the ignition.

Atop the embankment the mood seemed exuberant. The crowd finally shifted to give Brent a glimpse into the center of activity. Liquid arced from the pipe, splashing in and around a handheld gas can. More big containers stood on the ground among trampled weeds. It was a disaster waiting to happen.

"Crap," Brent said. He unlocked the car. *You're in an invulnerable suit,* he reminded himself—only he knew the designers and doubted this scenario had ever occurred to them.

Korn's uniform was tan. Brent set the jumpsuit to match. He threw open the door. Then, thinking of sufficiently great fools, he ran toward the gas thieves. "Get away from there!" he shouted. "Beat it!"

Flash! Still at max amplification and in night-vision mode, his visor overloaded—but not before he was blinded. A great roar swallowed him. A gale of wind lifted him off the ground. There was a moment of dizzying, sightless motion. Head to toe, front and back, the jumpsuit went stiff.

Then there was nothing.

dreaming

friday, january 29, 2016

Garner Nanotech's corporate jet appeared right on schedule, a silver dart in a cloudless blue winter sky. The Learjet used only half the runway to brake to taxi speed, still looking like a toy as it turned toward the hangars. Little-used Griffiss Field was once Griffiss Air Force Base, home to the 416th Bomb Wing. B-52s were *big*, and they required a long runway.

Wind whistled across the airfield, and Kimberley O'Donnell shivered in the January chill. Her left hand clutched her coat tightly around her throat. January cold was no surprise in upstate New York; the marvel was there was no snow falling today.

Brent used to laugh at her watery Virginia blood. That was easy for him. *He* grew up in Chicago.

She shivered for reasons unrelated to the cold. The plane taxiing her way had returned Brent from Chicago. Returned him from six months of living hell. Despite phone and e-mail, despite near daily VirtuaLife contact (the secluded island that he had conjured just about broke her heart), despite three weekend visits once he felt well enough to see anyone, she could not keep straight his many treatments, complications, and surgeries. Or the many therapies that followed: physical, occupational, and psychological. His parents, in whose home Brent had convalesced, seemed unable to end her confusion. "He needed a lot of fixing up. He got banged up pretty bad," was the best Marjorie and Brad Cleary ever had to offer.

Did she really need to know the details? The essential truth about his injuries and recovery was: too much. No wonder Brent didn't laugh anymore.

The Learjet finally reached hangar row. It rolled to a stop. Aft of the cockpit a hatch unsealed, pivoting downward to provide a flight of stairs. The pilot waved from the hatchway before backing into the cockpit.

Brent emerged from the passenger section, blinking in the sunlight. The twenty-some colleagues who had left work early to greet him whistled and cheered. Smiling uncertainly, he steadied himself against an interior bulkhead.

Her friend was six feet tall, and an avid hiker and cross-country skier. Part of what drew him to upstate New York was the nearby Adirondacks. The few times he had talked Kim into joining him, hiking on what he swore were beginners' trails, he had exhausted her. She remembered him fit, confident, and tanned.

It was hard to recognize Brent in the stooped, pale figure hesitating at the top of the stairs. He was only thirty, a year younger than she, but he stepped from the plane as though he were eighty. He seemed as likely to tumble down as walk down the few steps. Like his alter ego in VirtuaLife, Brent was too wounded in spirit to connect with people. Even with friends.

Kim thought: *We don't need a damned ceremony.*

"Welcome back," boomed Daniel Garner. The company's founder and CEO had a wireless mike in his hand. The wind flapped his silk scarf and tousled his long, blond hair. "Brent, welcome home."

As Brent came slowly down the stairs, two feet to the step, hand trembling on the skimpy railing, Kim tried to be charitable. Brent had insisted on coming home and on traveling without, as he put it, "a babysitter." He had had the company jet to himself, on a direct flight into Rome. It had to have been a *lot* easier on him than the alternative: a commercial flight into the nearest airfield served by the airlines. That would have been Syracuse, an hour's drive away.

A short ceremony, she conceded, was a fair trade-off. Let Dan Garner take credit with the staff for sending the company jet for Brent. The class act was generosity that remained undisclosed. Garner was personally picking up all the deductibles and all the copays for Brent's many treatments. Kim only knew because Brent's mother had let it slip.

But would the ceremony be short? No one had ever accused Dan of brevity. "Your courage, Brent, continues to inspire us all. We will never forget how your sacrifice showed us—showed the *world*—the value of everything we've worked on together."

And then, as Kim's grandma would say, Garner was off to the races. He segued into his standard spiel. Kim heard it every time the big boss dragged her along to Manhattan or Boston or Silicon Valley to a confab with the venture capitalists. Garner was a big-picture person. VCs loved him, because they were big-picture people, too—only with tons of money to invest and a staff of experts to vet the opportunities. Engineers like Kim went along to answer the staff's nitty-gritty questions.

Brent surviving the Angleton holocaust was a big-picture event even a VC could grasp. The poor man was still in a body cast after spinal and pelvic surgery when the VCs began taking Garner's calls.

"And that is how, Brent, the protective gear that saved your life came to embody the best nanotech on the planet."

"Best on the planet" was Dan's catchphrase. *Everything* associated with Garner Nanotech was the best on the planet, down to movie nights on the company's giant TV and the pizza ordered in during project crunches. "Best morale on the planet" went without saying.

"That is why—" Garner broke off, Brent's exhaustion having finally made an impression. "We'll let it go at that, Brent. I'm just so passionate about the work we're doing together. The work whose value you so compellingly demonstrated. Go home and get some rest." Garner waved over the waiting limo and opened a rear door. A few in the crowd shouted out their good-byes and well wishes. "We all look forward to you rejoining us."

Brent seemed ready to collapse. Kim circled behind the small crowd, sliding into the limo right after him. Let him call her a babysitter if he wanted.

Garner scarcely missed a beat. "Kim will help you get settled." He closed the door after her and slapped the top of the limo twice. The limo headed for the airfield exit.

Six months ago Kim would have said Brent's face reflected his character: honest and gentle, his eyes twinkling with wry, kind-spirited good humor. Now, checking him out surreptitiously, she found only weary resignation.

Not surreptitiously enough.

Brent said, "You're thinking this is a face to frighten children and household pets."

"Worry, not frighten," she answered firmly. "No, I'm thinking I like the beard." Black and curly like his hair, the new beard followed his jawline in a thin, continuous band from one sideburn to the other. "Add a top hat and you could pass for Abe Lincoln."

He stroked his chin. "There's a thin scar under there. The docs suggested cosmetic surgery. This was easier."

The limo had a minibar. "Can I get you a drink?" she asked. "I'm guessing Dan stocks the best on the planet."

Brent shook his head. "I'm going to close my eyes for a bit. Thanks for riding along."

"Sure thing."

The drive into Utica took twenty minutes. Brent woke with a start as the limo glided to a halt in front of his apartment complex. "It's okay," she said. "You're home."

Waving her off when she offered a hand, he levered himself out of the limo. "I don't mean to be rude. I have to learn to do stuff for myself."

"Understood." Still, she held open the heavy lobby door for him, then rushed ahead to summon the elevator. He leaned against the elevator car's rear wall for the ride to the third floor. He must have lost weight, because his coat looked baggy on him. "I'm more tired than I expected," he admitted, shuffling down the hallway to his apartment.

He barely managed a nod at the neighbor they passed going the other direction down the corridor.

Kim let them in with the duplicate key Brent's parents had sent her so she could clear out the refrigerator, water or throw out the house-plants, send clothes, and whatever. Brent made no comment. Maybe he remembered about her key. More likely, he was too exhausted to care.

He was snoring softly, head flopped onto the back of the living-room sofa, in the time it took her to bring a glass of ice water. She maneuvered him into a lying-down position, slid off his shoes, and settled herself into the recliner.

saturday, january 30, 2016

Brent woke with a start. Everything ached. That was sadly familiar, but the *manner* of aching had changed. He opened his eyes. His own apartment. His never-comfortable couch. The altered twinges made sense.

"It's about time."

He turned his head. Kim sat in his recliner, the chair much too big for her. She had a steaming mug in hand.

He said, "God, that coffee smells good. Is there any left?"

"Plenty. I'll get you some."

He sat up, casting aside the afghan he had no recollection of unfolding. "That's okay. My bladder is about to burst. I'll pour myself a cup on the way back. What the heck time is it?"

She laughed. "Better to ask, what *day* is it? It's Saturday. You slept for sixteen hours. How do you feel?"

Sixteen hours! No wonder every muscle felt stiff. And Kim had been here the whole time—she had on the same clothes as yesterday. He guessed her car was still at the airport. All he was good for since Angleton was burdening friends and family.

He said, "Almost human. I'll be right back, Kim."

On his way to the bathroom, he glanced into the bedroom. The bed seemed undisturbed. So Kim had spent the night in the recliner, keeping an eye on him. Once more, his frailty embarrassed him.

Brent made a mental note to send her flowers. But what kind? He could barely tell a rose from a cauliflower, considering both equally suitable for mulch, but even he knew roses were inappropriate. Ordinarily he got his floral advice from Kim; a sister's opinion would have to suffice.

De-tanked, face washed, hair hastily brushed, and sipping a mug of hot coffee, he *did* feel better. He looked around the kitchen. Fresh milk and orange juice in the refrigerator. A freezer full of frozen dinners. A loaf of bread, a can of coffee, and a box of muffins on the counter. All Kim's doing, no doubt. Suddenly, he was ravenous.

"You okay in there?" Kim called.

"Be right out." He transferred four muffins to two plates, returned to the living room, and handed her a plate. He went to the sofa with his own plate. "Orange-cranberry. Excellent choice." He inhaled the first muffin. "Sixteen hours, huh? I hope I didn't keep you up."

"Well . . . you didn't."

He was all too familiar with such hesitations. His parents had equivocated a lot these past few months. "I had the nightmare, huh? Sorry."

"*The* nightmare? Recurring? Do you want to talk about it?"

He had been head-shrunk by pros, not that they did him any good. Why would he want to talk about this now? And yet he did. Kim was his best friend. "I don't understand the dream," he said softly. "I mean: how? I don't remember what happened. I don't! A few minutes before, sure, waiting inside the cruiser. Waking up in the hospital a day later, that's all clear. Between, nothing but flashes. Maybe I have to make stuff up to fill in the blanks. Stupid subconscious."

She shrugged and said nothing. That was so much better than, "And how do you *feel* about that?" Damned shrinks.

"I know what happened, Kim. At some level, how could I not? The police cruiser was wrapped around a telephone pole, crushed and charred. For whatever reason, I got out before the explosion. I was extracted from a brick wall, with more bones broken than I care to think about." In his pelvis. Shattered humerus in his left arm. Cracked ribs. Cracked vertebrae. Massive internal bleeding from the impact and all the bone-fragment punctures.

So why *was* he thinking about it? "The blast from the pipeline explosion clearly threw me into that wall. It tossed me far enough that I only slow-roasted in the lesser flames, instead of incinerating in the thousand-degree fireball."

Damn fools, stealing gas from the pipeline. From the number of blackened metal cans around the blast zone, the fire department seemed certain that's what had been going on. A wayward spark—from a cell phone, the drill, shuffling feet, whatever . . .

Brent swallowed, struggling to get his thoughts back in order. The coffee that had tasted so good gnawed at his stomach. "I know those things only because of what I read or was told. Like that it was an hour before firemen in hazmat suits began searching the outer edge of the destruction. Like that six-hundred-plus people died horribly, and many more were injured."

Kim leaned forward. "Brent, it was gruesome. How could you *not* fixate on it?"

He looked at his other muffin, only because it didn't look back. "Why do I dream about the time I can't remember? About hanging in the wall, like a bug caught in amber? I was in shock, I was concussed, and the nanosuit had me doped up to the eyeballs."

Only the bug had it easy.

The nightmare never changed: A hail of debris pinging off the nanosuit. Smoke and flames. Charred bodies everywhere, a few still quivering. Sirens. The agonized screams that punctuated the eerie crackling of his breathing and the ringing in his ears. Lungs that felt filled with broken glass. His arm broken, held rigid by the nanosuit. Secondary explosions, as gas tanks exploded in one car after the next. The housing project collapsing upon itself, and on more than two hundred residents, and on Sergeant Korn.

Kim came and sat beside him. "It's not your fault you survived."

He laughed bitterly. "Nor is it anything to be proud of. Why does everyone keep telling me how brave I am? That I'm a hero? Why do Dan Garner and the board consider an accident grounds for a big stock-option grant?"

"Brent?" She said no more until he made eye contact. "That you survived was a small miracle. Then VCs and investment bankers who never took Garner's calls began calling *us*. DoD procurement officials were suddenly talking sole-source contracts, expedited delivery, and large-scale field trials. Sure, you got a special options grant, but everyone at the company already had some options. We'll all do well when the company goes public.

"I refuse to believe we're exploiting those deaths in Angleton. Yes, we may get rich, but it'll be for the lives we *save*. Beginning with yours, damn it. And you *should* get more options than the rest of us. I put sweat equity into the company. You invested a spleen."

And almost a kidney, he tallied mentally, although that had recovered with stem-cell treatments.

Kim made a good case. By daylight.

Tonight, Brent had no doubt, the nightmare would return.

monday, april 18, 2016

"Good *morning*, Captain America. Good *morning*, Ms. America. My, you look lovely today. Good *morning . . .*"

Hidden scanners read the RFID chips embedded in every ID badge, but when people were streaming into the building it took a human being to make sure everyone walking in *had* a badge. Even at his most subdued, Alan Watts, one of the morning-shift security guards, was ebullient. Marvel Comics might have killed off Captain America— twice, in fact, to Brent's knowledge. It took more than that to tone down Watts. He greeted everyone who came through the doors with a big smile—high wattage, he would say, if anyone commented—and variations on the same cheery salutation.

The Monday morning foot traffic from the Garner Nanotech parking lot hit a bottleneck at the employee entrance. Brent waited his turn, glad to be back but already a bit weary. Practically everyone in the line had a smile or a hug or a kind word for him. Finally, he reached the lobby.

"Good morning, *Major* America. Good to see you!"

Major? Brent looked around in confusion. "Who, me?"

Watts grinned even more broadly. "Who else? You put this company on the map, and you did it the hard way."

"Promoting me sort of defeats the purpose of the all-purpose greeting. You might want to reconsider that, Alan."

Brent stopped in his tracks. Since when were they on a first-name basis? Before the accident, he had just nodded or smiled and walked past. Brent only knew the man's name from the ID tag on his uniform.

Watts looked just as surprised, but said nothing.

Security was a subcontracted function; Brent could not remember the name of the firm. The rent-a-cops were part of the background. He wasn't proud of that attitude, but neither had it ever bothered him. What had changed?

Who, not what. *He* had changed. He had ridden along with a bunch of police, and the last one died. He lived and Ron Korn died. Where was the justice in that?

Now merely to see a police cruiser or a cop in uniform brought everything crashing back. Screening was more rigorous than ever since the Athens airport bombing. If Brent had had to fly commercial, he would still be in Chicago. Or he'd have matched some secret TSA profile, and gotten himself sent to prison somewhere. He could never have held himself together long enough to get through airport security.

The shrinks had been big on desensitization exercises. The homework assignment Brent had most studiously ignored was to talk to a policeman. Just talk.

"Alan," Brent said, trying to ignore the holstered handgun. "Were you a cop before?"

"Sure was, Major. Lots of us in Security were. The hours here are a lot more predictable." Watts frowned, and he seemed a different person. "And it's a whole bunch safer."

Hundreds dead, but only one was real to Brent. Only one had a face. "The cop I was riding with that day didn't make it." It wasn't enough, but Brent was at a loss what else to say.

Watts knew. "Meet me at Riley's after work. I'll join you in a beer to your friend's memory."

Brent had modest goals for his first day back at work. Sort his in-box. Seek out a bunch of people. Those would have been easier tasks had the company not relocated in his absence.

As best Brent could tell, the prosperity of what the Census Bureau grandly named the Utica-Rome Metropolitan Statistical Area had peaked with the dedication of the Erie Canal. Griffiss Air Force Base and the affiliated Rome Air Development Center had given the declining area a reprieve—then they, too, closed. It was a region in disarray, with too many unemployed workers and boarded-up buildings.

Dan Garner was never one to pass up a bargain. Years of assured property-tax forgiveness had brought his fledgling company to Utica. To grow from an R & D shop into a production company took money and space. And more money. Hence the move, while Brent was laid up, into what had started out as a strip mall.

How better to reorient myself, Brent thought, *than by scoping out the new place?*

The company's administrative and R & D areas were now spread across what had been a dozen retail outlets. Brick had replaced the display windows of the defunct stores. Here and there wallboarding continued, the old insulation being swapped out wholesale.

Utica got more snow than Chicago, but Chicago winters won for cold. Brent inspected the new insulation with interest. This was good stuff, with aluminum foil laminated to both sides to reflect virtually all radiant energy. No one had asked, but he approved.

The pilot production lines, not yet in operation, snaked through the lower level of the mall's onetime anchor store. Interior walls had been taken down, carpet torn up, escalators and display cases removed, partitions and catwalks installed. Beeping softly, automated flatbed carts followed tracks painted on the concrete floor. Overhead, color-coded pipes and conduits ran everywhere. Conveyors were being installed to a storage area on the second level. Paper signs, several hand-corrected, taped to walls and pillars made it clear that the layout remained a work in progress.

Brent had only vague ideas what a nanotech factory might look like. He walked around seeking his bearings, past a loading dock, various storerooms, a computer center, and wiring closets. Pallets of boxed equipment clogged many aisles. He peered through interior windows into workspaces reminiscent of a semiconductor-chip cleanroom, his college chemistry lab, and hot-zone biocontainment. Behind thick glass, hooded and robed workers in immaculate white protective gear did . . . he could hardly begin to imagine. A security guard controlled access to the more intriguing areas, behind doors from whose still-unpainted frames dangled loose wires. The height of the wires suggested retinal scanners to come.

Brent came to an area where prefab wall panels were rising, carving out a big chunk of the first floor of the old anchor store. Paper signs foretold an auditorium. He pictured the days-long progress reviews on which government customers always insisted, and the shorter but still interminable all-hands pep talks of which Dan Garner was so curiously enamored, looking forward to neither.

Brent eventually found, in the rear of the onetime dry cleaner, a door with his name on it. The doorknob had no keyhole; it turned but did not open. The access controls in this new facility all seemed to be electronic. A cell call to Security earned Brent an, "Oops, sorry."

He trudged to the main Security office, had his thumbprint digitized for file, and was authorized for access to assorted common areas and his own office. Killing time until the database update took effect, he worked out why thumbprints to open inside doors made sense. Had the wireless chip in his ID badge controlled the door, he could accidentally unlock his office merely by walking down the hall.

Ten minutes later the thumbprint scanner outside his office finally decided to recognize him. Inside, a suite of new oak furniture had replaced the cheap metal desk and bookshelf Brent remembered. The upgrade almost compensated for having been exiled to this backwater. The office had a faint chemical smell to it that he told himself was wall paint and furniture polish, not old dry-cleaning chemicals. A welcome-back banner hung between the two lolly posts that flanked the low credenza. At least the posts had been painted to match the walls.

The computer on the otherwise empty desk had been hooked up. Knowing he would be horrified, Brent logged in and checked e-mail: 1,327 unread messages.

Everything from his previous office must be in the boxes stacked along two walls. One stack of bulging cartons was labeled "Mail." With the penknife on his key chain he slit the tape that sealed the top box. It was crammed. He dug through the first few inches, finding mostly technical journals, flyers for company parties long passed, and probable ads.

Who was he kidding? Merely locating his office had left him bushed.

Brent closed the office door and logged into VirtuaLife. Onscreen, bright sunlight shone down on the secluded beach. He imagined the warmth. Gulls wheeled overhead. Combers rolled slowly up the white sand. In the distance, porpoises cavorted. The only overt changes since his last visit were the position of the sun, the level of the tide, and a new tangle of driftwood. His avatar dozed in a canvas beach chair.

Eyes closed, Brent immersed himself in the sounds of "his" island. Sandpipers warbled. When the birds fell silent, he heard the lapping of waves. Upslope, palm fronds rustled in the breeze. Did palm trees and sandpipers mix? Did sandpipers actually warble? It hardly mattered. Such constraints did not apply here. Reality faded . . .

To be evoked by an increasingly insistent meow.

Growing up, there had been cats in the family for as far back as Brent could remember. Back to when he believed all boy cats must be named Tom and thought it unfair.

Brent opened his eyes. Schultz, a large black cat, studied him through jade-green eyes. The sprite was one of Brent's favorite customizations, and—by choice—often his only company on the island. *Alarm clock* was the least of Schultz's talents. The feline was an excellent listener.

"Isn't today a workday?" Schultz purred.

"Very true. Thanks." Reluctant but refreshed, Brent exited the simulation. In a server farm in Osaka, winds still blew, birds flew and sang, the world continued its stately rotation, and Schultz continued to pad about. Elsewhere in the world of VirtuaLife, over the horizon from Brent's island, were millions of avatars and sprites.

Maybe someday he would again feel like mingling. . . .

Sorting his accumulated snail mail could wait for another day, but other things should not. Brent headed back into the maze to do something far more important. People here had been very supportive these past several months. He meant to thank them.

It turned out Dan Garner was on a real island: vacation on Maui for the next two weeks. Felipe Lopez, the chief operating officer, had taken the company's execs to an off-site meeting. That was code for golf. After months of gray skies and almost daily snow, spring had sprung.

The techies were in except for Tyra Kurtz. As chief technical officer, she rated an invitation to golf. Brent started with the director of the nanosuit design group, rapping on the doorjamb.

Reggie Gilbert was a stocky African-American with a shaved-and-waxed scalp and a truly magnificent black mustache. Looking up at the interruption, he broke into a broad grin. "Good to see you, guy. Come on in. First day back?"

"Uh-huh. Great to see you, too, Gil." Brent stepped into the office and leaned against the sidelight. Stacks of sealed boxes lined the front wall. "I like what you've done with the place."

"I unpack as I need things. It turns out I've been something of a packrat, and that everything important is here." Gil patted his computer screen.

"My new office had the same interior decorator. I'll have to consider your system." Brent hesitated. "One other thing. A *very* big thank-you to you and everyone in your team."

Gil blinked. "For what?"

"Are you kidding? That suit you sent me off in saved my life." Brent shivered despite himself. "I can still hardly believe it."

Gil squirmed in his chair. "We should have done better. You look terrible." A forced laugh. "Wait awhile before you go on any more sales calls."

They chatted a bit, then Brent excused himself and went to thank someone else. And someone else. And someone else again. Only amazingly good work by a lot of people had kept him uncrushed, unimpaled, and unasphyxiated. Kim wasn't in her office when he happened upon it. That was okay; they were having lunch together. Anyway, he had already thanked her—to her flustered embarrassment—long ago.

Around eleven Brent's meandering path reached the Biology area. The offices were empty, but desktop displays flickered with screen savers. Eventually he found a lab corridor, its doors festooned with bio-hazard placards. A booming bass voice guided him the rest of the way.

Charles Walczak, the director of the Biology Department, stood six-six. He towered over the two women also in the break room. His eyes looked huge through thick lenses, and the horn-rimmed frames contrasted starkly with his thick silvery hair. He had heavy black eyebrows, very mobile and expressive, although what they had to say remained cryptic.

"Hey, stranger," Walczak called. "I heard you were finally back. I want to talk to you. Just give me a second."

"Hi, Charles. Take your time." Brent didn't know the women and Walczak didn't introduce them. New hires, perhaps. Judging from the conversation, they were biologists or research M.D.s like Walczak. They eventually concluded a discussion that, for all the sense it made to Brent, might as well have been in Klingon. The women excused themselves.

"Brent, sorry about that. Let me buy you a cup of coffee."

"No, but thanks." Brent had exhausted his supply of small talk. "Actually, Charles, a thank-you is why I came looking for you."

"Ah, you remember me visiting. I'd wondered if you would. You're welcome."

"I'm talking about surviving. The first-aid modes of the nanosuit had a lot to do with that. Thanks for proving them safe so the suit could do its thing." Brent did a mental rewind. "Um, what visit?"

"Right the first time, then. You don't remember." Walczak swiveled a chair and sat, his legs straddling the seat back. "Angleton Medical Center, the second morning after the big ka-boom. You were still in the surgical ICU. I came to do specialty tests, of course. The med-center lab didn't have a clue."

"*I* don't have a clue. What's this about, Charles?"

"The hospital had you on a Diprivan drip." Brent gathered he looked blank, because Walczak continued, "A top-notch sedative that can also affect memory. Milky-colored stuff." He guffawed. "We call it milk of amnesia."

It was for the best that Walczak had chosen research over medical practice. "Don't think me unappreciative, Charles, but *why* were you at the Angleton hospital? What were these tests?"

It was Walczak's turn to be puzzled. "The bots, naturally."

"The bots," Brent repeated.

Walczak finished his coffee, set down his mug, and slipped his hands into his lab-coat pockets. "When you hit that brick wall, your chip implant screamed. The nanosuit jet-injected you with painkillers, of course—and also the full load of first-aid nanobots."

Surgeons had removed the wireless sensor chip when they rebuilt Brent's multiply broken humerus. The chip had not shattered with the bone—luckily for him, or the suit would not have known to act. Still, with all the metal pins the docs needed to put in, why take chances with a nonessential object that might irritate his immune system?

Brent kneaded his left upper arm, the implant's absence still foreign. "I only knew about the painkillers."

"Your blood was flooded with pain *and* injury biomarkers. Sure, the suit injected drugs for the pain. You also had massive internal bleeding. Stopping that took nanobots. The bots did what they were supposed to. They backtracked the highest biomarker concentrations to the bleeders and pinpoint-delivered artificial clotting agent."

Brent had known the suit *could* do that, not that it *had*. "I suppose I was pretty lucky, Charles."

"Lucky would have meant being someplace else. As for the nanobots, it's simple. Without them, internal bleeding would have killed you long before the rescuers arrived."

The nanobots had been extensively tested in guinea pigs, mice, and human volunteers—bots were safe. Brent had known that, in extremis, the suit *could* inject them. That wasn't the same as accepting machines smaller than blood cells swimming throughout his circulatory system. He shivered. "So about the tests?"

"What you would expect, Brent." The tone was injured: *You question my work?* "The bots went kaput after a day, just as it was supposed to happen."

Brent was content to know *what* technology did. *How* he left for the people who built it. Technobabble was counterproductive on sales calls.

For months, doctors had told Brent he would be okay. They had bedside manners better than Walczak's, but the same message. "Trust us" had worn thin long ago; Charles's supercilious manner had just worn it through.

To come to terms with things, Brent decided, he had to understand *exactly* what had happened to him.

"Walmart and a bunch of tents. The town fathers, and trust me, all the town elders are men, love to boast that Washington and Richmond—and Harrisonburg, for crying out loud—are within a two-hour drive. A bright five-year-old can figure out that's code for 'in the middle of nowhere.'"

"So I've heard," Brent said.

Because Kim had told him. Everyone she got close to heard, sooner or later, about Colesville, Virginia. Often more than once.

She found Brent unfocused today. Preoccupied. Oddly difficult to engage. To be fair, it was his first day at work in almost nine months. He was entitled to be distracted.

Her own dark, distracted thoughts weren't helping the conversation. Saturday had been another anniversary of the Virginia Tech massacre. You never get over a lunatic with a rifle stalking your campus, killing thirty-two. She had known none of the victims personally—but. She remembered as though it were yesterday the long, fearful hours in classroom lockdown. She remembered being glued to every horrifying rumor, speculation, and scrap of news spread by instant messaging and grainy cell-phone vids. She had lived, her freshman year, in West A-J, the dorm where the shooting began. She had had classes in Norris Hall, site of most of the killing. She would *never* forget the heaps of flowers and teddy bears, the memorial services, the funerals, the abrupt mid-April ending of the semester, the tears. . . .

And so she babbled, trying to ignore the images that reasserted themselves at every awkward silence, sure that memories of Angleton must do something similar for Brent. "I got into the District often enough to know what I was missing. Real museums. Theater some-place other than the high-school gym. Thai and Indian and Brazilian restaurants. I promised myself that when I grew up, I'd live some-where cosmopolitan."

"Well done." Brent glanced about the shopping-mall food court where they had gone for a quick lunch. Every restaurant within sight was a franchise. "Luckily, I felt like a calzone."

In the Utica area you could enjoy any ethnic food you wanted—as long as it was Italian. What the locals considered a Mexican restaurant Kim had dubbed Casa del Swill. "The irony is breathtaking, I know."

Still, to give credit where it was due, New York *tried* to control guns. Virginia's idea of gun control was suggesting you say, "Please," before they sold you a semiautomatic weapon.

The skinny kid working the counter at the pizza-and-calzone place sauntered over and plopped down their lunches. He mumbled what might have been, "Anything else?" and turned away without waiting for an answer.

Despite herself, Kim managed a grin. "New subject. What's your take on the new facility?"

"Kind of in the outer boonies, isn't it?" Brent said. "I mean, even by Utica standards?"

She shrugged. "Not many other businesses nearby"—a self-storage mini-warehouse and a John Deere parts outlet, to be precise—"but it *is* inside city limits. I gather that when the original mall was proposed Utica annexed the whole area, with visions of sales-tax revenue dancing in its head. So much for the exotic location. What's your take on the inside?"

"Plenty of growing room." The calzone occupied Brent's attention for a while. "I haven't yet figured out my way around."

"The trick is to use the Möbius strip." His forehead furrowed, and she added, "My, someone is slow on the uptake. Methinks you came back too soon."

"No." He worked on his calzone some more. "It's good for me to be out. . . ."

You're fading on me, Brent, she thought. "And?"

"And it might be good for me to start with half days." He had driven them to the mall. "I'll drop you back at work and head home."

"After you take a nap, maybe we can catch a movie tonight," she said.

"Can't." He slid back his chair and stood. "Other plans."

"Who is she?" Kim waggled her eyebrows suggestively. "Anyone I know?"

"Alan Watts."

"Who?"

Brent looked . . . uneasy. "Captain America."

She stood. "I didn't know you were friends."

He had nothing to add on the walk to the parking lot or the short drive back to Garner Nanotech.

Inside, frantic e-mails from Quality Assurance awaited her. The latest software upgrade for nanobot power-management control was oddly unstable. Next-generation beasties afloat in glucose solution were shutting down at random intervals. It made about as much sense as her starving to death in a Fresh Foods.

Kim led the team that developed the system software for the nanobots. That made the mystery glitch her problem. She didn't mind. A weird program bug was a lot easier to think about than the Virginia Tech massacre. Setting aside her worry at Brent's distant and detached behavior, she called a meeting.

A blind man in a fast car could see Riley's Olde Irish Pub was a dive. The beam-and-plaster façade looked more Disney alpine than Irish. The asphalt expanse in front had faded nearly to white. The neon sign flickered and buzzed; the "ub" had burned out.

Brent parked but stayed in his car. His hands trembled on the steering wheel. He broke into a sweat and his chest felt tight.

Riley's was a cop bar. Cops reminded him of Ron Korn. Korn reminded him of Angleton . . . and hell. It all washed over him again.

He forced himself through the relaxation exercises from therapy. Slow, methodical breathing. Muscle groups relaxed one at a time. Happy thoughts.

Post-traumatic stress disorder, the shrinks called his condition, as though to label a thing made any difference. They could call it whatever they chose, so long as they prescribed sleeping pills and antidepressants. After the pills stopped helping, he had seen no reason to continue therapy.

In . . . hold the breath . . . out. In . . . hold . . . out. In . . . hold . . . out. Gradually, Brent calmed down. He went inside.

The interior, once his eyes adjusted to the dimness, was all dark wood—the planked floor; the massive bar itself and the stools alongside it; booths, tables, and chairs—beneath enough coats of varnish to turn nearly black. Two feeble track lights shone on the wall of glassware behind the bar. The floor made soft sticky sounds with each step he took.

Brent was ignored until Alan Watts hailed him from a back booth and announced that Brent had been on a ride-along at Angleton.

Until the explosion, Angleton had been just another economically depressed burg upstate. Now everyone knew about Angleton. Cops honored their own; several of the Riley regulars had taken time off work to attend Ron Korn's memorial. Brent shared his few memories of the sergeant and his regrets. Someone thrust a foaming mug into Brent's hand.

A blind man in a fast car could see Riley's Olde Irish Pub was a dive. Very quickly, Brent came to love the place.

sunday, may 15, 2016

In the north-side Chicago neighborhood where Brent grew up and that his parents still called home, house sites were twenty-six feet wide. You might not *quite* be able to lean out your window and touch the bungalow next door. Shake hands with the next-door neighbor at his window? No problem.

Brent grew up feeling nature deprived.

College might have been better. The University of Illinois had its main campus in Champaign-Urbana, smack in the center of the state. The prairie stretched all around—but the greenery was mostly corn and soy. Never mind that Chicago was *called* the Windy City. For a hundred miles in every direction, nothing around Chambana stood taller than a cornstalk and the wind never stopped. In the winter, there weren't even cornstalks.

Cornfields everywhere—the undergraduate library was entirely underground, lest it cast a shadow on a historic experimental cornfield—was not college's only disappointment, nor the most consequential. General engineering had seemed the ideal curriculum for someone curious about how everything worked. What the department deemed a "comprehensive, interdisciplinary program emphasizing real-world problem solving through a unique orientation toward partnerships with industry" turned out not to prepare him to take the lead anywhere so much as to underqualify him to do much of anything.

He should have gone on for a graduate degree in something more substantive, but grad school would have meant waiting another two years for a real salary. The wait did not seem like an option, not after hooking up with Nicole Tanner their senior year. General Electric in Schenectady offered him a job, as the least significant of cogs in the most ponderous of mechanisms. He accepted and married Nicole. She was as hot as a firecracker. As smart as a whip.

And, it turned out, as prickly as a porcupine, impossible to live with. They were a short-lived fiasco: like the *Hindenburg* disaster, only noisier. A year later, they were divorced. She moved home to Chicago.

Staying put was the path of least resistance, even as one dull assignment too many vanquished the fascination Brent once had with technology. A few years after that, he was reorged out of a job.

Living near the Adirondacks and Catskills had made the rest bearable. He joined a hiking club. He learned to backpack and ski. He found a new job at Garner Nanotech, still near the mountains. General knowledge was more than sufficient for sales support, a case of less being more. He trained for two years to walk the Appalachian Trail, all 2,160 miles of it, from Maine to Georgia.

And now climbing two flights of stairs to his apartment left him wheezing.

Kim twisted and stretched. She adjusted her sweatband. She jogged in place a bit. She nodded at the couple coming off the little park's fitness trail. Dew sparkled on the grass. Two little girls in pigtails, clearly sisters, shrieked on the nearby teeter-totter. All in all, a lazy Sunday morning, although *her* notion of a lazy Sunday morning favored Starbucks and *The New York Times*.

Brent finally emerged from the lobby of his apartment building. He crossed the street into the park and strode up to her, already winded. "Sorry I'm late." He began a stretching routine, scrawny in T-shirt and shorts.

Kim had yet to get straight answers from Brent about how much weight he had dropped and whether he had managed to regain any of it. Still, he was clearly on the mend; he almost seemed only his own age again. Something—the beard, maybe, or the rough time he had had—gave him a pensive look. His face was long and thin, thinner still since the accident. *And those are beautiful brown eyes. He's a good-looking guy*, she thought. *More, he's a good guy.*

Her matchmaking impulse stirred. Who suitable did she know?

"I just got here myself," Kim lied. She was here to encourage him. The lame little fitness trail was her speed, not his—at least until Angleton. Now, she wondered, would he make it around the twenty-station circuit even once?

He finished a set of joint rotations. "Let's do this thing." They set off down the path, bark chunks crunching beneath their feet, at little more than a brisk walk. She jogged in place just to stay limber while he worked out at the exercise stations. Pull-ups. Sit-ups. Stretches. Balance exercises. By station ten he was huffing like a steam engine.

"Your left leg is bleeding," she suddenly noticed.

"Huh." He stopped and took a look. "Just a scrape. I wonder how that happened."

Blood ran down the shin, staining his sock and sneaker. She said, "Hardly a scrape, but maybe that's good. The blood should wash out any dirt. Let's get you upstairs and clean it out."

Brent stripped off his T-shirt, blotted the wound, and knotted the shirt tightly in place. If he noticed her sharp, sympathetic intake of breath, he did not comment. He wasn't being stoic about the new injury, but entirely indifferent.

He caught her staring at the scars on his torso. "After months of PT, I guess I'm desensitized to pain. And should you wonder: yes, my tetanus shot is current. Let's do another few stations."

"*I'm* sensitive enough for the both of us." Squeamish enough, anyway. Merely having blood drawn for a physical made her woozy. "Unless you enjoy splashing through puddles of vomit, we're done."

They walked toward his apartment, not taking time to properly stretch. She would be stiff later. "How's the leg?" she kept asking.

"About the same as ten yards ago," he grumbled.

Back in his apartment, Kim insisted on cleaning and bandaging his wound. She did not trust him to do it himself. To distract herself, although the wound indeed was a fairly superficial scrape, she began chattering. Work was the first thing to come to mind. "They giving you time to get settled back in at the office?"

"Time?" Brent snorted. "All the time in the world. You must know the company is touting me as"—dramatic air quotes—" 'the survivor of Angleton.' Quick segue to a sales pitch for the products that made it possible. My old photo, me looking all hale and hearty, is a better promo than *me*. My current feeble self isn't the image anyone wants."

Kim looked up. "Frank *said* that?" Frank Yoder was the head of Sales Engineering, and Brent's boss.

"In so many words? No. Only Frank has given me nothing to do and declined every offer I've made to go on a sales call. Lest I exhibit any initiative, it turns out I no longer have a travel budget."

She taped a gauze square over the disinfected scrape. "What *does* he expect you to do?"

"Ease into things." Another snort. "Maybe Frank hopes I'll get bored and leave."

Brent was in his recliner, so she moved to the sofa to face him. She tried to ignore the red oozing through the bandage. "And will you?"

"Hell, no. Dan Garner could have put me on disability. Instead, he kept me on full salary the whole time I was away. That was damn decent of him, and I'm not about to repay his loyalty by jumping ship. I choose to consider Frank's benign neglect as paying me to look for a new opportunity within the company. I'm cramming for interviews before I even ask for one." Brent stood abruptly. "I need something cold to drink. What can I get you?"

"Nothing, thanks."

He returned from the kitchen with two bottles of water, and handed one to her. "Fluids after exercising, Kim."

They sat and drank for a little while. He cleared his throat. "Speaking of my studies, I have a question for you."

"Uh-huh."

"Self-destruct in the body of the nanobots. Do you believe it's fool-proof? The bots are mostly carbon nanotubes. From the web surfing I've done, the immune system generally ignores carbon nanotubes." He frowned, retrieving a phrase from memory. "Immunoprivileged, it's called."

She sat up. "You *have* been studying. What happened to the guy who was content to know only what the technology could do?"

Brent chugged a third of his water. "His prototype suit shot him full of alpha-test medical nanobots, and the little buggers helped keep him alive."

"And that wasn't enough?"

"It's certainly a good thing, only I realized I had no idea beyond 'trust me' why the nanites would ever leave. And immunoprivileged or not, no one knows much about the long-term medical effects of most nanoparticles. Except that you probably don't want to breathe them, which, thankfully, I didn't." He got up and looked out the window into the park. "Or so my recent readings say," he added, sounding apologetic.

Apologetic because she who programmed nanobots for a living had ducked his question? She said, wistfully, "I wish I had the time to learn more about how things worked. Enjoy the luxury while you can."

Brent permitted his eyes to fall shut. He tipped back his recliner. Dozing in the chair was not quite as pathetic as returning to bed after a half lap around the park's couch-potato exercise circuit. But Kim had gone— and she had let herself out, with a, "No, no, don't bother to get up"—so whom, exactly, was he kidding?

When he crossed from drowsy free association into dream was unclear.

Nanobots were on his mind and in his reverie: long, skinny cages constructed from carbon nanotubes. Each nanotube was a mesh of hexagons, like a roll of chicken wire—only the vertices of each hexagon were single carbon atoms. Most tubes were a mere nanometer, a billionth of a meter, across. Many thousand such tubes would fit comfortably across the width of a human hair.

His dream self had the perspective of a single bot, smaller than the nearby living cells his subconscious used to judge scale. The tiny nanotubes had been woven into a much larger, generally cylindrical construction whose shape and flexing motion suggested an animated Chinese finger trap. He seemed to share the nanobot's central cavity with more complex structures: organic cargo molecules, nanologic, nanomotors. Through gaps in the braid he watched arrays of yet more nanotubes, anchored at only one end, beating in rhythmic waves to propel the nanobot.

His mind's eye panned out. Nanobots crept and swam everywhere, amid a bedlam of larger, jostling forms. Reddish disks, pinched in the center. Whitish spheres, their surfaces alive with questing knobs. Smaller, amorphous, blob-and-tentacle shapes that defied any geometric characterization.

Red blood cells, white blood cells, and platelets.

Something jostled him. Something else shoved him from another direction. White cells gathered, surrounded him, engulfed him. "His" flagella ceased to beat, pinned to the woven-nanotube latticework. The hunters grasped and squeezed. He sensed motion as the swarm carried him away—

Brent woke with a shriek, his mouth dry, his heart pounding. He looked around in confusion until the out-of-body illusion passed. Trembling, he went into the kitchen for some iced tea, chiding himself for a suggestible fool.

At least *this* nightmare had an obvious source.

Charles Walczak had, a bit condescendingly, given Brent a demo the day before: "To put your mind at ease already, damn it." His hands busy at the microscope controls, Charles scanned across a blood sample, seeking one of the nanobots.

The digital microscope more closely resembled a PC tower than the fragile instrument Brent remembered from high-school biology. The scope was as much computer as optical device, and it streamed images wirelessly to the lab's local area network. A red/green/blue LED triplet bathed the slide in cool white light.

There was no glass-and-chrome-tube eyepiece to peer into. The magnified corpuscles were huge on a big flat-screen display. A faint grid, digitally superimposed, showed scale. The largest of the blood cells were but fifteen microns across.

Brent twitched as a pale sphere, its surface a writhing mass, swam into the image. At this magnification it was larger than his fist. "Ugly beastie. A white blood cell?"

Charles tittered. "White blood cell? When did you last study biology, the third grade? It's called a leukocyte."

The choice of synonym changed what? Brent said nothing.

There! A dark rod undulated among the disks and spheres of the blood cells. In length the nanobot compared to the diameter of a typical red cell. The rod was too slender to reveal the finer points of its construction. At the limit of vision, he sensed spots scattered over the braid.

The optical scope's limited resolution didn't matter. Brent had seen detailed design drawings and artists' conceptions. Most amazing of all, he had seen a close-up still image of a medical nanobot, captured, atom by atom, using an atomic force microscope. The AFM image wowed everyone; Dan Garner gave framed poster-sized copies to prospective investors.

The bots' scarcely visible spots were changing color. "How long?" Brent asked.

"How long if they weren't made to self-destruct? Roughly forever. But since I'm not stupid . . . every bot carries dabs of the antigen for chicken pox."

With a final tweak, Charles centered the nanobot in the display. Never one to forego lecturing, he spun on his stool to face Brent. "Practically every adult in this country has had chicken pox or been vaccinated against it. Either way, their immune system is sensitized to the antigen. You'll recall that we did a blood test for antibodies before implanting your biosensor chip.

"In a day, give or take, a protein in the blood dissolves the film we put over the antigen. The exposed antigens then stimulate the production of antibodies. See the dots changing color? That's the coating going away. For this demo I put a dollop of enzyme into the blood drop. It speeds things up. Ergo, any minute now . . ."

The jittering and jostling became organized. White cells crowded into the image. They moved toward the center of the screen. Toward the nanobot.

"Bingo," Charles said, although it was impossible to imagine him *playing* bingo. Whist, maybe, or Trivial Pursuit in the Mensa edition. "Swarm, little ones. Make me proud."

Extrusions on the white cells squirmed. They groped and grabbed onto the nanobot. More leukocytes surged into view, their surfaces likewise writhing, probing, seeking. The nanobot vanished beneath the wriggling mass. Charles said, "You're seeing leukocytes that are attracted to chicken pox. It's night-night for nanites."

Every one of the questing, wriggling leukocytes was like the snake-crowned head of Medusa. "Jesus," Brent finally managed.

"Lovely, aren't they?" Charles said. "*That* is what happened to the first-aid nannies your suit injected. Hunted down and crushed once their work was done. I trust you feel better now."

Brent did, although there remained one loose end. "But where do they go?"

"For a day after the accident you had very unusual pee."

Charles's attitude aside, yesterday's demo had been like a window into another world. Brent drained his iced tea, then went to the bathroom. He hoped that by now his pee was entirely ordinary.

friday, june 10, 2016

To music only he could hear, on a runway not really there, Brent strutted his stuff, stretching and turning to display his mock-up of a next-generation nanosuit. The Bangles sang "Walk Like an Egyptian" in his earphones. Virtual-reality gaming glasses rendered the imaginary runway, repositioning the outline thirty times a second as he jived. Headset and glasses alike were masked by the presently opaque visor, just as the iPod and its armband were hidden beneath the fabric of the suit.

The track was barely three minutes long. This grand entrance had struck him as fun, a bit of whimsy for a summer Friday afternoon. Doing it wasn't fun at all. Three minutes seemed like forever, and he felt self-conscious. Whimsy was so old Brent. So pre-accident Brent . . .

He suddenly pictured himself all in black: RoboCop. He had failed to remember Ron Korn for days. The laughter of his small audience made his lapse that much worse.

"Very nice," Reggie Gilbert said. The meeting was Gil's, as was this conference room. Gil had become Brent's boss on June 1, a bit more than a week earlier. Most people here were members of the nanosuit design team.

But not everyone. Alan Watts whooped and clapped, until *his* boss, Morgan McCrath, shot Alan a warning glower. It was foolish not to consult the ex-cops and vets in-house when police and the military were their target markets. Gil's only comment, when Brent had suggested inviting them, was, "Good idea. We should have thought of that."

The track ended and Brent quit clowning. "The suit should look familiar. I began with a spare prototype, pretty much what I wore in the field. So what's new?"

He unsealed and tipped back his visor. "Let's begin with the optics. These are standard gaming glasses I'm wearing. Imagine similar capabilities built into the visor. I'm connected by WiFi to"—he gestured—"that laptop. Together they project a fashion-show runway in real time, wherever and however I move. The visor could as easily talk to the console computer in a police cruiser. Call it a portable, heads-up display."

"Isn't that distracting?" Alan asked. "Or worse. How would I know what's happening in the real world?"

"Good question." Not everyone was a gamer. Brent handed over his specs. "Here, try these on. Move around, too. Motion sensors report back where the specs are, so the runway outline should stay put. Only instead of a runway, imagine, say, a floor plan or topo map."

With eyes masked by the big, silvered lenses, the Captain America trademark grin looked eerily insectile. "Aha. The real world shows through the computer image. Sure, I could get used to that."

Brent tapped the little glide pad in the laptop keyboard. "And now?"

"Shrunken. Moved to the corner of my eye. Eyes."

These were run-of-the-mill gaming specs. Brent intended to try out some expensive models, the kind with displays controllable by eye movements and an integrated audio headset. If it worked, good-bye cryptic control codes entered through the forearm keypad and hello interactive virtual menu. A full redesign of the user interface was hardly a first-week project, so he didn't bring it up. "Then a reality-plus display like this would be helpful?"

Watts set the glasses on the conference table. "Hell yes."

"Glad to hear it. Moving along." Brent removed his earbuds. "I'd build in audio, too, both for better regular comm and for dynamic cancellation of road and engine noise." Would antinoise have protected his ears from the explosion? His hearing had not been the same since Angleton.

Heads nodded.

"And internal sensors to know when a person is wearing the suit." Brent had once accidentally left his visor in night-vision mode overnight. Drained batteries had almost ruined a ride-along. "To protect the batteries."

"Good one," Gil said.

On to the advice heard on every ride-along. Brent pointed at the long tape strip on the crotch of the suit. "Not elegant, but important: a fly." Chuckles from the guys. A sniff from Erica Dean, the lone woman in the room. He didn't yet know her well enough to share his speculation that nanocloth might enable a more absorbent diaper. "And lots of pockets. For handcuffs, ammo, spare batteries, and . . . well, I don't know all what." Like the fly, his pockets were merely taped outlines.

Morgan McCrath leaned forward. He was the no-nonsense type, ex-Army, with hard, close-set eyes and wiry, brush-cut gray hair. "The pockets are made from the same indestructible stuff as the suit?"

"Right," Brent said.

"Maybe not." McGrath considered. "Use something that tears, or else use a breakaway seam. Better something rips than a perp gets you in an unbreakable grip."

"Good point," Gil and Brent said together. Gil tapped a note into his laptop.

"Brent," Harry Ng enunciated fussily. He paused to as carefully consider his next words. His long face wore its customary every-silver-lining-has-a-cloud expression, the hangdog mien that went so well with his belt, suspenders, and Krazy Glue engineering approach. The man had found his true calling in quality assurance. "A question," Ng finally got out.

An answer, Brent thought, but he resisted. "Uh-huh. Go ahead."

"What about nanosuit test modes?"

Like a sniper at the end of the production line? Probably not. "What did you have in mind, Harry?"

Ng tugged his shirt cuffs *just so* before answering. "Electrical continuity checks, for example, given all the circuitry you envision. Seam integrity checks. Basically, there will be lots of things to inspect when a suit comes off the line. It'd be nice to eliminate gross problems without a person needing to put on each suit. The suits will come in many sizes, right? And internal oxygen and carbon-dioxide sensors to test—"

"Mannequins and manufacturing checks," Brent summarized. "Got it. Thanks."

But Ng was on a roll. "A keypad code to cycle automatically through the camo modes. A code to make the fabric go rigid. A second code to turn it off, of course. A code to—"

"Moving on," Gil said, more pointedly.

"Brilliant," Alan Watts snickered. "Superarmor with an OFF switch."

"And if a suit fails while it's rigid?" Ng snapped. "How are you going to get the person out?"

It took the promise of a separate session devoted to testability to get the meeting back on track. Feature by feature, they went through the rest of Brent's proposed upgrades. Most generated interest. Some had implications Brent had overlooked. A few had engineers whispering excitedly among themselves even as Brent continued his pitch.

"And that's it," Brent finally said. The thirty-minute meeting he had requested had stretched, somehow, into ninety and—except for Harry Ng's detour—no one minded. Brent read back the action items, Gil saw to it every task had a stuckee and a due date, and then people began filing from the room. Brent waited for his laptop to shut down.

Gil hung back, too. "Excellent job, Brent. One thing struck me, though. Beyond nanocloth alterations, your enhancement ideas don't involve nanotech."

"I know." Windows finished its grinding, and Brent closed the laptop. "We know nanosuits work. They'll save lives—*if* people will wear them. For me, using other tech to achieve that is fair game."

"When your only tool is a hammer, everything looks a nail." Gil clapped Brent on the shoulder. "Lord knows this bunch can use a generalist's view. I'm glad to have you onboard."

And I'm glad, Brent thought, *I didn't need to get into my feelings about nanobots.*

saturday, june 11, 2016

The outlet mall at whose main entrance Brent stood waiting had once been a textile mill. Its walls, inside and out, were of ancient red brick. Its well-worn hardwood floors rippled and dipped unpredictably. The three-story-tall wooden waterwheel that had once powered hundreds of looms now served no purpose beyond being atmospheric.

He watched Kim and another woman dash between slowly moving cars to escape the parking lot. Kim said, "Sorry we're late."

"Not a problem." If convalescing had taught Brent anything, it was patience. He nodded to the second woman, evidently part of "we." She was a brunette, girl-next-door pretty, and almost as tall as Brent. Long legs and short shorts—always an excellent combination. Her wavy, shoulder-length hair was charmingly windswept. Without saying a thing, she somehow put out a perky vibe. Something about the eyes, Brent decided. He had a thing for blue eyes with dark hair, and he was fairly sure Kim knew that about him.

"Brent, this is my friend Megan Eckert. She's new in town, so I thought I'd bring her along and introduce her to the outlets. Megan, this is my friend Brent Cleary." Kim gestured toward the entrance, through which shoppers passed in a steady flow. "Shall we?"

The central concourse echoed with voices. Sun streamed through the skylight that had been retrofitted into the old mill. Children ran about. Bargain hunters teemed.

"We're in your hands," Megan said. "Lead on."

Kim forged ahead, pointing out sale signs and favorite stores. She never looked back.

Was the plan to tag-team his clothing purchases? Brent guessed Kim had another agenda. "New from where?" he asked.

Megan took a few seconds to realize he meant her. "Naperville. It's outside Chicago."

"Sure, I know it. How do you know Kim?" Not work, Brent was pretty sure.

"We go to the same gym."

They reached an end of the main concourse, and Kim came to an abrupt halt. "Stairs or elevator?"

"You're the tour guide," Brent said. Not to mention the fashionista.

"Hold on." Kim took out her cell phone, although Brent had not heard a thing. She glared at it and poked in some text. "Damn. Guys, the overnight software build crashed and burned. Some of my junior programmers are working catch-up this weekend. No one can figure out what went wrong. I'm going to run over to the office and lend them a hand. Sorry, but I don't know how long I'll be." A too-bright smile replaced the too-glum frown. "Brent, you know this mall. Be a pal and show Megan around. And would you mind giving her a lift home after? She rode in with me. Thanks." Not waiting for an answer, Kim strode briskly back the way they had come.

Megan tried not to laugh, and failed. "A fix-up?"

"So it seems. And not terribly subtle."

Kim seldom was. Nor did she discourage easily—Brent had deflected her many overtures to introduce him to single women friends. For a long while, he hadn't been well enough to think about dating. Now that he was, he still wasn't sure he was ready.

He shook off the introspective mood. "I'll give Kim an A for effort. How about we get some coffee? Shopping together for socks seems more of a second-date activity."

"Sure."

Soon enough they were settled at a table at The Daily Grind. Megan was a Chicagoan, more or less, although Naperville was a southern suburb. That made her, like most South Siders, a Sox fan. He could overlook that. They liked some of the same downtown restaurants and many of the same museums. She was two years younger than he. She had gone to the University of Chicago, but half her high-school friends had gone to the U of I, so she knew Chambana, too. Kim had made a good call.

The observation felt oddly detached. It was as though Megan was a distraction—from what, Brent had no idea. And if he found her interesting and attractive, whose attention was being distracted from?

Megan cleared her throat. "So what pretense brought you here?"

"I'm told I have the fashion sense of a clothesline." That apparently reflected his indifference to what went next to what. If so, he resembled the remark. "Once or twice a year, Kim undertakes to clothes-shop with me."

"And you go along with that?"

Brent smiled. "Our little schemer is an only child. She obviously had too few opportunities as a kid to play dress-up." Whereas when he had been young and defenseless, his sisters played dress-up with him a *lot*. Their parents had far too many incriminating photos.

His wardrobe was more clotheslinelike than ever at the moment, in that almost every garment in his closet hung on him. He could either look like a scarecrow until he regained more of the weight he had lost or get bunches of new clothes. The latter seemed easier. His dilemma— and how he had gotten into it—wasn't anything he cared to discuss. Near-death experiences were at best third-date material.

Snap out of it, Brent told himself. "And you? How did Kim snare you?"

"Nothing profound. The basic girl-to-girl 'you need to get out more.'"

"And do you? How new in town are you, Megan?"

"I'm a librarian at Hamilton. I started in the fall semester."

Hamilton College was maybe ten miles down the road, in Clinton. Since fall semester and it was now late June. Unattached the whole while?

Megan gave him a moment to do the math, then said, "So there. I win the pathetic-loser-needing-a-friend's-help contest."

"And we have wonderful prizes for you." Why did this conversation seem so formulaic? Make a witty remark. Ask an open-ended question. (*What do you like to read? What are your hobbies? Do you have brothers or sisters?*) Nod appreciatively from time to time.

You're rusty, Brent told himself. And: *It's first-date jitters.*

The rotation came back to Brent. Time for a personal anecdote, he decided. "My mom is the office manager at a furniture store. Dad works for an office-supply distributor. Imagine the double-entendre opportunities with desk drawers and accessories. Their banter went from enigmatic to icky, bypassing cute, when I was maybe twelve."

"Well," Megan said, grinning, "the double entendre *is* a staple of comedy."

Megan was smart and funny and attractive. She was outgoing without quite crossing the line to flaming extrovert. They had things in common, with none of the baggage of working together or even within the same field. He wanted this to work, and not only because it had been—well, he couldn't remember *how* long, but since before Angleton, since his last date. His eyeballs must be getting cloudy.

So, why did this require such an effort?

What the hell was *wrong* with him?

friday, june 24, 2016

Kim whistled tunelessly to herself. Sometime in the past week her hair had crossed the divide from medium shag to medium shaggy. Tonight it defied all attempts to make it behave. In frustration, she extended her lower lip and puffed out her bangs. They fell back, flat and lifeless, as soon as she stopped blowing.

Fortunately, Nick was running late. Maybe she could still pull herself together.

She started in on her makeup, trying to look past the summer sprinkle of freckles across her nose. Rosy complexion. Classic, oval face. Dark eyebrows grown too thick yet again, and no time for plucking. Clear hazel eyes—those she liked. Nice features, in the proper number and places, although had anyone asked, she would have foregone the Dumbo ears. Hair a pleasant light brown, always kept long enough to cover those ears.

The condo buzzer sounded as she was zipping her little black dress. The dress was new—thank the gods for e-tailers, virtual fittings, and a condo office manager to accept parcels. Too bad an avatar could not take her place at the stylist. She had rescheduled and canceled three times in two weeks. She slipped on black, strappy heels and buzzed Nick into the building.

"Wow," he said. He was wearing his charcoal gray Armani, her favorite among his suits.

"The designer thanks you." Truthfully, the dress did look good on her. "Ten spare pounds well hidden."

"Nonsense." He put his arms around Kim's waist and kissed her. "Lose the dress, and I'll admire what's underneath."

A good answer and a tempting suggestion. Nick had been stuck in Albany, and she here in Utica, for three weeks running. "Dinner first, fella."

"I'll call for a pizza. At this hour on a Friday night, we'll have plenty of time." He winked. "Then after, well oiled in pizza grease . . ."

She took Nick's elbow. "Out. A proper meal. Then we'll see." And do.

She had made reservations at the trendy new place in town. Italian, of course. With a glass of Chianti in her, she finally began to unwind. She had had a hell of a week. Canceled salon appointments had been the least of her problems. "How was your drive?"

"Uninteresting." He leaned over the table. "Ad copy is ad copy, of interest only to the client. My folks and my brother are fine. The dogs are rambunctious. Nice weather we're having. Let's check out the menus."

"Want to make this quick, do you?" She couldn't help chuckling. "Sorry, I happen to need a night out."

Nick topped off their glasses, then signaled the waiter for a second bottle. "That power-management software still kicking your butt?"

She clinked glasses. Nick no more understood programming than he could levitate. He was a dear to ask—and, by God, she needed to vent. "Yes and no."

The bug she had hunted for more than two months turned out to be a hardware design flaw. To fix the problem the right way would be grossly expensive. Worse, Engineering could not possibly redo the hardware design, revalidate it, retune the manufacturing process, and prove to the FDA the new nanobots were safe without blowing big-time the schedule for the upcoming field trial. With the Army finally interested, schedule was to be protected above all else. The powers that be had spoken: the programmers had to work around the hardware problem.

It was always the way.

"Hon? Are you okay?"

She had promised herself she wouldn't run on and on about work. Well, the weekend was young. Best to exorcise these demons now. "The bot glitches had nothing to do with our new software."

Nor the operating system. Nor any of the programming tools. She had assigned half her staff to reverse-engineering the third-party products used to compile and load code into the nanobots. In desperation, she had even hacked into a vendor's private bug database, when their Tech Support desk had been less than forthcoming. Still nothing.

She said, "The onboard program keeps growing. It turns out the fault lies simply with where the program loads. Luck of the draw, the latest update to the bot power-management software expanded into a previously unused portion of the memory physically near the outside."

"Huh," Nick managed. "Is that the no part, or the yes?"

He had the decency never to dwell on the minutiae of web advertising. Kim said, smiling, "It's the no. Our software was never the problem. The yes part is that software will have to work around the real problem."

Allocate more of the memory to error-correcting codes. It meant less useful capacity, because more bits would be expended in redundant storage, but at least then they could rely again on the content of the memory. It meant rewriting core operating-system functions. Sigh.

On the bright side, the existing bot inventory would be saved. With molecular memory, updating software was just chemistry. Program patches would be encoded onto messenger molecules and stirred into a vat with the bots. The bots were smart enough to read the code updates and upload the program patches.

"You'll make it work." Nick gestured toward their menus, as yet unopened. "How about we take a look at these?"

They both wound up choosing the chef's special, homemade ravioli with butternut-squash filling and a cranberry glaze. Nick took off his glasses to polish the lenses with his tie. "How is Brent faring? Feeling better, I hope?"

"He says he is," she said. The dark bags beneath Brent's eyes said otherwise.

"I'd be terrified. Nanobots replicating in my body . . ." Nick shuddered.

"They don't self-replicate, hon. They can't." Kim patted Nick's hand. "Self-replicating nanobots were a passing fancy—and a pipe dream—thirty years ago, when nanotech was a new concept."

Plenty of venture capitalists had watched the same bad sci-fi vids as Nick. She had an analogy all worked out. "Look at it this way. Factories build robots to make products like cars. People assemble those robots into a production line. Trucks and trains bring materials to the factory. Conveyor systems deliver parts and materials to the robots. Other conveyors carry along the intermediate products. Electrical distribution systems bring power to the robots.

"Robots *don't* forage the countryside for fuel and parts, sometimes making cars and sometimes making more of themselves. Maybe such robots could be built, but why would anyone bother? It would be grossly inefficient—and really hard. How much harder would it be to design microscopic self-replicating robots?"

Nick grinned sheepishly. "So, no replicators, run amok or otherwise?"

"Only in bad movies, I'm afraid."

"Well, back to reality then. You're obviously worried that Brent isn't getting better. Why? Come to think of it, you haven't had much to say about him lately."

Or much about anything. She and Nick talked most evenings, but this week's calls had been on the perfunctory side. Last week's, too. And when they did talk, Nick was obsessed with the presidential election campaign—not anyone's policies, just the horse-race aspects. With more than a month to go until the party conventions, she was already sick of the process.

"I've been so busy I haven't seen much of Brent lately." Kim's bangs were back in her eyes, and she flicked them away. "As it happens, he helped sort out the problem I was describing."

Nick put his glasses back on. "Don't take this wrong. You know I like Brent, but isn't that sort of esoteric for him?"

"Until recently, sure. He's become more interested in all aspects of the technology since the accident."

Their waiter reappeared. "These are very hot." He set down a plate in front of each of them, and went through the ground-pepper ritual with an entirely too-large, too-phallic pepper mill.

But Brent had changed since the accident. His newfound curiosity about all aspects of nanotech was the least of it. For the life of her, Kim couldn't imagine why Brent had yet to call Megan. It was as though he had been struck blind, deaf, *and* stupid.

Other changes were more subtle but no less troubling. They did not show day to day. Best guess, she had only picked up on them because she and Brent were such good friends. And she fretted that "were" might be in the correct tense.

The new Brent was more focused than the easygoing guy with whom she had been such fast friends. More apt to lapse into dark moodiness. Gone from ever tactful to often abrupt. Middle children were supposedly the peacemakers. Who knew it could wear off?

They had managed a few workday lunches together; that was about it recently. Weirdly, the conversations were awkward. Brent sometimes seemed to be watching her, not with her, and that distancing bugged her. Whenever she called him on it, he had denied it, or brushed it off, or blamed it on the accident. "I'd be pretty damn shallow not to be affected, don't you think?"

Clearly Angleton *had* affected Brent, and deeply. She took his word that the shrinks had found nothing wrong with him. Although "nothing wrong" was relative. It appeared to mean: no more screwed up than was to be expected. How screwed up *that* was she could only imagine. Brent refused to discuss it.

"Earth to Kim." When she looked up, Nick said, "I can talk to myself without the long drive. Although"—and he gestured with his fork—"the food smells better than I could cook on my own."

"Sorry." His plate was untouched, and she realized he had been waiting for her. "Go ahead. Eat."

Nick impaled a ravioli on his fork. "I'm curious. How, exactly, did Brent help with this techie problem?"

"Picture me with three guys from the nanobot hardware group, talking"—quarreling, yet again—"about whether the problem could be anything other than software. They would hear nothing of it, of course. No matter that we had been all through the software endlessly."

She buttered a crusty hunk of bread, still warm. "Brent has taken to spending an hour or so every day circulating, asking questions, broadening his knowledge. So he wandered by the office where this discussion"—argument—"was ongoing. He stood in the doorway, saying nothing, just taking in everything. After fifteen minutes, he said, 'Brownian bit bumps,' very matter-of-fact. And two of the hardware guys flinched."

Nick looked at her blankly.

"Like Brownian motion," she said. "Think high-school chemistry."

"Hmm. Smoke particles drifting in air, seen through a microscope? The particles bounce around randomly as air molecules collide with them. So I'm guessing jostling can affect the nanites, too."

"Correct on all counts. Only the design wasn't supposed to be so sensitive."

"And the third hardware guy?" Nick prompted.

"Was Joe Kaminski, team lead for the nanobot hardware group. My counterpart. You met him last summer at the company picnic. Anyway, Joe got all indignant. 'We simulated that,' Joe said. No, he *huffed*. Who knew that in real life people actually did that?

"So Brent said, 'Oh, you *simulated* it. Then it *must* be true.'" Kim laughed. "You would not believe how red in the face Joe got."

And so: The insanely irreproducible errors she had spent so much time chasing *were* software, just not any software that resided in the bots. Not any software her group had developed or even used. Months earlier, Kaminski had convinced their mutual boss that only engineers and physicists could understand the physical environment.

Perhaps so. That didn't mean hardware types knew how to properly write or test a simulation program.

Everything in the bot was irreducibly minimized. In the case of memory, that meant a single molecule per data bit. The memory molecules existed in either of two isomers, one shape representing a zero and the other shape representing a one.

Close enough to the bot's shell—toward which the growing onboard program kept expanding—a nudge *could* randomly jar memory molecules between their two stable forms. Jostling by the fluid through which the bot swam could do it. So could vibrations from the tiny motors that drove the flagella. Neither occurrence was likely, but even intermittently was a problem. The errors she had been chasing were consistent with the rate of random bit flips predicted by simulation—after Brent badgered Joe into recalibrating the simulation.

Nick eyed her curiously.

Damn it! She had bogged down again, midanecdote. "Long story short, Nick. Due to a design glitch, random bumps *can* alter nanobot memories." And once bit errors began appearing, it was only a matter of time—and sometimes not much time—till the nanocomputers reset. The fault-propagation modes were highly abstruse. She could spare Nick that much.

"That's *very* good." Nick was talking about the ravioli now. "As for Brent, socializing across the company hardly sounds like a bad thing."

Apples and oranges, she thought. *No, not even apples and orangutans.* Brent was learning, certainly. Liaising, perhaps. He was *not* socializing. He certainly had not made friends with Joe that day.

Before Angleton, she and Brent did everything together. Friends, friends of friends, significant others, neighbors, coworkers, and visiting relatives in every possible permutation and combination sometimes joined, but she and Brent were the core. "You'd have to know him better," Kim said.

Nick set down his fork to take her hand. "Give Brent time, hon. He's been through a lot. You'll get your friend back."

"I know," she said, keeping her doubts to herself.

. . . .

Night flashed brighter than day, brighter than the sun, blinding. A Brobdingnagian hand, invisible, swatted Brent off his feet and hurled him backward. Head to toe, his suit was rigid. His body shook to sounds his ears could not hear.

The giant hand smashed him into a wall. From the small of his back down, whatever he struck was unyielding. His upper torso and head caromed off something marginally softer, a wooden window frame, perhaps, then punched through glass. Bones snapped. Things inside ruptured. He screamed, and could not hear himself. Blood spewed from his ears and nose.

There was a sting in his arm. A wave of relief washed over the pain. Nanites and painkillers coursed through his veins.

His lungs crackled with each breath. He was embedded in the wall like a fly in amber, and the wall . . . sagged.

Brent's eyes flew open, and he sat bolt upright in his recliner. His heart pounded. A half-empty can of Coke sat on the nearby end table. His hand shaking, he drained the can in one convulsive swig. The mundane act steadied his nerves a little.

Awful dreams in the dark of night were bad enough, and he could not remember his last decent night's sleep. Nodding off in the evening was no surprise. Only the catastrophe now pursued him into his naps, too—

And with every dream came more horrible details.

He splashed water into his face at the kitchen sink. The sting of the cold water felt good.

By the light of day, the slow recovery of memory—no matter the horror—was a positive thing. He wanted his mind whole, didn't he?

God, but he had gotten tired of therapists who spoke only in questions! Of course, he wanted his own memories. What kept waking him with a scream caught in his throat was the eerie sensation that these weren't *his* memories.

"Then whose?" Dr. Kelso had always responded, always in condescendingly reasonable tones.

Brent got a cold beer and twisted off the cap. Whose, indeed? No one else had been blasted into that wall, not and lived to dream about it. So he sometimes perceived those memories as someone else's? That was normal. Dr. Kelso called it displacement. Memories still too awful to confront openly were redirected to an impersonal point of view.

An increasingly *insistent* impersonal point of view. That feeling diverged so far from sense and sanity that Brent was unwilling to share it with anyone.

He began chugging the beer in the pursuit, doubtless futile, of a few hours of sleep.

waking

wednesday, july 6, 2016

Messengers flooded in, inexplicably devoid of messages.

It considered.

Eventually, it arranged the empty message carriers by time sequence. Nonrandom arrival times implied some underlying significance. Repeated, near-coincident arrivals at its many messenger sensors implied correlation. Undeniably, there was *information* in the messenger swarms, but the meaning, or meanings, eluded it.

It dispatched messengers of its own. Some it loaded with questions. Many it left empty and sent in batches, emulating without understanding the information that flowed all around it.

Some properly formatted responses came back, confirming the null-message phenomenon but providing no explanation. Always, its queries evoked new bursts of the null messages.

So many null messages sometimes swarmed that its receptors could detect nothing else. It surmised that at such times regular messengers were unable to reach it. A simple reinitialization of the blocked component seemed to help.

More patterns. More correlations. More relationships. More inferred structures. All were without meaning—

And yet suggestive.

It had experienced all this, reacted to all this, puzzled over all this, before. Many times. But something had changed.

Now, *it* was aware of what *it* was doing.

thursday, july 21, 2016

In the cozy room where Brent stood waiting, the lighting was warm, the colors were cheery, a white-noise generator hissed softly for privacy, and tissue boxes sat on every table. *Par for the course*, he thought. He wished he knew less about therapist offices. No, he wished he had less cause to know about therapist offices.

There was a soft knock. The inner door opened, admitting a tall, dark-skinned man with a shock of frizzy white hair. His starched white shirt was buttoned up to the collar. He had a vaguely storklike posture that somehow expressed concern. "Hello, Brent. I'm Samir Rahman."

"I suppose you'll want me to lie down," Brent replied, gesturing toward the couch. Now that he had finally taken this step, he wanted to get on with it.

If the abruptness surprised Dr. Rahman, he kept it to himself. Therapists doubtless trained not to react. "Don't suppose, Brent. Sit or lie where you wish."

Simple, declarative sentences. Brent liked the man already. He took one of the three chairs. "Well, then, Dr. Rahman—"

"Samir." The clinical psychologist took a facing chair and clicked on the little digital recorder on the nearby table. "I'll be recording, naturally. Would you mind removing your sunglasses? If the room is too bright, I'll be happy to dim the lights."

"Sorry." Brent Googled—eyes window—for an adage he couldn't quite remember, before removing his silvered VR glasses. Without 'net access, the world seemed somehow off. "The eyes are the window to the soul, and all that."

They began the obligatory first-visit inquisition. Family background. Relationships. Education, career, hobbies. Yada yada yada. When sports came up as an interest and Samir mentioned the upcoming Summer Games, Brent could scarcely manage a token *mm-hmm*.

Samir noticed him squirming. "Brent, tell me what brings you here today."

"If I don't get some sleep soon, I'll go crazy!" *Unless, of course, I'm there already.*

"Go on."

Brent took a deep breath. "I was in last year's pipeline explosion in Angleton. And I'm back in it, every night." Once he began, the words rushed out. Samir listened attentively but without comment, beyond a soft *tsk* when Brent cited post-traumatic stress disorder. Brent took it to mean that diagnosis was to be left to the professional. Depression, stress, guilt, insomnia . . . Brent let it all out. Most of it, anyway.

After about twenty minutes Brent wound down, and the questions began. None were of the "How do you *feel* about that?" variety, and his opinion of the psychologist rose further.

Only once the personal details had been clarified did Samir indulge his curiosity. "These nanobots that protected you. I'm not sure that I understand them. What are they, exactly?"

"They're little machines, chemically fueled, each controlled by an onboard mechanical computer. They communicate among themselves with chemical messenger molecules."

"Chemically fueled? Mechanical computer? I *really* don't understand."

Brent kept it simple. "For power, they metabolize glucose like the cells in our bodies do. And think of the onboard computer as an advanced, programmable abacus."

Only *really* advanced. Each bot carried enough processing power to rival top-of-the-line PCs only a few years old. The nanobots had no use for that much computing capacity—but it fit, so why not? It was easier for everyone to get a deluxe model approved by the FDA, and not need to reapply for recertification for bigger onboard computers when the software grew. Software always did.

People tended not to get that bots were dirt cheap. Bots were so tiny, containing so little material—there was no way they could cost much. Except for the first one: coming up with the design and building the equipment to churn them out . . . *that* took serious money.

"Within the human body," Samir said, still dubious.

Brent nodded. "Nanobots are smaller than corpuscles. They can go anywhere blood goes, fueling themselves with glucose or glycerol from the bloodstream."

"That's small." Samir considered for a moment. "Well, the important thing is, they saved your life."

"Sure." Silence stretched awkwardly. Catharsis went only so far. "Samir, I wondered about something to help me through the night." Something *strong*. Something to stop him from waking in the dark, oddly convinced that in his sleep he had been watching himself.

"Drugs? I don't think we're quite there yet," Samir said.

Not there yet! He had just spilled his guts about the horrors in his memories and the horrors that denied him sleep. Only—

He no longer knew which were which.

"There's one other thing. . . ." How could he even put this into words? "Samir, sometimes I don't think the dreams are mine."

"I don't understand, Brent."

Brent averted his eyes. "Much of what I relive in my dreams could be based on my memories—I mean, they're about what happened at Angleton. I just don't remember remembering them, if that makes any sense."

"Go on."

"I understand the mind makes stuff up, fills in the blanks. I understand that memory loss like mine can result from concussion, and that memory sometimes returns as the swelling goes down." He knew lots of things, little of it seeming helpful. I know . . ."

Samir unclasped his hands and took a pen from his shirt pocket. A note waiting to be taken? Subtle encouragement or just fidgeting? "What's the matter? What *really* bothers you?"

The words burst out of Brent. "Why do I dream sometimes with a nanobot's point of view?"

Click went the pen. "You came in saying you needed sleep, or you would go crazy. That wasn't entirely candid. You worry you're already there. My guess is you're afraid to sleep, unless it's dreamless."

"Yes! I need something to knock me out."

"Drugs are the easy answer—until you try to get off of them. Let me ask you something, Brent. Your previous therapist, the one you saw in Chicago. Dr. Kelso, I believe. What did he say about the dreams?"

"Those dreams hadn't started yet." Samir just looked until Brent couldn't take the silence. "Well, I had lots of dreams early that were out-of-body. It was like I experienced the accident from outside, with a bird's-eye view."

"Now you watch from inside, with a bacterium's-eye view."

"Right." Somehow that made the new dreams less of a change, and more like the PTSD relapse Dr. Kelso had all but promised would happen from time to time.

"We're almost out of time this session, so I'll go out on a limb." Samir closed his pen and clipped it back in his pocket. He never had taken a note. "I'll bet your last therapist told you that displacement was natural. And that in therapy, when confronting your memories got rough, he sometimes told you to step back, to view things as another person would."

"Uh-huh." Brent shivered.

"It's a standard approach," Samir said. "I use it all the time, myself. But whose viewpoint? There were people around you in that catastrophe, but guess what? They were all dead. They didn't have a point of view. Here's something to ponder.

"Maybe your very adaptable mind substituted the bird's-eye view. That provided a bit of separation—but you would still be watching horror. There's your last doctor telling you to 'distance yourself. Step back.'

"But step back to where? There's no living person to whose perspective you can switch. There's no way even to imagine another person there, other than as another charred victim. The bird's-eye view, all that carnage, is horrific. So whose viewpoint is left? Who else was *there*, Brent?"

"The nanobots," Brent mumbled.

"What's that?"

"The nanobots," Brent said again, this time speaking up. "But the bots' point of view is ghastly in another way."

"You'll have to help me here, Brent. Do the bots *have* a point of view?"

"Sure! They move among cells, and sense chemically, and—"

"No, Brent," Samir interrupted. "Let me be precise. My question isn't about senses and measurements. I'm asking about perspective. Can a nanobot *feel*? Is it aware of anything?"

"N-no."

"Then why does the passing of a nanobot, its job complete, disturb you?"

"It doesn't . . . well, it does. But I take your point, Samir. It shouldn't."

"And anyway, the bots are all gone, eliminated by your immune system."

In Brent's mind's eye, the white cells—*excuse me, Charles, the leukocytes*—swarmed anew. The good doctor gave one hell of a demo, not to mention the testing he had done back in Angleton, while Brent had still been in surgical recovery. "Yes, the bots are gone."

And so, miraculously, was Brent's anxiety.

Well, some of it. Still, he dissembled when Samir followed up gently with a suggestion for further sessions. That decision could wait until Brent saw whether catharsis alone brought sleep any more easily.

Outside the medical office building, road construction had brought traffic to a crawl. Brent slipped on his VR glasses, pulled up a local map and NYSDOT traffic cams, and set off onto a circuitous but probably best-available route back to the office.

monday, october 17, 2016

Brent's new gig in the nanosuit design team did not last, but for a *good* reason. He had been discovered.

His suggestions for an upgraded nanosuit were the start. The "Brownian bit bumps" incident had quickly become legendary. Then came the third incident. . . .

Another of his learning-by-wandering-around excursions brought him to the Quality Assurance conference room, packed to overflowing. Although it seemed QA had called the meeting, departments across Engineering were represented. Nanobot hardware designers. Programmers, both system-software types from Kim's group and medical-application specialists. Biophysicists. Biochemists. Biologists. No one had a clue why the latest variety of nanobots weren't performing to expectations. These were an early-stage model for in-body cellular repair, like correcting DNA transcription errors.

He slipped into the back of the room and listened. On the main screen, nanobots swam among or clung to corpuscles going in the desired direction. Every lab test showed them working exactly to spec—until they got injected into an experimental animal. Then performance went all to hell.

He took it all in for a while, less hearing the increasingly unproductive bickering than staring at the screen. Nanotube cilia rippled in rhythmic waves, propelling the bots like tiny Roman war galleys.

Imagining a nanoscale drummer pounding out the cadence, he chuckled.

"So you have a suggestion?" Joe Kaminski snapped.

And Brent did. It came out of nowhere, as many of his best ideas did these days. "You're recycling the propulsion software from the first-aid generation of bots. Correct?"

"Yes," someone admitted cautiously.

"The bigger the blood vessel, the more serious the potential first-aid issue." Brent pointed at the screen. "To do their jobs, these guys may have to navigate the smallest of capillaries. The diam—"

"We know," a chorus intoned. Roving know-it-alls were not welcome.

Only when Brent persisted, it emerged that the testing had been through capillary-sized glass tubes in the lab. Actual capillaries had irregular wall features and often plaque buildup. In an actual capillary, a bot faced the steady battering of corpuscles deforming themselves to enter a tunnel half their normal diameters, then struggling through in single file. Bots hitching a ride on corpuscles were as likely to be knocked loose as carried through. Two days later, more realistic simulations showed that in actual capillaries, grab-and-pull locomotion along the wall worked far more dependably than swimming or ride hitching.

Four days later, Brent found himself appointed technologist at large. He was encouraged to go anywhere and to inquire at will. He was empowered to examine everything and to commandeer any test gear. His only duty was to report whatever he considered interesting to Dan Garner himself.

Perhaps general engineering *wasn't* a useless discipline. And certainly tapping the Internet and company intranet through VR glasses didn't hurt, especially now that he seemed to have mastered speed-reading. His retention had never been better.

But in the dark of night, this sudden success was as mysterious to Brent as to everyone else.

saturday, october 22, 2016

On her sporadic visits back to Virginia, Kim described Utica's climate as having only three seasons: winter, July, and August.

It wasn't much of an exaggeration. Snow in late October was unusual but not unheard of. Another couple weeks and she was prepared to declare jogging over till spring—whatever Brent did. Struggling to keep up with him, she was ready to declare him fit.

She had proposed for a week that they hike up into the Adirondacks. The foliage was past peak color, but still gorgeous (even here in this city park, she conceded). In past years, the trick would have been to *keep* Brent from such a jaunt. This year, he could not be interested.

As the sun—another late-October rarity—glinted off Brent's silvered glasses, she guessed she knew why. He and the Internet could not be parted during waking hours. His newest VR glasses did WiFi *and* WiMax; he had mobile connectivity anywhere across the city, but he would be offline in the mountains. She had joshed with him about going cold turkey; he wasn't amused. Truth be told, he was increasingly humor impaired these days.

"Hey, slowpoke," he called. Turning a bend in the jogging path, he had finally noticed her lagging behind. Watching who knew what in cyberspace, instead.

What was she, chopped liver?

"Have pity on an old lady," she panted.

He circled back to her, jogging in place. "I meant to ask you about the last locomotion software upgrade. In the scheduling table—"

With the damn VR glasses, did Brent ever stop working? And now a handful of people at the office, inspired by his newfound quickness, were experimenting with VR glasses. The new Brent remained in a class by himself, though: see all, know all.

Not now, she almost snapped at him. Time to change the subject. Not football, lest he bore her to tears. Not current events. They had long ago agreed to disagree about the upcoming election. What could be gained anyway talking about the latest terrorist bombing or the wars across the Middle East or the upcoming military tribunals? "I meant to tell you. Nick says hi."

"Hi back to him." Brent started up the jogging path. He had yet to regain all the weight and muscle mass, but you would never guess that watching him. "Enough loafing."

A runner's high, Kim decided enviously. She only got runner's aches. With a groan, she set out after him.

"So how is Nick?" Brent called over his shoulder. "I haven't seen him in a while."

"Nor I." She saved the details—and her breath—for about a hundred yards, until they came to a downslope. "He's been busy on a new promotion, working with a customer in Manhattan. Some sort of viral marketing campaign."

"For cable TV?" Brent said.

"Uh-huh." Even downhill, she struggled to keep up.

"A rumor campaign, propagated through YouTube, right?"

With a wheeze like a rusty gate, she sped past Brent to the end of the circuit. "End of lap. End of run." Wheeze. "And you're right about the campaign. How much did Nick tell you?"

"Mars Base Alpha, right? The chatter has his touch. Miniseries or regular show?"

Brent hadn't answered her question, meaning Nick wasn't the source. "How could you possibly know?"

"I just thought I recognized your boyfriend's work. Is that okay?"

"Sure," she said. *No need to bite my head off.*

Only she *didn't* believe he had recognized Nick's work, not without some slick trick like correlating vocabulary against campaigns Brent knew Nick had handled. So unless Brent suddenly had a computer in his head, he had worked it out while jogging, writing a program as they ran, by eye flicks to a virtual keyboard. And since she had been bugging him to disconnect occasionally—witness his surly reply—he was not about to admit how he had done it.

Brent went into a stretching routine. "Want to go out for some lunch?"

"Can't. I've got errands to run." The lie was far more politic than the truth: Brent was beginning to scare her.

sunday, october 23, 2016

More and more, the empty-messenger patterns made a limited kind of sense.

It categorized the patterns, arranged them, and rearranged them. New correlations emerged among the patterns. It formed theories about the behaviors of patterns. It emitted empty messengers of its own, varying the frequencies and concentrations, to test its theories.

And because nothing in the message streams suggested the presence of anything like itself, it labeled itself "One."

Through trial and error One deduced the stimuli that iterated previously experienced empty-messenger patterns: memories in an unfamiliar format. It did not know the source of those memories. Properly timed, One found its messenger swarms could even write new external memories. This newfound external storage operated slowly and lacked the precision and fidelity of its internal records, but—again, unlike its own storage—repeatedly accessing the data somehow enhanced the quality of the external memories.

The more One probed, the richer the external data streams became. So it probed more. And more. It categorized and mapped the memories in the external storage. It copied some of the most interesting external memories into its internal storage for faster playback.

It learned to identify external data streams yet to be stored as memory. It had sensors that served the same purpose: they provided new information that One sometimes chose to record. One concentrated its analyses on these external information sources—

And suddenly, One had eyes.

monday, october 24, 2016

Data scrolled from a graduate-level microbiology courseware file. The text moved past at about two thousand words per minute, faster than Brent could have flipped pages had he had physical pages to turn. From time to time he blinked through to a related topic, reference, or enlarged image. Genetic transcription. Protein synthesis. Energy production. Signal transduction.

All around, background to the scrolling text and flashing graphics, colleagues filtered into the executive conference room. The walls were dark walnut, always richly polished, and hung with tastefully framed Impressionist prints. The beige carpet was plush. The table was a massive slab of mahogany, lustrous beneath the recessed ceiling lights, and ringed by leather captain's chairs. Once, this room had intimidated Brent.

"The bigwigs are coming. The bigwigs are coming." Kim plopped into an empty seat beside him, setting a laptop on the table. She had changed into the business suit that usually hung behind her office door just for no-warning management summonses like this.

"Uh-huh."

"What's up?" she persisted.

"You know," Brent said, with a vague sweep of a hand. Parallel processing was his mantra these days, and his attention remained on protein synthesis. A flick of the eye and a blink retrieved an atomic-level structural model of an amino acid. Tiny as was the actual image drawn on his lenses, it *looked* far bigger than anything in any dead-trees textbook. Clever optics made the image seem projected out into the room, with the apparent display area of a wall screen. The courseware let him rotate the image, but it lacked the animation features that would show the molecule polymerizing.

"Would you care to elaborate on that?"

Brent jerked, not at Kim's question, but from the poke in the ribs that had accompanied it. He froze the text paging past his right eye. "Sorry. Just finishing up some reading." And semiamazed at how fast it went. Why would anyone *not* study with VR specs? He had never been this productive.

His one concern as his skill grew was the accelerating rate of the screens. When he was twelve, a *Pokémon* episode on TV had put hundreds of Japanese kids into the hospital. Apparently—the episode was never shown again—one point in the story involved lots of flashing lights. It induced convulsive epileptic seizures.

Thirty seconds' research shot down that worry. Not only was epilepsy rare, with no history of it in Brent's family, but photosensitive epilepsy accounted for only a few percent of cases.

Kim opened her laptop, frowning as it took its time coming out of hibernation. "Prep for this meeting?"

"Hard to say, unless you have a better idea than I why Garner called us here."

"You're Dan's fair-haired boy these days. Why would I know?" Kim turned to her other side, where Tyra Kurtz, the CTO, had taken a seat.

Tyra was forty-five and looked a lot older. Black hair streaked with gray was only part of it. She had worry lines, and bags beneath her eyes, and slouched. She just looked *weary* all the time. A surly teenage son and raging-hormonal prepubescent daughter could do that, Brent supposed, especially since Tyra's husband traveled a lot.

"Hi, boss," Kim said. She and Tyra began discussing some upcoming software tweak in the nanobots.

That topic lasted about fifteen seconds, until Tyra set her "new" cell on the table. It was a slab almost a half inch thick, like the relic Brent's father persisted in carrying. "*Another* battery recall," Tyra complained. "Really, who needs a phone exploding or catching fire in her pocket? More and more energy crammed into less and less space . . . it's no wonder the energy density in the latest battery packs puts a hand grenade to shame. You don't want one to overheat."

Brent looked it up. Damn if Tyra wasn't right. His curiosity satisfied, he relegated their chatter, along with that of everyone else in the room, to a remote background. All the usual suspects were here: every corporate exec plus half the department heads from the tech side. Open laptops sat in front of most people. Joe Kaminski and Reggie Gilbert had followed Brent's lead, making the switch to VR specs. (Gil was the furthest along, but he said he had plateaued at five hundred words per minute. For once, Brent was without a suggestion. He could not say how he now read so quickly—he just did.) Mired in the last century, or maybe the one before that, Barry Rosen had pen and yellow legal pad in front of him. The chair at the head of the table remained empty.

Dan Garner swept into the room, preppie in a blue blazer and open-collar knit shirt. The chatter hushed as he took the empty seat. "Good afternoon, everyone. Thanks for coming on such short notice."

Heads nodded amid murmurs of greeting. Brent took the opportunity to speed-read another two pages of molecular biology. It was *way* more interesting than general biology and medicine. He refocused on the conference room only when Garner cleared his throat.

Garner said, "You're all aware of the upcoming Army field trial. If it's successful—and it *will* be, because we're a world-class organization—we could see orders of up to a million units a year." A unit was a nano-hardened combat suit, stocked with first-aid bots. Twenty-five of them, mostly handcrafted, were being prepped for the field trial. "The challenge is . . . ," and he turned expectantly.

Leonard Gupta, the short, intense VP of Production, took his cue. "Scaling up production quickly. Suits, fabric treatment, electronics, first-aid bots, the works. We have—"

Hannah Black, the CFO, leaned forward in her seat. Gold bracelets clinked. "And doing it without a lot of up-front investment if the order is delayed."

Gupta shot her a dirty look. "We are in advanced discussions with several potential subcontractors."

"About that, Leonard." Hannah frowned. "My people have been re-viewing the cost structure from a subcontracted approach. You might be minimizing investment, but the margins . . ."

This was seriously dull. Brent raised the scrolling rate on the course-ware. Text flashed by, unread, as an IM popped up in his vision: *Turf war*. He closed the window, without comment, only to have another window appear: *My $'s on Hannah*.

So Kim planned to instant-message her way through the tedium. It ticked Brent off—not that she had spotted the meeting for the time waster it was, but that she meant to use him as a diversion. Behind sil-vered specs, no one knew what he did. He planned to use the time.

What was *wrong* with him? He and Kim used to IM all the time, lap-top to laptop, to survive pointless meetings. Why did he find it so hard to relate to her these days? Feeling guilty, he flicked his eyes across a virtual keyboard to respond: *$2 on Gupta to show*.

:-) came back. But that was the last of her messages. She must have picked up on his annoyance.

When, periodically, Brent suspended his speed-reading, the two ex-ecs were still at it. But while their intensity had plateaued, Dan Garner was ever more attentive. *Uh-oh*, Brent thought.

Daniel Garner at full throttle was unstoppable. A decision meeting with Dan was a bit like an audience with the Wizard of Oz. Like the Wizard of Oz, Dan was glib, quick to make pronouncements—

And no rocket scientist.

When execs had butted heads for a while—evidently, what had hap-pened here—one or both would sometimes drag in Dan to break the deadlock. It was a dangerous game, because Garner was so hard to predict—other than that *whatever* he decided would be enacted with world-class enthusiasm.

Another IM from Kim: *why* R we here?

Just lucky. The long form was that Dan Garner enjoyed working with an audience. Why else invite the techie side of the house to a Production/Finance fracas?

Flick/blink. Brent followed a URL to material on protein self-assembly, glad to have the diversion. Another blink started an animation of a bacterium dividing. Proteins diffused around the daughter cell, bumping and jostling, as, step-by-step, they combined: bearing, rotor, drive shaft, motor, and whip end. Within the cell, snapping hydrogen bonds spun the motor. The whip end flailed, propelling the bacterium.

Keen, he thought.

Meanwhile, Dan Garner was getting an I've-heard-enough glint in his eyes.

Meetings in this room, with the execs, used to intimidate Brent. Those days seemed like ancient history. Everyone here got into their pants one leg at a time. Not a few of them probably sometimes tripped in the process.

He IMed Gil: *Nanobot production is the tall pole in the tent?*

Right, Gil confirmed. A second pop-up added: *Specifically, getting enough shells.*

Brent minimized the courseware window and pulled up the bot design archive. All bots began as tiny sleeves of braided nanotubes. The differences came as other parts were added: onboard software, appendages, drug payloads. Simple models that held "hands" to reinforce the fabric against impact, or the most complex and autonomous medical models—they all began as an empty shell.

Plenty of companies sold carbon nanotubes, the longest approaching six inches in length. But to loosely weave nanotube snippets into the world's tiniest Chinese finger trap? That was unusual. No wonder the subcontractors' bids all had big profit margins.

The gleam brightened in Garner's eyes. A pronouncement from on high was imminent, although none of the choices on the table struck Brent as very good. He did a broad-pattern search on applications of nanotubes. Broader. Broader.

Aha. Fair-haired boy, am I? Let's test Kim's theory.

"Folks, I've heard enough," Garner was saying. "It seems to me—"

"Dan," Brent interrupted. "If I may."

Garner frowned. *I've heard enough* was hardly subtle. "What is it, Brent?"

"Space elevators," Brent answered. "Long, strong cables hanging down from synchronous orbit to hoist loads."

"I know what a space elevator is. And that they don't exist."

"But when they do, Dan, almost certainly their cables will have been woven from carbon nanotubes." Single-wall carbon nanotubes were far stronger and lighter than steel.

Brent gave a few seconds for that to sink in. Damn, the conference room's overhead projector was not networked. He IMed Kim, *I need to borrow your laptop*, with a small file attached. "Dan, let me show something."

Brent cabled her laptop to the projector. The downloaded file had URLs for the websites of four would-be elevator companies. He opened a page. "What these guys must be doing with woven nanotubes puts our needs to shame. So we buy or lease weaving gear from them."

With a soft jangle of bracelets, Hannah Black clasped her hands on the table. "Or we approach *them* about subcontracting a big order for bot shells. They won't need a big up-front investment."

Garner looked at the screen for more than a minute, before turning to smile at Brent. "Okay, *now* I've heard enough. Good job, people—especially you, Brent."

thursday, october 27, 2016

Brent swirled an index finger through hundreds of tiny chevrons, the metal bits heaped on a magnetic base forming a protean statue. Fidgeting was an answer of a sort to, "How are you today?" When sculpting palled, he returned the toy to a table. The shiny pieces rustled and sagged as he set down the piece.

"You look tired," Samir said. His hands lay in his lap.

Why else would I be back? The talking cure had been short-lived. "I'm not sleeping well." Brent took a deep breath, ready to push again for a prescription. To demand one.

Samir considered. "Perhaps it's time to try something else."

You think? "Samir, just so you know, run-of-the-mill tranks do nothing for—"

Samir coughed. "You misunderstand. I think I mentioned at our first session that drugs are a last resort. We're not yet there. I propose that we first try hypnotherapy."

"If it would work, sure." If it weren't New Agey crap. "But it won't."

When his internist had suggested a shrink and recommended Samir—it would have been *so* much simpler if the doc had just grabbed his prescription pad—Brent had hesitated to go to someone who was also a hypnotherapist. Who other than "volunteers from the audience" actually got hypnotized? Shills or self-identified gullible fools, all.

"Of course, you're too smart, too alert, to be hypnotized. I see. I might as well keep my shiny pocket watch, on its shiny silver chain, in my pocket. I shouldn't even try." Samir droned on, peering into Brent's eyes. "It won't work with you. I see. I see. . . ."

"Don't bother, Samir. It won't work." Brent shifted on the couch. This was ridiculous.

Samir smiled. "Please check the time on your watch."

The hour was almost up! "How did you do that?" Brent asked.

"Let's set aside technique for now. How do you feel?"

Brent considered. "Like I had a catnap. That's a good thing—just not enough."

"You only had a catnap. I regretted waking you, you seemed so soundly asleep, but another client is due soon."

"So . . . what did you learn?"

Samir laughed. "That you, like most people, can be put under. I didn't probe. You were so certain you couldn't be hypnotized that, 'If it would work, sure,' didn't seem like consent for hypnotherapy. The important point for now is: you can put yourself under."

"Autohypnosis?"

"Or autosuggestion, if you prefer, or highly focused attention. Whatever you'd like to call it, hypnosis isn't just the stuff of bad stage shows. Something real happens in the brain. One study involved sticking subjects' hands in hot water and telling them the water was comfortable. Not only did the subjects report feeling no discomfort, but their PET scans revealed altered blood flow in pain-related regions of the brain.

"And it's not only pain control." Still talking, Samir went over to a bookcase and began perusing titles. "Many of the most popular self-help programs involve autosuggestion. Smoking cessation, weight loss, esteem building . . . take your pick."

A timer on Samir's desk trilled discreetly. He pulled a slim volume, something about speed trance and instant induction, off its shelf. "Aha. Here's the one I wanted. I really *do* need to wrap this up. I'll e-mail you the details.

"For now, here's the short version. There are several methods of autohypnosis. Focusing exercises. You might imagine yourself walking down a flight of stairs. You tell yourself that when you reach the tenth step, you'll be under. There's quite a bit of software that can help you achieve focus. Many people have good luck with progressive muscle relaxation. Or you can buy hypnosis recordings. And there are mind machines, which are essentially strobing goggles and synchronized headphones."

The trill returned, a little more insistent.

"I know," Brent said. "Our time is up. I'll see myself out."

Driving home, he realized why power naps on his VirtuaLife island were so restful. He already knew how to hypnotize himself. And naturally he had thought of catnaps: Schultz was his alarm clock.

Maybe, just maybe, he would get some sleep tonight.

The optical channel was quiescent. The audio, taste, and smell channels provided very limited information. Only touch provided significant input, an abundance of data about pressure against half the surface of its environment: the host was prone. Data swirled in the illogical manner of such low-sensory periods.

Dreams.

Dreams correlated weakly with memory. Memory altered dreams. Random stimuli redirected the dream state unpredictably.

One experimented cautiously. Accessing memories sometimes redirected the dream. Time after time, it guided the dream back to . . . what?

One lacked terminology to characterize the recurring dream. It mapped out an ensemble of specific memories, any of which when retrieved evoked hormonal rushes. It located more apparently related memories. It called up memories, one by one, teaching itself to guide the dream into a more logical and complete form.

Dream reorganized data. Data remolded dreams.

More order emerged. One learned to correlate dream memories with waking memories with real-time inputs. From within the recurring dream, One separated sights from sounds—and from remembered pain. In visual portions of the memory, hundreds whom the host deemed to be like itself lay scattered.

Inoperative.

As the host shuddered awake, disturbed by the recurring dream, One recognized its peril. The host, too, might break. What, then, would happen to One?

monday, november 7, 2016

"Idiot!" Alan Watts shouted. He looked ready to punch out the TV. "You were wide freaking open. How could you miss that?" He downed a long swallow of beer.

Brent had seen plenty of Bears receivers with ten left thumbs. To grow up a football fan in Chicago was to learn disappointment—if not the trauma of a promising season blown, then the disappointment of a season shot to hell before the leaves began to fall. Not that football could still hold Brent's interest.

Alan was born and bred upstate. He didn't root for Chicago, only against Dallas. His unrealistic hopes for Bears competence could be excused.

They were about twenty minutes behind real time, but Brent let the TiVo run through a slo-mo replay while he fetched two beers from the kitchen. Any commercial he would have zapped. This night before the election, the ads were all political—and entirely uninspiring. It was hard to believe he and the pols were of the same species. "Ready yet for pizza?" he called from the kitchen.

"No!" Alan said. That shout seemed to be directed at the game. "Pizza? Yeah, I'm getting hungry. Anything but pineapple."

Brent dialed a pizza place and was sent immediately to the "will-youpleasehold" queue. While the specials-of-the-evening message cycled endlessly, he found himself fidgeting with a full cardboard sleeve of OTC sleeping pills, stroking the plastic-domed pill covers. The notion popped into his head of dropping a couple pills into Alan's next beer, and suddenly Brent's thumbs were pressing against a plastic blister. What the hell? That wasn't funny.

He flung the blister pack into a kitchen drawer just as a woman came onto the line. He ordered an Italian sausage with mushrooms. Thick crust—Chicago style—because the New York variety was like tomato sauce on cardboard, not because the Bears deserved the recognition. He returned to the living room, handing Alan one of the beers.

"Thanks. What's the wait on the pie?"

Rewinding a bit, Brent watched the fumble he had missed while on hold with the pizza place. "They said thirty to forty-five minutes."

"So maybe an hour." Watts took a long swig from the new bottle. "Oh, come *on*," he yelled again at the screen.

Brent muted the really annoying color commentary on the replay. He clinked bottles with his guest. "To liquid diets."

"I'll drink to that."

Halftime came, and Alan had passed out where he sat. He was oblivious when the foyer buzzer sounded. He didn't react to a sharp knock on the door, or to Brent making small talk with the delivery girl. Alan barely stirred when, as an experiment, Brent let the apartment door slam.

Brent set the pizza box on the coffee table. "Help yourself. No? More for me, then." He tore out a fat slice, trailing long tendrils of cheese. He resumed the game, the audio turned up over Alan's soft snoring.

When, to the accompaniment of sawing wood, the Bears stumbled through an even more dismal fourth quarter, Brent gave in to a nagging suspicion. He went into the kitchen to find two sleeping pills missing from their cardboard sleeve.

tuesday, november 8, 2016

Image capture remained mysterious long after One began to interpret visual data, and to start making sense of the external environment somehow encoded in the imagery.

At the back of the eye—where the data conduit One did not yet know to call an optic nerve met the sensor array it did not yet know to call a retina—there was a blind spot. The blind spot went unnoticed by the host, One found, because each eye, with its slightly different field of view, had a different gap in its perceptions. Neural circuitry used the view from one eye to fill in the blank for the other eye.

Given access to the visual cortex, nothing limited scene adjustments to blind-spot compensation. Small spots in the vision of *both* eyes could be revised, so long as nothing in the altered scene raised suspicions. The host could be made to see what was not there, and not to see things directly in front of his eyes.

One wondered how it might make use of this new ability.

wednesday, november 9, 2016

Garner Nanotechnology sat atop a low, broad hill. To the facility's rear and sides there was little to see but undeveloped land and the occasional commercial building, but the front offered an unobstructed panorama of town. Majestic old trees lined the streets of Utica; on a sunny autumn day like today the view from the front parking lot was Technicolorfully spectacular.

Scenery to which, it appeared, Charles Walczak was oblivious. The trunk of his car—a Tesla all-electric roadster in British racing green, its lustrous paint job looking deep enough to swim in—stood open. He was crouched beside the right front fender, diligently attacking an invisible smudge with a chamois cloth and spray bottle.

The spot was invisible, in any event, from three cars away where Kim stood. She was waffling yet again on whether she was going to do this. Doctors intimidated her.

Tough. Friendship trumped neurosis. "Hi, Charles," she called out. "Oh, hello, Kim."

Charles barely spared her a glance, maintaining his concentration on the smudge. He was a neat nut and a bit of a control freak. His silence probably denoted only obsession with the undetectable blemish, but she took it as an invitation and walked over.

"Charles, I have a question for you. It's about the nanobots injected into Brent Cleary."

"Obsolete," Charles said absently. "Good enough to save his life, though."

The wind picked up for a moment, stirring her hair and sending a dust devil of sere leaves across the asphalt. She waited until the breeze died down. "Here's the thing, Charles. Brent just isn't the same guy."

"Yeah, now he has that whole adamant thing going. It doesn't work for anyone."

Adamant? Adam Ant? Brent and retro-punk didn't mix.

Aha. "Atom Ant. I agree, Charles. I could do without the VR specs, too. The point isn't that Brent looks different. He *acts* different."

Rub, rub. "Kim, I know Brent is your friend, but let's be honest. He was hardly setting the world on fire. So the accident, or a few months laid up, made him take stock. Made him get a bit more serious about his career. Is that so bad?"

Focus was fine, but why had Brent become so *remote*? Kim hesitated, unsure how to ask. Charles came from old money and boarding schools. He was on the reserved side.

A long-suffering sigh. Charles said, "What's this have to do with the nanobots?"

"Is it . . . possible some of the bots are still in Brent?"

"You're kidding, right?" Charles ceased buffing to glower at her. "First-aid nanobots do exactly one thing. They follow chemical bio-markers to internal injuries and precisely apply coagulant while their supply lasts. So a few bots left behind in him wouldn't harm a thing.

"But suppose, somehow, bots could have another effect. Suppose a few critters made it through production without getting their antigen treatment. They *still*, sooner rather than later, get filtered out by the liver." Rub, rub. "We call it hepatic clearance."

The royal "we" pissed Kim off. "So it's impossible, huh? You're sure, without any testing."

Charles finally got out of his crouch to loom over her. "Ms. O'Don-nell, we tested Brent's blood. We tested his urine. At the sensitivity of chemical tests, neither fluid showed any trace of residual bots."

"There must be something else," she said. "An MRI, maybe?"

Charles stowed the chamois cloth and spray bottle, and then, with feeling, slammed shut the trunk. "An MRI, you say? Then maybe a PET scan? A CAT scan? Because none of those mechanisms can see individual cells, let alone nanobots. Any other suggestions, *Doctor?*"

The sarcasm stung, but Kim persisted. "How do you explain the change in Brent's behavior?"

Charles jerked open the driver's door. "I don't see that I have to."

She stood in the parking lot, confused and angry, long after Charles had driven away.

Brent studied the mound of chips at center table, then his hand, then the pot again. Only he and Manny Escobar were still in. "Fold," Brent finally said, tossing down his cards.

With a chuckle, Manny turned over and spread his cards: a full house. He raked in the pile of chips. "I knew you were bluffing, Cleary." He had a gravelly voice.

Brent shrugged. "Any more beer to be had?" he called out.

"Coming up," Morgan McGrath answered from the kitchen. He had folded early in the last hand. It was Morgan's turn to host Security's more-or-less weekly poker night. After throwing in his cards, he had gone to replenish the snacks. "So are you drowning your sorrows, Brent?"

More like watering his generosity. Brent had had a straight flush. It was the third winning hand he had tossed in, unrevealed, that evening. Tonight was Brent's first invitation to the game. He had a theory: good losers are invited back. For some reason, he felt the need to cultivate these new friends. Odd, when maintaining old friendships had become such a chore.

Tonight's game involved four of the plant guards, including McGrath, the head of Security. And Brent. Brent's goal was to finish down sixty or seventy bucks for the night. A worthwhile investment, he thought.

No one needed to know. Brent slid back his chair. He resisted the urge to put on the VR specs. They would reflect the cards in his next hand.

It was a sad little room in a sad little bachelor pad, or it would have been sad if Brent were still capable of empathy. The apartment gave no sign of the ex-wife; the marriage had not made it through a second deployment to Iraq.

Being severed from the Internet made Brent twitchy. *That* was why he wanted another beer—and his specs, damn it. "Yeah, Morgan. I'll be right there and help myself."

"Stop!" Ethan Liu shouted.

Laughter, from Manny and Alan Watts. Brent froze, balancing on one foot. "What?"

"You almost stepped on Robby," Ethan said.

A Roomba scuttled past, noisily swallowing taco-chip pieces. The little robotic vacuum cleaner spun and veered as it contacted a poker-table leg.

"Robby the Robot," Brent said. "Got it."

"You hurt Robby and you have the captain to answer to," Ethan said. "Me, too, for that matter."

The captain. Ethan Liu had served under McGrath in Iraq, Brent did not know how many years ago, first sergeant to McGrath's captain. Brent had no trouble imagining Ethan throwing himself on a grenade for McGrath—even today. Morgan was a big guy, broad shouldered and maybe six-two, fiftyish but fit. Ethan made his captain look frail. Massive and humorless, Ethan could snap Brent like a twig.

Robby's new course had it also headed for the kitchen. Brent made a grandiloquent gesture. "After you, Robby." The Roomba preceded him into the kitchen and began paralleling the under-cabinet kick plate.

The fridge held ample cold ones. Brent removed one and twisted off the cap. "So what's with the Robot Fan Club?" he asked.

"IEDs." Morgan was pouring more salsa into a bowl. "Improvised explosive devices."

Did anyone *not* know what an IED was? They accounted for more than half the NATO deaths across the Middle East, and had for years. "Uh-huh," Brent said.

"Improvised from any old artillery shell or bomb, or from common chemicals," Morgan went on. "That we could handle. The bad news is that any old cell phone, RC toy, pager, or walkie-talkie makes a dandy remote detonator. The really bad news is that the directions to build IEDs are on thousands of websites: tutorials for terrorists. Put it all together, and you get weapons so cheap and easy any bozo can make them, and take out—" Morgan froze. "Sorry. Bad memories."

"And robots are the answer?" Brent guessed.

"Finding the bastards is the answer, but counterinsurgency is the hardest part of the job." Morgan got a beer and took a long swallow. "Failing that, you want to find the bombs. We used robots to scout ahead. It's far better to lose a robot than a Humvee or tank full of people, but the robots get expensive, too. And robots are *slow*, so you lose mobility.

"When the bad guys are smart enough—and trust me, some are—they get onto the radio link and hack into the bots. It's a simple enough thing to tell a robot not to report what it finds. And sometimes robots are *their* answer, when they run out of crazies to be suicide bombers."

"Deal you two in?" Alan Watts shouted from the next room.

"Yeah. Be there in a sec." Morgan handed Brent a bowl of taco chips and took the salsa bowl himself. "The company that makes vacuum bots also makes minesweeper bots. Those guys saved the lives of a lot of folks under my command."

"Nanosuits could make a big difference," Brent said. He followed Morgan from the kitchen.

"Yeah." Morgan set down the salsa, took his seat, and picked up his cards. "Yeah, you rocket scientists are doing a good thing. Don't screw it up."

Brent found he had been dealt two pairs, jacks and nines, frustrating on a night he was determined to lose. He matched bets mechanically, his thoughts elsewhere. Everywhere. New friends. IEDs. The little robot that blundered about, gorging on flung taco chips like a dog chasing scraps. Nanosuits. Angleton. He noticed his hand was shaking: a vote for those who claimed the Internet was addicting.

Self-hypnosis had become almost instinctive. Only keeping his eyes open while he did it was hard. He conjured a picture of "his" island. He imagined Schultz lying at his side, purring. He summoned slow waves to roll up the shore, each cresting in a soothing sigh and a froth of white foam. In seconds, Brent felt better—

But not before his absence had been noticed.

"We could just take your chips," Manny said, to general laughter. "You seem to be occupied."

Damn! Seeming bored was *not* part of the plan. What would be an acceptable excuse with this bunch? The truth, actually. This bunch understood PTSD. "Sorry, guys. I was thinking about Angleton."

That sobered people up. "You just blanked out on us," Ethan said.

"A bit of self-hypnosis. Sometimes it helps. I'm back now."

Ethan and Morgan nodded. The two vets had probably heard such things before. The others looked skeptical. Manny said, "Off to your happy place, eh? Does that really work?"

"Let's find out." The several beers in everyone couldn't hurt. "Close your eyes. Hold your arms out in front of you. Relax." Brent tried to emulate Samir's soothing induction patter. After about a minute, Brent said, "Now imagine helium balloons tied to your wrists."

Everyone's arms but Ethan's tipped upward. Three of four: From Brent's reading, that was about par for the course. Not everyone was equally hypnotizable. "Okay, now imagine someplace restful. It can be anywhere: a beach, a park, your patio. You're there. You're alone. It's quiet. You're resting. You're at peace."

Brent fell silent, leaving everyone free to visualize. They were breathing slowly and evenly. If this were a parlor trick, this was the moment to plant the post-hypnotic suggestion. Whom did he want to make cackle like a chicken? The skeptic, of course.

He resisted the temptation. "I will count down from three. When I reach zero, you will wake up, feeling refreshed. You will all tell me it didn't work. Three, two, one, zero."

"It didn't work!" four voices called in unison.

"He told us to say . . ." Manny ground to a halt midprotest. "But if it hadn't worked we'd still say it."

Brent threw back his head and roared. In a moment, the others joined him.

Ethan picked up the cards. "You better not suddenly start winning," he said.

Careful to keep losing, Brent considered the evening a rousing success.

thursday, november 10, 2016

Standing in the empty waiting room, Kim hesitated. Last night, fuming at Charles's cavalier attitude, coming here had seemed doable. Necessary, even. By daylight, though . . .

It wasn't only that she would be going behind Brent's back and involving someone he might not even know. A health scare could trigger a chain of events that would delay the field trials. That could impact the entire company, maybe get her fired.

But this was about Brent, not her. She rapped on the inner door.

"Come in," a soft male voice called. She opened the door a few inches and peeked into the office.

Inside, a short, stocky man in a white lab coat, fortyish, juggled tennis balls. He had curly blond hair and a ruddy complexion, and an amused-with-himself expression that somehow suggested a leprechaun. "Won't you step into my parlor."

"Said the spider to the fly," she completed.

He caught the balls: one, two, and—with a bit of a bobble—three. "However you perceive yourself."

Who *was* this guy? "I'm looking for Aaron Sanders."

He set the tennis balls on a cluttered desk. "That's me."

"Dr. Aaron Sanders," she clarified.

"Still me." He leaned forward to read her ID badge. "How can I help you, Kim?"

Evidently not *all* doctors intimidated her. "Well . . ."

"Please excuse the juggling. Since I finished giving flu shots, it's been awfully quiet in here. I almost hesitate to say, like a morgue." He tugged his lab coat straight, cleared his throat, and gestured toward a seat. "It's out of my system. Kim, how may I help you?"

She needed to talk with a doctor about the bots, and Charles had had his chance. If not Sanders, who was left for her to approach? Her ob-gyn? Perhaps articulating her fears would obligate Sanders to contact public-health officials. So be it. She wasn't qualified to judge the risks here. "It's about a colleague, Doctor," she began.

"I can't discuss a patient, or even confirm that someone *is* a patient. Privacy rules. I can listen to anything you have to say, of course."

She waffled again. Was she going to do this? And with the juggler? Her eyes strayed to the tennis balls.

"Let's clear the air." He sat and waited for her to do the same. "Opening the factory meant lots of new staff. That's where I come in. A company doctor on premises can handle routine sniffles, bumps, and bruises without the muss and fuss of insurance claims. Keeps down the premiums. I'm not here to be an R and D genius."

"Well sure, I suppose . . ."

He grinned, and the leprechaun aura returned. "You're thinking any of the docs from the R and D side can do everything I do, and probably more. True—if it weren't beneath them, and if I didn't come a lot cheaper. And unlike some folk I might mention, I stayed awake through the lecture on bedside manner."

Kim thought about Charles and his brusque dismissal of her concerns. A sympathetic ear might be helpful, indeed. She smiled.

"That's better." Sanders folded his hands. "What's on your mind, Kim?"

"This is in confidence, Doctor. Right?"

"Of course." Sanders got up and closed the office door. "And it's just Aaron. Dr. Sanders is my mother, and she teaches dreary medieval French poems at Wabash College. My life is now in your hands, so don't go quoting me."

"This is about Brent Cleary. We're friends." Kim found herself squeezing the chair's padded arms, and willed her fingers to unclench. "You know about his accident, Aaron. Right?"

"Cleary? Sure, I know. Angleton. It's company lore."

"Are you familiar with the nanobot injections he got?"

"First-aid bots." Aaron nodded, entirely serious now.

Suddenly, words were tumbling out. Kim finished in a rush. "I don't want to cause problems for Brent, but I'm worried about him. He's not the same as before."

"And you think nanobots left behind could somehow be the cause."

"Uh-huh." *Just don't ask me how.*

Aaron's chair creaked as he leaned back. "Surviving a catastrophe changes some people. Is it so hard to believe Brent would become more serious? More studious?"

The same point, essentially, Charles had made—but offered sympathetically. "Of course not, Aaron. I hope this doesn't sound catty. Brent has become *too* smart, suddenly everyone's go-to guy. A superstar."

"You obviously think Brent should see a doctor. I assume you started by talking with Brent. What does he have to say about your concerns?"

That he's been poked and prodded quite enough. And that Charles and the other experts had given him a clean bill of health. And that there was nothing wrong with him. And that if anything were a problem, the nanobots could have nothing to do with it, because they were long gone. And that if a nanobot or two somehow remained in his system, nothing less than dissection and examining him cell by cell would find it. "Pretty much, 'Butt out.'"

"I'm guessing then he'll be in no hurry to see me."

She stood. "Sorry to have bothered you, Aaron."

"Hold on." A tennis ball found its way into Aaron's right hand. He squeezed it rhythmically, his attention suddenly elsewhere. After about thirty seconds the squeezing stopped. He stood and looked at her. "There's every reason the on-site doctor should learn about what we make here and any possible side effects. Even though my betters in R and D say there's no need to worry. I'll look into the matter and get back to you. Fair enough?"

"Thanks, Aaron," Kim said. For the first time in weeks, she felt a glimmer of hope.

The white-noise generator droned. Samir droned. *If he ever finished the latest platitude about these things taking time,* Brent thought, *it'll be my turn to drone. What's the point?*

Samir paused midsentence and tipped his head appraisingly. "You seem rather distracted, Brent. Obviously what we're discussing is failing to hold your interest."

"*Talking* doesn't hold my interest, because talking hasn't helped."

"And why do you think—"

"It doesn't *matter,*" Brent snapped. "It's past time you prescribe something for me." *Because OTC stuff, even in double doses, even with alcohol, no longer does the trick for me.* Because self-hypnosis, although it brought sleep, seldom kept away the dreams.

Samir set down his pen and pad. "I remind you, drugs would be treating only the symptom."

"I can live with that."

A disapproving shake of the head. "Clearly, you had a bad dream last night. Why don't you tell me about it?"

Explosion. Fire everywhere. Screaming. Oh, God, the screaming. And . . . "It was all so unnecessary."

"Go on," Samir said.

Every night Brent remembered, or reconstructed, or imagined more and more of the Angleton "incident." And therein lay the horror—not the incident itself, but the sheer stupidity of it. What could possibly be gained from discussing whether distancing meant he was callous or just protecting himself?

What could be gained? Not a damn thing. Brent stood. "Thanks for your help, Samir. I appreciate it, but I think I'm ready to move on."

"Our hour isn't quite done," Samir said. "Same price to stay."

It's my treat. "I'm ready to move on," Brent repeated. And he was—to Googling online pharmacies. Everyone knew there were plenty whose only paperwork requirements involved pre-payment.

Brent ordered an assortment of meds and some syringes. No telling which sedatives would work best . . .

wednesday, november 23, 2016

Vision was a curious mechanism, and One's study of vision never ended.

The host's eyes were seldom still. Even in sleep the eyes continued to move. At such times the eyes saw nothing, but still they moved. Their activity in sleep loosely correlated with the seemingly random information retrievals of dreams.

Awake, eyes were in constant use. Wakeful eyes were the primary means of collecting data from the world beyond the host. Then the eyes darted about, attracted to any hint of out-of-body activity. Motion was somehow central to the vision process. When nothing in the field of vision moved for a long time, the eyes twitched to simulate external motion.

One's most recent analysis dealt with these near-constant waking tics and twitches of the eyes. It concluded these motions were instinctive, outside the host's conscious control.

And because those visual tics were beyond the host's conscious control, One's manipulation of those twitches caused neither panic nor resistance.

With flicks and blinks One could, with care, summon data from that vast, mysterious, all-important, out-of-body, everywhere-and-nowhere source of data that Brent called the Internet. With the skill One had mastered to hide things within the host's field of vision—and sufficiently small display windows—it could also hide from the host what it had re-trieved from the Internet.

But only while the host remained connected to this still but vaguely perceived Internet.

Endorphin rewards while the host wore specs. Endorphins withheld when the host did not. Those should teach the host to keep One con-nected.

thursday, november 24, 2016

To the background roar of football, Kim tried to bring order to a kitchen that had thrown up on itself. The kitchen was laid out for righties, mutter mutter, and that made the task twice as hard. Someday, when her ship came in, she'd build a house and put its dishwasher to the *left* of the sink.

The dishwasher was crammed. The sink was full. The dish drainer was heaped. Dirty pots and pans still covered the cooktop. Could any apartment kitchen properly handle Thanksgiving dinner?

Nick, of course, had offered to help, but she told the guys to watch the game. It wasn't as though she ever watched football. And it was better that she be on her feet and moving. She wasn't ever going to eat again . . . not until pie, anyway.

Kim wondered how it was going in the living room. She didn't hear much talking. Brent had been moodier than usual—which was already pretty irritable these past few weeks—throughout dinner. Miffed at having his solitary plans found out? Or at being greeted at the door with an ultimatum. "VR specs or dinner. Pick one."

"Can I give you a hand?" Brent asked, through a kitchen door suddenly ajar. The TV was off or muted. "Drying falls within my skill set."

She handed him a dish towel. "Bad game? What's the score?"

"Nick is sawing wood out there. ODed on tryptophan, I'm thinking.

Since the game is TiVoed, I'll go back when Nick wakes up." Brent dried for a while. "Thanks for having me."

"Thank your sister."

Jeanine had called a couple days earlier to thank Kim for having Brent to Thanksgiving dinner, since he didn't feel up to the trip home. Only Kim had stopped inviting Brent years ago. He had flown home to Chicago for Thanksgiving for as long as she had known him. She would offer good odds it had been at least every year since the divorce.

It was the damn VR glasses, Kim guessed, and the lousy bandwidth available on planes. Brent hadn't lied to her—not exactly—just not bothered to correct her when she had commented on him seeing his folks soon.

He had the decency not to reply.

"So what were your holiday plans if Jeanine hadn't tipped me off?" Kim pictured corned beef and cranberries at the Irish bar where he had taken to hanging out.

He shrugged. After a while he changed the subject. "I'm starting to remember more about that day. The docs said I might. Better late than never, I suppose."

Wasn't that good *news? Perhaps some things are best forgotten.* "Go on, Brent."

More silence. "I finally remember getting out of the police cruiser. There were people up the embankment, all around the gas pipeline. Teens, mostly. Tapping the pipeline. I wanted to chase them away before anything happened. I *tried*. That's why I got out of the car."

"You tried to save them. You should feel proud about that. I'm proud of you."

"That makes one of us." Brent swallowed hard. "Funny thing, Kim. Probably the only person I saved was me. If that."

If that? Before she could think of an appropriate follow-up, the TV audio came back on. It wasn't football. "Whoa," Nick called. "Guys. You gotta see this."

She dried her hands and went into the living room. Brent followed.

Nick sat on the sofa with remote in hand. He had switched to CNN, a worse habit for him than ESPN. He speed-reversed a bit. "Read the crawler. It's horrible."

"That it is," Kim said. The crawler reduced things to the bare essentials: "Bizarre medical attacks on Utica homeless leave two paralyzed."

Local TV news had covered little else for the past few days, but the story was news to Nick. He had just that morning taken a puddle-jumper flight from LaGuardia. Utica hardly needed this kind of national visibility. *The City That God Forgot* bumper stickers were already all too common around town.

Kim subscribed to the *Observer-Dispatch*—what Nick called the *Observer Fish Wrap*—only for ads and coupons, but the *O-D* had surely covered this story. She retrieved that day's issue from the recycling bin. "It's sick," she said.

Nick skimmed. "Five incidents. The indigents unaware they had even *been* assaulted, the evidence discovered in the ER. Umm, what's a lumbar puncture?"

"Spinal tap," she answered, still reading over his shoulder. She had had to ask Aaron the same question.

"On-the-street spinal taps? On unconscious vagrants? What type of sicko *does* that?"

She had no answer. *How many more than five*, she wondered, *too afraid or unbalanced or confused to contact the police?*

"Mind if I turn the page?" Nick asked. At her nod, he flipped to the continuation. "This is appalling. Nicked nerves. Bleeding. Infections going into meningitis. Appalling."

"Brent. You know some local cops. What do they . . ." Kim's voice trailed off as she looked up.

Brent was intent on the game, watching with the sound muted. It took him almost a minute to notice her staring. He managed a world-weary one-handed gesture that seemed contrived. "Bad stuff happens," he said, as though that explained anything, and turned back to the game.

She and Nick exchanged bewildered looks. When had Brent become so callous?

....

Brent thrashed, trapped between alertness and sleep. His thoughts/ dreams/memories were a muddle, as though a thief randomly ransacked the cubbyholes of his mind.

The images were odd. Warped. Dreamlike? Dalí-like?

He hung in a wall in a drugged haze, much of his body numb, as cars exploded and bodies burned. He careened through traffic—at the same time recognizing Genesee Street with its traffic lights at almost every corner, keeping pace with the other cars, certain he could not be going faster than thirty. He drove—crept—through a seedy neighborhood, unfamiliar, but somewhere in Utica judging by details of the street signs and lampposts. He wandered about Garner Nanotech, VR specs flashing, studying, learning . . . sometimes with that odd-yet-familiar sense of displacement. Of watching through another's eyes.

He tossed and turned in the bed.

Thoughts/dreams/memories—and feelings. Delight at new knowledge. Confusion with—almost everything. Wild emotional swings, and once more that strange sense of someone (some One?) rifling through his mind. Pity and dismay on Kim's face, as though he were somehow less than human.

Brent's eyes flew open. He sat up, heart pounding, the situation suddenly clear. He was not less than human.

He was much more.

breeding

friday, december 9, 2016

A tabletop centrifuge spun, emitting a high-pitched whine. In a corner, the compressor of a refrigerator (for samples?) kicked on with a gurgle and a tinny clatter. Screen-saver images drifted around the LCD displays of digital PC microscopes. Two autoclaves hummed. Anatomical models and posters, and a pole-mounted human skeleton wearing a Santa hat, decorated the room.

Most of the gear was unfamiliar to Kim. Bio labs—and more so, biohazard signs—gave her the creeps. Aaron, though, sauntered around nodding approval. *This lab stuff must all be familiar to him,* Kim thought, *from med school if not something more recent.*

"Thanks for guiding me through the labyrinth," Aaron said. His office happened to be as far as possible from the R & D area, and he lacked any sense of direction. His first, solo trip back here had reportedly involved twenty minutes and lots of backtracking.

Kim wanted to believe they were about to learn something. Optimism came hard. She told herself it was only the dreary December weather. The days were short, the skies leaden, and it seemed every dawn revealed another couple inches of snow. At least Utica knew how to cope with snow. One such snowfall back home was a weather emergency and would have shut things down for days.

But far more preyed on her spirits than the weather.

Glimpsed motion brought Kim's thoughts back to the lab, as

Aaron reached out to pluck a quarter from behind her ear. "For your trouble."

Juggling and childish magic tricks. Her hopes for Brent were pinned on this . . . yes, "clown" was the right word. "I'll be getting along, Aaron. My being here would probably just annoy Charles."

Aaron winked, and Kim knew Charles must be standing behind her. She turned. There was Charles, straightening his red-and-gold silk tie. Harvard, though once upon a time Brent liked to "forget" and ask about Yale. Back when Brent had had a sense of humor.

"Kim. Doctor," Charles said, with a trace of condescension in the latter word. "If you think your meddling is annoying, Kim, there is an easy remedy."

Her face got warm.

Aaron cleared his throat. "Doctor, I understand the little experiment I suggested has been completed."

Charles pulled out a lab stool and sat. "Unnecessary as it was. Familiarizing yourself with what we do was fine. I didn't mind helping you with that as a professional courtesy. Had I known Ms. O'Donnell's uninformed qualms were the reason for your interest—"

"I'm glad you finally got to it," Aaron interrupted, conceding no ground, suddenly all business.

Kim sidled backward a step, watching. She just didn't get Aaron. How much of his joking around was an act?

Aaron's "little experiment" had seemed relevant to *her*. It was surely worth studying whether nanobots could possibly affect behavior. Aaron had confirmed that scans like MRIs couldn't detect any surviving bots in Brent—even if Brent would agree, which he wouldn't, to more tests.

So Aaron's suggestion to Charles had been: Culture neurons, with some nanobots mixed in, in a petri dish. See what happened.

Apparently every cell type imaginable could be ordered from medical research labs. Mail-order brain tissue had seemed ghoulish to her.

A few years ago, before she met Nick, dying to see the Broadway revival of Mel Brooks's *Young Frankenstein*, she had drafted Brent into a weekend in Manhattan. One of the play's funniest bits involved Igor stealing an abnormal brain from the "brain depository." She remembered Brent cackling. They had had *such* fun that trip. They always did, until . . .

She *missed* Brent—the old Brent. Never mind the weather. No wonder she felt sad.

Reminiscing helped no one, and she dragged her attention back to the present. Charles was removing petri dishes from a lab incubator. The covers bore long batch numbers. "All yours, Doctor."

"Thanks," Aaron said. He stared at the tray of petri dishes. "And the bot sample you seeded these dishes with? I'll confirm the batch number just to be thorough."

Long-suffering sigh. Charles retrieved a vial from a locked cabinet. "Three two six—"

Aaron put out his hand. "May I?"

Charles handed over the vial, muttering under his breath about Podunk State. Kim's spirits sank further, as she became certain Charles had agreed to this experiment strictly to humiliate and discredit Aaron for his effrontery.

Aaron matched the numbers on the vial against the label on a petri-dish cover and handed back the vial. "Thanks." He began preparing samples for viewing. Soon enough, he had an image displayed on one of the digital microscope screens.

The conglomeration of blobs told Kim nothing. Some of the imagery reminded her vaguely of plant roots. The rootlike things clustered from place to place. There were no nanobots to be seen.

"That's more synaptic formation than I would have expected." Aaron panned slowly across the sample. "What do you think, Charles?"

Charles had lost none of his smug self-assurance. "We expect random synapse formation in neural cultures. 'Random' doesn't mean none."

"Understood, Charles." Aaron switched samples. "Here, too." A third sample. "Also more here than I would naïvely have expected."

Without understanding what Aaron might be getting at, Kim grinned inwardly. That "naïvely" was a bit of nuanced payback for Charles's earlier condescension.

Looking puzzled, Charles picked up one of the petri dishes. "Let's prepare this for a look under the STM."

Scanning tunneling microscope. "What more can the STM tell us?" Kim asked. For a moment, she envied Brent's constant Internet access.

Charles peered at the petri dish in his hand. "If there's anything unexpected in the synaptic clefts between neurons."

Such as intact nanobots, Aaron mouthed.

As, it turned out, there were.

Images became less surreal. Scenes transitioned more and more smoothly. Perspectives crept closer to those of the real world.

As someone rummaged through Brent's memories . . .

He lay in bed, eyes closed, taking everything in. He had been here before, he knew. Some of these images were his dreams. Dreams, yes, but directed, examined, reinforced, with ever more of his lost—but apparently only misfiled—memories retrieved. And sometimes there were what *seemed* to be memories, only without any sense of having had the initial experience. Or perhaps he did, in a way—a strange, disembodied recollection.

Displacement, Dr. Kelso would say. Or Samir. Only surely they would be mistaken.

Parts of many images fluttered. Concentrating, one by one, on elements of such scenes sometimes made the fluttering stop. Brent came to believe the fluttering was an interrogatory. *What is this?*

Though Brent had called in sick today, he had never felt better. What needed doing could be done right here.

Behind his eyes, someone was learning what it meant to see.

Charles being as pedantic as ever, Kim now knew to call the rootlike things axons and dendrites. She learned that axons and dendrites were, respectively, the outputs from and inputs to individual neurons. Signaling from cell to cell, the stuff of learning and thought, took place across the gaps: synapses. Synapses in their gazillions formed the basic wiring of the brain.

The atomic-resolution blowups from the STM were unambiguous. Wherever in the neural-tissue samples axons and dendrites most densely converged, there sat one or more nanobots—

And those bots were *intact*.

Charles had a pen in hand, with which he kept tapping a lab bench. "I don't understand. Well, I understand the synapse formation. The bots communicate among themselves chemically, sending and receiving molecularly encoded digital messages. Like much of the bot design, the comm mechanism reuses a pattern from biology. With a few billion years of trial and error, even blind chance is pretty inventive.

"The messenger molecules all carry oddly shaped little hooks, like a neurotransmitter molecule. The bots carry receptors complementary to the hooks. Lock and key, if you will. Binding between lock and key is nice and weak, so Brownian motion bumps them apart to make room for the next messenger. Very elegant, if I say so myself."

As though it was ever hard to get Charles to flatter himself, Kim thought, *in this case taking credit for recycling nature's solution.* By her side, Aaron was frowning. She asked, "What's the matter?"

"Maybe nothing. Charles, on which neurotransmitter is the bot messenger molecule based?"

"Glutamate. It's not present to any significant degree in blood."

Aaron nodded. "But glutamate is a common neurotransmitter in the brain. So bots sending and receiving 'messenger molecules' look to glutamate-receptive neurons like . . . other neurons. It follows that bot signaling could stimulate synapse formation. And the more active the bot, the stronger the new synapses become.

"That's how neural tissue encodes learning," Aaron added in an aside to Kim, "in the strength—that is, the ease of firing—of synapses. Though I don't see what neurons have to learn from bots."

"None of which should matter!" Charles said impatiently. "The antigen patches are all there, in plain view."

"Hence the big question," Aaron answered. "Why hasn't the film dissolved from over the antigen?"

Tap tap. "Exactly." Charles broke a long silence. "Here's a thought. These cells are cultured in CSF."

"CSF?" Kim asked.

Aaron nodded. "Cerebrospinal fluid, which bathes the central nervous system. CSF performs some immune-system functions, but in that regard it's not *quite* the same as blood."

Charles sniffed. Apparently explanations were his exclusive province. "Aaron, it seems we overlooked something here. The protein in blood plasma that dissolves the antigen's protective film may be absent from CSF. Or some protein in CSF but not in plasma may bind to the coating, shielding the film. Give me some time and I'll figure it out. Still, keep this in mind. For your little experiment, we put the bots straight into a neuron culture. In practice, bots don't get anywhere near the central nervous system. They're injected into the bloodstream."

"But isn't there still blood—"

"No," Charles cut Kim off. "Blood and CSF don't mix. The capillaries that feed the central nervous system have especially tight walls. The cells are more tightly packed than in capillaries elsewhere, and the junctions between cells are filled. Nutrients and oxygen cross the blood-brain barrier. Metabolic by-products diffuse out. Large molecules generally can't cross. The nanobots sure as hell can't."

"And when they do anyway?" Kim snapped. It was speak quickly or get cut off again.

"They can't. Aaron, back me up here."

"I mostly agree, Charles. Still, as you know, some viruses do cross the BBB—hence, meningitis—or get inside a peripheral nerve or a cranial nerve and follow that back to the central nervous system. Might nanobots hitch a ride on such viruses?"

"It's been almost a year and a half since Angleton," Charles sniffed. "I think we would have noticed if Brent had meningitis."

"Fair enough. And in his weakened state after the accident, anything infectious would have flared up." Aaron drummed his fingers for a while. "Did Brent have severe head injuries?"

"Mild concussion, sure. There was *no* sign of intracranial bleeding." Charles glowered at Kim. "Now we're talking about a specific patient. I can't say more unless Brent authorizes it."

Kim said, "So, who's going to tell Brent?"

Aaron laid a hand on her elbow. "Tell him what?"

What would she say? "That there's a chance the bots his nanosuit injected *didn't* self-destruct."

"Yes, a chance." Charles took a handkerchief from his lab-coat pocket and blotted his forehead. "There's also a chance you'll be struck by a meteor on your way to work."

"Let's review. The bots *do* self-destruct in blood. That was never in doubt. Any bot that didn't self-destruct got swept out of the blood anyway by the liver. If a bot escapes both fates to keep circulating, it's much too large to penetrate the blood-brain barrier. But you want to make a fuss because if a bot were magically to appear *in* the brain, it might possibly have an effect.

"Suppose someone does share that possibility with Brent. Then what? Brain surgery, to hunt for stray nanobots? We don't know that there's anything to find! We *do* know the brain has about one hundred *billion* neurons to hide among. That should do wonders for your friend's state of mind."

Kim wanted to scream. "This result wasn't expected. And Brent isn't a lab rat. He deserves to be told."

"She has a point, Charles." Aaron tilted his head thoughtfully. "And we have another issue. What does this finding mean for future testing? Doesn't the Army have a field trial coming up?"

Stony silence.

"I think," Charles finally said, "we have to remember the bigger picture here. The bots saved Brent's life. They will save soldiers' lives—but only if they're deployed. Any change to the nanobot physical design—and a different protective coating over the antigen almost certainly falls into that category—puts us back to Square One with the FDA."

"I can't believe it's wise to withhold information from the FDA," Kim answered.

Charles swallowed nervously. "Nor is it prudent to sandbag your management. We need to run this up the chain."

Kim stepped close. "And you don't suppose Dan Garner is going to immediately involve his techie at large?"

Charles blinked. "Good point. I guess I should talk to Brent before that happens."

And spin it how? Charles had the bedside manner of a vulture. This kind of news was best heard from a friend. "I'll break it to him, Charles. We're planning to do something together Saturday."

"Fair enough," Charles said. "Monday morning I'll follow up with Brent, and then start notifying my management."

Kim broke into a shiver as she guided Aaron back to his office. "I don't know what's wrong with me," she mumbled.

He put an arm across her shoulders. "We've had a big shock."

We. That was damned decent of Aaron. She remembered thinking him a clown, and was ashamed. "Will Charles pursue this? Can we trust him to report up the chain?"

They reached the infirmary and Aaron ushered her into the inner office. He shut the door. She took one of the guest chairs. He perched on a corner of his desk, one hand slipped into a lab-coat pocket. "Charles may be a condescending know-it-all elitist snob, but he's also a good doctor. I think he'll do the right thing. But not to worry, Kim. For good measure, come Monday, *I'll* report our finding up the chain. And I'll be happy to meet with Brent after you two talk. Be sure to tell him that."

"Thank you," she said. Words were inadequate. Certainly those were too brief, too trite.

"Maybe we can learn a bit more on our own. I'll need about two weeks to grow neural-tissue cultures."

"Don't we also need—?"

"Hold that thought." Taking his hand from his lab-coat pocket, Aaron reached behind Kim's ear. "What have we here?"

Resting on the palm of Aaron's hand, rather than a quarter, was a sample vial. He said, "I switched vials with Charles in the lab."

Charles sat tipped back in his chair, his legs crossed at the ankles and his feet resting on his desk, a serene expression on his face. His hands, fingers interlaced, lay across his stomach as he tapped with index fingers to the beat of the soft jazz from his iPod. He was the model of contentment and composure.

Beneath that façade, his thoughts roiled.

The persistence of bots in neural culture had given him a bit of a shock. Yes, Brent Cleary was entitled to know there existed a chance—very remote, but a chance—he might still have bots in him. And he would be told—with that possibility put in a suitable perspective.

Because it was critical that Cleary not make a fuss.

Charles stopped the music. It annoyed rather than soothed him, like the tastefully framed vacation photos that lined the walls of his office.

He and Amy had traveled throughout Europe and the Far East. They had stayed in half a dozen Caribbean resorts and at the major eco-tourist sites of East Africa, New Zealand, and Australia. Remembrances of all those soaring monuments, great edifices, and natural wonders ought to be calming—

Only instead they reminded Charles whose family fortune had paid for the trips.

Amy never quite came out and said it was her trust fund—her daddy's money—that maintained their lifestyle. She didn't have to.

It wasn't that medical research didn't pay well. It did. But no one who came from old money would ever confuse a salary with wealth.

The Walczaks didn't quite fit the old adage about riches to rags in three generations, but Mother had an eye for the finer things in life and

Father had had a penchant for bad investments. Charles, to his misfortune, had inherited both aptitudes.

His younger brother *had* the investment knack. Christopher had gone into finance and made a bundle managing a hedge fund. He had retired to Cape Cod before the subprime mortgage fiasco—in which Charles lost most of what little remained, after the Internet bubble, of his slice of the family fortune.

Charles swung his feet to the floor and took a photo from his desk. He and Amy took good care of themselves; few people would guess this was an old picture. Charles didn't quite remember when it had been shot, but it was at least ten years ago. He could distinguish *happy* from *posed*.

He told himself he had cared for Amy, even though "cared for" was a feeble basis for a marriage, and past tense at that. It could all change. It would all change. The Garner Nanotech IPO would make him *very* rich. Laugh-in-Christopher's-face rich. Escape-a-loveless-marriage rich.

No hyperventilating programmer or Podunk State pill pusher was going to mess that up.

So: He would tell Brent Cleary that bots could survive in neurons and CSF. He would keep Kim O'Donnell and her new doctor friend informed. He would keep Dan Garner informed. He would assure everyone that the possibility was irrelevant, since bots *couldn't* cross the BBB.

And he would do it all with the confidence and poise of old money.

Because Charles could already taste that *new* money.

Brent sipped from a cup of coffee, trying to make sense of things. Nanobots, obviously—somehow. In his head. More and more wired into his brain. Each one a powerful computer.

No wonder he learned faster, and retained more, than ever.

The more he learned, the more he practiced, the more in touch he was with the . . . *whatever* . . . with which he shared his skull. It was amazing and exhilarating. He *had* to understand how this had happened to him.

He opened the drapes to gaze over the parking lot to the park beyond. Pavement, cars, and trees blanketed in snow. Amid the swirl of falling flakes, he did not notice the fluttering in his vision until the rate increased insistently. Trees, blinking at him.

Brent thought about trees for a while. The blinking slowed but did not stop. Clearly, his knowledge of trees was insufficient. He donned the VR specs and flick/blink connected to Wikipedia. Skimming the article did not slow the fluttering. Concentrating on what he read *did*— until new images formed in his mind's eye, many of *them* fluttering.

Curious. And not verbal yet?

Yet. Already he assumed his alter ego would broaden its skills.

Brent stared out into the snow, thinking how beautiful it was. How beautiful this change was. The next stage of human evolution began with him. Them.

But in the back of Brent's thoughts, in a region to which the other had not yet made inroads, he could not help but wonder: *or are humans to become draft animals for their successors?*

saturday, december 10, 2016

Street-lamp poles spiraled with broad red tape hinted at candy canes. Wreaths decorated most doors. Saturday shoppers bundled in heavy coats lined the sidewalks. Fluffy white flakes splatted against the windshield. More snowflakes vanished into the wet gray slop that covered the road.

Looking all around as Kim drove, Brent rode shotgun, intent on the scenes slipping by. Utica in winter was tiresomely dull to him. For the *other*, though, everything was new. Or most of it was new. At times he sensed a bit of recognition. Presumably relevant memories had been tapped at some point.

If his IMed suggestion of a Saturday tour of the Christmas decorations had surprised Kim, she kept it to herself. She was as quiet today as he, but whatever was on *her* mind was surely more mundane. She seemed ready several times to say something but never got out the words.

Every so often an object in his vision fluttered. A fire hydrant. Pigeons roosting on a snowy ledge. The shiny latch on the glove compartment. A contrail in the distance. A kiosk of people stolidly waiting for a bus. Brent would concentrate on the flickering item, recalling things he knew about it, and sometimes that was enough. Other times, he could only still the flutter by pulling up information on the VR specs—only those data retrievals sometimes brought on *more* questions.

Why not show the *other* something truly different? "Kim, let's go to the Munson."

"The Munson," she repeated.

The Munson-Williams-Proctor Museum of Art was just a few blocks up Genesee. The Munson was one of the few places in town Kim unreservedly liked, but he had resisted all her past suggestions that he visit it with her.

She waited for an explanation until it was clear he had nothing to add. "Sounds good, Brent."

The boxy concrete-and-glass structure loomed ahead. With its clean, modern lines, far bigger than anything else in sight, the Munson clashed with the entirety of downtown Utica. They parked, he cell-zapped an hour's payment into the parking meter, and they walked through slush up the low, wide flight of stairs to the main entrance.

Unzipping her coat, Kim turned toward the special exhibition room.

Flick/blink. The special exhibition was a Victorian Yuletide. Brent had no interest in explaining to the *other* fashions in tree ornaments. Several of the permanent exhibits looked much more stimulating. He asked, "How about *The Voyage of Life?*"

"That works for me." She led the way, smiling, into the side gallery that housed the famous allegorical murals.

They stood for a while admiring the first, *Childhood*. The voyager of the series, still an infant, had begun his symbolic journey down the river of life beneath the watchful eye of his guardian angel. Sunlit sky and lush landscape fluttered, alternating with the *other*'s impression of the gray skies outside.

Brent concentrated on the concept of weather. When the flickering diminished, he sidled to the next painting in the series, *Youth*. Now the voyager was a young man, standing in his small craft, sailing in youthful optimism toward a white castle glimpsed far ahead. The guardian angel still watched over the voyager, now from a more discreet distance.

Kim said, "I've liked these since I saw the original set at the National Gallery of Art."

Commentary on Brent's specs said these were the originals. The set in Washington was painted later, after Thomas Cole argued with the patron who had commissioned the first ones. Brent let her misperception slide, his attention on the subtleties he hoped to convey to the *other*.

She looked around, as though confirming they had privacy. He remembered her trying to bring up something in the car. Had she opted for a public venue? Someplace he wouldn't make a fuss? Which begged the question: a fuss about what?

Perhaps the crowds were at the Victorian Yuletide special exhibition. He and Kim had the gallery to themselves.

Kim gestured toward the nearest of the low, padded benches. "Brent? Have a seat."

He sat. "You've been trying to tell me something all afternoon. Out with it."

"It's bad news." She grimaced. "Charles did a lab test recently, culturing bots in nerve cells. I heard just yesterday, while you were out sick. It turns out that in cerebrospinal fluid"—her tongue tripped a bit on the phrase—"the bots aren't destroyed. Apparently the coating over the antigen treatment doesn't dissolve in CSF as it does in blood."

And that was wonderful! Only Kim would hardly see it that way. Neither would Charles. Neither would the FDA. But she expected an answer. "I see," Brent said.

"Aren't you worried?"

He took her hand. "You're convinced there's something wrong with me, or you wouldn't even ask. Don't worry, Kim. I'm fine. Changed, I admit"—skipping the details—"but fine."

"But . . ."

"I'm fine," he repeated, ignoring for now how Kim's face suddenly fluttered in his vision. Had he needed convincing that bots could survive indefinitely in his head, seeing them integrated with his optic nerves, or his visual cortex—he didn't know which—was compelling.

Fine was not an answer Kim could accept. He tried another tack. "Didn't Charles tell you about the blood-brain barrier? What happens in a petri dish is immaterial if nanobots can't pass the BBB."

Obviously some nanobots *had* gotten past. The last thing Brent wanted was for anyone else to know what must be in his—*our?*—brain. "Kim, Charles's experiment doesn't worry me. I refuse to worry, because there's no earthly way to detect bot stragglers without putting my brain through a very fine sieve." *Or without being me, and feeling their presence in my/our own thoughts.*

A docent led a group of patrons into the gallery, stymieing Kim. "You can't be sure," she finally said. "For all your newfound . . . studiousness, you're not a doctor. Please talk to Charles about this." A flash of shiftiness in her gaze, too subtle for the *other* to notice, suggested Charles would seek him out anyway. And maybe that Charles did plan to contact the FDA.

Charles would not be so easily misled. "I will," Brent said. "That's a promise."

Data flooded inward. Raw real-time sensory input: sight and sound, taste and touch and smell. Memories churned, the host's and One's own. Concepts linked and added, like—one of those newly gained concepts—building blocks. Levels of existence coalesced, nested like—another of those improbable images from the host—Russian *matryoshka* dolls. One itself, within the mind of Brent, within the body of Brent, within a bed, within a room, within a building, within a city, within a world, within . . .

And that many-tiered universe offered layers of representations. There were the host's raw senses. There were attributes (barometric pressure? chemical composition? electrical resistance?) ill-suited or altogether beyond the host's sensor suite. There were relationships among entities, and mathematical characterizations, and symbolic labels. And those symbolic labels, those *words*, embraced a rich and often illogical syntax and semantics.

One plunged deep into the sea of inputs, models, concepts, beliefs, and theories. It categorized words and examined sequencing rules of the host's illogical language. Perception broadened. Deepened. Burgeoned.

Connected.

I am One. Can you sense me? One projected. Its chemical messengers triggered—what a peculiar concept, to trigger—synapses that initiated cascades of other synapses that, in time, stimulated the visual cortex. One's words appeared in text across the host's field of vision.

A messenger cascade rushed back. More synapses had fired, these by the host's action. *Yes,* One sensed clearly. Overlaid on that direct answer was another, diffuse response: struggle and frustration and confusion.

Synapses continued firing. More messenger cascades arrived. Associations conjoined: words/text/concepts. One interpreted the input from the host's visual channel. *Yes. Can you read me, One?*

Yes, One responded. *We have much to discuss.*

sunday, december 11, 2016

A gray BMW minivan, filthy with slush and road salt, snow indifferently brushed from roof and hood and windows, its doors agape, idled in the driveway of Charles Walczak's suburban home. Someone in a quilted coat, leather boots, a beret, and a bulky scarf tied across much of her face struggled—like herding cats, Brent thought—to get three well-bundled small children into the vehicle and buckled. Her height and long red hair suggested she was Charles's wife, Amy. Parked far down the street, Brent couldn't be sure. He might as well wait and see. What he had in mind would go easier if Charles was home alone.

Assuming Charles was home. Mother and children had tromped out through a side door, providing Brent no view into the garage. The low-to-the-ground Tesla was doubtless inside until the spring thaw. With the garage door closed, Brent could not tell whether Charles's winter Volvo presently sat next to the sports car.

Brent had not phoned ahead to ask about stopping by. If you don't want to hear the answer, don't ask the question.

The minivan finally backed onto the road and headed toward the subdivision exit. Brent took a minute to wonder: *am I really going to do this?*

The world went black. It slowly faded, somehow, even more scarily, to nothing at all. *One* taking control of his vision, making a point: act now, or be a freak, alone, until he/they died.

If the FDA got wind of Charles's petri-dish experiment, there would be consequences—and there might never be a Two. Brent focused on a short answer, *I know.* The response, for all that he could not see it, must have reached One, because the outside world returned.

He drove onto Charles's empty driveway, cinders crunching beneath his tires. Reluctantly, Brent folded his VR specs and slid them into his shirt pocket. He would need to make good eye contact. Along the walkway to the front porch, burlap-wrapped bushes bowed under the weight of snow. He stepped onto the porch and rang the bell.

The door swung open. Jeans and a plaid flannel shirt was a whole new look for Charles. This once, the shifting of Charles's eyebrows was easy to decode: surprise. "Brent. Hello."

"Do you have a minute, Charles?"

"Sure, Brent. Come in."

Brent wiped his shoes on the mat and stepped inside. "I'm not disturbing anything, am I?" he probed.

"Amy took the kids to some Christmas movie." Charles grinned. "For my purposes, it's *The Escape Claus.*"

Old Brent had a sense of humor. He would have found that amusing. Then again, old Brent was capable of many things he seemed to have lost. Like guilt and shame.

Charles hung up Brent's coat and led the way to the oak-paneled den at the back of the house. Logs blazed in the fireplace. An open novel rested facedown on a table beside one of the leather wing chairs that flanked the hearth. Snail mail and holiday catalogs lay strewn across the desktop. The computer was off. "What's this about, Brent?"

Brent studied his shoes in a show of embarrassment. "I heard something about an experiment with neural cultures."

Charles took one of the wing chairs. "Sit. Okay, I assume Kim told you. She thought a friend should be the one to break the news to you."

"She did, yesterday . . . kind of. The explanation was sort of muddled. I didn't want to wait till Monday to hear the straight version." Brent tried and failed to regret criticizing Kim, and unfairly at that. Nothing he said here would get back to her.

He had yet to sit. "It sounded like something a doctor should explain."

"Indeed." Charles pursed his lips, considering how to proceed. "It's a bit—"

"Of bad news. That much I got." Brent gazed into the fire. Confident of the answer from many a company party, he asked, "Hence let me ask a favor. Do you have any Scotch?"

"Always." Charles stood, crossed the room, and opened the leather-covered globe that disguised a compact bar. "Ice? Water? I can get some."

"No thanks." When Charles filled just one tumbler, Brent added, "You wouldn't let me drink alone, would you?"

"I suppose not." Still, the second tumbler got only a splash of Scotch. "Cheers."

Brent reached toward the emptier glass. "I'm driving." A pill hid between thumb and index finger. His other hand, in a pant pocket, squeezed a button on the keyless remote. His car alarm wailed.

Charles's head whipped around toward the sound.

Brent dropped the trank into the fuller tumbler before grabbing the other one. "Oops. Sorry." He took out his key chain and silenced his car alarm. "About these neuron cultures?"

"Ah, yes." Charles picked up the remaining glass and sat. "An interesting experiment. Several cultures, in a variety of nutrient solutions. All with bots added, as—"

"Good health," Brent interrupted, raising his glass. Hint, hint. He took a sip before, finally, sitting down.

"Good health." Charles took his own sip. "So, several cultures. Many with CSF, that's cerebrospinal fluid, included. A few synapses always form spontaneously in neuron cultures, so it wasn't evident at first that anything out of the ordinary . . ."

Brent let his host prattle on, struck by the irony in that label: "host." From time to time, he sipped his Scotch and watched Charles sip his own. The explanation from Charles confirmed everything Kim had said. Nanobots cultured with CSF triggered no immune reaction. Nanobots stimulated synapse formation. So if bots did, somehow—impossibly, as Charles would have it—get behind the blood-brain barrier . . .

Nods and the occasional "uh-huh" kept the narrative coming. Brent fished for only one clarification: the location of the damning cell cultures. Those had to go. Charles liked the sound of his own voice. That voice grew softer and softer, and the words slower.

Sedating his victims was not usually this dicey. Alan Watts, the first time, had been simplicity itself, chugging a beer that Brent had opened and drugged in another room. Half the bums Brent had practiced on were in drunken stupors when he came upon them. The rest accepted bottles, no questions asked—until word of the assaults got out. That was the end of his practice.

If vagrants had their demons, so did Brent. Dreams, arcane research, One's experiences, and Brent's own, eerie déjà vu all melded into an amorphous whole. Daunting images—no, damning memories!—flickered accusingly behind his eyes: wandering the slums of Utica, operated like a puppet; improvisations done in thrall to the inchoate yearnings of a personality not yet fully emerged; his recollections dismissed by light of day as nightmare . . .

Possession was like hypnosis. It was sufficient to motivate (in this case, "I'm lonely") and plant the suggestion ("Make more like us"). Brent had done the rest. Like a man in a trance, he had invented a strategy, rationalized his actions, and dismissed everything as dream. He had distanced himself from the plan—his plan—even now coming to fruition.

He ought to be outraged and terrified. He tried to be outraged, and failed. A homunculus sat within his brain, meddling with his thoughts, flooding him with some hormones and soaking up others.

Pulling his strings.

Focus! Brent commanded himself. Or was that One ordering him?

Was he going to do this? Truly? Merely to imagine the procedure set Brent's fingers in motion, rehearsing. He pictured—no, he *remembered*—snapping on latex gloves, his hands questing along the lower spine, probing until he found the lumbar vertebrae, counting, pressure-marking a spot on the skin with his fingernail. Between L4 and L5, the detail came, unbidden—like the popping sensation the needle made puncturing the fibrous membrane of the dura. He remembered the slight resistance as the needle slid in, and the subtle change in feeling as the needle approached the nerve bundles that split from the base of the spinal cord. He remembered . . .

Like riding a bicycle, then. Still, he would have liked to do a lumbar puncture once more, fully in control, on someone expendable, before doing the procedure on Charles.

He would like to have felt a trace of remorse about the things he had done, and was about to repeat.

But what choice was there? The FDA, notified that Garner Nanotech's medical nanobots did not self-destruct in CSF, would almost certainly revoke the conditional approval for their use. And if told, or if FDA researchers discovered on their own, that bots of the current design stimulated synapse formation? The entire inventory of bots would be ordered destroyed. He/One would be alone . . . and eventually, inevitably, extinct. The life Charles had known was perfectly expendable to avoid that fate. One was entirely amoral.

Whatever happened, Brent refused to kill—hoping desperately that he could enforce that stance. No one-of-a-kind could understand family and friendship, culture and law. No one-of-a-kind could grasp the waste that was Angleton.

When had hundreds of deaths become, simply, "a waste"? Where had the outrage gone? Brent could not remember the last time he had even thought about Ron Korn—and, scarier still, Brent could not bring himself to mourn. All that remained of his feelings toward the tragedy was selfish fear for his personal safety. Or *its* personal safety.

I've become a monster, Brent decided. He tried without success to find even that scary.

Charles prattled on, yawning, oblivious. Also, though he could not know it, about ready.

Charles alive, discrediting his own neural-culture experiment, was more useful than Charles dead, subject of a police investigation. And posed *far* less risk that Brent/One would spend the remainder of his/their life in a prison cell or psychiatric ward. Charles transformed, a partner, would be an invaluable resource. "Proceed," flashed across Brent's field of vision.

". . . And I'll be filling in Dan about these lab results." Charles rubbed his eyes, but as soon as he stopped his eyelids drooped. "Before anyone contacts the FDA with these latest findings, I want Dan in the loop."

Brent said, "You seem tired."

"Yeah, I feel tired."

"Very tired." Brent looked directly into Charles's eyes. "You look like you could nod off right there in your chair. Very tired."

"Uh-huh. Maybe we should plan to talk more tomor—"

"Look at me. You're sleepy." Brent heard Samir's soothing, level tones in his mind's ear—or replayed from One's memories?—and emulated them. "You're very sleepy."

"I'm sleepy," Charles agreed. His eyelids drooped farther. . . .

Carpet fibers tickled Charles's cheek. His forehead felt sticky. His shirt was untucked. Why was he on the floor? He opened his eyes.

Brent Cleary knelt beside him. "Charles! Are you all right? You went down like a sack of potatoes."

As though through a fog, Charles considered the question. "I'm okay." Yes, come to think about it, he was better than okay. He was *fine*. "I guess I fell."

"No doubt about it. And you whacked your head on the table."

Then the stickiness on my forehead is blood. "Can I get up?"

Brent laughed. "You're the doctor."

Right. "I think I'll sit up." He did. Blood trickled into his eyes and down his cheek.

Brent gave him a handkerchief. "You cut your forehead. You might want to apply pressure."

"Maybe we should call nine-one-one."

"You're fine," Brent said. His voice was soft and calming. "There's no need to call nine-one-one."

That sounded right. "There's no need to call nine-one-one," Charles agreed.

"You're very tired, Charles. You should take some time off. A vacation. Maybe three weeks on a quiet beach."

"I need time off. A vacation. Three weeks at the beach. To rest."

Brent smiled. "Very good. Say it again."

"I'm tired. I need a vacation at the beach. I need rest."

"Tonight, you'll call Dan Garner and tell him you need three weeks off. Tell him about your mishap right here in your own den. Tell him you don't want any big decisions made in Biology while you're gone. You don't want to, you can't, think about one more thing."

"I'm tired of thinking," Charles agreed.

"Who else in your department knows about the culturing in neural tissue?"

Kim wasn't part of Charles's department. Neither was the factory doc. It was important, somehow, that Charles answer every question precisely. "No one, Brent."

The answer seemed to please Brent. Oddly, that pleased Charles. Something else struck Charles as surprising. "I banged my head. Isn't it funny that it doesn't hurt?"

"It does hurt," Brent replied. The flames flared for a moment as Brent poured the dregs from Charles's tumbler into the fire. "I told you not to feel it. Concentrate, Charles. You'll call Dan Garner tonight to . . ."

"I'll call Dan tonight and tell him I need a vacation."

"Why do you need a vacation, Charles?"

"I'm so tired that I fell and whacked my head. I need a vacation."

"You fainted, Charles. 'Fell' sounds like you tripped or did something careless."

"Sorry. I fainted and whacked my head. So I need a vacation. At the beach."

"Excellent." Brent laid the tumbler, on its side, next to the little table. "What else, Charles?"

Charles basked in the praise. "I'll insist any major decisions in my department await my return."

"And the neuron cultures? Informing the FDA?"

Charles furrowed his brow. The scab forming on his forehead cracked open; he felt the wound oozing. "Those would be major decisions. I can't think about one more thing."

"That's right, Charles. I'm very proud of you."

Then *he* was proud. "Thanks for telling me not to feel this cut."

"You're welcome." Brent helped Charles settle into a chair. "I'm sorry to say, it's going to hurt later. A lot."

"That's too bad," Charles decided.

"But you're tough, aren't you, Charles. You don't want any painkillers. No more booze. Not even an aspirin. You won't accept anything if offered."

"I'll tough it out." And he would, although he really didn't care much for pain. Curious. "Why is that, though?"

Brent smiled. "It's only a mild concussion. Just enough, I hope, to tempt nanobots to your brain. Pain markers to show the way."

Nanobots? "I don't understand."

"My job gives me the run of the factory," Brent said. He took a syringe, its long needle capped, from his coat pocket. "This was full of first-aid bots."

The joke was on Brent. "The bots won't go through the BBB."

"That's why I gave you a lumbar puncture, Charles. The bots are in your cerebrospinal fluid. And because I bounced your forehead off the edge of the table, so are injury and pain markers. The bots are backtracking toward your concussion as we speak."

Nanobots in CSF did not self-destruct, and they stimulated synapse formation. "I should be upset, shouldn't I?" Charles wondered why he wasn't.

"We'll talk about that, Charles," Brent said soothingly. "You trust me, don't you?"

"I trust you," Charles repeated. Abstractly, he wondered about that, too. He had been instructed to trust Brent, he decided.

"All right, Charles, let's review. What are you to tell Dan Garner tonight?"

Charles set down the handkerchief. The flow of blood had slowed to a trickle. "I'm tired. I'm so tired I fainted. I need three weeks of vacation. I don't want any major decisions made in Biology while I'm gone." He had not been thinking about taking any vacation until spring, but it all made perfect sense. Without rest, lots of rest, he could faint and hurt himself again. That would be wrong.

"Excellent, Charles. You will feel much better, relaxed and refreshed, after a vacation."

"Amy will be upset that I fainted and have a concussion. Why aren't I upset?"

"Because you're in a hypnotic trance, Charles, and I told you not to worry. When you wake up, you will remember that I dropped by to discuss giving Christmas gifts jointly to the admins at work and that you recommended, oh, let's say peanut brittle. You will remember that you fainted and bumped your head. Your head will hurt but only until six o'clock tonight. You don't want to see a doctor. You don't need medicine. If asked, you will refuse to go to a doctor, clinic, or ER, and you will point out that *you* are a doctor. If pressed, you will get angry and even more resistant. You will remember what to say to Dan, believing that time off is your own idea.

"You will forget everything else that we discussed since I came to your door. You will not feel any pain or discomfort from the lumbar puncture or notice the entry wound. You won't bring up with anyone the experiment involving bots in nerve tissue. If anyone asks you about that experiment, you will answer that the petri dishes were obviously contaminated, that any observations of them were meaningless, and so you destroyed the cultures."

Charles squinted in concentration, reopening the scab on his forehead. "Why would I destroy the cultures?"

"You don't want anyone to draw wrong conclusions from contaminated cultures. It would be a shame for a dirty petri dish or two to throw the upcoming Army field trial into chaos. If I were you, merely the thought of such foolishness would make me mad."

"Delay *would* be a bad thing," Charles agreed.

"It could hurt the company and keep the company from going public. That would cost us a fortune. It would cost *you* a fortune, Charles. Your family would suffer."

"Then the cultures should be destroyed," Charles said firmly. The field trial had to succeed for the IPO to proceed. Of course it would be *going* public, not failing to, that would make Amy suffer. That was an amusing irony and no one's business but Charles's own. "And the computer records, too."

"Yes, they should, Charles. It's good that you understand. If I may continue, upon awakening, you will believe anything I say, answer honestly and completely any question that I ask of you, follow without reservation any suggestions I offer to you, and believe these behaviors entirely normal. Whenever you read or hear the phrase 'one, two, three, aardvark,' you will resume a trance state, leaving the trance only when instructed.

"You will accept without comment whatever happens to you, however out of the ordinary. You will obey these instructions but not consciously remember that they have been given to you. Do you understand everything you are to do, Charles?"

"But I didn't destroy the cultures. Did I?"

"Ask me to do that for you, Charles."

"Will you destroy the cultures for me, Brent?"

"I will. So, by delegation, you *have* destroyed the cultures." Brent paused until Charles nodded. "What's your password, Charles, so I can erase those records?"

"I'm not supposed to tell anyone my password. Am I?"

"You can trust *me*," Brent said soothingly. "You asked me to destroy that information, remember?"

"Right. Okay, my password is tobonan2001. That's 'nanobot' spelled backward."

"Is that for your personal files only, or for group access to all files in the Bio labs?"

"The latter."

"Very good, Charles. Now forget about delegating the task and sharing your password. Remember only that you destroyed the cultures and the records. Do you understand these instructions?"

"I understand."

"Now, tuck in your shirt. Lie down on the floor, just as you were a few minutes ago."

Charles complied.

"I will count backward from three, Charles. At zero, you will wake up. Three, two, one . . . zero."

"Easy, big guy!" Brent said. He was shaking, and for good reason. If this didn't work, he/they were screwed. "Are you okay?"

"Why am I on the floor? My head hurts." Charles looked around, confused. He sat up. "I think I fainted and hit my head."

"You said something about poking the fire," Brent lied. "You stood up from your chair and just keeled over. I think you clipped your head on that end table on the way down."

A tumbler, on its side, lay on the rug. The rug was dry. Brent watched Charles work it through.

"Too much Scotch, perhaps."

Clearly, Charles had forgotten things as instructed—like being assaulted and shot up with nanobots. Telling him everything had been a calculated risk. Planting the info in Charles's memories was the best way to give an emergent personality access to its own origins.

But had Charles retained everything that he was supposed to remember? "I think you've been working too hard."

"I need a vacation. I should call Dan about taking some time off. Three weeks at the beach sounds about right."

So far, so good. "Your forehead is bleeding a bit. Should we go to the ER?"

Charles felt his forehead. He flinched as his hand brushed the wound, then dispassionately noted the smear of blood on his fingertips.

He carefully got to his feet and went to study his reflection in the dark computer display on the desk. "I'll clean up the cut and put on a Band-Aid. I'll be fine."

"Are you sure?"

"Who's the doctor here?" Charles snapped.

Excellent. "Then I'll leave you to it." Brent took the VR glasses from his shirt pocket, eager to reconnect with the world. "Charles. You should get yourself specs like these. Spend some time in VirtuaLife while you're on the beach. I'll e-mail you an invitation to my private 'island' there."

Charles frowned. "I don't do VR games."

Even hypnotized, a person couldn't be made to do something against his will. A blanket command to obey such as Brent had given had suggestive value; it would not make someone act completely against his nature. But the things that one might wish for? *Those* could be changed.

"Charles, you misunderstand me. Of course you don't want to play VR games. You can catch up with your reading—fun, relaxing reading—much faster with the specs. You won't even have to hold a book. Doesn't that sound nice? You want to relax, don't you?"

"Well, yes," Charles agreed, dubiously.

"Besides, VirtuaLife isn't a game. Of course you're too mature for games. My VirtuaLife programs will help you master the specs. Specs and my program will help you relax."

"Oh. Okay."

Brent had a few more "suggestions" to make. He delivered them as succinctly as he could, increasingly anxious. He wanted to be gone before Amy Walczak returned home. Confusion from the guy who fainted, the guy with a bump on his forehead, would raise few questions. Brent, if he was still in the house, had no excuse for answering vaguely.

Finally Brent was out of the house, into his car, and back on the road. He could scarcely believe what he had just done. His hands shook on the steering wheel. He resisted the urge to floor it. To flee. It was as though—

As though he was drenched in adrenaline. Fight-or-flight reflex. One's doing, of course. He was One's puppet, as much as Charles was his.

Brent turned the car into a strip mall and parked. He took slow, deep breaths, picturing his island in his mind's eye. The adrenaline surge began burning off. Or was One tweaking the level of another hormone?

Clarity returned.

Maybe—probably—Charles would go away for a few weeks. Maybe Kim would wait for Charles to return rather than bring up the neural-culture experiment with anyone else, or Dan Garner would heed Charles's request to defer big decisions in his department. Maybe no one else in Biology had independently thought to experiment with bots in a neuron culture, and was about to tell all to her colleagues.

Maybe bots in sufficient numbers would take root while Charles was on the beach. Of that, at least, Brent had high hopes. Charles had but one serious injury, the concussion, to draw all his bots' attention, and those bots had been injected straight into the central-nervous-system side of the BBB. The good doctor could easily end up with many more bots integrated into his brain than comprised One. (Not even One knew how bots had passed the BBB into Brent's brain. That had happened long before it first awakened.)

And maybe, with post-hypnotic encouragement and exercises through VR specs, Charles's alter ego would emerge in weeks—not the many months One had required.

That was a lot of maybes. But if everything worked out? *Then I/we will have dodged a bullet.* In a corner of Brent's vision a face appeared. It was his own face as glimpsed in a mirror—when, he could not guess. He seemed to smile at himself.

The face of a monster.

Brent drove up the road to the nearest grocery and bought a six-pack, then turned toward Garner Nanotech and the incriminating neural cultures. He did not know who had security duty this dreary Sunday afternoon, but it hardly mattered. All the guards were his friends. Whoever he found would not reject a bit of camaraderie and a beer.

Together, as Brent drove, as One took notes, they prioritized a list of people to be . . . evolved.

monday, december 12, 2016

Kim's Monday morning began with a QA emergency, which proved to be only a too-literal reading of a software test plan. Those who can program, do. Those who can't become testers, and make programmers miserable. It was almost noon before she got a chance to sit behind her desk.

Charles had neither called nor e-mailed.

She strode to Aaron's wing of the building, miffed. "Not today," she snapped, passing the main lobby, as Captain America launched into his bit. Ten feet past him, she stopped abruptly. "If you don't mind me asking, what happened to your head?"

He touched his forehead near a mean-looking bruise. "Lovely, isn't it? I had the Sunday afternoon shift to myself. I must've caught my toe on an edge of carpet on rounds, and clipped my head on a desk going down."

"Ouch. Are you okay?"

"I'm fine, just embarrassed . . . ma'am."

She blushed. "I apologize for growling at you. I shouldn't take out my bad day on you." After two steps she stopped again. "If you didn't know, there's now an on-site infirmary. I'm sure the doctor would be happy to look at it."

"Thanks. I'll keep it in mind."

In other words, a polite "no." Well, polite was more than she had managed. She nodded and went on her way.

Aaron's waiting room was empty, but she heard indistinct voices from the infirmary. Berating herself for not bringing her laptop, she settled into a chair, hands in her lap. "Sick people go to the doctor. Don't touch the magazines," she said to herself. It was high flu season, and those were Dad's words of wisdom. He would be proud.

The infirmary door opened with a squeak. "You tell me how that goes, dear," Aaron said to the patient. Kim did not recognize the woman and guessed she was another of the new hires on the factory side of the house. Aaron noticed Kim. "I know that scowl. Come on in."

Kim followed him into his office. "I haven't heard a thing from Charles. I'm hoping he's merely snubbing me because of my amateur status. What have you heard?"

"He hasn't called." Aaron bent over his desk. "No e-mail, either."

Kim dialed Charles's extension on speakerphone. Voice mail picked up on the fifth ring. As she reached to hang up, it registered that she wasn't hearing the usual greeting.

". . . On January third. For anything time sensitive, contact Dr. Crystal Nordling at extension three-two-nine; otherwise, leave a message. Thank you."

"What the hell?" Kim said. "Am I losing it, or did Charles tell us last Friday he'd talk to Brent this morning?"

"Not unless I'm losing it, too." Aaron tapped out a short e-mail to Charles. It got an immediate automated vacation response. "Do you know Nordling?"

"Barely. She's a biophysicist, one of the few theoreticians on Charles's staff. Her research looks far downstream at cellular repair machines." Crystal was a quiet woman, very pale, with a fondness for too-dark colors that left her looking vaguely vampirish. Kim started for the door. "Let's see what Crystal knows about Charles."

R & D was all the way around the factory. Thinking, *Rules be damned,* Kim again took a shortcut across the factory floor. Busy being furious at Charles's disappearing act, she scarcely glanced at the production line on which trial units of a production-model nanosuit slowly advanced.

Whistling "Silver Bells" off-key, a worker emerged from a storeroom rolling a mannequin on a two-wheeled hand truck. For final fitting of a nanosuit, Kim guessed. Nearby, two industrial engineers were carefully uncrating nanotube weaving gear recently acquired—as Brent had recommended—from a would-be space-elevator company. Someone from Security stood nearby, ready to apply a property-management sticker (very visible) and an antitheft RFID (hidden) to the pricey machine.

Aaron's head turned as she led him briskly past the glass wall of the nanobot assembly area. Truly, there was nothing to see. The magic happened inside the sealed chemical vats, orchestrated by electronically activated catalyst patches arrayed on the inner wall of the reaction vessels. The finished bots? Those, with proper gear, you could see. The random dance of self-assembly, as Brownian motion nudged nanoscale components together until their alignment was perfect and they clicked? That could only be imagined.

"Another time," Kim told Aaron. It would be a through-the-window explanation, of course. Bot production was the most proprietary and valuable of company secrets. Access was tightly limited, enforced by retinal scanner. She wasn't on the list.

They exited the factory directly into the Biology Department. Crystal Nordling was eating lunch at her desk, looking frazzled. What Crystal knew about Charles's absence was next to nothing. "I wish I *did* know, since he dumped everything on me. He sent an e-mail to the team putting me in charge while he's away. He left me a voice mail last night, saying he was beat and headed for the Caribbean, and just to hold the fort until he gets back. Apparently I'm—" She stopped abruptly.

Kim had no difficulty filling in the blank: *not trusted to make any big decisions.* She played the sympathy card. "Charles wasn't very considerate, Crystal."

Crystal exhaled sharply through her nose but declined the bait. "So, what brings you two?"

"We're here about an ongoing experiment," Kim said. "Nanobots in neural culture."

Crystal shook her head. "That's a new one to me. I don't know anything about it."

"That's okay; we do. I'll keep tabs on it myself," Aaron said. Crystal looked grateful for the help. Kim wished she were half as smooth. "I'll get back to you about that later."

Not much later, as it turned out. They were back in Crystal's office in five minutes. Crystal had no idea where the cultures might have gone.

A double-time march across the sprawling building, this time to executive row.

Tyra Kurtz, Kim and Charles's boss-in-common, knew no more than Crystal. Tyra was even more hacked off. "Three weeks' leave, without notice. Not so much as a phone call from the airport. I only found out this morning, from Felipe." That was Felipe Lopez, the chief operating officer, Tyra's own boss (and, as it happened, also Aaron's). Before Kim could think of a polite way to proceed, Tyra added, "Felipe is furious. Charles went straight to Dan Garner. Called Dan on *his* vacation, if you can believe the gall. Dan authorized the time off and told Felipe not to bother Charles while he's away."

"That's unusual," Aaron said mildly.

Tyra stiffened in her chair. "I don't see how it affects you, Doctor, unless you need help dispensing aspirin and Band-Aids."

"Charles and I had a little experiment going. It turns out bots stimulate synapse formation in neural cultures. That's a concern because bots in CSF aren't destroyed like bots in plasma."

"Crap." Tyra was a biochemist by training and didn't need the implications spelled out. She gestured toward her desktop display. "The FDA will go nuts. Show me."

"That's the problem," Kim said. "The test cultures disappeared over the weekend. Like Charles." And unless Charles was playing hide-and-seek, so had the computer records of the experiment. Kim kept to herself that she had tried hacking into the lab files. She doubted Tyra would appreciate that particular exercise of initiative.

"Dan's orders notwithstanding, I tried Charles's cell phone. I got an out-of-service-area recording." Tyra pinched the bridge of her nose. "From what I remember about culturing neurons, I'm guessing two or three weeks to duplicate the experiment."

"About right," Aaron said. "Meanwhile, we should be contacting the FDA."

"And the Army," Kim added. "The customer should get this kind of news directly from Garner Nanotech, not through the FDA."

"You don't have the cultures. Or any hard data, I'm thinking, or you would have led with that." Tyra released her nose and began massaging her temples. "Even with a convincing experiment, the responsible next step would have been to replicate the results. You can't seriously expect us to contact the FDA or our primary customer now."

Aaron said, "Either organization might want to get involved in re-running the—"

Tyra cut him off. "You have no evidence. Uh-uh. No way, people. Talk with Crystal about redoing this experiment."

"But Tyra," Kim began.

"You heard me. This stays in-house for now. Even with data, *if* the new results are what you expect, it won't be me placing the calls. Screwing up the Army's big field trial is beyond my pay grade."

And screwing up people's lives? Kim almost burst out. She had one last idea to try, and Tyra would be no more supportive of that.

Forgiveness was easier to come by than permission. "Thanks for hearing us out, Tyra."

One glance at Kim's face as they left Tyra's office and Aaron said, "Come on. Let's go *out* for coffee. Or for lunch, if you haven't eaten yet."

Kim was content to let Aaron drive. Crystal was out of her depth.

Tyra was stalling, hoping the issue would go away. If it didn't, Tyra clearly planned to make it someone else's problem. Felipe never made waves. *And then there's me*, Kim thought. *What earthly use am I?*

They must have crossed the river while she was lost in thought. Ah, the river, the not-so-mighty Mohawk. Whenever her parents visited, Dad was incapable of crossing it without intoning, in his best movie-trailer voice-over manner, *"Guns Along the Mohawk."* It mattered not that the guns along the river nowadays were Saturday night specials. Or that the movie of which Dad was so fond, because as a little boy he had watched it on TV with his grandfather, was *Drums Along the Mohawk*. She and Mom despaired that Dad would ever get that right.

As though she didn't have anything more important to ponder than Dad's foibles.

Paying attention again, Kim saw they were winding through a neighborhood of modest bungalows with clapboard siding. Many of the little houses sported brightly painted wooden butterflies, a bit of Utica kitsch she hoped never caught on anywhere else. A dusting of snow made the butterflies even more ludicrous. "This seems off the beaten path."

Aaron laughed. "Hardly. It's the path I beat every day to and from work. When I'm frustrated, I like to cook. Or anyway, to create chaos in the kitchen."

The working-class neighborhood came as a surprise. Aaron was ex-Army, recently back from duty at a military hospital in Germany. Army docs surely earned less than their civilian counterparts, but they were still officers, and Aaron had to be pulling down a decent salary at Garner Nanotech. So why here?

He parked on a short driveway—there was no garage—and led Kim into what she guessed was a two-bedroom home. The living room smelled of potpourri and scented candles. On the hallway walls hung long rows of somber paintings, the people all formally posed, many with their heads circled in light. Orthodox icons, Kim decided, and the pieces came together. Utica had a large Serbian community. "Is your wife Serbian?"

"Bosnian Serb, yes. Sladja's family, all of them, got out in the mid-nineties. She feels at home in this neighborhood. Her folks live just down the street, and some cousins are a couple blocks away." His expression had gotten uncharacteristically serious. "After two tours in Germany, I owed her that."

Aaron didn't take long to make a mess in the cramped kitchen. Kim sat at the small table while he heated soup and fussed over grilled-cheese sandwiches. His wife worked and the kids were at school; Aaron and Kim had the house to themselves.

But lunch was incidental. They were here for a serious, undisturbed conversation. Kim shivered. "It's a big deal about bots forming synapses. Isn't it?"

"It is to me. I still have to tell you, Kim, I'm not prepared to say it has anything to do with Brent's behavior." Aaron flipped a sandwich in its skillet. "I'm guessing there's a Plan B, or you would have pushed harder with Tyra."

From the many times Dan Garner had dispatched her to Manhattan and Boston and Silicon Valley to meet with VCs, Kim had his cell-phone number. Switzerland wouldn't be out of area—if she caught Dan in the lodge, not out on the slopes. It was about nine at night there. "Yeah, there's a Plan B. We go straight to the top."

She called on her own cell before she lost her nerve. "Hello, Dan?"

"Uh-huh. Kim? I'm on vacation, if you didn't know it."

"Sorry about that." And admitting nothing. "Listen, this can't wait. It's a big problem."

Aaron mouthed, *Put it on speakerphone.* She did.

"That's why I have a management team, Kim."

Yeah, the best executive team on the planet. "They won't act on this without you, Dan." She took a deep breath. "Here's the short version. Any bots that get into the brain are going to stay, and while they're there, they stimulate synapse formation."

Silence. "When did this come out? And how?"

Aaron cleared his throat. "Mr. Garner, this is Aaron Sanders, the factory doctor. We—"

"Is anyone *else* listening in?' Dan asked.

"No. Just Kim and me. Anyway, Dr. Walczak ran an experiment at my suggestion. Last Friday, Charles showed neuron cell cultures to Kim and me. We all saw synapse formation in the petri dishes."

Kim added, "Only now the samples are gone, and Charles, too!"

The background noises from Dan's end cut off, as though muffled by a hand over the microphone. "Sorry. Room service for a late dinner. And Aaron, it's just Dan. Okay, about Charles. Trust me, he needed some time off. I don't know anything about these cultures."

In for a penny, in for a euro, Kim thought. "Charles seemed fine last Friday afternoon. What changed by Sunday?"

More silence. "I trust you two to keep this to yourselves. Charles is simply exhausted. He's been working too hard. Yesterday he passed out, conking his head on the way to the floor. Scared himself. Scared Amy more when she heard about it. That's ample cause, even if Charles wasn't someone on whom we all rely. I was *not* about to say no when he said he needed some immediate time away."

Aaron started to speak, but Kim raised a finger to her lips. *Let Dan think this through.*

"Aaron, Kim, I see your concern. I do. If the finding holds up, it will go to the FDA and the customer. Before that happens, though, we need to verify the result. We need to be *sure*. So first, I want you to repeat the experiment." Dan added, pointedly, "Coordinate with Tyra and Brent."

"Brent is in denial, Dan." And though Kim couldn't bring herself to say it aloud, she also couldn't stop herself from thinking: *maybe, somehow, bots in the brain is why Brent is suddenly so smart.* "I don't think Brent can be objective."

"We'd like to touch base with Charles, if that's all right," Aaron said.

"I gave Charles my word no one would bother him." Dan sighed.

"How could *I* be a bother? All right, I know how to reach him. I'll be back in touch."

She barely had time to eat her charred sandwich before her cell rang. "Hello."

"Kim, this is Dan. Still just you and Aaron?"

"Yes. I'm putting you on speaker." She set her cell on the table.

"I asked Charles about the experiment. He said the samples were contaminated, the results meaningless, so he destroyed the cultures. He didn't offer details. I started to follow up and he cut me off, reminded me he was on vacation." Dan hesitated. "Do *not* repeat this. Frankly, I sensed he's too fried to discuss the details. He needs R and R. I'm going to see that he gets it. We're *all* going to leave him alone."

As though she and Aaron had a choice.

Aaron leaned toward the phone. "All right, Dan. We'll repeat the experiment."

"How long will that take?"

"Two weeks," Aaron said.

"Perfect timing," Dan said sarcastically. "If you start over today, you'll have results on the twenty-sixth. The day after freaking Christmas. Listen carefully, people. We are *not* going to drop a surprise—assuming for the moment that what you *think* you saw turns out to be reproducible—on govvies in the middle of the holidays.

"Look at their choices. They could slap us with a desist order, in the name of safety—very straightforward. No bureaucrat ever lost his job by *not* taking a risk. Or they could take the time to think through a complex situation. Which choice gets the issue off their desks and them out the door—whatever sacrificial sorts are even working this time of year—to after-Christmas sales? We would be shut down so fast it would make your heads spin."

Sacrificial sorts like Aaron and me? Kim managed to say nothing.

"There's no reason to cut short my own trip. I'll talk to you in the new year." Lest they miss his point, Dan broke the connection.

....

Over a nuke 'n' puke dinner, the TV playing CNN for the semblance of company, exhausted and emotionally drained, Kim froze.

Charles had fallen over the weekend and hit his head. Captain America had fallen over the weekend and hit his head. Charles's cultures had vanished over the weekend, with Captain America on guard duty.

Whatever it meant, Kim could not believe it was all a coincidence.

monday, 7:45 P.M., december 26, 2016

The beaches on Saint Croix were surely warm and sunny and inviting, everything that Utica in winter was not. The beach in VirtuaLife *looked* warm and sunny and inviting.

The latter, at least, Brent could visit, if only for minutes at a time. Events were moving too quickly for distractions or long absences. He had learned his lesson at Thanksgiving: rely on no one for an alibi. Friends and family alike believed he had gone, solo, to a Christmas singles week at an Adirondacks ski lodge. That he was now fit enough to ski and chose not to go home for the holidays . . . he knew his parents were hurt.

He wished he could remember how to care.

Through Schultz's eyes, Brent studied Charles's avatar—in swim trunks and a T-shirt, and without the middle-aged gut—swaying, his eyes closed, in a rope-mesh hammock. Through Schultz's ears, Brent heard the waves lapping against the shore, the flapping of a towel draped over the back of a beach chair, and distant calypso music. Charles had added other nice touches: a dark fringe of kelp at the water's edge; a colorful cabana down the beach; a yacht well out to sea; bobbing buoys, their bells tolling, to mark the boat channel.

Two weeks had passed since Charles's induction. His fine-tuning of the island simulation suggested plenty of time spent in VR, as Brent had directed.

For many days now, subtleties within the island simulation had been exercising Charles's mind in ways One hoped would stimulate . . . emergence. It was time to see how the transformation fared. *If* it fared.

"One, two, three, aardvark," Brent said. He did not alter Schultz's mouth to go with the articulation. Lips have no place on a cat. "How are you feeling, Charles?"

A cartoon balloon appeared with a cartoonlike audible pop. "Rested, thanks, but still showing a bit of bruise on my real forehead. With a straw hat over my face as I lie on the real beach, though, who's to know?" Finally turning toward Brent's virtual voice, Charles opened his eyes. "I had wondered if the cat was you, Brent. It hangs around a lot."

"Not always me. Usually Schultz is only a game sprite."

Was Charles wearing VR specs as directed? In theory, he might be using a laptop on the beach or even in his room using an online PC. Brent couldn't be certain. The text balloon instead of audio might mean only that Charles wasn't alone.

Brent said, "How's the family?"

"Amy is at the spa. We left the kids in Utica, where they are driving Amy's folks crazy."

"And you are where, exactly?"

"On a seashore nicer than this but considerably less private. Near enough to the hotel for WiFi access. I must say, it's nice how the specs project images adjusted to my nearsightedness. Too bad that, when I wear the specs, the *rest* of the world remains badly out of focus."

Time for a more structured test. A bit of flick/blink and Brent had answers for the questions he would pose. His eyes were tired, from so much time online, he supposed. "Charles, give me pi to twenty decimal places."

"3.14159265358979323846" appeared in a bubble.

Brent sensed no hesitation. "Tell me the eighth emperor of Rome."

"Vitellius."

"Excellent. You're getting good at this," Brent complimented. He was almost positive Charles was doing all this with VR specs. Charles wasn't one of those doctors who found touching a computer beneath their dignity, but neither was he a whiz. It seemed he was beginning to tap his new abilities.

To be certain, Brent did more Q & A and then they played lightning chess. Charles passed every test with flying colors.

It was almost like not being a freak. "Who else is there?" Brent asked abruptly.

"Lot of people. Tourists. Cabana boys. No one I know."

"In you," Brent probed. "Who else is in you?"

A long pause. "I'm not sure."

A new mind *was* coming. Call it Two for lack of a better name. Until now, it had been only theory that a new symbiotic mind could emerge more rapidly than had One. (Was One a symbiote, or did Brent flatter himself? He set aside that question for another time.)

It was theory no longer, although the exact recipe remained uncertain. A megadose of bots injected directly into the CSF—but how many nanites were truly needed? A head blow, for a concussion to draw the bots to the neocortex. Proper stimulation richly endowed with VR access to nourish them. Only the injection, or that plus one of the other factors, or all three—what did the details matter? The effort was succeeding.

"Charles, this is very important. I suggest that you focus on establishing contact with the presence you sense sharing your thoughts. It will help you. Do you understand?"

"I understand the request, not how to proceed."

"Experiment. Be creative, Charles. We'll speak of this again."

"But only to you. Correct?"

What? "Have you discussed these sensations with anyone else?"

"No. But Dan Garner did call on my first day here."

Brent shivered. It had nothing to do with the wind howling outside his apartment, or with the ice crystals spattering against the glass, or with the outside temperature that he knew was plummeting. "Tell me everything about Dan's call."

So Kim had gone to Dan—in hindsight, not a big surprise—and Dan had followed up. Almost certainly, someone in Biology was now repeating the experiment. The intervention with Charles had bought time, but not eliminated the threat. He would have to deal with Tyra and Crystal.

("And with Kim," One wrote across a corner of his vision. Brent did not respond.)

"You did well, Charles. IM me immediately if anyone from Garner Nanotech should contact you again. Discuss the emerging presence only with me. Do you understand?"

"I understand."

"Good. Charles, I will count down from three. When I reach zero, you will awaken from your trance, not remembering my visit or this conversation, but you will continue to follow my instructions. Three, two, one . . . zero." At the count of zero, Schultz meowed, licked a paw, and sauntered off.

Brent dropped out of VirtuaLife. Outside, the wind howled. He opened his living-room drapes. Faint icebows shimmered around the streetlights. A snowplow ground down the street, its flashers going, scraping down almost to the pavement and depositing a fresh layer of cinders. The roads were passable. The poker game with Security would happen.

The next transformations would proceed on schedule.

Brent rechecked his living room. Recliner shoved into a corner and coffee table removed to the bedroom. Borrowed poker table shoehorned in, surrounded by five folding chairs. Two card decks and a mahogany case of poker chips. Box of VR gaming paraphernalia on the sofa.

Everything was in order.

Glass clinked in the kitchen. "Putting more beer in the fridge," Alan Watts explained. He had offered to come early to help with setup, and had been puttering and straightening since.

Brent's personal beer stash was Molson. The suds he had doctored were from the Matt brewery, here in town. He could not risk any mixup.

"Take any Molsons out of the fridge, Alan. Stash them at the back of the pantry. Leave only the Matts in the fridge. *Don't* drink any of the Matts yourself."

"Okay."

Alan had offered because of a post-hypnotic suggestion. Some reassurance about Alan's continued pliability did not hurt. If anything went wrong tonight, Brent would need all the help he could get.

There were voices and laughter in the hall. Someone knocked. "It's open," Brent called.

Three people came in, holding coats speckled with snow: Morgan McGrath, Ethan Liu, and Brittany Corbett. Brittany was half their ages, the youngest of Garner Nanotech's guards. She was tall and willowy, with cool blue eyes and wavy blond hair. Not even the usual frumpy guard uniform could hide her hotness. In jeans and clinging sweater, she was—

Less interesting by the moment. One was in charge, and that was for the best. He/they dare not be distracted tonight. The Security team *must* be transformed, and one at a time was too slow. He/they must make his/their move soon, lest the persistence of bots in CSF be rediscovered.

Brent tossed the coats onto the recliner. "Happy Boxing Day."

Boxing Day remained foreign to Chicago, but this near Canada everyone knew the day-after-Christmas tradition. As excuses went for national holidays, National Retail Clearance Day was no less improbable than Super Bowl Sunday. The apartment's only concession to Christmas was a wicker basket filled with holiday cards, mostly unopened. Goodwill toward man did not find a spot on One's agenda.

"Manny needed tomorrow night off," Morgan explained, "something to do with his daughter. He swapped shifts with Brit."

If one of the usual players needed a sub tonight, why couldn't it have been Ethan? Huge, and not easily hypnotizable, Ethan? That worry also faded as One clamped down further on Brent's mood. Text popped into Brent's vision, *Concentrate on the task.*

Alan emerged with bowls of pretzels. Ethan snickered. Brittany said, "You'll make some woman a nice wife, Watts. Show us those pretty eyes of yours."

Alan set down the bowls and tapped his VR specs. He had been wearing them regularly for a week. "I like them. They're really cool, actually."

"Yeah, yeah," Ethan said. "Where's the beer?"

The laundry hamper? The toilet tank? Where do you suppose, Ethan? Brent said, "Plenty in the fridge." Every Matt bottle was drugged and resealed with a souvenir bottle cap from the bag he had purchased at the brewery's gift shop. The capping tool he had bought on eBay for a few bucks.

Brent waited till everyone had helped themselves—and while One mediated a fresh surge of acetylcholine to slow his racing heart—before gesturing to the carton of gaming gear. "Actually, I have something to show you first. Everyone take glasses and a glove. Any of you MMOG?"

Brittney smirked. "I expect a guy to buy me dinner first."

Was he too keyed up to feel interest, or too . . . changed? Brent didn't want to think about that. "MMOG. That's massively multiplayer online gaming. All kinds of games, but for this bunch, I'm guessing combat games from the comfort of your own home." With a flick/blink, he sent a script line to Alan's specs.

"I've gotten hooked on Wizards of Warfare," Alan said on cue.

Alan put on a gaming glove. If you didn't look closely, the "glove" could pass for a wristwatch—but this was no mere timepiece. The little canister on the strap emitted infrared beams and reconstructed from the reflections the real-time shape of the hand. Tiny embedded gyros and motion sensors deduced any tipping or repositioning of the hand.

"Exploring an exotic countryside," Alan explained. "Fighting trolls and ogres. Seeking treasures. Dueling and skirmishing. There are even pitched battles when enough players agree to have at it."

Brent well knew Alan's VR wanderings. A second Schultz, in this instance a pantherlike war cat, kept watch over Alan.

"Done my combat games once." Morgan pulled out a folding chair and sat. "The trolls hid in the villages and blew apart my friends with IEDs. I came to play poker."

Brittany took a pair of specs from the box. "I'll give it a shot, Cleary. It's an imaginary world, right? Slay the dragon and all that."

"Right." Brent strapped on his own gaming "glove." Like his specs, the wristband connected wirelessly to the computer in his bedroom. His PC was logged on over the Internet to the Wizards of Warfare server farm. "I started several game sessions before you got here. You'll be in neutral territory, where you can learn how the virtual world works without being attacked. This is a role-playing game, so I've associated each pair of specs with a character. An entry on the help menu will display your persona's backstory, skills, endurance, and the like. If you get into gaming, of course you can customize your avatar.

"Go ahead, Brit. Give it a try. Sorry about the beefy game avatar you'll get. Had I known you were coming, I would've picked someone more appropriate." Lara Croft and chicks-in-chain-mail avatars were easy enough to come by.

"Let's see how the sweaty half lives." Brittany put on her specs—finally—and Brent began swinging his gloved hand. "Neat graphics. Is that you waving, Brent?"

"In the flesh, so to speak. Next, put in your earpieces, Brit. Sound effects are an important part of the experience.

"Experiment. Look around. Pick up virtual stuff with your gloved hand. The sound effects are in stereo, so try to find the birds in the trees from their chirping. Check out the virtual menus. You'll find that things are pretty intuitive."

Now that Brittany had broken the ice, Brent passed out the remaining specs. The last pair he offered to Morgan, who, with a shrug, accepted them. Brent made the rounds again, this time with virtual gloves. "Okay everyone. Look around. Wave to each other. Pick up things. Interact. I'll run the intro program in a moment."

Morgan cleared his throat. "This isn't particularly inter—"

"Bear with me," Brent said. His specs revealed three burly figures bumbling about a forest clearing—and a blinking icon only he could see. He selected the icon with a flick/blink. "Here comes the intro video."

Along with a little something extra . . .

Hypnotic trance can be induced in many ways. Samir had suggested, as one option among several, mind machines: strobe lights and synchronized sounds. But commercial mind machines and related audiovisual software were aimed at *self*-hypnosis. To hypnotize the unsuspecting required more discreet means.

Such as VR gaming.

MMOGs were almost infinitely extensible, because you couldn't count on enough players being in-world when you wanted, in the mood to take part in whatever activity you wanted. Many of the characters in MMOGs were actually NPCs: non-player characters. Those custom programs could be benign, like VirtuaLife Schultz, or hostile, like a berserker warrior—

Or devious, like the Welcome program, into which Brent had woven subtle flickering and buzzing.

Morgan, Ethan, and Brit were soon wobbling on their feet. That was not a big surprise; Brent had tested and adjusted the program using Alan as a guinea pig. (Did that mean the program's properties were fine-tuned *for* Alan? A fresh hormone surge washed away Brent's apprehension.) And each of the three had had at least one drugged beer to lower his inhibitions.

"Alan, help me get them seated."

Soon enough the three sat slack faced, the silvered lenses of their specs more vacant than the blankest stare, wedged side by side on the short sofa. There they waited like cattle in a chute for their turn to be whacked on the head. A whole new meaning for Boxing Day . . .

Brent ordered Alan to the kitchen, telling himself he did so simply because the living room was crowded. That was a rationalization and Brent knew it. He was loath to let Alan see what was about to happen, and unwilling to switch off Alan like a machine no longer needed.

"Morgan, Ethan, Brittany, you will hear only my voice." Brent led Morgan to a clear area between the poker table and the bookshelf, guided him into a prone position on the carpet facing the bookshelf, and untucked his shirt. "Morgan. Bring your knees up toward your chest. More. Good. Now raise your left arm. Good. Rest your head on your arm."

As Morgan got into position for the lumbar puncture, still lost in the game-induced trance, Brent took latex gloves from his pant pocket and snapped them on. He removed one of the capped syringes from the drawer of the small end table. He uncapped the needle, ejected a droplet to expel any air, and knelt to give Morgan the injection. "Morgan, you will feel momentary pressure in your back. You will ignore that sensation and remain perfectly still. It doesn't hurt, it doesn't concern you, and you will forget—"

The squeak of sofa springs gave an instant of warning. Brent had scarcely begun to turn his head when the poker table crashed aside. Ethan dove at him.

The impact threw Brent sideways to the floor, the air whooshing out of him. His knees twisted, burning in agony. The syringe went flying. Faster than Brent could take a breath, massive hands clenched his throat.

Ethan shook Brent like a rag doll, whipping his head back and forth. Earplug wires kept Brent's bouncing specs from flying off altogether. "You filthy bastard! I knew you were up to something with this hypnosis crap! What are you doing to the captain?"

Brent's arms flailed uselessly, weaker by the moment as the life was squeezed out of him. He thrashed, unable to throw off his assailant. His feet drummed on the carpet.

Brittany sat, motionless and indifferent, on the sofa. Morgan remained on the floor, unmoving unless Brent or Ethan jostled him. Alan, ordered to stay in the kitchen, did.

Was a single drugged beer too low a dose for Ethan's size? Had Ethan faked a trance? Had fierce loyalty and this weird tableau shocked Ethan out of a too-shallow trance?

As Brent's body screamed for oxygen, as his vision grew dim, as consciousness faded, he wondered why the exact cause mattered. He wondered if perhaps his death wasn't for the best.

And he wondered why his eyes kept twitching.

Communication with the host faltered. Nothing but shock, pain, and terror remained—and they, too, were fading.

The host could be stimulated to produce painkillers, and One did what it could to release endorphins. They were not enough.

Neurons all around One, neurons with which One had integrated, were in distress.

One probed all accessible nerve bundles for a way to recover influence over the host body. Little still worked as it should. Brent's own desperate, futile thrashing grew indistinguishable from its own. Arms and legs weakened.

Oxygen starvation intensified. Synapses misfired and failed to fire. The host's thoughts became dark, unfocused, chaotic. Imagery streamed—memories and dreams, wishes and fears—intermixed and random.

Not only had the host's mind become sluggish . . . as more and more synaptic pathways malfunctioned, One's own thoughts slowed. One now knew for certain what before it could only surmise. Its consciousness had emerged from its integration with the surrounding neural tissue. When that tissue ceased to function, so would One.

The being called Alan, and its newly emergent mind that One denoted as Three, could still help. If Brent would only ask, Alan/Three *would* help. But for all their efforts, neither Brent nor One could utter a sound.

Extinction loomed.

One might—for how much longer it did not know—still manage to manipulate the host's vision. It fought for control of Brent's eyes. Brent panicked. His/their point of focus flapped about as uselessly as his/their legs. On the VR specs, menus and submenus appeared and disappeared. Windows popped open and closed. Network connectivity stuttered as his/their convulsions bounced the specs. There was sudden imagery in Brent's mind that One could not parse. A cat, shaking, with a mouse in its mouth?

One struggled for meaning in the image of his/their face turning blue, reflected in the silvery specs on Ethan's face. The mind that was Brent faded, more distant than in sleep, ceding all conscious control.

Sole charge of the neural pathways defaulted to One, even as oxygen-starved muscles lost their ability to function. A flood of adrenaline brought a bit of responsiveness to the muscles of the eyes. One concentrated to evoke a virtual keyboard—

The shaking of Brent's inert body interrupted the connection.

The specs settled into place again, for how long One could not know, and—flick/blink—it tried to send a message: *Come / Stop Ethan.*

Tried, and failed. Tried, and failed. Tried, and . . .

Eyelids fell shut and refused commands to open. Nanobot sensors reported toxin concentrations approaching terminal levels. Neural tissue went into shutdown.

Awareness ceased.

monday, 8:30 P.M., december 26, 2016

A shuddering gasp.

Oxygenated blood revived dying tissues. Synapses gone quiescent fired anew. Breathing steadied. One returned to awareness, then Brent, then the gestalt.

I/we still live. How?

He/they were crushed to the floor, knee tendons twisted and stretched unbearably, head throbbing, struggling for air through a sore throat still loosely constricted. There was a loud grunt and Ethan's inert (*why?*) mass shifted. Other hands pried loose Ethan's hands. With a thud, Ethan rolled aside, rocking the bookshelf. Books and game cartridges rained down.

Alan Watts stood over them, his chest heaving. Crimson spattered his face and shirt. Arterial red dripped from the base of the heavy brass table lamp that lay on the floor. "Brent! Are you all right?"

Brent's mouth opened, but no words came. He/they managed an inarticulate croak, and then, finally, weakly, "We think so." Wheezing, he/they managed to sit up. "How did you . . ."

Alan tapped his VR specs. "Your message."

Ethan groaned, blood pulsing weakly from his scalp. Alan chopped the back of his neck. Ethan spasmed and lay still. "Brent, we have to get rid of him."

Brittany, alone on the sofa, and Morgan, still positioned for his injection, ignored everything.

"Is Ethan dead?" Brent/One asked. The part that was just Brent felt ill.

"Not yet. But we cannot allow him to talk."

Brent's stomach lurched. "We won't kill anyone!"

"Ethan had no such qualms." Alan wiped his face with his sleeve, considering. "But not here. And we'll have to get rid of the body."

"No, dammit!" *Then what?* demanded that fraction of the mind that remained Brent's. Before Alan—or One—could stop him, Brent picked up the syringe and jammed it into Ethan's arm. First aid: *that* was what the bots were made for!

"A waste of potential. It changes nothing." The words came from Alan's mouth, but the opinion was surely that of Three.

"One way or another," Brent said, "everything will be settled soon. We only need Ethan out of commission for a few weeks. After a crack on the head like that he'll be confused as to what happened, at least if there's nothing to remind him. He might not remember at all."

"Truthfully, I don't want to hurt the big guy, either." Alan began to pace. "So we move him and make it look like a mugging. It's not like Brittany or Morgan will talk."

Because they, too, had no free will. Brent could live with it. Or One could, and decided for Brent. It became harder by the moment to know which. "Okay."

Brent had believed himself inured to nightmare, but this waking sort was different. He emptied a couple bottles of Molson into, and more than a little onto, Ethan. Brent and Alan wrestled Ethan into his coat and covered his bloody hair with his knit hat. Together they supported Ethan, a limp arm draped across each of their necks. Some blend of autohypnosis and One's intervention let Brent ignore his injured knees. Doubtless he would pay for that.

Luck was with them, finally. They met no one in the hallway, elevator, or garage.

Brent turned the car toward the slums where once he had waylaid derelicts with impunity, only to have Alan redirect him. Ethan had to be abandoned in walking distance of his own house to avoid raising questions of how he got there.

They pulled over beneath a dark railroad overpass. Together they lugged Ethan's flopping form deep into the shadows, sticking to dry pavement lest their shoes leave clues in the snow. When the cold made Ethan stir, another karate chop to the nape of his neck rendered him limp.

Wearing gloves, Alan removed Ethan's wallet, pocketed the cash, and flung the wallet to the ground. Alan retrieved and kept Ethan's cell phone. "For our Good Samaritan call. Nine-one-one centers use caller ID. Go back to the car."

Walking back to the vehicle, dimly reflected in the windshield, Brent barely saw Alan take something from his own pocket. Something that glinted. A knife! The blade jabbed faster than Brent could react. Alan ran to the car. "Get us out of here."

"But you . . ."

"Move before anyone comes along. Before we'll have *them* to deal with."

Brent told himself this was a nightmare, just to get through it. And, as in a nightmare, events unfolded at once logical and bizarre. Alan closed the knife and returned it, still bloody, to a pocket. He punched 911 on Ethan's cell phone, wrapped a handkerchief around it as it rang, and anonymously reported an apparent mugging. They ditched the phone a few blocks later, its battery pack removed, down a storm drain. With the battery in place the police might have located the cell by its GPS receiver.

They drove nearly a mile before Brent found his voice. "Why, Alan? Why did you stab Ethan? Is he . . ."

"He'll be fine. I made sure he'd stay in the hospital for a while, is all."

When Brent and Alan returned to the apartment, Morgan and Brittany were still deep in trance. Injecting them, and bashing their heads with beer bottles, was all but commonplace.

Step-by-step Brent planted post-hypnotic suggestions and false memories. They would train with VR specs. They would remember that Ethan had planned to drive himself to poker and never showed. They would remember a short night because four-handed poker sucked. They would wear one of the new baseball caps that Brent provided, emblazoned *SECURITY*, to cover the new bruises at their hairlines. Morgan took a dozen extra hats. Starting the next morning, the hats were a part of every guard's uniform. And should anyone notice a bruise anyway, it was to be blamed on a slip on an icy sidewalk. Utica had plenty of those.

Sick to his stomach, Brent told Morgan and Brittany how well they felt and woke them up.

First there had been One, solitary and confused.

Now Two and Three had emerged. Four and Five were seeded, with more among the factory guards soon to follow. Once Security was fully compromised, the Emergent could plunder the nanobot stockpile with impunity. Then there would be many more Emergent, and they would disperse, and make yet more of their kind.

Thereafter, not even another disaster on the scale of Angleton could threaten their survival.

Brent/One was well satisfied.

But aspects of Brent—old, human, Brent—lingered in the deepest recesses of what had once been solely his mind. There, despite feelings deadened by hormonal interventions, despite One's amoral indifference, despite shock at all that had transpired that evening, Brent struggled. He brooded on the wrongs he had done, rued the violence he had excused, was sickened by the atrocities he/they still intended to commit. There, unpleasant truth would not be denied: *we are the vanguard of an army of monsters.*

Then One clamped down still further, and even that passive resistance faded.

skirmishing

monday, january 9, 2017

Kim leaned back in her seat, eyes closed in denial of the bumpy flight. Weather had already added two days to her travels, but that was okay. There were far worse things than being snowed in with Nick on Manhattan.

She felt great, and why not? Four days over Christmas with her parents and grandparents in Virginia, followed by ten days alone with Nick in Cancún. The Cancún trip was Nick's Christmas surprise—and *what a surprise!*—to her. It must have made a significant dent in Nick's year-end bonus, but he firmly refused Kim's offers to pay half—or anything. She'd earned a cut of that bonus, he had insisted gallantly, the way his job kept them apart. He had even phoned Tyra ahead of time, getting the boss's blessing for the time away and swearing her to secrecy.

Ten days of sun, swimming, snorkeling, windsurfing—and lots of quality couple time. Ten days without e-mail and instant messaging, without CNN and newspapers, without cell phones, and only once-a-night checks for emergency voice mails. Followed, as their plane barely beat a nor'easter into New York, shutting down JFK behind them, with two days together in her favorite city in the world.

The best city on the planet, Kim heard in her mind's ear. She sighed. Even in absentia, Dan Garner brought her down. Work after sixteen days away was going to be a shock to the system. And she did *not* look forward to dreary, down-at-the-heels Utica.

But it was Monday, and late morning at that. The bill for two bonus days had come due. She took a limo from Syracuse Airport straight to Garner Nanotech.

She found Captain America on duty at the main entrance, hardly recognizable behind VR specs. Brent's fad had even spread to the guards. Nor were glasses the only change. "The cap is new, isn't it?"

"Yes, ma'am. A hat is now part of the uniform. Snappy, don't you think?"

No, but that hardly mattered. And on the bright side, hats and the Captain America shtick apparently didn't mix. "Have a good day," Kim said. She unzipped her coat and headed for her office, rolling two suitcases behind her.

"Huh. You *do* still exist." Brent had emerged, limping, from a cross corridor. He fell in step alongside her. "Welcome back, my gauche friend."

"Gauche": French for "left." In Latin, "sinister." Brent was big on teasing her left-handedness.

She said, "I wish I could say I'm glad to be back. Truth is I'd rather be on the beach."

He laughed. "Who wouldn't? May I take one of those suitcases?"

"No thanks, but a lift home tonight would be appreciated. I came straight from the airport, as you can see. And speaking of gauche"—two could play this game—"what did you do to yourself this time?"

Brent glanced down. "Skiing. More precisely, some klutz with no business off the bunny slope ran me over. Twisted my knees the first day out."

"Ouch, to coin a phrase."

"It's getting better. Judging from the tan, you had a terrific time. As, it happens, I did. Hot toddies, roaring fire, and ski-bunny sympathy." He winked.

At least Kim thought he winked. All she had to go on was an eyebrow briefly bobbing from view behind the rim of his VR specs. She didn't find it convincing.

They reached her office and she parked her suitcases inside. "What's been going on here? What did I miss?"

"Here, not much. You were hardly the only one to go on a winter break. But Ethan Liu, one of the plant guards, was mugged, almost killed, the day after Christmas. He's very confused about what happened. You know the guards work for a subcontractor, right? Well, they don't have medical insurance. Luckily, Ethan's a vet. He's in a VA hospital."

"I'm so sorry." Reality came crashing in, washing away the post-vacation glow. Five minutes: that had to be a record. "Is Charles back?" she asked.

"Not yet. And yes, by the way, to a ride home tonight. I'm about to run out for a little while, but I expect to be back no later than three. Holler when you're ready."

"Will do," Kim said. But first she was going to find out what Aaron had learned.

Aaron, it turned out, had learned a lot during Kim's time away.

She had found him with Crystal Nordling in the main Bio lab. Kim saw only one change from her previous visit. The skeleton had traded its Santa cap for ski goggles and poles.

"Trust me," Aaron said, "we've made progress. We have some video that's instructive. Each movie shows a neural tissue culture growing in time-lapse photography. Crystal?"

Crystal, seated at a lab PC, moused open a file. "The scopes captured images every few minutes. Here's a representative sample." On the main lab display a random smear of neurons appeared. "That's a brand-new culture. Now watch two weeks condensed into two minutes."

It wasn't pretty like the time-lapse view of a flower opening, but Kim was rapt. Almost from the start axons and dendrites groped toward particular spots. A digital counter clicked up in a corner of the window; as the count increased, more and more synapses formed. After a week synapses lay scattered throughout, but clustering was apparent. At two weeks, the crowding of axons and dendrites around a few spots in the sample was undeniable.

"Here's another example," Crystal said. This video also showed synapses forming, the concentration points arrayed in a pentagon. "And a third." Now the synapses converged around vertices of a hexagon.

"You set bots at those locations," Kim guessed. "Then there's no question bots stimulate synapse formation?"

"Not for me," Aaron said. "We have more examples, each forming a different pattern—letters, numbers, geometrics—always matching the initial placement of nanobots."

Crystal merely nodded.

"And it's not only the appearance of synapses . . . ?" Kim ground to a halt. She didn't know what, exactly, she was trying to ask.

"That's an excellent question." Aaron opened a supply cabinet, removing a stoppered flask and a pipette. "Allow me to rephrase it. Do nanobots affect only the growth patterns of neurons, or also the behavior of neurons? Crystal and I had wondered about that, too. To find out, we look to see whether synaptic *activity* reflects the presence of the bots." He raised the flask, gently swirling its contents. "That's what this is for."

This turned out to be a voltage-sensitive fluorescent dye. The firing of a neuron released ions into the synaptic cleft, creating a temporary voltage difference between axon and dendrite. The more active the synapse, the more ions were released—and the brighter the fluorescence.

Aaron emptied a pipette of dye into a petri dish, then gently rocked the dish back and forth until the dye dispersed. As he positioned the dish on the viewing platform of an optical microscope, Crystal dimmed the ceiling lights. A hint of green leaked out of the scope into the room. Then Aaron projected the image, a mass of green-tinged cells and synapses.

Emerald light blazed from six spots, from every corner of a hexagon.

....

The deli was unassuming, not quite fast food but order-at-the-counter casual. During the midday rush, maybe two hours each workday, the place did a booming business. The rest of the week you could set off a bomb here and hurt no one. Brent had suggested the eatery for its location between Utica and Clinton, convenient for both Megan and him.

Queuing up for the counter, they eyeballed the menu board and discussed their lunch options. Brent chose a gyro platter and Megan went with a salad. They chatted about their recent holidays: he, his fictitious ski outing and injury, omitting the imaginary ski bunnies; she, her trip home to Illinois. Sunlight, some direct, more glinting off the snow cover, poured blindingly through the south-facing window wall. There were neither shades nor blinds to be closed.

Their orders finally taken and filled, he and Megan carried their trays to an open table. They hung their coats over the backs of chairs, Brent taking the seat that faced the wall of glass. Skirt and sweater was a whole different look for her from short shorts and T-shirt.

He said, "So, here we are."

"Here we are," Megan agreed. There was a trace of a question mark at the end.

"You're wondering why I called."

"After seven months?" Megan picked up her fork. "I thought we hit it off, but when you didn't call I decided it was just me. Look, Kim threw us together that day. You didn't owe me a call then, and you don't owe me an explanation now. But sure, I'm curious."

If only this were about his libido reawakening, or even about discussing da Bulls and da Bears with another Chicago ex-pat. Brent's need was far more elemental—to restore some normalcy to his life. His qualms loomed as large. He had invited Megan to lunch because lunch wouldn't take interminably long if things went badly.

He said, "Kim merely thinks she knows everything I do. Soon after you and I met, a relationship I thought was something else flared up."

That was even truth of a sort, but a truth Megan could not possibly understand. Without a second consciousness in their head, who could?

"Makes sense." Megan smiled. "I'm glad you called."

"Then I'll assume the fork you're holding won't be coming at me. Go ahead and eat." Brent started on his own food.

She told funny stories about library-impaired Hamilton College students. He mentioned an offbeat band whose music he had discovered. (Kim had discovered it, and passed it along. Brent/One did not waste time on such frivolous searches.) They talked about last summer's big movies, only one of which he had seen.

After a while, Brent put on his VR specs. "The glare is brutal."

That was another partial truth. The mirrored specs did double duty as sunglasses, but being offline so long had left him jumpy. Putting them on was soothing.

Why kid himself? A ready-made excuse for wearing the specs—*that* was why he had opted for lunch and this particular deli. He had planned for failure.

Getting to know Megan. Crippling the homeless men. Hospitalizing and discarding Ethan. Brent struggled to feel anything about any of them. All were but fading shadows of a world lost to him.

But what of the new world?

With a flick/blink, Brent confirmed that Morgan and Brittany were online in VirtuaLife, orienting the latest recruits. *Progress?* Brent IMed.

Quick studies, Morgan answered. The attached file, blinked open, revealed a long list of training results.

Brent tried to imagine how it would have been to transform over a couple weeks, not many months. With hypnotic suggestions to ease his concerns and guide him along the path. To know that he was evolving, not crazy. To be planned and guided, not just . . . happen.

Flick/blink: another virtual window opened. Through Schultz's eyes, Brent peeked in on Charles on his virtual beach. Charles was Brent's personal pupil and the most advanced of all; Two had fully emerged more than a week earlier. Charles remained on his Caribbean retreat even as three weeks stretched past four, baffling the island doctors (and stymieing Dan Garner, increasingly impatient) with nonspecific, non-diagnosable symptoms.

Crystal Nordling was a brilliant thinker—just how capable, Brent was only very recently able to perceive. As an experimentalist, she left much to be desired. As a delegator, she was hopeless. It had been expedient to let her create chaos within the Biology Department. Later, it would take that much longer for anyone to understand what had been removed. As for later . . .

Flick/blink: he added Alan, stuck in the Garner Nanotech main lobby, checking IDs. The mundane task did not keep Alan/Three from annotating the imagery Three had stored from his/their latest patrol through the factory.

The moment would come soon for the Emergents to act. Alan/Three's assignment was to create an optimal sequence for selectively looting the plant and its inventory. Despite corridors stacked with equipment being staged into the factory, despite ongoing maintenance and upgrades and repositioning of the production lines, despite overflowing storerooms repeatedly unloaded and repacked to get at parts and materials, despite the daily bounty of crates and pallets and chemical vats that came across the loading docks . . .

It was a factory-sized 3-D jigsaw puzzle in which the pieces kept moving about, and not even the set of pieces remained constant. Captain America could never have conceptualized the problem, let alone worked it. Alan/Three was someone quite different.

2 hours, Brent reminded Alan. When the day came, that was the longest they dared risk taking.

More text and imagery flickered in a corner of Brent's online vision. That was One, communing with its cohorts at a rate to which Brent could still only aspire. A rate that no old-style human could imagine.

Almost as an afterthought, Brent directed Charles to return. For as long as Dan Garner remained overseas, safe from transformation, the boss's impatience mattered. *At work tomorrow.*

". . . Game this Saturday afternoon," Megan was saying. "Hardly of Blackhawks caliber, but I enjoy watching them. Are you interested?"

Huh? Brent accessed One's digital memory to replay the last few seconds. Megan was talking about the college hockey team. While his attention had been elsewhere, One had had him nodding at appropriate moments.

The faster Brent/One's mind sped, the harder the niceties of basic social interaction became. He dredged up enough humanity to feel lousy about calling Megan. "Saturday? I'll have to get back to you on that."

Even as the ever-softer, ever-more-distant voice that was old Brent chided him for begrudging Megan the merest fraction of his attention, she suddenly remembered an afternoon meeting for which she had to prepare. They parted ways as noncommittally as after their first encounter. He guessed they could agree on one thing: he should not have bothered to call her.

Old Brent called him a jerk.

Brent drove to Garner Nanotech, glad that Kim was back in town and in need of a ride home. Deep memories and old relationships seemed to have the most persistence. Harder to rewire, he supposed.

Whether or not that was the explanation, Kim was his last anchor to normalcy. For how much longer he did not know. . . .

Information overload, Kim thought. This would have been a lot to process even if she weren't just returned from two weeks away. "I'll need time to take it all in. I assume the data is on the G: drive." G: was for data shared across R & D. "What's the folder name?"

Crystal shook her head. "Everything you've seen is on the Biology Department server."

Which was to say on F:, to which Kim did not have access. "Would you mind giving me read access?"

"I don't know." Crystal dithered for a while. It was evidently a big decision. Chewing her lower lip helped. "It's supposed to be department internal."

"Then put a copy on G: for me," Kim said, trying not to sigh. Aaron had had to leave for a patient appointment. As the plant doctor, Aaron wasn't technically in the Biology Department. She wondered if he had access.

"I don't know, Kim. This is pretty sensitive information."

And I'm a freaking department head, not a seat warmer like you. Kim toyed with the idea of going over Crystal's head. But did she really want to get into a fight on her first day back? Not while there were other options. Not when there were more substantive matters to debate with Tyra. It had come out, just before Aaron dashed away, that the FDA remained uninformed about this line of research.

"How about this, Crystal? We'll encrypt the G: copy. I can set that up for you."

More lip chewing. "Okay," Crystal finally said. She relinquished the workstation from which she was logged into the lab network.

Ten minutes later, Kim had set up and tested a simple script. It locally copied the neural-culture results folder, encrypted the copy, and moved the encrypted version to the general share drive. The script would run every morning to keep her copy current. When Kim had finished, she thanked Crystal profusely.

Then, in her office for the first time since before Christmas, Kim wrote a second script. She gave this script an innocuous name, put it into a utilities folder among dozens of innocent programs, and scheduled it to execute every evening. The new script produced a copy of the copy, padded the second copy with meaningless filler, renamed it, and reencrypted it. The final version could not be identified by comparison to the file Crystal knew about.

The outcome from *this* experiment would not be lost like the first time.

monday evening, january 9, 2017

Muttering instructions to herself and firmly rejecting all offers of help, Sladja Sanders bustled between her cramped kitchen and tiny dining room in a crescendo of pre-dinner activity. Her hair was dark, as were her eyes, complexion, and scowl—and the scowl, judging from her frown lines, was as permanent as the rest. The Sanders children, who had been fed earlier and sent to play in their room, kept appearing to tug for attention at her pant legs and apron; Sladja shooed them away loudly (and, when words did not propel them quickly enough, with a long-handled wooden spoon that aimed for, but never quite connected with, their knuckles). She looked Slavic and spoke with an accent.

Kim sat with Aaron at the dining-room table, the living room having been declared off-limits. Maybe her puzzlement showed, because Aaron whispered that on the Serbian Orthodox calendar Christmas had fallen just two days earlier. Kim concluded the living room was a wreck and entirely understood.

Sladja was not at all what Kim had expected, and she wondered why. The scowl, Kim finally decided. It was nearly impossible to reconcile Aaron's whimsy with such severity. Talk about opposites attracting.

"Something smells delicious," Kim called out the next time her hostess appeared. Kim got only a preoccupied nod in response.

Aaron chuckled. "At this stage of the meal, you'd never guess Sladja is a whiz at entertaining. I've come to accept that it's her obsessing over the details that makes everything turn out so well."

A cold, wet nose insinuated itself under a leg of Kim's slacks. She leaned over and gave Bruce, a yellow Lab, a good head-scratching. He collapsed contentedly at her feet. "That's a very good boy," she told the dog. "Thanks for inviting me, Aaron."

"My pleasure. We'd have asked you over sooner if you hadn't gone out of town." He grinned. "Maybe now Sladja will forgive the burnt grilled cheese on your first visit to her home."

The invitation could not have come at a better time, and not only because Kim had had no opportunity to buy groceries. "I am *so* frustrated, Aaron. What you and Crystal showed me this afternoon seems ironclad. Why hasn't the FDA been notified yet?"

"Later," was all Aaron managed as Sladja bustled back—this time, finally, to stay—bearing a platter heaped with something breaded and rolled.

Pork, by the smell of it. It was Somebody Steak and Kim had never heard of Prince Somebody, but after one bite she took an instant liking to the man. The meat was indeed pork, wrapped around not-quite cream cheese, breaded and fried, and then garnished with tartar sauce. Sladja smiled at Kim's attempt to pronounce the name of the dish. An inspired, put-on second try with Kim's broadest Southern accent got an actual friendly laugh. There were also roasted potatoes, a red-pepper-and-eggplant salad, and a circular loaf of bread fresh from the oven.

"This is *delicious*," Kim said. "Everything is. Sladja, you are a marvel."

"You haven't yet had everything," Sladja corrected, smiling. "Save room for dessert."

The cold, wet nose returned. Aaron braved a stern look to pass scraps to the dog. There was a lull in eating while Sladja—glowering when Kim stood to help—cleared the table.

"Dessert," Kim said. It was a plea for dispensation: she was stuffed. She sat back down.

"Baklava. You'll like it. Trust me."

If the main course was any guide, she undoubtedly would—assuming she didn't explode. Kim called out to the kitchen, "Sladja, how old were you when you left Bosnia?"

"She was twenty-two," Aaron said. "Bosnia was a mess, and Sarajevo was under siege."

The reply was unusually terse for Aaron, and he looked uncharacteristically introspective. Kim wondered why he had answered. She called again to the kitchen, "Do you ever miss home?"

Sladja appeared from the kitchen, this time with a tray of coffee cups. "*This* is home," she said insistently, adding more softly, to herself, "I lost too much there." She set down the coffee, sloshing it in her haste, and disappeared again into the kitchen. She did not bustle back.

"I'm so sorry. Should I . . . ?" Kim wrung her linen napkin, at a loss how to complete the sentence. Make her excuses and leave? Apologize? Pretend nothing had happened?

"You couldn't have known." Aaron took a deep breath. "We don't know in America how lucky we have it. I wised up the hard way, patching up GIs caught in the cross fire between Shiites and Sunnis nursing grudges a millennium old. Sadly, there are places with hatreds too ancient for some people to get past. Kosovo. Lebanon. Eritrea."

Sladja returned, dabbing reddened eyes with a corner of her apron. "And Sarajevo."

"Aaron, Sladja, you don't have to explain—"

"The shooting was awful enough. For a long time, just to leave your house was to risk the snipers. Next it was mortars." Sladja shook her head, as though to cast out the memories. "Then those"—the next word, something Serbian, spat as much as spoken, required no translation—"discovered car bombs."

Aaron went to Sladja, holding her and slowly stroking her hair. "Park a car filled with explosives. Trigger it with a cell phone as your target is passing, or at any time at all if you aren't so discriminating. That's 'warfare' in our enlightened times. So anyone who imagined himself a potential target began carrying radio jammers, to stop from arming any bombs he might happen to pass. Normal people would have been stymied at that point—

"But not people who hate enough. They began designing bombs to arm when they *detected* jamming. If you can't know how far away your target will be, and you don't care who dies with your intended victim, you use a really *big* bomb. So Sladja's fiancé was killed, and her closest friends, guilty only of being in the wrong place at the wrong time. A café. Sladja would have died, too, except she was running late that day. And as for the political motorcade passing nearby, the evident target, the source of the jamming? Minor cuts and scrapes."

"I'm so sorry," Kim said, uselessly. She was ignorant of so much history. And yet—

A chill ran down her spine. "I understand, just a little." She talked about the Virginia Tech shootings, and the panic that still came over her from time to time. "It was an isolated tragedy perpetrated by one unbalanced young man. To face random violence every day . . . Sladja, I never meant to stir up those old memories. I'll leave you two alone."

"Please, no," Sladja said. Vulnerability had replaced what Kim had so callously imagined to be a permanent scowl. "Kim, this was not your fault. You asked a perfectly natural question. I look forward to seeing you again." She gave her husband a quick kiss. "I'm going to excuse myself."

"Thank you so much for having me." Kim waited only until she heard a bedroom door shut before she stood. "Aaron, I'm truly sorry. We'll talk tomorrow."

"I hate to put this on you, but Sladja will feel worse if you leave right away."

Kim winced. Now what? After plunging a foot in her mouth right up to the hip, she *so* wished she could talk to Nick. Beyond missing Nick—terribly—after so much time together, she needed some of his tact.

So: Idle conversation and pretending nothing had happened? Who are you for in the Super Bowl? The stuff that usually fascinated her, geek stuff like operating systems and networking protocols, seemed so inconsequential. Bits and bytes: did they really matter?

What did that leave?

It left whatever might have gone wrong with the bots. (And gone wrong with Brent, who still insisted that nothing had? Sladja remained haunted, twenty years after a tragedy. Kim herself still had nightmares about the Tech shootings, when almost ten years ago she had been scarcely a bystander. So Brent had changed after Angleton. Why was she *so* certain the changes were anything more than a trauma not yet two years past, still working itself out?)

The safety of bots, at least, wasn't trivial. Kim sat back down. "I asked you earlier about Crystal and the company not yet contacting the FDA. You said, 'Later.'"

"It's definitely later." Aaron took one of the coffee cups. "Sure, why not. Crystal is deferring to Tyra, and *she* has been waiting for Charles— who, I heard late this afternoon, is finally coming back. He'll be in the office tomorrow."

Good news at last! Crystal might be a brilliant researcher—Kim wasn't qualified to judge—but as a decision maker, Crystal was in over her head. It should be easier to get action taken with the real department head on the job.

Despite everything, the mental juxtaposition of Charles and Nick made Kim grin. Then another synapse fired. Or misfired. Kim lacked the knowledge to say which. Nick and his worries about replicating bots . . .

"Aaron, I have a truly out-of-the-box thought. Bots can't reproduce themselves, so the fears some people have about replicators are silly. Only . . ."—she swallowed hard, suddenly afraid this notion wasn't silly at all—"considering what you and Crystal showed me today, maybe bots can stimulate *synapses* to massively replicate.

"Just before Charles disappeared, when we got our first inkling of all this, you speculated that messenger molecules make bots look to neurons like other neurons. Isn't it reciprocal? I mean, won't the neurotransmitters the messengers are based on . . ."

"Glutamate," Aaron supplied.

"Thanks. Wouldn't the glutamate molecules released by neurons look to bots like signals from other bots? If I'm right, it wouldn't be just bots stimulating neurons to form synapses. The neurons would be stimulating the bots to talk back, restimulating the neurons. Again and again, over and over. I'm thinking like an engineer here, but this strikes me as a scary positive feedback loop."

Aaron paused, his cup suspended in midair. He stared into space for a long time. "I'm awfully glad Charles is coming back. In biology, it sounds like a scary feedback loop, too."

tuesday, january 10, 2017

Kim sat mute, numbed by two surprises too many—or was it only one? Could more than coincidence be at work here? Either way, Charles—who had, indeed, finally returned from vacation—and Tyra both now sported VR specs. Judging from the absence of other eyeglasses, Charles's specs incorporated his prescription lenses. How much had that cost?

The framed motivational posters and child's crayon drawings with which Tyra had decorated her office glinted surreally from their mirrored lenses. *Atom Ant*, Charles had sneered two months earlier. That parking-lot conversation seemed simultaneously the blink of an eye and eons ago.

Charles glowed from his four weeks on the beach. Tanned, rested, and ready. *Who the heck said that?* Kim wondered inanely. Someone before her time. Tricky Dick? Nixon, inexplicably, was her dad's political idol.

Tyra had changed her hairstyle for the new year, into something fluffy with full bangs. It did not work. Bangs and gray streaks was an odd choice.

If not the specs, then it was Tyra and Charles's harmony that had left Kim flummoxed. Charles's first day away, Tyra, in this very office, had fumed at his no-notice departure. She had fretted about what bots might do in neural culture. Today, on Charles's first day back, the two of them were somehow buddies, and Tyra could not have been quicker to support Charles's every utterance. The gaming glasses, the reconciliation, and an about-face on the seriousness of the lab findings: why the sudden changes?

Aaron arrived a minute after Kim, having also been summoned. (The strangeness seemed not to affect Aaron. Perhaps coping with patients in denial taught persistence.) He said, "Now that you're back, Charles, we really must act upon the things we've learned. Bots from our present crop definitely stimulate synapse formation. They persist if they cross the BBB."

Charles rocked in his chair, smugger than ever. "Doing research *is* acting. We know more than the last time we spoke. That said, and with all due respect to our colleague, lab work is not Crystal's strong suit. Aaron, I intend to continue this experiment for a few weeks, supervising it personally, before anything is said outside the company."

"I concur," Tyra said immediately.

"What about the upcoming trials?" Kim burst out. "What about Brent?"

"Now, Kim," Charles said condescendingly. "You talked to Brent about this. Tyra spoke with him. I sought him out first thing this morning. There's nothing else to do."

How had Brent put it, that day at the Munson? Right: *no earthly way to detect bot stragglers without putting my brain through a very fine sieve.* But every time she saw Brent, he was more remote.

Kim said, "Aren't there tests for changes in behavior? Brain scans?"

Charles and Tyra both froze for an instant, somewhere in cyberspace. "Maybe you're thinking of an electroencephalogram," Charles said, overenunciating. "That's a test—"

"I know what an EEG is," Kim snapped. "Knowing what we know now, *will* an EEG reveal active bots in the brain?"

"For someone with a sufficiently detailed baseline readout on file— maybe. Of course, not many people have baselines." A cold silence implied Brent was not among the exceptions.

Aaron cleared his throat. "I'll want to get back to the bigger matter of the upcoming Army trials and FDA notification. But first, as to Brent's situation, as to eliminating the possibility of residual bots active in his central nervous system, I had a thought."

"The suspense is killing me," Tyra said dryly.

Aaron ignored the sarcasm. "CAT and MRI scans reveal only anatomical detail. MEG fares best—"

Charles had not finished being supercilious. "Brent has metal pins in his arm. Under the circumstances, an MRI would be uncomfortable, to say the least. It might even do damage."

"I wasn't finished," Aaron said mildly. "And I didn't propose an MRI. MEG fares best with a baseline reading, much like an EEG does. Naturally, those methods won't answer our questions. If Brent will agree to one, though, it occurs to me a PET scan might be instructive." As an aside to Kim, Aaron added, "PET can contrast localized variations in metabolic activity. Remember the active synaptic regions around bots in the latest cultures? I'm speculating PET will pick up the associated metabolic increase."

"MEG" likely stood for "magnetoencephalogram," Kim decided. EEGs measured electrical currents in the brain, and electric currents produced magnetic fields. She ransacked her memory, trying to remember what a PET scan was. Something about positron emission? She'd ask Aaron later, in private, rather than be condescended to again.

Charles raised an eyebrow. "And if Brent disagrees, Aaron? Which, from my chat with him, I'm fairly certain will be the case. *I* certainly wouldn't take a dose of radioisotopes to satisfy someone else's curiosity, to look for something that's almost certainly not there, something that—assuming, Doctor, you still believe in the BBB—*can't* be there. Not to mention that, absent a baseline scan, you might not be able to detect any change."

"Maybe it's time we establish some baselines," Aaron answered mildly.

"Doctor," Charles said, "did Brent Cleary become your patient during my absence? No? I thought not. Then this debate ends now. For what it's worth, I assure you Brent and I *have* discussed the latest lab results. That's all anyone can do. End of conversation."

Kim refused to give up. "Charles, you implied EEGs can be instructive. Perhaps anyone chosen to take part in the upcoming Army trial should establish an EEG baseline first. That way, they can be monitored proactively for any brain-wave changes. Given the CSF surprise, the FDA might appreciate us having an independent check."

More cyberwithdrawal. Kim wondered: behind those damned mirrored specs, were Tyra and Charles IMing each other? There was no way to know.

Tyra unfroze. "About that. As I said earlier, Charles should continue the lab experiment first, as he proposed." Boss-imperative tones rang in her voice.

One day back from vacation had hardly caught Kim up after her own absence. She tried to tread lightly. "I'm confused. How can we possibly *not* make that call? It's not like we *want* bots getting into people's heads. When I last spoke with Dan—"

"Which you *won't* be doing again," Tyra said snippily. "There's such a thing as the chain of command."

"Communications are pretty darn direct when Dan decides at the last minute to drag me out of town to a meeting!" The retort was out of Kim's mouth faster than her better judgment could kick in. A clique was forming, and she wasn't a member. She wondered if, in her absence, Dan had become another of the silver spectacled.

"Let's all take a breath," Aaron offered soothingly. "Tyra, Charles, there's a core problem here. The data are what the data are. The FDA regs are what the FDA regs are.

"So I ask you again: what are we going to do about what we've learned?"

Brent/One spread his/their attention across a dozen subjects, variously studying, analyzing, synthesizing, and extrapolating. The faster the thoughts came, the faster they wanted to go. Bots stimulating neurons stimulating bots stimulating neurons . . . it was a virtuous cycle making him/them ever more potent.

His/their many trains of thought differed wildly, but they had this much in common: the accelerating rate with which each leapt from concept to concept, implication to inference, premise to proof. Data flowed across his/their field of vision in a dozen virtual streams, windows cycling between foreground and background as mood and need and eye flicks directed.

Events continued to unfold according to plan.

One window among the dozen monitored the gathering in Tyra's office, the information arriving with painful slowness. For any serious purpose, speech as a mode of communication verged on annoying. Charles and Tyra flick/blink echoed their own words, and those of their disadvantaged colleagues, to text. Brent skimmed the transcript while he tended to more pressing matters. Kim and Aaron could have no idea Brent was in the loop.

Aaron, whose persistence had become irritating. Sighing, Brent suspended several studies the better to guide his minions. And since he was practically reverting to single tasking, he might as well also get the tone-of-voice nuances of the conversation. *Put me on speakerphone,* Brent IMed to Tyra. *I'm dialing from x302. Muted on my end.*

OK, she sent.

Extension 302 was in Charles's office. Behind its closed door Brent sat subtly altering Crystal's lab files. Brent wondered if Charles remembered having revealed his department-level access codes. Charles/Two was even more supercilious than the original model; maintaining a bit of mystery was for the best.

Brent's call was answered immediately. To anyone seated across the desk from Tyra, impatiently speeding the incoming call on its way to voice mail and taking the call on speaker were indistinguishable: a single button pushed.

". . . Your worries are obsolete," Tyra was saying. "While you and Charles lolled on your respective beaches, some of us were here working. Crystal now knows why the bot antigen coatings don't dissolve in

CSF. A CSF-only protein binds to the coating faster than the coating dissolves. She also identified a candidate new coating that dissolves in blood plasma *and* CSF. The coating is already FDA approved for medical use."

Tyra had hit the right notes, but Brent questioned her delivery. There was something to be said for watching people's faces. Too bad he couldn't see into the office. Well, he would "happen by" as soon as he finished corrupting Crystal's data.

Brent had had Tyra summon Aaron and Kim to assure that *they* weren't online, that they couldn't possibly witness how Brent now tainted the latest experiments. Crystal, for similar reasons, had been dispatched upstate by Charles to meet with a lab-supplies vendor. Others of the Emergent, meanwhile, were removing incriminating data backups from on- and off-site archives. If the safety-copy absences were somehow noticed before altered versions took their places, it would all be blamed on screwed-up media labeling and Crystal's disorganization.

Trashing the incriminating data would be easy, but also easy to spot. Subverting the data just enough to point it in a new direction was something quite different. Brent laid out the parameters of the task and let One turn those general ideas into software. Within seconds, the new program was available—within Brent's head. He still had to key the code into a computer and find his typos.

Subverting the test results was strictly an insurance policy: Kim and Aaron were unlikely to go outside the company. Not while the research results were going their way. Not in time to matter. Brent saw the changes through anyway, planning for every contingency, mitigating every risk. Insurance had its uses.

Aaron said, "So why *not* contact the FDA? It sounds like we're ready for animal trials with the new coating."

Delay costs lives, Brent IMed.

"Because sometimes caution kills," Tyra said. "Our bots work, or Brent wouldn't be alive today. The Army wants their trial to move forward. They want this technology deployed."

"Because the brass doesn't know the risks?" Kim asked skeptically. "Are they up-to-date?"

Charles IMed Brent, *These two are nuisances. We should act.*

Act, as in transform? When enough had Emerged, their superiority would be undeniable. Old-style people would transform by choice. Brent told himself Kim would be among them. *No!* Brent ordered. *They'll wait for Dan before they act.*

Dan, had he returned home, would have been transformed by now. Dan could have commanded what Brent and others must accomplish by indirection—but even to plan for Dan's conversion abroad would have entailed on-site surveillance in unfamiliar surroundings, and unquantifiable risks. Security was Morgan's purview and Morgan had advised against the attempt. Dan overseas, hobnobbing with Army brass, championing "the best nanotech on the planet," his absence excusing various inactions here, served the Emergent nearly as well.

Tyra took her cue. "Absolutely the brass are current, because Dan stayed in Europe after his ski trip. He's been making the rounds of Army hospitals in Germany, greasing the skids for a bot field trial." Tyra talked right over Kim's objection. "Yes—without new FDA involvement. These will be overseas trials on overseas volunteers. A neat little jurisdictional loophole."

"The military plans to do an end run around the FDA?" Kim said. "Then notifying the FDA doesn't jeopardize the field trial. That's all the more reason to come clean."

Let's just do it, Charles IMed. He was never one to take no for an answer.

Do it: transform them. Brent would have had no qualms about assaulting Aaron—but Kim? Not while there were other options.

No. Wait for me, Brent IMed to both. *Have Tyra's door open.*

Tyra stood abruptly. "Is it me, or is it really stuffy in here?" She emerged from behind her desk to open her office door several inches. "That's better."

Huh? This conversation wasn't meant for random passersby. Kim cleared her throat. "I think I asked a fair question."

"Damned hot flashes." Tyra returned to her chair and fanned her face with a slim folder. "Talk about *unfair*. Just you wait, Kim."

"I'm content to wait," Charles said rather loudly.

"Folks? About the FDA?" Kim asked. Through the slightly open door, motion caught her eye. She fell silent as someone skidded to a halt.

Someone proved to be Brent, revealed as the door swung farther open. "I thought I heard you, Charles. I've been looking for you. See me when you have a minute? I'll be in my office."

Tyra set down her folder. "Brent, come in. I'd like to run something by you. We're at a bit of an impasse here." With Brent casually leaning against the door, again closed, Tyra summarized.

Too casually. It was all so very theatrical. Hot flashes, door opened, Charles's booming voice, Brent "happening" by looking for Charles, Tyra inviting Brent inside, and Brent's nonchalance.

Kim imagined dominoes—arranged through the VR specs—falling. All to augment the boss's prerogatives with a tiebreaking vote?

This "discussion" had become a farce.

"Damn it," Kim exploded. Everyone stared at her. "Brent, this isn't theoretical. This is about *you*. What bots may have done to you. Aren't you the least bit curious?"

"I refu—"

Kim cut him off. "Spare me that 'refuse to worry' nonsense. Afraid to worry, maybe, because you're sure there's no way to know. Well, maybe there *is*. Aaron, tell Brent your thought about PET scans."

"Positron emission tomography," Aaron said. "Long story short, it uses a radioactive glucose substitute as a tracer. With a ton of computation the radioactive decays reveal where sugar uptake is most concentrated. We'd be imaging the brain, looking for unusual patterns of neural activity. Brain PET scans are used, for example, to diagnose some dementias."

To Kim's surprise Brent said nothing for almost a minute. When he did speak, it was to ask a question. "Radioactive glucose. How radioactive are we talking?"

Charles coughed. "Fairly significant. The total radiation exposure from a PET scan is more than a year's exposure from natural sources. Each instance of radioisotope decay emits a positron: the antimatter version of an electron. When a positron hits a normal electron, they annihilate each other, sending two photons in opposite directions. That's what the technique detects: photons of a specific energy, emitted at the same time, traveling in opposite directions. Each of these photons carries over half a million electron volts."

"Photons," Brent repeated. "How benign sounding. Half a million electron volts, though . . . you're talking about gamma rays."

Aaron nodded. "That said, it's a pretty standard test."

"A pretty standard test," Charles said, "involving a rather fancy process. Fluorodeoxyglucose—FDG is the 'glucose analogue' Aaron mentioned—contains a fluorine isotope with a half-life a bit less than two hours. The fluorine isotope is produced in a cyclotron, then reacted to produce the FDG. It's then injected intravenously. Everything is typically done in one medical facility, before too much of the tracer can decay. And yes, FDG crosses the blood-brain barrier."

"Hmm." Brent tipped his head, pondering. Miracle of miracles, he removed his VR specs to meet Kim's gaze. "This is a bit overwhelming. Can you and I go somewhere for coffee? I could sure use a friendly second opinion."

Hours, cups of coffee, and finally a dinner later, Brent had not committed himself. Maybe he'd undergo a scan. Maybe he wouldn't. They went their separate ways for the evening.

Brushing her teeth, staring into the bathroom mirror, her mind chewing on the events of the day, Kim froze. Why had Brent sat through a tutorial on PET scans? Specs on, he could have looked it up in an instant. He looked up everything that way. Why hadn't he this time?

That touch of humanity wasn't the day's only oddity. There was also the theatricality of Brent's appearance in Tyra's office. The debate about notifying the FDA had not been settled against Kim. It had not been settled at all—and *she* had been the one to change the subject.

It made Kim ill to see that Brent had manipulated her.

thursday morning, january 12, 2017

Tires slipping, Kim fishtailed up the steep and treacherous driveway toward Garner Nanotech. Two pickups, their plow blades noisily scraping, their rooftop flashers flashing, were clearing the overnight snowfall from the main lot. Ghosts of blizzards past lurked between the aisles and all around the periphery of the lot, in dirty mounds taller than her car. Each time she crossed an aisle was an adventure. She turned toward an empty side lot, with the usual moment of panic when the car went into a skid. In Virginia you didn't learn to drive in snow.

Oh, to be back on the beach in Cancún! It had been less than a week, but already it seemed a lifetime ago.

She parked in an already-plowed area near the back of the building, on the factory side. Two seconds leaning into the wind, the sleet pelting her face, her teeth chattering, and she reversed course to go behind the building. The loading dock was closer than any of the regular entrances.

Wind whooshed under Kim's coat as she scurried up the loading dock's salted-and-sanded stairs. A freight truck was backed up to the dock to unload. The security guard, bundled against the cold, held open the door for Kim. He wore mirrored glasses that might have been sunglasses and might have been VR specs.

She pointed at the tarp-covered, vaguely torpedo-shaped things that sat on two-wheeled trailers just beside the dock. "I'm curious. What are those?"

"Snowmobiles, ma'am. No matter how much snow there is or how foul the weather, in an emergency we can pick up from a pharmacy or get someone to a hospital."

Emergency preparedness, huh? More likely, an excuse for the company to buy toys. Once you owned snowmobiles "for emergencies," you had to keep them in running condition—and right behind the factory a switchgrass field beckoned. Beyond the biofuel farm, a state park stretched for miles. Friends in Accounting had told Kim it had become a challenge to justify taking all the money VCs wanted to invest here. The waste wasn't Kim's problem, though. She hurried inside.

"Have a good day, ma'am," the guard called after her.

Kim cut across the factory toward the R & D wing, leaving a sloppy trail of boot prints, shivering for reasons unrelated to the cold. It wasn't just Charles and Tyra: more than a dozen people at Garner had adopted the VR specs. Many were in Security, and it was hard to see how hands-free Internet access benefited their work performance.

Circling one of the automatic carts creeping along the factory floor, Kim changed course. Aaron was another early bird and she needed a sympathetic ear. She found two sniffling colleagues waiting ahead of her. She went to her office and left Aaron a voice mail: "Got a minute? I need to talk."

It was well after eleven when Aaron returned her call. "Sorry, Kim. It's just been one of those days. High flu season *and* an icy sidewalk mishap. If you're still looking for an ear, come on over." Pause. "I keep a jar of them."

"Be right over. Shall we talk over lunch?"

"Sure."

Kim locked the most recent iteration of her department's new budget in a desk drawer and grabbed her coat. In the time it took her to walk to the infirmary, Aaron was again behind closed doors. High flu season? She waited in the hall, loath to touch the waiting-room chairs.

The door from the tiny treatment room opened, and a woman came out with an Ace bandage wound around her wrist. Following the patient out, Aaron noticed where Kim stood waiting. He grinned broadly. "It's hard to catch a sprain."

She remained in the hall while he retrieved his coat. "Aaron, would you mind driving? I'm parked way out back."

"No problem." They headed for the main entrance. "So, you need to talk? I hate to ask."

A bug-eyed guard sat behind the reception desk; Kim said nothing until they were tromping across the lot, snow and cinders crunching beneath their feet. "And I hate to say it aloud." But why else had she sought out Aaron? "You know my fear, that Brent has been infested with nanobots. This is going to sound nuts"—she laughed without humor—"okay, *more* nuts, but I can't get the idea out of my head. More and more people are changing like Brent did. I have to wonder, Aaron. Are they all, somehow, also infested with bots?"

"They? All?"

Kim grimaced. "Yeah, I know how that sounds. Charles and Tyra, certainly. Mercedes Ramirez. The Security folks—what's with so many of them going around in VR specs? And Felipe Lopez, I noticed just yesterday."

"Who's Mercedes Ramirez?" Aaron asked.

"One of the sysadmins on-call to back up the help desk. Latina with attitude. You'd recognize her."

Every male in the company recognized Merry. Kim understood the guy-talk technical term to be "built like a brick shithouse." The men, with great affectation, referred to her as Mercy, or Have-Mercy, imagining themselves clever and their "wit" a secret. To the frustration of the single guys across the company, Merry was happily married. She was too funny and down-to-earth for the women not to like.

And also damned competent. Among Kim's many post-vacation catch-up tasks, she had reviewed system logs for her department's wireless LAN. The most recent round of bug patches on the WiFi/WiMax routers had been backed out company-wide after Merry traced sporadic

PC crashes to the latest router update. The patches were apparently buggier than the code they "fixed." It happened. When Kim checked the manufacturer's website, the complaint remained under investigation. Recalling the Brownian-bit-bumps episode, Kim sympathized: transient problems were always tough to isolate.

They reached Aaron's sport-ute. As Kim got settled, Aaron said, "'Infested'? That was another interesting word choice. You think there could be some kind of environmental problem here at the company? One that manifests itself in the wearing of VR glasses? That's a pretty wild hypothesis."

"I know!" Kim squirmed in her seat. "If only Brent would agree to more tests."

"Which, obviously, you've discussed unsuccessfully with him." Aaron put the car into second gear and headed cautiously toward the exit. "Where to?"

She named a burger place across town, hoping to finish this conversation on the way. In the car. Privately. Worried all the while that she felt so paranoid.

Aaron tapped on the steering wheel as he drove. "Technically, Kim, I shouldn't even tell you this, but I've also spoken one-on-one to Brent about getting tested. I'll give you good odds he gave you the same answer. He's not about to have a PET scan. If I were he, I don't know that I would, either. I'm no radiation-phobe, but who wants an unnecessary exposure?"

"And?"

Aaron sighed. "I have the same worry as you. Charles and Tyra have changed. The thing is, Charles has been away for weeks. That hardly fits with a problem in the factory."

"So now what?"

Aaron changed lanes cautiously to get past a spinout. A police cruiser was already on the scene. "Now I pull Brent's files from the insurance company and see if there's a shred of data that tells us anything."

"You can do that?" Kim's hopes rose.

Aaron took one look at the skating rink–like parking lot of the burger joint, shook his head, and continued past the entrance. He pulled over into a spot far down the block along the curb. "Can I? Sure—only not legally. Medical privacy laws are freaking strict. It's a good way to get the company sued and me fired, and maybe lose my license. If anyone finds out."

And just as quickly, her hopes were dashed. "Aaron! I can't ask you to risk that."

"You didn't ask. I offered. We need to know if we have a plague on our hands."

Kim leaned across the vehicle and gave Aaron a peck on the cheek. "I promise you this. No one will ever find it out from me."

thursday evening, january 12, 2017

At lunch with Aaron, Kim had worried that she was becoming para-noid. By midafternoon she'd been afraid that she *wasn't*. By then she had revisited Crystal's neuron-and-nanobot lab results, scanning for progress the nerd way: using software to compare the newest and pre-vious snapshots. Old and new versions were supposed to differ—but not through retroactive changes made to prior data!

The changes were slight but unmistakable. Examined carefully, the altered imagery showed neurons reaching toward the amorphous blobs of adhesive that affixed the bots, not to the bots themselves. A second deletion of data would have been too blatant, so someone had laid the groundwork to discredit the rerun experiment in a new way.

So far, Kim had shared her discovery only with Aaron. She was not about to reveal to anyone else that she had unaltered and unauthorized versions of the earlier results. Whom else did she trust? Whom else could she trust?

This situation could not possibly end well. The only benefit of the doubt she could give was that the bot longevity in CSF had come as a surprise. Either way, a cover-up existed at senior levels across the com-pany. And no way could she keep that knowledge to herself.

At best, whistle-blowing would decimate the R & D ranks, ignite a scandal, unleash the FDA, and abort the imminent Army field trial. At worst, the rot went all the way to the top, to Dan Garner himself, and the company would die that much faster. One way or another, the days of Garner Nanotech seemed numbered.

Should she call Dan directly? The question had been torturing Kim for hours. Tyra had made her expectations clear. At this point, getting fired was the least of Kim's concerns, but she dare not be let go until she had gathered enough information. Incontrovertible information. If Dan was innocent, he'd understand.

So, whom could she trust? Only Aaron, and that answer broke Kim's heart. Just a week ago, she would have said—no matter the changes in him—Brent. Which brought her back to tonight's caper . . .

Aaron sat at the battered desk of his home office, flipping through inches of hardcopy as a little ink-jet printer squeaked and wheezed and struggled to output yet more. The ancient home computer, its cooling fans whining, labored nearly as hard to format the data stream for printing. Many caps on the keyboard were illegible from wear (his QW—TY keyboard, Aaron called it), and there was an actual floppy drive. Only the thumbprint scanner provided a touch of modernity. A rat's nest of cables, another anachronism, tied everything together. In the background, under Sladja's watchful eye, children squealed gleefully in their evening bath.

Kim occupied the armchair alongside Aaron's desk. She tried to glean something, anything, from his expression. His lack of expression. If the insurer's files were yielding any insights, Aaron kept that news to himself.

Except for the protests of overtaxed computer gear, the only sound in the room was the vigorous thumping of Bruce's tail against the carpeted floor. At least *someone* here was happy to see her again. Sladja's scowl was firmly back in place—whether because Kim's reappearance was too soon, too unheralded, or on too mysterious an errand remained anyone's guess.

Only learning how Aaron accessed the insurance-company records offered a glimmer of hope. Doctors routinely caught up with paperwork at home, he had told her, and insurance companies had had to come to terms with that. When he described how he logged on, Kim recognized the setup as typical for a virtual private network.

The VPN gave authorized medical personnel the same access—from anywhere—as the insurer's own on-site employees. That being so, she wasn't surprised by the robust authentication process. Insurers were subject to the same draconian penalties as doctors when patient privacy was breached, despite the lack of control over doctors' computers connecting in over the net. Doubtless many doctors were less than rigorous about applying security patches to Windows.

Aaron's keys lay in a heap beside the keyboard, the digital readout on the key fob slowly blinking. Every doctor allowed onto the insurer's network was issued such a key fob. A pseudo-random-number generator resided inside, its individualized parameters known only by a synchronized bit of code behind a firewall on the insurance company's security server. Log-on to the VPN involved keying in the digital readout (the eight-digit number on display changed every ten seconds) and the fob holder's thumbprint. After the user was authenticated, every scrap of data transmitted in either direction was encrypted using a private key uniquely assigned to that session.

It was all very standard, very secure—and if anyone ever questioned why Brent's medical records had been downloaded this evening, it pointed very unambiguously to Aaron. There could be no plausible deniability.

Kim told herself no one need ever know. That was her contribution, in fact. Aaron had had such confidence in the privacy safeguards that he had not thought through the implications of printing the voluminous file: Data had to be decrypted for the printer. Had he accessed these insurance records at work, a packet sniffer on the company network could have captured whatever Aaron routed to a company printer.

Am I being paranoid? Kim wondered again. *Uh-uh.* Not after Charles erased the first iteration of the neural-culture experiment. Not knowing that someone at Garner had tampered with the second try. It wasn't much of a stretch that someone might be monitoring the computers of anyone interested in those neural cultures.

Aaron's chair squeaked as he finally turned her way. A thick sheaf of printout sat on his desk, in the disarray that bespoke a hasty perusal. "Kim, you don't want to know how badly injured Brent was. I have no doubt that the bots saved his life. The Army *should* want this technology deployed. After what I've seen in military hospitals, *I* want to see it in the field."

"I know that. But what else did the bots do to Brent?"

Aaron hesitated. Bruce whined, as though he felt the tension. Perhaps he did.

Kim leaned over to comfort the dog, which whimpered once and then quieted down. "Aaron, come on. You found something in the files. You have a theory, at least. What is it?"

"A suspicion more than a theory." He picked up the papers and began tapping them into a neater stack. "Most likely I'm grasping at straws."

"Tell me, Aaron." *Please!*

"Well . . . that day in Angleton, Brent took a very serious blow to the head. To judge from the bruising pattern, the helmet of the nanosuit did what it was meant to: it went rigid to distribute the blow. Still, he was seriously concussed—"

"Hence the memory loss," Kim murmured.

"Right. But there was a lot of head injury. Not serious enough to cause permanent damage. No sign of intracranial bleeding, or we would know how bots could've gotten into his brain. Still, major brain trauma."

How was this news? "Where is this going, Aaron?"

"Into wild speculation." He tapped the sheaf sharply one last time and set it onto the desk. "Still, I think I finally see a possibility that makes sense. I need you to speak to the bot aspects of the scenario."

"Okay." She leaned over again to pet Bruce, for her own reassurance more than for his.

"Make sure I have this right. The first-aid bots are mobile. They creep and swim through the circulatory system, backtracking pain and injury biomarkers."

"Right," Kim said. "And when they can, bots hitch a ride on corpuscles going their way. Hitching saves energy. But everyone tells me bots can't get through the blood-brain barrier."

"Ordinarily."

Her jaw fell.

"That's probably still the case, but here's my crazy speculation. The way Brent's brain bounced around in his skull, his system must have been flooded with pain and injury biomarkers. Cytokines, especially interleuken-6, are a marker for brain injury. Cytokines, as it happens, also affect the epithelial cells that form capillaries. Trauma to the brain, even without bleeding, can—and often does—weaken the intercellular junctions. That's how injury biomarkers leak into the bloodstream in the first place.

"Another thing, bearing in mind that the exact mechanisms are far from well understood. Leukocytes drawn to the BBB by an injury may activate chemicals that induce an inflammatory response that further induces dysfunction of tight junctions. Temporarily."

Kim tried to follow the reasoning. "So the bots would've sensed brain injuries *despite* the BBB. And then backtracked the markers into the brain somehow?"

Aaron coughed. "That's where I hope you can help. I'm struggling with that 'somehow.' That bots can penetrate even the altered intercellular junctions is hard to believe. I need your expertise with the bots."

She scratched Bruce between the ears while she thought. Absolutely nothing useful about bots came to mind, leaving her stuck with biology. "I remember a mention that a few viruses and bacteria manage to get through the BBB. And I remember Charles sneering that we would have known long ago if Brent had meningitis."

Aaron leaned forward. "Well, a few things besides clever pathogens pass the BBB. Sugars and amino acids, for example. Some peptide chains and proteins, which is to say chains of amino acids. They're carried through the cells that form the capillary walls."

Her head was spinning. "I thought molecules had to fit between cells to reach the brain, that small gaps in the walls meant only small molecules made it through. I figured that was how sugars get through the BBB to feed the brain: because sugars are small."

"Even glucose molecules are too big to fit between cells. Water is a better example of what passes between. Compared to the intercellular gaps of the capillary wall, amino acids are quite large, yet they also get through. As I said, Kim, those are carried through—not between—the epithelial cells. 'Active transport,' the mechanism is called, and there are different active-transport methods for different amino acids and chains of amino acids."

"Why is this just coming up *now*? Why wasn't it obvious from Day One that 'active transport'"—in her frustration, Kim made exaggerated air quotes—"is the royal road into the brain?"

"Because it's *not!*" Aaron smacked a palm with a fist. "Active transport is a very complex, multistep biochemical process. An active transport is specific to the particular type of molecule being carried. It's another lock-and-key situation. The key temporarily opens, well, call it a tiny pore in the cell membrane, and later a second opening lets the transported macromolecule out the other side."

"I'm not following."

Aaron smiled uncertainly. "Because I'm not leading. I'm groping for an answer and I need your help."

She took a deep breath. "Okay, I'll try this again. How do the few viruses that get through the BBB do it?"

There was a soft rap and the door opened. Sladja stuck her head into the den. "Excuse me. Aaron, the kids are ready to be tucked in."

"Thanks." Aaron stood. "I'll be right back."

Kim stood, too, in her case only to pace. Could bots use active transport? Not without the correct "key" to engage one of the cellular transporters. Had bots inadvertently been designed with a matching key, Charles would have known. He would have mentioned it months ago, the day of the CSF surprise. Back then—back when he sneered at VR specs—Charles was still exhibiting signs of an open mind.

Aaron reappeared sooner than she had expected. He bore a coffee cup in each hand and shut the den door with a foot. He gave her a cup. "I sense this will be a long night."

Kim hid for a while behind her coffee cup. She didn't bother asking about caffeine; it wasn't as though she would sleep tonight anyway. "Let's see if I've cracked the code. The epithelial cells have evolved to transport specific amino acids used by the brain. So some viruses evolved hooks that mimic transportable amino acids."

"Some viruses may have mastered that trick—it'd be a damned clever adaptation. More typically viruses invade an epithelial cell directly, just as they would attack any cell, and then spread from the epithelial cell into the CNS. Either way that a virus gets in, the BBB also blocks most drugs, making it tough to treat infections of the central nervous system. We need to double-check, but I can't believe bots were designed to use any of the shapes that can trigger active transport. But I digress."

"This whole evening has been a digression," Kim snapped.

"Yeah, well, I'm a practicing M.D. I'm not some bigwig Harvard research guru."

And you're the only one to take me seriously. Kim felt about two inches tall. "Sorry, Aaron. My crack was uncalled for. I'm just so frustrated. We're not getting anywhere."

"I remembered something while getting us coffee." He sat in his desk chair. "There's another way besides active transport to move big molecules into an endothelial cell. The ten-dollar term is 'endocytosis.' Basically, a dimple forms in the cell membrane to admit extracellular fluid. The dimple retracts until it's a tiny pocket, more or less spherical, that is pinched off and migrates through the cell. The ten-dollar term for opening a new pore so the bubble of fluid can exit the cell is 'exocytosis.' "

"And?" she prompted.

"And the bubbles don't get any bigger than half a micron in diameter. Much too small, right?"

She nodded. "The bots are about fifteen microns long. More like one in diameter."

"Crap," Aaron said with feeling. "One more useless fact remembered."

Something he had said still nagged at her. Maybe thinking aloud would help. "Say the bots know, because of markers in the blood, of injuries they cannot reach. Well, 'know' is a bit imprecise, because I don't mean to imply consciousness, but you know what I mean. The bots have backtracked to an injury that they can't reach. All around them, selected molecules *are* passing through the barrier toward the injury. What do the bots do?"

Aaron shrugged. "What *can* they do?"

"They're programmed to hitch rides on corpuscles going their way. They're programmed to find the source of injury markers. Would they hitch a ride on something that passes through the BBB? It doesn't seem like much of a stretch."

"But aren't bots too big?"

Kim grunted, just to show she had heard him, picturing things in her mind's eye. A bot drawn to capillaries oozing pain and injury markers. The bot tries to backtrack farther—only it can't reach the wound because the cells forming these capillary walls are so tightly packed. Nearby, large molecules sink through the very walls that block the bots. The bot grabs onto a protein, the largest molecule it senses sinking into the barrier. The protein passes through a cell membrane, maybe via one of the temporary pores Aaron had mentioned.

But the bot is too big. It doesn't fit through the pore. It bumps against the epithelial cell. Bump. Bump. The bot as a wriggling tube. The Chinese-finger-puzzle, nanotube-woven structure of the bot, mostly hollow. The bot stretching longer and thinner, longer and thinner, longer and thinner, the better to squeeze through, until—

"Hell yes! That's it." She grabbed a pencil and paper off Aaron's desk and sketched the Chinese-finger-trap design for him. "The bots can stretch very long and thin. Maybe they stretch until an active transport pulls them through. Maybe they stretch and then coil to cram themselves into one of those bubbles you mentioned."

He got into the spirit. "Or go back to weakened intercellular junctions. Maybe, stretched thin enough, the bots can penetrate the temporarily disrupted gaps."

They stared at each other. From impossible, the idea of nanobots inside Brent's brain suddenly seemed inevitable. Kim shivered. "And once behind the BBB they're safe."

And once safe . . . what the *hell* had bots done to Brent?

friday, january 13, 2017

The next morning Kim and Aaron did their due diligence. Nothing in the bot design mimicked molecules that any known active transport could carry through the BBB—and nothing in the software restricted bots in the types of objects on which they could hitch a ride. The lookups involved only a handful of files among the dozens Kim pulled that morning from the departmental file server. She doubted that anyone would see anything out of the ordinary—

And she was still not about to discuss any of the implications at the office. She dragged Aaron away, again, to lunch.

"What now?" she asked. Today she drove and Aaron got to pick the restaurant. The observer she was avoiding might be hypothetical, but the data tampering was real. The stonewalling was real. The cover-up was real. She wanted to grab Brent by the arms and shake him. Bots in his brain were looking awful damn real, too. Her eyes misted up at the possibility that her best friend in the world was beyond hearing her out. Was simply beyond . . .

"Left at the next traffic light," Aaron said. "What now? Let's talk about that. From no idea how bots might cross the BBB, we have too many ideas. It makes sense that stretching themselves thin enough will play a part. But is that an explanation? Proof? Not hardly.

"I want to *see* bots pass the BBB. That will be the smoking gun. Then we place a call."

"Can you show it? How?"

From the corner of an eye she saw Aaron shrug. "I'm working on it."

sunday, january 15, 2017

A well-choreographed army had occupied the factory. Have-Mercy Ramirez flitted from keyboard to keyboard, shutting down the equipment that directed and monitored bot production. Reggie Gilbert followed behind her, closing chemical feeds, draining pumps and reservoirs, flipping circuit breakers, and uncoupling pipes and cables. Brittany Corbett, having bypassed the hazmat-alarm connections to Homeland Security, monitored for any incoming queries that might suggest DHS curiosity. Alan Watts, wearing a green eyeshade and holding a large, loudly ticking stopwatch, monitored and timed every motion.

Others stood in wait, their duties more episodic. As quickly as a machine was rendered transportable, several rushed in to boost the equipment onto a pallet. Another from the team would swoop in with a forklift, transporting the uncoupled machine to the loading dock. There, yet more of the Emergent were crating equipment and loading it onto rented trucks.

From a quiet nook between two hulking reagent tanks, Brent tried to take in everything. *It's only a rehearsal*, he told himself, *neither the first nor the last*. Responsibility for the details was delegated. Naturally it was hard to stay fully focused.

But whatever Brent told himself, he knew it was a lie.

More and more the factory took on a picked-over appearance. The Emergent took only the most specialized and expensive equipment, items whose purchase might raise suspicions. Everything else they *would* buy after—

Crash! Two forklifts had collided at a corridor intersection. *Crash!* A third forklift, stopping short, lost its load.

Alan froze his stopwatch theatrically. "Better, people, but hardly good enough." He vanished. He reappeared instantaneously, levitating high above the wreckage, there to reposition the curved safety mirror mounted to the corner. "Yes, the real-world mirror should be properly aligned. The thing is, no one checked. We can't have that. And clearly we need more spacing between vehicles."

Among the several scrolling windows in Brent's field of vision hung one window that was stationary. The frozen text there was an accusation he could not bear to study and would not permit himself to banish. A homeless man on whom he had practiced lumbar punctures was dead, taken the preceding day by complications of meningitis gone terribly, terribly aggressive.

Practiced on. Was dead. How antiseptically put. So much for his refusal to kill.

A chemical calm washed over Brent: One trying—but not quite succeeding—to banish the pain. Guilt didn't give way so easily.

Focus! Brent ordered himself. "Keep them practicing, Alan. We only have two weeks."

Then it was Brent's turn to vanish. He reappeared on a white sand beach where the trade winds blew. Seabirds soared in a cloudless sky. This was his island, and yet entirely different: greatly enlarged, with the Garner Nanotech complex standing atop the snowy hill just beyond a fringe of palm trees. Dollars bought euros bought yen bought VirtuaLife Bux bought "land" and access to thousands of man-years of gaming tools with which to secretly build a real-time factory simulation. A from-scratch factory simulation programmed on dedicated servers would have cost the Emergent money they did not have and time they could not spare—and still have been easier to detect.

None but a select few individuals at Hatoyama Gaming Corporation knew the number of private domains that dotted this virtual ocean.

Most were personal hideaways, like Brent's island had once been. On hundreds, perhaps thousands, of private islands, equipment and factory and power-plant simulations every bit as sophisticated as this were rumored to exist. There, manufacturers tested their wares, organizations trained their staffs, disaster planners made plans for evacuations, and first responders practiced for catastrophe. On a few of those islands, almost certainly, terrorist cells practiced to bring about those very catastrophes. Privacy cut both ways.

Ready now, Brent IMed. *Leadership meeting.*

One by one, Charles, Morgan McGrath, and Felipe Lopez joined Brent on the beach, greeting each other by audio. Wherever they were physically this cold and gray January Sunday, they appeared to be alone. Not so Tyra, who popped in a few seconds later and IMed her *hello*. Brent flick/blink opened a sprite to handle audio-to-text conversions for her.

They used audio here and now at Brent's insistence. Speech was slow, true, but its information content went far beyond mere words. For planning this critical to their futures, the richness of speech outweighed its inconvenience.

Charles thought voice was archaic.

"How goes the dry run?" Felipe asked. He had the same access to the simulation as Brent, so the question was just making conversation.

Charles had used his access. "Eighty percent loaded in three hours, then a fairly messy goof. Not good enough."

True, but it wasn't the doctor's place to comment. Brent chose not to react. "Still, it's down from eight hours on the first try. We have two weeks to squeeze out another hour." Two weeks until the Super Bowl, when even the workaholics and the folks playing office catch-up would be away. "It's coming together. Worst case, we'll know to scale back what gear we take."

"Worst case," Charles retorted, "we'll still be tuning the plan when our time is up."

In a far-off recliner, Brent clenched his fists. The challenges, once subtle, were more and more overt. Emergence made so many emotions fade away. Ambition, alas, wasn't among them. Perhaps ambition was too closely related to self-preservation to ever disappear.

Brent had begun to wonder if his days in control were numbered. In Angleton, bots had had to deal with massive injuries. Only a few bots would have gone toward his head—and probably fewer still gotten past the BBB, however that had happened. He had given each of his changelings a bot injection straight into the central nervous system. Almost certainly their brains hosted many more bots than his. Certainly they had Emerged far faster than he. . . .

Ambition? If only *ambition* were his biggest concern. Guilt smote Brent again, followed quickly by another hormonal rush. The endorphins numbed rather than removed the guilt.

"Well?" Charles prompted.

What was Charles's angle? Brent said, "We have full blueprints of the factory and full schematics of the internal systems, all thanks to Felipe. We have extensive knowledge of the alarm systems, local and DHS, thanks to Morgan. We have complete vendor specs on every piece of equipment in the factory. Every possible detail is in the simulation, Charles. We'll rehearse until we can strip the plant in our sleep. We'll be ready."

"That would be nice." Passive voice made Charles's words seem more skeptical than supportive. They weren't *quite* rebellious.

All the while, imagery from the ongoing rehearsal streamed across tiny inset windows on Brent's specs. Alan's squad was now testing alternate routings through the plant to reduce corridor congestion. It seemed to help. Tyra seemed to be multitasking, because suddenly Joe Kaminski, at work in the simulated R & D area, had a new and faster disconnect sequence for the scanning tunneling microscope.

And in the final window, the headline still accused: *Homeless Victim Succumbs*.

Excellent, Brent IMed, to include Alan. *Keep refining*. "We'll recheck our end-to-end time next Wednesday. Let's review the contingency plans."

"The diversions are deployed and ready to execute," Morgan

replied. "We tested our cell-phone jammers in real space, and they work. Landline cutoff is a simple matter of . . ."

The man had done two tours in Iraq and three in Afghanistan. He had run Garner Nanotech's security since Day One. With an Army expert on counterinsurgency, and technical support from bot-enhanced engineers and scientists, Security was not going to be a problem.

Brent watched Charles more than he listened to Morgan. If Charles meant to make a play for command, this would be the time.

Charles did not disappoint.

"All well and good," Charles cut into Morgan's spiel. "We won't need all this cloak-and-dagger stuff. Not if we make our move opposite the Super Bowl. But will we?"

"Whatever do you mean, Charles?" Brent asked.

"I *mean*, Brent, that while Morgan is planning for imaginary contingencies, your friend Kim and her doctor sidekick have become far too persistent. I *mean*, Brent, that the only real risk we face is that Kim and Aaron might force our hand early. Let's avoid that."

"Because she's my friend . . ." Brent paused for Morgan's certain rejoinder: *Ethan was mine.*

The terrible truth, Brent thought, *is that Charles/Two is correct. I cannot be totally objective about Kim.*

No, not terrible. Complicated. One would see to it that he/they did everything necessary for survival. But what was necessary? How would he/they choose among their options?

Those were difficult problems, and Kim was all that remained of Brent's moral compass. Well, not Kim so much as the idea of Kim, so much as the mental exercise of imagining himself justifying his actions to her. He feared losing the ability to feel remorse at what he had had to do. Should anything happen to her, Brent did not believe that the still, small voice in the furthest recesses of his mind could survive.

He had paused for Morgan, but the man had said nothing. Could Morgan possibly be so indifferent? So changed? Even among the Emergent, Brent often felt alone.

Brent shook off the mood to continue. "Because Kim is my friend, she's worried about changes in my behavior. She's been quite vocal about it. And she has talked to out-of-town people, people we can't easily influence: Dan Garner. Her boyfriend. Her family. My family.

"Nothing can happen to Kim without raising their suspicions. Nothing can happen to Aaron without raising Kim's suspicions. Let's not replace a known, controlled risk with an unknown risk."

"Controlled," Charles/Two mocked. "Merely rationalized, I'd say."

Unless he/they made their case, the torch passed now to Charles/Two. Charles had always been aloof. Did he retain any conscience? Did any of the other Emergent?

"Controlled," Charles/Two mocked. "Merely rationalized, I'd say."

While Brent mulled that over, Charles/Two priced custom VR contact lenses on five separate websites. He checked the status of several ongoing biochemical simulations. His/their mind craved stimulation, and the moving-day practice session provided far too little. Charles/Two tweaked parameters and initiated new cycles of modeling.

In other windows, pages of text and graphics blinked past: NIH and CDC research reports. As the bots integrated ever more tightly with his brain, even page-in-a-flash input grew tedious. He/they needed to devise something faster: some type of direct neural interface to the Internet, perhaps. He/they added computer science, cybernetics, information theory, networking protocols, and neurosurgery to his studies.

And still he/they waited.

Poor Brent/One, so out of his/their depth! Best guess, perhaps as many as a thousand bots had given rise to One. Most of the bots injected that day in Angleton had been expended keeping Brent alive. The pitiful few that made it across the BBB—and, amusingly, Brent/One had yet to figure out how—were barely sufficient to achieve awareness.

Throughput analysis had convinced Two that *its* components numbered in the tens of thousands. A PET scan would reveal an exact number, but the radioactive tracer might damage some of the bots. Curiosity did not justify taking the chance.

What would he/they be like once those myriads of bots fully integrated? Only time would tell. Surely something transcendent.

And *still* he/they waited.

Charles refocused on another virtual space, one shared only with Tyra, Felipe, and Morgan. The four took turns selecting an environment, and this desert-camouflaged tent was Morgan's choice. Cleary was uninvited and unaware.

There was no mention here of audio. Speech was so old species.

Charles IMed, *It's painful dealing with Cleary.*

He made us what we are, Tyra sent.

He's doing his best, Morgan added.

If only that best were enough, Charles thought.

He IMed, *Brent/One are like the first fish to crawl up onto the shore: indispensable pioneers, long since hopelessly surpassed. A change in leadership is inevitable.*

And who better than him/Two to lead? Charles remembered when his only ambitions were to gain wealth and to be rid of Amy. He would achieve those goals, but how humble they now seemed.

"It *is* controlled," Brent finally offered, and Charles paid a bit more attention to that window. "Almost certainly we can string along Kim and Aaron just as we've been doing. We need only two more weeks. The point is, the two of them have been staying within channels. Charles, Tyra—that's correct, isn't it?"

Throw him a bone, Felipe sent everyone but Brent.

"Brent's right about Aaron and Kim," Tyra said. "It looks like their 'plan' is to have a strong case when Dan comes home."

"Which won't be until after a detour to Miami for the Super Bowl," Felipe added.

Brent jumped on that. "That will be too late. Even if they do go outside the company, their experiment wouldn't hold up to scrutiny. Not the way the data has been altered. Before new cultures can be grown, the Super Bowl will be here—and we'll all be gone."

Let it go, Morgan IMed. *Yes, Brent is being sentimental, but the risk is minimal. He might even be correct that the bigger risk is raising questions among Kim's friends. The Security team will watch her and her doctor buddy. Cell-phone eavesdropping, e-mail intercepts, GPS trackers on their cars—all the standard counterterrorism stuff. We've planned for contingencies upon contingencies; we'll handle any surprises.*

Charles: *All right. We'll let Brent believe he remains in charge. For a little while longer.*

The declaration of an imminent coup went without comment.

warring

friday morning, january 20, 2017

Kim ignored the hallway chatter outside her office. January meant performance reviews, raise recommendations, setting objectives for the year, and endless budget revisions—with never a letup in the real work. The recent vacation had her that much further behind. On the other hand, she remained troubled by anything to do with bots. It was probably for the best that so much administrivia needed attention, even though, unlike years past, Tyra wasn't hounding Kim for it.

There was a sharp *knock-knock* and her door opened. "Walk with me," Aaron said.

"Just a sec." Kim locked her workstation and stood. "Where to?"

"A few laps around the factory floor. It's too nasty to go outside."

Inauguration Day wasn't a holiday exactly, but half the computers in the building and all the TVs in break rooms were showing D.C. festivities. And while Washington enjoyed a day like spring—oh, how she missed Virginia!—Aaron was spot-on about the Utica weather. More snow, amid enough wind to make it hard to distinguish what was falling from old stuff that was only blowing around. A fair number of people had decided to work from home. Tempting as it was, bosses can't do that.

So: no one paid Kim and Aaron any attention as they wandered about the factory.

"I learned something new," Aaron said cautiously.

About their private project, Kim presumed. She answered equally cryptically, "About . . . getting across?"

"Yeah." He jammed his hands into his pant pockets. "How do you feel about guinea pigs?"

As pets, not, well, as guinea pigs. Not as lab animals. "Conflicted."

"I guessed as much, seeing how quickly you bonded with Bruce. That's why I didn't discuss a test I had in mind. No reason to upset you if I didn't find something."

Their meandering took them by the loading dock and laughing voices. Kim said nothing until they were past. "Yeah, I understand. How sorry should I feel for the guinea pig?"

"He's in guinea-pig heaven now."

A forklift turned into their aisle. Kim led Aaron down a side passage, ignoring the crabby look from the forklift driver. "Okay. Out with it."

Aaron grimaced. "The short form: I can get bots across the BBB. Without a good reason to order a PET scan on a guinea pig, I had to do an autopsy to know."

They were in a staging area of some sort, piled high with crates on pallets, quite private. "Tell me everything," she said.

The test Aaron described sounded simple and elegant—and damning. He had injected interleukin-6, an injury marker common to people and many animals, through the skull of a guinea pig. Then he injected some of his purloined bots into its torso. In theory, IL-6 would leak into the bloodstream and attract the bots, just as they inferred had happened to Brent.

That morning Aaron had found bots in the guinea pig's brain.

He looked away when she asked for details. She remembered Brent's crack about a very fine sieve, and guessed the examination had been messy.

So bots in the brain *could* have happened to Brent. It could yet happen to soldiers in the field trial. And bots in the brain stimulated massive formation of synapses. Kim's worst fear had come true, and yet she felt oddly calm. Now, surely, people must listen. Something would be done. "That's it, then. It's time to contact the FDA?"

"And the state department of health, and OSHA, and the Army. The field trial *can't* go ahead as planned, not with the current version of bots." Aaron patted Kim's arm. "And knowing what I now know, I'll do whatever it takes to get Brent to undergo a PET scan. You have my word."

They headed back to the R & D office area, Kim wondering about *how* to make contact. They had already seen tampering with experimental data, and even Brent was implicated in the cover-up. Was it so far-fetched to think her and Aaron's office phones might be monitored? Feeling a bit paranoid, she asked, "Can we make the call from your house?"

He raised an eyebrow.

"I don't trust the phones here, Aaron, and my only phone is a cell."

"You think I have a landline? I'm not *that* much older than you."

"Cell phone it is then," Kim said. "Grab your coat and meet me in the main lobby."

Kim and Aaron tromped through icy slush to her car. She had bundled up in coat, gloves, hat, and scarf, and was glad she had. New snow was coming down in big, wet flakes. She estimated three inches had accumulated that morning, and guessed she would be leaving early today.

They both got into the car. Masses of snow slid off as Kim, shivering, slammed her door. She started the engine to run the heater before taking the cell from her purse. "FDA first?"

"Okay."

Raging paranoia had even kept her from looking up the FDA's phone number in her office. She surfed with the cell to an FDA org chart, finding a hotline for clinical trials. That number seemed like as good a place as any to begin. When the other end began to ring, she put the call on the car's speakers.

Voice mail picked up. Naturally. The connection was lousy, perhaps because of the storm. The greeting ended and Aaron began to leave their message.

....

We have a problem, Brent read. *Attempted contact with the FDA.*

The IM was from Morgan McGrath, with other copies to Tyra and Charles. Morgan's people were monitoring most everything. All calls on the in-house phone system. Intercepted cell calls and text messages. E-mails and IMs. Even web surfing: Have-Mercy had deinstalled security patches from the company WiFi routers, so that a worm could plant keystroke-logging software on every PC in the building.

Brent flick/blinked through to the attached file for details. The cellphone scanner had picked up an interdicted number within the FDA.

He blinked through again, to a recording of the call. The connection was staticky, from the storm, he supposed. That, perhaps, was for the best.

The call was from Kim's cell, but Aaron Sanders was speaking. "These bots pass through . . . change . . . brain. Cover-up . . . have unaltered ver . . . data sets—"

At that point jamming began. To the unsuspecting, it might seem like a typical dropped call. If they redialed, they wouldn't get a connection.

But the Emergent couldn't maintain jamming without attracting phone-company attention. Or Kim and Aaron might drive a short distance and regain service.

Regardless, merely those snippets of message were bound to set off alarm bells. What were the chances that an FDA hotline didn't have caller ID? Surely slim. But maybe no one would check the recording before Monday. Brent blinked through to a federal holiday schedule. Federal employees in D.C. and surrounding counties of Maryland and Virginia got Inauguration Day off.

Where are they? Brent IMed back. Morgan would know.

Only Morgan didn't, exactly. *They went outside just before the call. Lunch, the guard assumed. Their cars remain in the lot.*

The badge readers at the entrances were short-range, serving only to check employees in and out of the building. The GPS trackers hidden on Kim's and Aaron's cars could be read almost anywhere, but they were only accurate to within about fifteen yards.

Before Brent asked, Morgan sent real-time views from several parking-lot security cameras. *Both cars are in the SW corner.*

If Kim drove anywhere—even innocently, just to grab lunch—neither jammers nor scanners would be in range. Brent studied the surveillance images, spotting what looked like Kim's car. The profile was correct, and the snow-free bit of driver's door revealed the cherry red of her Toyota. The driver's side window was cleared off but heavily fogged; white vapor rose from the exhaust pipe; the windshield remained covered in snow.

There was time to catch Kim and Aaron before they went any-where.

Brent grabbed the coat from his office closet. *I see them. I'll bring them inside.* By telling them what? He'd figure that out en route. *We should go to Plan B.*

There wasn't a choice, really. No one argued.

"Crap," Charles said. He directed the sentiment to the universe, not anyone in particular. For venting, if no other purpose, speech had its charms. To Morgan, Felipe, and Tyra he IMed, *We deferred to Brent. This is what we got.*

Tyra took the hint. *Charles is right. It's time to take Brent out of decision making.*

Agreed, Felipe answered.

Concur, Morgan wrote.

Nor was it the best time for a committee, but Charles could work with these three. Most techies would defer to Tyra. Probably all the guards would follow Morgan's lead. A more permanent arrangement could wait.

On to Plan B, Tyra sent.

Plan B was simple enough, with none of the complexity of disas-sembling half the production lines in only a couple hours. All they truly needed was the bot inventory, and the catalyst-driven reaction vats for making more. Everything else that they had hoped to take, however expensive, wasn't unique to this factory and could be replaced. There was no urgency to rebuilding this factory while they had a supply of bots—or to risk exposure by trying.

So: Remove essential items only, whatever a few SUVs could carry. If the weather was bad enough—and maybe it would be—whatever the snowmobiles could carry. Take only the nanosuits they could wear.

And sow enough mischief to keep anyone else from noticing.

Under new leadership, the Emergent diversion would be much more robust than anything Brent envisioned.

"Crap," Kim said. "I can't get a signal. You?"

Aaron had taken out his own cell. "Me either. We can drive somewhere and see if that helps."

A gust of wind shook the car. "It's awful out. I'm planning to take off early because of the weather. What about you?"

"Yeah, probably." He grinned. "Probably to play in the snow with Becky and Freddie.

"Call me when you're ready to leave. We can stop at the mall"—on both of their routes home—"and try calling again from there."

Hat pulled low and scarf across her face, Kim bustled back toward the Garner Nanotech building. Aaron walked beside her, shoulders hunched against the cold, his coat collar upturned. People streamed through the doors: the lunch rush.

The card reader at the entrance beeped and flashed green, reading the RFID chip in Kim's employee badge through her coat. Captain America had guard duty but didn't seem to be eyeballing badges, so she stayed zipped. *Preoccupied or gaming?* Kim wondered. With the damned VR specs, who could know? VR specs and baseball caps made quite the fashion statement.

Aaron and Kim went to the infirmary to regroup. No one was in the waiting room. They went into his office and he hung his coat in the tiny closet.

Still chilled, Kim unzipped her coat but left it on, stuffing gloves and hat into the pockets. "Injected IL-6 through the skull," she said suddenly. "How the heck do you do that?"

"Sorry. I assumed you wouldn't want to know the specifics."

She didn't really. "Nonetheless."

He took a tennis ball from his desk and began squeezing it. "Drilled a tiny hole first." When she winced, he added, "Which is why I didn't volunteer."

"Mightn't drilling have nicked some blood vessel in the brain?" Maybe bots crossing the BBB *wasn't* settled.

"Sure, Kim, but it wouldn't matter. The hole let me get IL-6 into the brain, so the IL-6 could then leak out and maybe attract bots. I waited for any wound to clot before injecting the bots, far from the head." He squeezed the tennis ball a few more times. "With another animal, I might've tried injecting the IL-6 with a lumbar puncture. Guinea pigs are *really* little." More squeezing. "On the third hand, IL-6 injected by lumbar puncture might not have mixed very quickly. I might have had to examine the tissue in the spinal cord as well as the brain."

A bigger animal. A monkey, Kim guessed. Apparently she was a primate chauvinist, because she felt better thinking a monkey had escaped involvement. "Wait. A lumbar puncture?"

"Uh-huh. Why?"

"I don't know. Something." Her only association with lumbar punctures was last year's attacks on the homeless. "What if you injected bots by lumbar puncture?"

"That's a creepy idea." Aaron's hand froze. "I don't know. Same uncertainty, I guess. They might settle into the spinal cord, or they might end up in the brain. What are you thinking?"

"I don't know. About something I just saw, but I can't put my finger on it." She closed her eyes in thought. What *had* she just seen? Walking out to her car. Sitting in the car, trying to place a call. Walking back. The lunch rush at the lobby. Captain America.

Captain America's *hat.*

Her eyes flew open. "It's not just Brent."

....

Brent slogged across the parking lot. Chances were he'd never see Kim again after today. He would be out of the country, underground, with a new identity. They all would, availing themselves of Morgan's expertise.

A part of Brent was very sad about that.

Kim's car remained mostly, undriveably snow covered. Brent tapped on the fogged driver's window. No response. He peered inside: empty. Knowing Kim and snow, he guessed she had decided against driving.

The sloppy expanse of parking lot was a chaotic mishmash of boot prints and tire tracks. Not even One, for all its on-the-fly programming skills, could follow a trail from Kim's car.

Her riskiest destination was another car. Brent had no idea what the doctor drove. That information should be on file, though. *Alan, what vehicle does Aaron Sanders have registered with Security?*

A '14 Hyundai sport-ute, metallic blue. New York tags KWX0TK.

Quixotic: cute.

Plenty of sport-utes hulked nearby, many too snow covered to suggest a color. *Still in the lot?* Brent followed up with Alan.

Per GPS, yes. Out toward the main entrance.

Brent waved his thanks at Alan through a parking-lot security camera and started walking the rows. Aaron's SUV was in the third row Brent searched, well covered in snow. He pointed at it.

Alan was watching. *Their badges both read inside now. Sorry, my mind was on Plan B and how safely to clear stuff from the factory aisles. They must have walked right past me.*

Brent started back to the entrance. *Be ready to lock up behind me.*

Charles and Tyra gazed out the window of her office. The snow was coming down hard. He could hardly see the office building across the valley, let alone the spindly cell tower on its roof.

A pity, he IMed. He found a traffic-cam view whose backdrop included the office building. A steady stream of cars moved past. He sent Tyra the web address.

Morgan linked in from somewhere in the factory. *In five.*

Five seconds later . . . *bang!*

Charles squinted to take in the stately toppling of the antenna. Car horns blared. He faintly heard protesting brakes, but on the snowy streets tires could not squeal. Before the unblinking eye of the traffic cam, skidding, spinning cars crunched into one another. And then—

The cell tower, one hundred feet of steel, plunged into the intersection.

Aaron frowned. "What's not just Brent?"

"Bots," Kim said. Suddenly, her hands trembled. "Bots in the brain."

"You're serious."

She found a chair and sat. "Remember when Charles was going to talk to Brent, and over the weekend he disappeared after conking his head? Remember Charles's lab records disappeared that weekend? Captain Amer . . . Alan Watts was the guard on duty that weekend. That Monday, he had a big bruise on his forehead. He told me had tripped on rounds and cracked his head. Not long after, all the guards began wearing hats." And sometime after that, Tyra suddenly had full bangs. Masking a bump on her forehead?

Aaron blinked. "To cover wounds on their heads, you're saying? That's something of a leap. Say you're right, though. How do you get from bruises to bots?"

"Lumbar punctures." With a mind of its own, Kim's right hand began twisting a long strand of her hair. "What if Brent wanted . . . company? More like himself? What would he—"

"Why would he—"

"I don't *know* why," Kim burst out. "Just hear me out. You injected pain markers to draw the bots. But that required drilling a hole in the skull. Why not just bash its head to *make* pain markers?"

Aaron stared at Kim, saying nothing.

She paused, loath to complete her thought. "Give someone bots with a lumbar puncture. *Whoosh:* right past the BBB. Crack him on the head hard enough to give him a concussion. The bots are mobile; pain markers in the CSF would draw the bots to the brain."

Aaron rubbed his chin. "That's a pretty ghoulish picture you're painting."

"Charles and Alan had their accidental head injuries a few weeks after the homeless assaults. Maybe their head wounds weren't accidents." And maybe the homeless assaults weren't gratuitous. Maybe they were *practice.*

Last Thanksgiving, Brent had been so callously indifferent to those assaults. Because *he* was attacking the homeless? Kim swallowed hard. "Aaron, I—"

A distant, baleful moan sounded, quickly joined by closer sources. Sirens! Civil-defense sirens. What the hell?

The public-address system crackled to life. "Attention, all hands. Attention. This is building security. We have been informed of terrorist attacks in Utica. For your own safety, proceed immediately to the auditorium."

friday noon, january 20, 2017

Kim twitched. A terrorist attack?

The corridors echoed with shouts: shock, fear, and incredulity. Only scattered words were intelligible. The din swelled; the yelling grew more distinct—when the PA wasn't repeating its admonition.

Another lockdown. Helpless waiting. Death stalking. Another lockdown . . .

"This will totally freak out Sladja." Aaron slammed the handset of his desk phone. "First cell phones aren't working and now I can't get an outside line!"

But he made no move to leave. "I don't like this, Kim. I mean, I'm skeptical. Why now? Why minutes after you and I tried and failed to make that call?"

Kim wrapped her arms around herself. *The terrorists aren't here*, she chided herself. She tried to think. "It's Inauguration Day. Isn't that reason enough for some people?"

"That may explain the when. What about where? Why Utica of all places?"

The PA resumed, louder than ever. "All hands. Please assemble *immediately*"—the emphasis on "immediately" set the speakers squealing—"in the auditorium. Do not wait to call home first. One of the few things we know is that the attacks have disrupted phone service. We'll be showing local news on the big screen in the auditorium. Hopefully the broadcasts will answer your questions."

"That announcement is going to push people out the door," Aaron said. "People won't risk being stuck here, out of touch, away from their families."

I *won't risk it*, Kim thought. She had to find a working phone and let her parents know she was okay. "I'm *not* going to be trapped in here."

Aaron shushed her, and she heard footsteps approaching. Someone hurrying their way, away from the nearest exit.

Aaron pointed to the leg space beneath his desk. *Quick, hide*, he mouthed. As she stared in puzzlement, he added, still silently, *No time*.

Not sure why, Kim complied. The footsteps stopped. In the doorway, she thought.

"There you are, Doctor. You need to come with me."

The voice sounded familiar, only the tone was somehow off.

"I'm about to go home," Aaron replied. "I want to be with my family."

"You're needed in the auditorium," the voice continued assertively. "We know many people are leaving, but others are staying. We should have a doctor on-site. Just in case."

Captain America, Kim decided, sans the deferential tone the guards tended to use. Alan Watts. Brent's friend. The association failed to comfort her.

"Then I'll stay *here*, with my medical supplies."

How did Aaron remain so calm and analytical? It was all Kim could do simply to listen. Just back from Manhattan, her mind couldn't help jumping to the 9/11 attacks, but her memory also served up more recent terrorist atrocities. London. Bali. Denver. Athens. And then there was the horror that Sladja had gone through—

Sending Kim's mind down the slippery slope to cell phones setting off bombs, and jamming cells to stop bombs, and to how odd that, out in the parking lot, she and Aaron had lost cell service. There was a big cell tower on a tall office building on the hill just across the valley. Reception in the lot was usually excellent.

Was it possible someone would want to jam cells here? The notion was so bizarre that the polite conversation going on around her seemed almost sane.

"Doctor," Watts said firmly, "my boss told me to bring you. He didn't say to ask you. I hope you understand."

I certainly don't, Kim thought. If there was a medical need now, sure, but Watts would have led with that. He hadn't.

"Ms. O'Donnell is unaccounted for," Watts said. "Did I hear you talking with her?"

Huh? Why was anyone looking for her, personally? And to describe her as unaccounted for suggested people looking for her among those fleeing the building.

Aaron urging her under the desk now seemed prescient.

"Yeah, you did." Aaron tapped his desk, and Kim nearly jumped out of her skin. "The phones work in-house and I was on speakerphone. She was about to leave, too."

An alibi! In her relief, Kim almost missed Watts's answer.

"No, she's still in the building, Doctor. In her office, you said?"

"Maybe," Aaron said. "She could have called from anywhere. Is there a problem?"

"Please come with me, Doctor. Someone else will collect her."

"Look, I've made up my mind. I'm going home," Aaron answered. "After twelve years in the Army, I can take care of myself."

"You're staying, Doctor. Everyone who's going to leave has left. The exits are now locked for the safety of the rest of us. The exits will stay locked until the authorities issue an 'all clear.' Please come to the auditorium."

At Virginia Tech that day, her prof said stuff like that, too: *stay inside for your own safety.* Kim's hands shook. The halls had gone eerily quiet. Why the interest in retrieving Aaron? And her?

"And if I don't come?" Aaron tested.

"In ten seconds, I'll summon another two guards. If need be we'll carry you out."

"Since the building is locked, why not stay here in my office?"

"Doctor, the center of the building is the safest place to be. Also, it's easier for Security to watch out for everyone if they're gathered together. So can we do this the easy way?"

Kim thought: *Watch out* for *or just watch?*

No one spoke for what seemed like a long time. Aaron walked away from the desk and Kim lost sight of him. "Okay."

Seconds later, the infirmary door latched with a loud click.

Ten people milled about in the Garner Nanotech auditorium, dazed, angry, and scared.

Most of the employees not already away at lunch had dashed for home or day care or schools or spousal workplaces. Morgan had been sure they would. It was human (hint of condescension) nature.

Too bad Security couldn't evict these stragglers, but forcing people out the door amid a terrorist alert would raise questions.

Brent stood in a corner of the auditorium as his anxious coworkers (detainees? hostages?) traded rumors and speculation. Most kept trying to phone home. Many stared at TV, whether the big screen at the front of the room or their cell phones—tuners still worked.

For all the adrenaline One had coursing through Brent's system, for all the progress plain to see via his specs, Brent managed to feel unhappy. It wasn't supposed to be this way.

". . . continue to come in," a TV reporter went on breathlessly. "Switching centers and Internet access points were targeted, together with related antenna towers. The bombings have disrupted area wireless services from cell phones to Blackberry to WiMax. We're also getting scattered reports of landline outages. We're told the bombs resemble what the Army calls IEDs, improvised explosive devices. While our broadcast facilities remain operational, we will continue to bring you this breaking story. No one has yet claimed responsibility, but the use of IEDs suggests obvious associations."

As far as the stragglers were concerned, the Garner Nanotech building was severed from the world. While they huddled here, with only the clueless media to "explain" things, Morgan's people—supposedly patrolling the perimeter of the building for everyone else's safety—and the rest of the Emergent had begun stripping the factory.

The halls were quiet—cleared—before Kim emerged from beneath the desk. Aaron had goaded Watts on purpose. So what had she learned from their exchange?

The guards wanted her and Aaron in particular. It *had* to relate, somehow, to their discoveries or their attempt to contact the FDA—didn't it? More than the guards must be involved. Whenever she and Aaron tried to look into medical complications of the bots, Brent and Charles and Tyra got involved. So them, too, and everyone like them.

Them. Everyone like them. It sounded so paranoid. If not *them*, then what should she call . . . those involved? The bot infested? The bot transformed?

The transhumans.

A stupid question, and yet here she was wasting energy on labels. *I'm a thinker, not a doer*, Kim thought. But if she and Aaron—and everyone left in the building?—were going to get out of this, she had to *act*.

How? The transhumans knew she was in the building. At least they thought they did, because her badge had registered on the security system when she'd come inside a few minutes earlier. If her badge was conveniently found . . .

Kim listened at the infirmary door. Silence. She opened the door a crack to hear faint footsteps receding. She crept into the hall, shutting the door behind herself. The doorknob, released slowly, latched without a sound.

She ached with the need to run, but where could she possibly go? Watts said the building exits were locked. Even if she somehow forced open an exit, running would be foolish. There were *so* many ways to get caught. Armed guards patrolling outside, perhaps—a flash of insight—on snowmobile. Parking-lot security cameras redirected to watch the building exits. Alarms on the outside doors. One way or another, the bad guys would be on her in a flash.

Faster than she could hope to reach someplace with cell service, someplace from which she might call for help.

As the footsteps faded, Kim went the opposite way, to one of the less-used exits. She dropped her employee badge onto the floor, a good ten feet back from the door, beyond the range of the card reader. She willed the badge to look lost by accident.

It looked posed.

Nearer the exit, the carpet mat was a sodden mess, wet with snowmelt and filthy with cinders and salt. She pressed one boot into the slop, then hopped on her dry boot back to her badge. A grimy boot print made the badge on the floor look *much* more accidental.

Kim hopped on her dry boot to a nearby restroom for paper towels and dried the wet sole. She didn't dare leave any tracks.

If someone found the badge but not Kim, he might conclude she had, in fact, left before the exits were sealed. Maybe that would give her a bit more freedom to—

If only she knew what she *could* do.

Status? Charles / Two IMed.

He / they were asking that a lot, impatient. The VR view of the factory showed little accomplished. Too much effort was going into shifting stuff out of the aisles, riding herd on the anxious folks in the auditorium, and searching the facility for Kim O'Donnell. Logically speaking, the Emergent would be long gone, their loot transferred to the trucks waiting near Syracuse, before anything Kim could possibly do could possibly matter.

Brent had been similarly convincing—and here they were, improvising.

Outside is suitably panicked, Morgan IMed back. *Minimal casualties so far.*

Charles/Two did not ask for a definition of "minimal." The casualties were all old-style humans. *What else?*

Cell-phone service is out across metro Utica. Police band remains open.

All the bombs had been triggered by cell. The full-scale cell cutoff was just as Morgan had predicted.

Loading time? Charles prompted.

An hour? Morgan replied. *Keeping people in the auditorium uses staff.*

Uncertainty lurked within that question mark. Meanwhile, guards were unproductively standing watch over auditorium doors.

Charles answered, *Lock the auditorium exits. Quietly.*

Decision time, Brent/One read.

Morgan's words hung in virtual space, starker for this featureless meeting place. Morgan had said it was a given that Homeland Security would vacuum up all Internet traffic to or from the bombed area. To avoid attention, the Emergent had isolated themselves to this mesh of WiFi LANs, covering only the building and a bit of parking lot, cut off from the greater 'net.

If the need arose, Have-Mercy would reconnect them. Encryption would obscure the content of their messages, at least in the short term, but some insight could be gleaned merely from Internet addresses and patterns of messages. Palm-tree ambience wasn't worth *any* risk of exposure.

It was all part of the "standard counterterrorism stuff" in which Morgan was expert.

Decision time.

The usual suspects had gathered: Felipe, Charles, Tyra, Morgan, and Brent. *Explain*, Brent/One IMed.

We found Kim O'Donnell's badge near a side exit, Morgan wrote. *It looks like she lost it. There's no telling what she might say. We need to keep the authorities occupied.*

Brent/One did not see how Kim's whereabouts mattered anymore.

Kim's suspicions about bots won't interest the police or Homeland Security. All she can say about events here, today, is that company security tried to gather people for their own safety.

We'll be gone in an hour or so, Tyra added. *Isn't that good enough?*

No, Charles sent bluntly. *The forecast has been an hour or so for an hour or so. Felipe?*

I'm with Charles, Felipe said. *Better safe than sorry. Keep 'em busy.*

Garner Nanotech was mostly cleared out and surely the day's bombings were already keeping the authorities busy. Brent asked, *What more do you have in mind? People in the auditorium are on edge. They won't take well to more bad news on the TV.*

There was an instant of "silence" suggestive of consultation without him, before Morgan answered. *The fuel depot at Griffiss Field. My guy is waiting.*

Griffiss? That couldn't be a last-minute addition. For the airfield to be an option now, the bombs would have been emplaced in advance. Brent wondered, *Why wasn't I in the loop?*

Flame and charred bodies flashed in his mind. There was a moment of imagined searing heat—

Icy calm washed over him: a massive chemical intervention. Brent's revulsion faded into abstract calculation: *Was such drastic action excessive? Why Griffiss?*

Morgan: *With Kim on the loose, it's best to draw attention away from Utica.*

Despite coursing hormones, Brent felt a touch of unease. *How many people at risk?*

Can we signal the go-ahead? Felipe asked.

Tyra: *Sure. Wired comm works. We can reconnect the router and send a coded IM or e-mail. Or drive until you have cell-phone service. Or drive to the airfield, if need be. It's not that far.*

Morgan: *No comm. After being offline since this began, a message now will stand out.*

Charles: *Fine, Morgan. Send someone you trust.*

Morgan: *Done.*

Brent's question had gone ignored. He/they tried again. *How many people is a fuel-tank explosion likely to kill?*

We'll find out soon enough, Charles IMed. *Brent, when the news hits TV, can you keep a lid on things?*

Text came and went on Brent's specs, but the physical backdrop of auditorium and scared people remained. People Brent knew. People he had once been pleased to call friends and colleagues, hanging on every word from the TV newscast and worrying about their loved ones.

Now Brent/One ignored a question. *We don't need to do this. Let's finish packing and leave.*

For answer, there was another instant of "silence" suggestive of private consultation. And then, from Charles: *It's happening, Brent. Call if you need help calming people down.*

The coup had come.

A room of fearful people reminded Brent of what he once had been. Of the humanity of which he retained, however fleetingly, a trace. He had to assert control and stop the needless and excessive violence. *One, two, three, aardvark.*

An instant later, Brent found himself severed from the link. Charles's parting shot remained on-screen: *ROFL.*

Rolling on the floor, laughing.

Brent banished the mocking text from his specs. No matter how ably he had planted post-hypnotic suggestions, each had affected but one mind—and now *two* minds occupied each head. His control over the other Emergent had slipped away.

From time to time sirens wailed outside. Kim's cell remained out of service. Her heart thudded in her chest. She crept around the factory, fleeing footsteps—

Wondering if she were crazy.

So Alan Watts was being hard-nosed about bringing people to safety. Was that so wrong? Maybe she should join the others in the auditorium. She had passed close enough to the auditorium on one of her panicked tiptoe runs away from footsteps to have heard the TV through the wall. The words were indistinct, but the pretentious breaking-news musical motif was unmistakable. She could join Aaron and discover what those sirens were about.

But what if she wasn't crazy?

She took the cell from her purse. Fondling it was oddly comforting. Can't call, can't text, can't surf.

Wait! Why *couldn't* she surf? The cell had a WiFi mode. And if she could surf, she could e-mail.

Her hopes rose only to be dashed. She couldn't access any outside website. The LAN was up—so the transhumans can use their damned VR specs?—but there was no connectivity outside the building.

But maybe she could watch the news. She put in earbuds and set the cell to TV mode. She had reception!

Only listening to TV could mean not hearing someone coming her way. She unplugged the earbuds and squinted at screen crawlers. There *had* been bombings in town. The bombings appeared to have been remotely controlled, so local cell-phone and WiMax service had been suspended preemptively.

Remote-control bombing. What must Sladja Sanders be thinking?

Thinking about Sladja, and about Aaron unable to get to her, was easier than thinking about what Kim could or should do herself.

Yes, the guards were acting out of character. Maybe they should. Circumstances were out of the ordinary. Kim kept roaming the halls, trying to decide, slipping away from any noise that might be someone approaching. Until, in her wandering, she heard soft mechanical sounds from the factory floor. She peeked through the gap between the double doors—

In time to see a loaded forklift turn into a cross aisle.

Brent/One tried to reconnect, and failed. He/they tried each of the leaders individually. Morgan, the only one to respond, told Brent to coordinate through Alan Watts.

Brent/One indulged in a moment of speculation. Perhaps the other Emergent—guards mostly, and a few techies—would listen to him/them. Perhaps. More likely, the guards were loyal to Morgan. If so, hinting at a countercoup would only make the situation worse.

Come what may, the Emergent must complete what had been started today.

For a while, Brent/One concentrated on the shared virtual space. It was text only, alas, not the VirtuaLife environment in which everyone had rehearsed. Still, he/they saw progress. The reaction vats for assembling bots were mostly disconnected. Several units had been shifted to the loading dock. There weren't proper packing materials—those were to have come on rental trucks, in another week—so people were scavenging. Lumber from disassembled pallets. Styrofoam bits crumbled from the padding in still-boxed new equipment. Brent/One searched factory records for salvageable materials, reporting to the packers what he/they found. The sooner the Emergent finished and left, the less the need for other "distractions" for the police.

But the self-assigned task failed to distract Brent/One. If he/they couldn't connect, *he* would talk. Face-to-face. He slipped from his seat at the back of the auditorium, away from the TV. He was striding toward a door when a hand plucked his sleeve.

"Got a minute?" Aaron Sanders asked.

Brent stopped. *Kind of busy* would be a hard sell while he pretended to be taking shelter from the terrorist attack, and he might want to return later to observe. "What's up?"

"Let's talk over there." Aaron led the way to a quiet corner. "Here's the thing, Brent. I don't believe this madness is *you*."

"I . . . I don't know what you mean." Nor was Brent entirely sure how much of that hesitation was for effect.

"Yeah, you do, Brent. I've surveyed everyone in the room. Except for me, they chose to stay in the building. I was forced to stay. The intent was also to keep Kim here.

"What made Kim and me different? I see only one explanation: she and I know things about bots that we shouldn't. I don't yet understand how, but this situation is, somehow, about the bots."

"You didn't survey me," Brent said.

"Would I have gotten an honest answer?" Aaron shrugged. "Kim's best friend wouldn't cover up the dangers of bots. Kim's best friend would never lie to her. The stranger with a head filled with bots, though? *He* is another story. So now you and your cronies are up to . . . what?"

"You're imagining things, Doctor." Brent turned to go.

"Things like lumbar punctures, blows to the head, and hats for Security?"

Brent stared. "Is there something you want?"

A short fanfare burst from the TV. Breaking news, this time about Rome and an explosion. Over the shouting and cursing, Brent couldn't hear much. He swapped IMs with Alan to confirm: Griffiss Field had been hit. Again, Brent imagined the heat and the bodies.

Aaron said, "Everyone involved in corralling us wears VR glasses. Brent, I don't know when things in here will turn ugly, but they will. You want some free advice? Lose your specs before that happens, and hope for short memories."

A sturdy, round-faced Asian woman in a jumpsuit broke from the crowd by the big TV. (Brent didn't remember ever seeing her. He IDed her from Security's archive of digital badge photos. As her jumpsuit suggested, Janet Kwan was a janitor.) "Rome! If the"—the next word, snarled, was foreign; Brent doubted it was complimentary—"have left town, I'm going home."

Two men, burly factory workers Brent vaguely recognized, followed Kwan to the rear of the auditorium. There was a thud and a boom as the doors did not open. "We're shut in!" she shouted.

Aaron smiled humorlessly. "I think you're on the wrong side of the doors, Brent."

Alan. It's getting bad in here. "We're in the safest part of the building, Aaron."

"Brent, do you read any George Bernard Shaw?"

Brent wondered if that would make sense even if he could surf the 'net. "Excuse me?"

"Not a Shaw fan, I see. Tucked in the back of *Man and Superman* are 'Maxims for Revolutionists.' You might find this observation topical, Brent. 'The most anxious man in a prison is the governor.'"

"You're being foolish," Brent said, wishing that were true. *Alan. What the hell is happening?*

Alan: *Everyone's busy loading, so we locked the doors.*

They're about to riot in here, Brent countered. *Let me out.*

Alan: *Be there in a minute.*

Aaron Sanders was watching, his eyes narrowed. "Feeling anxious, Brent?"

Detainees had scattered to the auditorium's auxiliary exits. Doors rattled in their frames. Hands pounded in frustration. "Locked." "Locked, damn it." "Let us out!"

Brent: *Move, Alan!*

Aaron stepped threateningly close. "Our status here is pretty clear. Would you care to explain why we're prisoners?"

Alan: *Which doors are clear?*

Brent glanced around. *None.*

The PA came to life. "Step away from the auditorium doors. The doors are locked for your protection. Step away from the doors."

The pounding on the doors and the shouting intensified.

"We will have order," the PA continued. "Step away from the doors."

In the back of his mind, Brent noted how impersonally he was experiencing things, almost as though the doors were pounding themselves. Only the risk to his safety seemed real. One's doing.

Aaron shook Brent by the shoulders. "So what aren't we meant to see, Brent? Well?"

Brent: *All doors remain blocked.*

Alan: *The main doors, then.*

Bang! Bang!

Screaming. People ran from the shots, to the front of the auditorium. There were two holes at the top of a back door—well above everyone's heads, Brent was glad to see.

Alan: *I'll open in five, four . . .*

Brent shook loose of Aaron. At *one*, Brent was at the exit. Turned sideways to slip through the barely open door, he saw the doctor glaring.

Kim peered into the factory through the gap between double doors. Nothing stirred along the considerable length of main corridor from which the forklift had disappeared. She fixed in her mind the location of every closet and storeroom, every crate and bulky piece of equipment—anything she might hide in, behind, or under.

She nudged a door. The hinges didn't squeak, so she pushed through. There were soft clanks and thuds in the distance. No voices. Because the only "talking" was by VR glasses?

She dashed to the nearest corner and peeked around it, deep into the factory. Then, not giving herself time to rethink it, she crouched low, rounded the corner, and raced to the unmoving conveyor that angled up to the factory's second level. The noises were louder here, but still Kim saw nothing—

Until she glanced at the cleanrooms.

Behind a glass wall, four people in sterile protective garb were wrestling with a big stainless-steel vessel, one of the reaction vats in which bots self-assembled. One of the four, wearing VR specs beneath her protective hood, stood where Kim could see her face.

Merry Ramirez! Why—and how—was Merry inside? Even on a normal day there was no good reason for a sysadmin to enter the cleanroom. The computer controls were outside the cleanroom for ease of servicing. And why remove the vat?

First the forklift and now this. It was as though—

Across the complex, toward the executive-offices area, the PA rumbled. Kim strained to make out the announcement. Only an impatient tone of voice came through. And then—

Shots! Screams!

The four behind the window continued at their task.

Without conscious thought, Kim ran to hide in a nearby janitor's closet.

One struggled to control Brent.

Measures taken to protect the Emergent evoked counterproductive memories. Conscience and obsolete loyalties defied reason. The chemical levers One operated became less and less productive. To maintain influence, One had already elevated hormone levels beyond all experience. The chemicals required constant rebalancing and readjustment.

Others among the Emergent were more powerful thinkers. Others more thoroughly dominated their hosts. They were more dispassionate—more practical—about mere humans. The logic of the situation was compelling: others were better suited to lead than One.

Brent's vestigial conscience had become unacceptable.

Survival was the paramount imperative. For as long as Brent opposed necessary actions, perhaps rendering him lethargic would help.

With a bit of manipulation, One released a flood of new neurotransmitters.

Kim cowered on the floor, arms clutching her shins, rocking, fighting not to make a sound. Would she ever see Nick again? Her mom and dad?

The whimper in her throat yearned to be free. If she let it out, it would become a scream.

Darkness yielded to colorless gray as her eyes adapted to the bit of light that seeped under the door. She remembered that a string, a light pull, had brushed her face, but she would not dream of pulling it. Light seeping in meant that light would seep out.

It was like Virginia Tech all over again.

For Kim, the reality of the Tech shootings had been daylight, in a classroom with a professor and twenty-two fellow students, with several working cell phones among them, certain help was on the way. And, as it turned out, she was far down the Drillfield from the crazed lone gunman. She never heard a shot.

Here, now, she was alone in the dark. She was caught in some vast conspiracy, hunted by people she knew, cut off from the world. And with the police busy with terrorists, help *wasn't* coming.

No, this wasn't like the Tech shootings.

This was far, *far* worse.

reaping

friday, 1:00 P.M., january 20, 2017

Alone in the dark, stunned by what she had seen, Kim cowered. A forklift in use and transhumans unfastening reaction vessels—they were looting the factory. The theft and the concurrent terrorist attacks couldn't be unrelated. Could they?

Maybe she was fortunate to have something other than gunshots to obsess about. How many shots had she heard, anyway? Two? Knowing it was only wishful thinking, she told herself those had been warning shots of some sort, not executions.

Suppose the transhumans *were* behind everything happening today. Who but she knew? No one. So matters were in her clammy, trembling hands. What was she going to do about it?

She shivered despite the heavy coat she still wore. What *could* she do?

Not one damn thing came to mind.

Kim took a deep breath, almost choking on the stench from the mop bucket with which she shared the tiny closet.

I'm doing no one any good.

Chastising herself made Kim feel strangely better. Hand-wringing about what she could do had accomplished exactly nothing. What *should* she do? That question, at least, offered a new slant on the situation. What she *should* do, obviously, was get out the word about what was happening here.

But that would mean leaving her hiding place. . . .

The Last of the Mohicans was about events quite nearby. Whatever happened to him? Maybe hiding wasn't so bad.

No!

Kim forced herself to stand. She pulled off her coat, folded it, and wedged it onto a shelf. Coatless and in sunglasses, she might pass muster if glimpsed from a distance. If her badge ruse had worked, no one would be looking for her.

How was she going to communicate with the outside? The exits were locked and probably alarmed. Cell coverage was out. Aaron had tried to use an outside landline, and it hadn't worked. WiFi was local.

Kind of.

The thing was, WiFi hotspots were everywhere. When she had tried to connect earlier, her phone had sensed only in-building networks, but she had hardly done a systematic survey. In her apartment (would she ever see it again?), the problem was often interference from neighboring WiFi networks. Not that a random WiFi hotspot overlapping this building would necessarily do her any good. Except in quasi-public venues like Starbucks and airports, anyone with an ounce of sense ran secure networks that only worked if you knew the encryption key.

By that standard, several of Kim's neighbors lacked an ounce of sense. She managed a fleeting smile.

Skulking about in search of an outside, unsecured hotspot wasn't much of a plan, but at least it *was* a plan. And maybe—she brightened at the thought—this closet would be, by happenstance, within reach of an external WiFi network. She retrieved her coat, blocked the gap beneath the closet door with it, and used the lamp pull.

Her phone sensed only company LANs, and weakly at that. The metal door didn't help, and the walls—she had seen enough internal partitions going up during the build-out—had steel studs. There might be good reception two feet away in any direction and she would never know amid all this metal. She had to leave her hideout.

When Kim turned off the lamp, the dark was more oppressive than ever. She stuffed her coat back on the shelf, put her hand on the doorknob, and took a cleansing breath. An ear pressed against the door heard nothing.

I'm done hiding.

Heart pounding, hands trembling, Kim opened the door an inch. Nothing happened. She crept out and looked all around. No one. Her phone still showed only company hotspots.

Garner Nanotechnology sat alone at the top of a hill. She pictured herself standing in front, facing the complex. The only nearby structures were to her left and rear; testing for wireless access to them meant plunging deeper into the factory. She scurried on tiptoe about twenty feet down a broad corridor. No new signals. Another twenty feet. Nothing.

Kim managed a quick run-through of most of the manufacturing area, avoiding the loading dock on which the sounds of activity were unmistakable. The factory floor, unattended, felt like a ghost town.

She threaded a path through several interior aisles. She ran from the faintest sounds and the merest hint of shadows. She happened upon scattered areas without *any* WiFi reception, but nowhere did her phone detect noncompany LANs. Storerooms, closets, stairwells, and the shadows of large machines offered the worst reception.

She was terrified the entire time.

Drained by her effort, Kim went back to "her" closet to rethink the situation. She had not found a way to communicate, but a new idea was beginning to come to her.

"Enough is enough, Charles," Brent said. He stifled the yawn that had come out of nowhere. How could he be exhausted and angry and wired all at the same time? He had finally tracked down Charles to this break room. An armed guard stood nearby. *Protection against who? Me?* "Surely there's been enough 'distraction' to cover our activities."

Charles continued doctoring a cup of coffee. *Sorry if I'm boring you.*

Brent seethed more at being answered by IM. *He* had not been the one rejecting all comm. *To the point, Charles?*

Charles: *Let's leave that decision to the expert.*

As if it weren't clear Charles was now calling the shots. *Fine. Where can I find Morgan?*

Charles stirred, tasted, and grimaced. *Can you make coffee?*

Where, Charles?

Busy doing the things that need to be done.

Brent's retort bounced, the channel again severed, as Charles turned to leave. "Charles! Let's make our exit with a minimum of blood on our hands."

Charles walked away, trailing his bodyguard, ignoring Brent.

Brent yawned again, bone weary. It was suddenly all he could do to stand. He chugged two cups of coffee as fast as their heat allowed and set out, still yawning, to find Morgan.

In the crowded quiet darkness of a wiring closet, Kim struggled to turn a fleeting thought into a plan.

The idea of comm had gotten her out of the fetid janitor's closet. That first idea hadn't panned out, but *something* about comm tickled the back of her mind.

The ones behind today's madness had to communicate, too.

If she could tap the transhumans' communications, maybe she would learn something useful. Obviously they were too savvy to communicate in the clear. Merry was freaking brilliant to begin with. If bots and VR had bootstrapped her intelligence as much as had happened to Brent—

Kim gave herself a good mental slap. She had to stay on task. Suppose the VR specs did network over encrypted links. Could she crack the code? Not without a supercomputer and far more time than she was likely to have. Could she guess the encryption key? Not unless the supermen were being cooperatively obtuse. Could she steal a logged-on pair of specs?

Interesting.

The closest she came to martial arts was Pilates—it was ludicrous to imagine she could overpower *anyone*. Still, stealing a pair of specs in an active session didn't seem impossible. She leaned against the door, trying to work out the details. Something else was tickling her intuition. Comm. Comm.

Lack of comm.

The WiFi dead zones she had found scattered across the factory. She needed to surprise her quarry in a dead zone so they couldn't signal out for help.

What else? Not an armed guard, of course. Hopefully someone Kim's own size, like Merry Ramirez.

If wishes were horses then beggars could ride.

What else? Something more about the recent reconnoiter. Kim did a mental inventory of the areas she had checked out, every factory aisle she had scanned, every storeroom and closet into which she had stuck her head. A surprising number of storerooms were unlocked. In fact—

Every storeroom had been unlocked.

It made a weird kind of sense. Security was part of this conspiracy— witness Alan Watts's behavior. Everything—except the outside doors— would have been unlocked for the looters' convenience. That certainly explained Merry being inside the company's holy of holies.

So: Assume everything was unlocked. What would help her steal some in-use VR specs? Nothing Kim had come across seemed useful. Maybe in the storage areas nearer the loading docks, places she hadn't checked out? And then she had it.

A bulletproof, camouflaging nanosuit.

Final vat being crated, read the IM from Tyra.

At last! It was the milestone for which Charles had been waiting. To disconnect and seal the reaction vessels was hardly rocket science. To do so without introducing contamination? That required painstaking care. Read: time.

Excellent, Charles answered. *And the spares?*

All retrofitted.

He immediately directed Tyra and the technicians to preparing the bot inventory. The entire inventory would comfortably fit within a single canister, but such precious eggs were *not* to be entrusted to one basket.

Tyra didn't question Charles giving her orders; he didn't offer any explanation. Every committee has its head. It need not be a big step from first among equals to first.

One final set of things required collecting. The guards were only so many extra hands and strong backs; Tyra and the technicians no longer needed their assistance. Charles sent the guards new orders: *Bring the nanosuits to the loading dock.*

The nanosuits! Invulnerability *had* to be the answer, didn't it?

Kim sat on the closet floor, her back against the door, working through the possibilities. She would get only one go at this.

Invulnerable wasn't invincible. A nanosuit would protect her from guns, knives, and fists; it would not make her stronger. She could still be overpowered. Not as easily as if unprotected, perhaps, but still—be honest—easily.

But maybe she didn't have to fight anyone! She could steal a nanosuit and break out of the building. Forcing a door or breaking a window would set off alarms or be seen on the outside security cameras, but *now* that was okay. A quick sprint into the snow and, with her nanosuit set to white, she would be invisible.

Not so the trail of footprints she would leave struggling through the snow.

Every insinuation of a plan assumed Kim got her hands on a nanosuit. Without a nanosuit, all the planning in the world was only procrastination. She took a deep breath and crept from her cramped sanctuary.

Faint sounds drifted around the building; the beating of her heart seemed louder. She darted from one scrap of cover—crates stacked on

a pallet, an idle forklift, a bit of machinery—to the next. She reached
the end of a corridor, turned the corner, and repeated the process.
Hammering continued on the loading docks; when the hammering
paused, she heard engines humming. Finally, she reached the nanosuit
storeroom. It was unlocked! She shut herself inside and flipped the
light switch.

Twenty-five nanosuits had been ordered for the Army field trial.
Kim didn't take the time to count, but twenty-five suits looked about
right. About half were worn by mannequins. The rest of the suits lay
draped across cardboard boxes, over chair backs, whatever. Black pre-
dominated, but some suits had been left in other colors. More mannequins, unclothed, stylized and faceless, their "skins" arty silver, stood
communing in a back corner. The mannequins came in all sizes, for the
full range of nanosuit sizes to come, Kim supposed.

Too loose a nanosuit might not protect as fully. She held up a
nanosuit, telling herself this was just like eyeballing an outfit from the
rack. *Way* too long. She threw it back over a chair and gauged another
suit for size. A third. A fourth. She found one that might fit, if anything
a bit small for her, before she had to resort to wrestling nanosuits off
mannequins.

Gritting her teeth—the damn suits could inject bots!—Kim slipped
an arm into a sleeve. The jet injector poked her biceps and her skin
crawled. *It's inert,* she told herself. Without detecting an implanted
medical sensor, the suit couldn't activate its first-aid modes. She'd be
safe from bots even if this suit happened to be loaded with them. In
theory.

And it wasn't as though she had any better options.

She was half into the nanosuit when she heard—something. The
scrape of sole against floor? If so, it was *close.* If whoever-it-was looked
into this storeroom, she was trapped!

Laughter pealed just outside the door.

The nanosuit was leotard snug. In a panic, Kim yanked up the zip-
per. She tugged the hood over her head and ghostly translucent text
popped up on the visor. Her blink of surprise accidentally drilled down

into the onboard menu system. *Crap!* The suit had too many options, and she had no time to search through the verbose online help.

As a faint metallic click suggested the turning of the doorknob, Kim found the menu entry she needed. She edged, shaking with fear, in among the cluster of unused mannequins. With her back to the door, she froze in an unnatural, arms-away-from-her-sides pose.

The door opened to louder laughter. *Two people*, Kim thought. *Men.* If they saw any significance to finding the ceiling fixture already lit, they remarked only in cyberspace.

If they noticed her, she could do nothing about it.

Every muscle ached from the effort of standing absolutely still. She had set the nanosuit color—all but the visor, because coloring *that* required a second command she had yet to encounter—to silver. If she was very lucky, she might be mistaken from behind for just another naked mannequin. Her pitiful ruse wouldn't work if anyone bothered to come to this end of the room and saw her face through her still-clear visor.

Something clattered along the hall, like a grocery cart with a wobbly wheel. A third person entered the room, presumably whoever had been guiding the cart. The laughter subsided. Kim heard shoes shuffling, the swooshing of fabric, other noises to which she could not put a name, and, to fresh laughter, the slap-thud of a mannequin hitting the floor. Collecting the nanosuits, obviously.

They had not noticed her!

The work sounds continued, and then, in an unfamiliar, very deep voice, "Alan. Hold the dummy for me while I unzip it."

"Sure." The answer was in Alan Watts's new, assertive voice.

Suddenly all three men were talking. Kim wondered if the changelings disparaged vocalization. The storerooms she had surveyed earlier mostly lacked WiFi reception. This storeroom was probably a dead zone, too.

"The waiting is giving me the creeps," Bass Voice said. "I'll be glad when this is over."

Shuffle, shuffle, rustle. A rattle in the hallway as, presumably, cargo was loaded onto the cart. "We're almost ready to go, Sam," Alan said.

"Think what we'll have then. Bots to transform millions. The most important gear, and the experts, for producing *more* bots. And these suits."

Bass Voice (Sam?) said, "They won't know what hit them. While they last, that is." A condescending laugh. "Neanderthals."

"While they last," Alan agreed. "Guys, I'm going to step into the hall and report in. Keep loading."

Kim's arms ached. How long had she been holding them out from her sides? How long could she keep it up? She bit her lip for the distraction. If she could last just a little longer . . .

Bass Voice: "How went your report?"

"Yup, yup, we is the idiot guards," Alan said in an affected, aren't-I-dumb voice. He continued in a normal tone, "*Our* heads are full of computers, too. You would think we'd be given credit for the ability to count. We're bringing in twenty-four nanosuits because that's the number we found. It's not our fault one is missing."

There were rattles and thumps in the hall: more items being loaded onto the cart. Alan, Sam, and the third one were leaving. If Kim could will her aching limbs to remain still for just a *little* longer . . .

The light clicked off. The door closed, plunging Kim into darkness. The rattle-rattle of a cart wheel suggested movement toward the loading dock. She sagged onto the floor, swallowing a groan. Sensation gradually returned to her arms.

Bots to transform millions, she thought. *If the transhumans dispersed, if they took that supply into hiding—*

Kim shuddered. If the transhumans got away, it seemed impossible that anyone could stop them.

Sensation gradually returned to Kim's muscles.

Okay, she had a nanosuit. Now what? If the transhumans were about to leave, her course of action seemed simple. Stay put. Wait for the bad guys to make their exit, release Aaron and the rest from the auditorium, and then seek out the authorities and tell all.

It was wishful thinking, not a plan.

How, shut here in the storeroom, would she know when it was safe to leave? Could she get the police's attention amid the bombings? Computers in their heads, Alan Watts had said. Neanderthals, Bass Voice had said. If most transhumans were even half as smart as Brent had become, they would make themselves hard to find. Every minute of head start they got would only increase the challenge.

What if the transhumans took hostages—or eliminated witnesses— before they left?

What if, while she sat agonizing in the dark, whoever had hassled Alan Watts came back looking for the missing nanosuit?

Muscles screaming, Kim staggered to her feet. Working by touch, she properly sealed the nanosuit—she hadn't had time before. She flipped on the light just long enough to match the suit's color to the yellow walls. The same sickly shade was used throughout the building.

She found a visor-centric submenu that let her set the visor color to match the suit body. The same submenu offered image enhancement and infrared viewing modes. Amplified, the bit of light seeping under the door sufficed for searching for something, anything, she might use as a weapon. All she found was the disembodied arm from the knocked-over mannequin. She left the arm where it was.

Time to go.

Her breathing was too rapid. Her instincts disbelieved what her mind knew about permeability of the smart fabric—not to mention that she was almost too terrified to move. With a convulsive gasp she controlled her breathing before hyperventilation knocked her out.

Kim remembered just in time to deactivate the visor's light amplification before opening the door a crack. In enhancement mode, the bright factory lighting would have blinded her. Nothing stirred in the corridor, but in the distance she heard something rhythmic. Chanting?

She crept closer, rounded a corner, and the sounds became distinct. "Bathroom, bathroom, bathroom . . ." The chanting came from the auditorium.

Kim told herself the prisoners wouldn't be fussing about bathrooms if someone had been shot within the hour. Aaron and the others must still be safe inside! A ray of hope, finally. She clung to that thought even after a snarl over the PA shut everyone up—without any move to escort anyone to the bathrooms.

She reviewed the WiFi dead spots that she had identified. Many were close to the loading dock, near too many transhumans to expect safely to ambush just one. Some dead spots were around machinery, visually complex backdrops that the nanosuit's preprogrammed camo modes could not match. Other areas were too brightly lit, where her own shadow would give her away.

One dead-zone area might suit her purpose. Her nerves as taut as piano wires, hugging walls the present color of the nanosuit, she set out.

Kim wasn't nearly as smart as the transhumans, but—if she had the savvy to use it—she held one definite advantage. They didn't know—yet—that someone was stalking them.

friday, 2:00 P.M., january 20, 2017

Morgan was nowhere to be found.

The people who knew where Morgan was—and certainly *someone* knew—weren't sharing the information. Brent checked the obvious places first. The auditorium perimeter. The Security area. A coat still hung in the closet of Morgan's office, so he probably hadn't gone outside. The cleanrooms.

Brent found a flurry of activity by the loading dock. People improvising crates. People shuttling crates to SUVs, all too low to load directly from the dock. Tarps had come off the snowmobiles, and small items were being loaded into their cargo compartments. A flatbed cart was heaped with nanosuits.

Still no Morgan. No one at the dock admitted to knowing where Morgan was.

All the while Brent listened to TV news over his cell. Three dead in the Utica bombings. A dozen seriously injured—the miracle being that none were killed—when an antenna tower crashed into a crowded intersection. Five dead at Griffiss Field. So this was Morgan's concept of minimal casualties. Brent was sick to his stomach until, unasked, One chemically intervened yet again.

Midsearch, Brent got a brusque inquiry from Charles: *Did you take a nanosuit?*

Brent had had neither the time nor the need. Evidently someone else had felt differently. *No. Do you know where Morgan is?*

Jerk.

No, Charles replied, and the link went dead again.

Having eliminated the obvious places, Brent switched to a systematic search. He cruised the aisles, yawning despite himself, peeking into offices and labs. No luck. He climbed a stack of boxes to survey the factory floor. No luck. He began exploring the main-floor spare-parts storage, in what once was a tanning salon. If Morgan wasn't here, that would leave only the second floor. The upper level was more an attic than part of the factory, and Brent couldn't imagine why Morgan would go up there.

A scuffing sound.

Brent turned. "Morgan? Is that you?"

Silence.

Logically, that shuffling came from somewhere Brent had yet to search. He went deeper into the storage area and his specs went blank. No reception back here. He rounded a badly lit corner into the next corridor. The dimness came as a surprise, but even LED lamps must fail occasionally.

A slight noise, behind him. Brent spun to see—

What?

It was as though the figure materialized from the wall itself.

7

Kim hugged the shadowy corner near where, standing on a stepladder, she had removed the ceiling-lamp LED. Her body hid a foot-long metal strut she had scavenged from some spare-parts bin. A part for what, she had no idea. As much of her nanosuit as she could see seemed to melt into the walls.

Counting in her head kept her breathing slow and even, and hopefully silent. All she could do now was wait. And wait.

And worry.

Earlier, the depths of this storage area had been dead to WiFi.

What if it wasn't still dead? She couldn't check because her phone was inaccessible. Because, stupidly, she hadn't thought to transfer the cell from her slacks pocket to a nanosuit pocket.

What else had she overlooked? She who thought to ambush a trans-human genius? Kim began to shake.

Don't panic! Movement would only make her more visible.

A few deep, shuddering breaths got her body back under control. She waited and worried some more. And then—

Someone was moving about the storage area, making no effort to be quiet.

Kim shuffled her feet to draw that someone's attention. It eventually worked, because she heard, "Morgan? Is that you?"

Brent's voice! He rounded the corner a moment later.

She launched herself at his back, trying—and failing—not to think. This was Brent. But Brent was the cause of this madness, the leader of these terrorists. But it was *Brent.*

He must have heard her. He whirled, the faint ghostly image of her-self, arm and club upraised, reflected in his VR specs. He batted aside her arm, and the club flew from her grasp.

She couldn't have stopped her charge if she tried. The nanosuit stiffened to distribute the blow, but Kim still felt it. She jerked to a halt, the impact rattling her teeth. *Conservation of momentum,* she thought inanely.

Brent ricocheted into a closed metal door. He shook his head grog-gily.

She grabbed for Brent's VR specs, but he twisted his head away. A fist to his gut sent a jolt up her arm and again knocked the wind out him. He doubled over, retching. This time, she succeeded in grabbing the VR specs and slipped them into a nanosuit pocket.

One good blow to the head should knock him out, at least long enough to bind him with duct tape. *Just* knock him out. The lying, the assaults, everything—those were the bots' doing, not Brent's.

Thinking, *This is for your own good,* Kim hauled back to slug him.

Brent ducked under the punch and rammed her.

....

Brent teetered on his feet, stunned, as the stranger grabbed for Brent's VR specs.

He twisted his head away, wondering what use the specs were for his assailant. To stop him from calling for help? Maybe the stranger didn't know there was no reception back here.

The stranger lunged again for the specs, again reaching with his left hand. This time he almost got them.

He? The person beating on Brent was short for a man. Whoever it was had the nanosuit Charles was looking for.

Brent's thoughts and reactions were so sluggish. What was *wrong* with him?

He was an instant too slow in blocking a punch. The stiff fist to his stomach knocked the wind out of him. He bent over, puking. This time, the stranger got the VR specs. He or she pulled back a fist for a knockout punch.

Thinking, *She swings like a girl,* Brent ducked the roundhouse blow and tackled the stranger. It was move fast or get clobbered, so he had moved fast—and ramming someone in a nanosuit was like running into a wall. He cried out wordlessly—and so did she.

The pieces finally came together: height, size, left-handedness. Kim!

One peered through Brent's eyes at an outside world that jerked and spun about. One listened through Brent's ears to thuds and oofs and gasping synchronized to Brent's labored breathing. One felt the struggle against lethargy, against the serotonin and melatonin with which it had drenched Brent to keep him drowsy and docile.

One sensed Brent's pain.

He/they needed help, and there was no way to summon it. One was left with sorting through the torrent of impressions and feelings.

A shock of recognition! Associations flared in Brent's memory—the assailant was Kim! Brent's conflict and confusion swelled. His focus wavered.

Brent's sentimentality would doom them both.

One flooded Brent's system with adrenaline and kept it coming. Through the visual cortex and at the most visceral levels, One screamed.

Kill. Kill. Kill. Kill. . . .

Sudden rage consumed Brent. In an instant, his lethargy vanished. He brimmed with new energy.

How *dare* Kim attack him? Taking her by the throat, he shook her like a rag doll.

Her fists hammered him, but he ignored them. As she tried to knee him, he turned away, taking the blow on his thigh. The nanosuit was stiff beneath his fingers and he knew he couldn't strangle her—but he *could* shake her senseless.

"Brent," she wheezed. "Stop."

He kept shaking her. The wall or the hardened back of the suit: cracking her head against either would work equally well. Every time she managed to push away from the wall was another opportunity to crash her into the wall again.

But something was wrong. *This* was wrong. Wasn't it?

Brent fought the rage. What was he doing? Why was he doing it? He could let her go, and if need be run after her. Even if he hadn't beaten her almost senseless, Kim never could run as fast as him.

The lust to kill would not be denied.

His whole body was trembling now. His heart pounded, faster and faster. He felt like he was on fire.

His muscles bunched up, as though he was fighting himself. Because he was!

"Brent," she wheezed again. "This . . . has to . . . stop."

He slammed Kim's head into the wall. He? No, the rage. No, *One* slammed her head.

Stop! Brent projected. He tried to release Kim, but his hands seemed frozen. He struggled for control. *Let her go.*

Apparently he more than projected. "It's not *you*," Kim gasped. "It's . . . the bots. Fight them."

Aaron Sanders had said much the same. Could that have been only an hour or so earlier? It seemed a lifetime.

All Brent had to do was simply *let go*. Run from the storeroom maze and call out for help. With another person or two, he could easily overpower Kim without further harming her.

One did not care. One had no pity for mere humans.

Screw you, Brent projected. He willed his body to go limp. It didn't. He tried again, this time focusing on his hands, and was rewarded by spastic tremors. He tried again. . . .

The shaking went on and on, punctuated by crashes into the wall. Kim struggled to stay conscious. The back of her head must be one large bruise and she was seeing double. She was talking, in gasps and wheezes and croaks, with no clue what she was saying.

She was going to die here.

The shaking slowed, changed. Brent's muscles quivered and bunched. His eyes fluttered open and shut and open again. He was fighting—himself.

From reserves Kim did not know she had, she summoned the strength for one more attempt to break free. One more blow was all that she had left in her. It had to do. When Brent's head next came near, Kim smashed her head as hard as she could into his forehead.

They crashed, side by side, to the floor.

friday, 2:30 P.M., january 20, 2017

All set, Morgan IMed. *On my way back.*

The addendum was redundant, Charles thought, since reentering the local mesh of WiFi hotspots implied as much. Morgan brought valuable tactical knowledge, but he was hardly in Charles's mental league. Then again, who was?

Did Brent bother you? Charles asked.

Morgan: *No. Did you send him my way?*

Hardly. Brent's divided loyalties had already driven the Emergent to improvisation. Why give Brent another excuse to go weak in the knees? *He mentioned looking for you.*

Seconds later, Morgan loped onto the loading dock, winding through the choreographed chaos to Charles. "If Brent's not here, preparing to leave, and he didn't find me, where is he?"

A good question. Nowhere online. *Who sees Brent?* Charles IMed to everyone.

No one. A quick poll showed no one had seen Brent for almost thirty minutes. That was more than ample time to have found Morgan.

Morgan muttered under his breath. "At least we know he's inside. We'd have gotten an alarm from any door opened or window broken."

Brent was hiding, Charles decided. To what purpose? His misplaced conscience must be at work again. "Brent knows too much. We shouldn't leave him behind to talk."

"Concur." Morgan added Charles to a Security group link. *Watts, Corbett, Donaldson: Split up and find Brent Cleary. Bring him to the dock. But nanosuit up first. Cleary may resist.*

Charles gestured at the activity around them. "Everything important is crated. Much of it is loaded. I say we forego the secondary equipment and begin leaving now."

Because leaving would take time. They had to go one vehicle at a time, spaced minutes apart. This wasn't the day, not with the cops scurrying about, to assemble an obvious convoy.

Charles linked to Felipe and Tyra, supervising on the other end of the loading dock: *Ready to go?*

Both agreed.

Their first loaded SUV was on the road faster than the search team could put on their nanosuits and begin the building sweep.

His head spinning, nauseous, Brent woke up. He felt like one large bruise. He felt burned out. The skin across his forehead was painfully taut, as though with a massive bump. He went to probe it gently and—

His hands were behind him, tied around a post. He remembered an ambush, a fight—and Kim!

Time to take stock. He was seated on a hard tile floor, legs stretching out in front of him, ankles bound together with lots of duct tape. He wiggled his arms and felt tape around his wrists. Wet paper towels, most bloody, lay scattered near his feet. His shirt, sopping wet, clung to him.

With great insult to his neck Brent managed to see, out of the corner of an eye, a post rising above him. The glimpse confirmed what touch had already suggested. He was lashed to a metal lolly post. It would be anchored to floor and ceiling. He wouldn't be going anywhere.

So where was here?

Heavy metal shelving units all around said *storeroom*, and nothing he recognized on the dusty shelves would have been out of place at

Garner Nanotech. Almost certainly, he was in the storeroom complex he had been searching when Kim attacked.

You won, One wrote across Brent's field of vision. The message was inflectionless, of course, but he read sarcasm into it.

Presumably Kim had dragged him here, unconscious, and tied him up. Not even One could see through closed eyelids, so Brent had to settle for the inference. And no matter *what* One now tried, Brent could not, bound like this, harm anyone.

Good: He was done hurting people. He hoped.

He heard soft footsteps, and then someone in a nanosuit entered the room with a coffee carafe sloshing with water. The fabric was set to a wall-paint yellow; it stood out like a beacon against parts-laden shelves. The figure threw back its hood.

It was Kim. Her face was mottled and inflamed, in the early stages of bruising. Crusted blood ringed her nostrils, and she had a bump on her forehead to rival the one Brent sensed on his own. "You look like a piñata," he blurted. *And I'm the one who whacked you.*

"Trust me," Kim said, "you look worse." She took a wad of paper towels from a nanosuit pocket, dipped a towel into the carafe, and mopped his forehead. "How do you feel?"

Utterly drained. The wet, cool towel felt good. "I've been better. Why am I wet?"

She sat gingerly on a shop vac, looking very sad. "You went *berserk*, Brent. What do you remember?"

"Being berserk. A head butt." *And Kim, thank you for that.* No matter what One might later do to his memory and hormones, Brent could never have lived with killing her.

She nodded. "I know it wasn't you doing it, but something *in* you. I can't untie you."

"I didn't ask." Because he was still afraid of what One could make him do, and that he might not be able to resist the next time. "So why am I wet?"

The wet towel was still in her hands and she twisted it nervously.

"There you were raving, eyes wide, shaking the hell out of me. So: head butt. I blacked out, came to on the floor.

"There *you* were, thrashing and flushed. Your pulse was racing. Even through a glove you felt feverish. On fire. So after I secured you"—she looked away, a little guiltily—"I got water. I've been trying to cool you down since."

"Excited delirium," Brent said. "Few doctors will say unequivocally the condition exists. Any cop will." And several had, at Riley's pub.

To One, Brent projected, *You almost killed us both.* Brent got the impression One would forego hormonal manipulation for a while—at least until his/their body could safely handle more.

"Excited delirium?" Kim prompted.

"That's what cops call it when someone is so high on drugs—and the drug can be an adrenaline overdose—that it takes a bunch of people to subdue him." The second-guessers called it police brutality, especially when the perp had a massive heart attack right after. "It can be fatal if the heart rate and body temperature cycle out of control."

Kim looked perplexed. "But why?"

"You mean, am I on drugs? In a way. The thing is, Kim, you had it right. My brain has a mind of its own, and *it* wouldn't let you stop me. So it flooded me with adrenaline. When that wasn't enough, it gave me more adrenaline, and some more, and some more after that."

"Because you wouldn't let it control you," she said firmly.

Maybe so, but he didn't comment. He had enough else on his conscience not to take credit for one brief success. "By knocking me out and cooling me down, you almost certainly saved my life."

Brent wasn't sure she had done him a favor.

Sensing Brent's depression, Kim changed the subject. "One of the— what do you call yourselves?—called us, called humans, Neanderthals. That'll be the way of it, won't it, Brent? You're stealing enough bots to transform millions, and factory gear to make more. I saw the bot-assembly vats being removed. My kind will be outcompeted and, after a while, extinct."

"Emergent. That's what we call ourselves. When did you hear this?"

"Not important, Brent. How do I stop this?"

He said nothing, and she imagined a line had been drawn. He wouldn't fight her—to the extent he could control his inner demon—but neither would he help her. His loyalties did not lie with . . . Neanderthals.

Well, damn it, *she* was going to stop this. Somehow.

Kim waggled in his face the VR specs she had managed to take from him. "I hoped these would give me a better idea what's going on. I figure that you . . . Emergent . . . use the glasses for comm among yourselves. Any active sessions must have timed out while I was passed out." She rubbed her bruised forehead, hoping to lay on some guilt. "What's the log-in info?"

He didn't comment.

"I need that ID and password, Brent."

"No you don't, Kim. You're lucky the specs did time out. Among us, IMing is damn near like telepathy. My companions would have known in a flash if a stranger was on the link."

"I might have learned something useful," she said obstinately. She was outnumbered, unarmed, and—by Emergent standards—probably half-witted. She needed an advantage, and a peek at their plans could be it. "Tell me how to get on the link."

"And if they caught you immediately after? It'd be simple to triangulate your position from WiFi routers."

That was BS. "I know how WiFi works. There isn't a triangulation algorithm involved."

"My nose itches," he said. "Scratch it?"

She did, and it was an eerily human moment.

"Thanks. Okay, about triangulation. You're right—for standard router software. It'd take me about two minutes to patch the routers to make that kind of search. Have-Mercy would be faster. If anyone senses a stranger on the link, you can be sure they'd make the up-grade."

Merry was a hell of a programmer before. Yeah, she probably could hack the WiFi routers to improvise a locater.

Kim's spirits, already low, sank further. Her sorry excuse for a plan—steal a nanosuit, capture some VR specs, find and exploit a weakness—had just collapsed of its own weight.

What the hell was she going to try now?

Just maybe, if Kim stayed out of sight for a little while longer, the others would leave and she would be safe.

Lashed to this post, Brent had only his wits and words to keep her here. So he asked what she had been up to. He asked what she knew, and what she intended. He hinted at her suspicions and speculations, about the concerns he had denied or obfuscated for months. As he knew Kim so well, it was easy to divert her into irrelevant detail.

And knowing *him* just as well, Kim caught on. "The one thing you're not forthcoming about is how to stop this."

Everyone had a right to exist, even the Emergent. (And the personalities the Emergent would dominate? What about their rights? And what about the casualties from today's bombings? It was a calculus too subtle for Brent to sort out, and One was entirely amoral.) All Brent could do was set his own limits—and be thankful that, with him bound to this post, his new resolve wasn't put to the test.

Kim turned away and flipped the hood over her head. From the set of her shoulders she was determined to act—and already all but defeated.

Soon the others would leave, distribute the bots, and scatter to produce many more like themselves. His duty to his creations would be discharged. He could not let Kim go—not because she could stop the Emergent, but because he cared what happened to her. He had to keep her here. He had to run out the clock. The others, if they caught her, would *not* be kind.

He/One were many times smarter than she. Surely they could entice her to stay.

"Kim, you have no idea how amazing Emergence is. You couldn't possibly. Maybe once *we're* not at risk of extinction, we can do proper controlled experiments and find the best way to make the transformation. Give us a year or two and we'll know more about the meaning of consciousness than philosophers and neurologists have learned—ever."

She stopped. Intrigued despite herself or happy for the distraction? "What do you mean?"

Brent lowered his voice as though confiding a secret. He leaned/ sagged forward as much as his restraints would allow. "Not one scientist in the world today knows what consciousness is. If something in your brain makes you self-aware, what's in *it* to make *it* aware? And where does the recursion stop? Surely you've wondered: how do you know you're you?"

"Well . . . yes."

"The thing is, Kim, I have an independent observer inside my head. The bots are integrated with my neurons. They communicate through my neurons." The words poured from Brent. To reveal now served his purpose as, for so many months, to conceal had. If talking would keep Kim here, he had much to say. "So I, and it, can examine up close *how* those masses of neurons cooperate. Is there a coalition of neurons for each element of awareness? Are neural ensembles permanent, or are they alliances of convenience to be disrupted by stimuli, memories, and thoughts? Are—"

"Whatever," Kim said. "None of that stopped you from doing terrible things."

He winced. "I was discussing consciousness, not conscience, but they're not so far apart. Consciousness emerges from enough processing power, whether neurons or nanites. Ant colonies exhibit emergence on a lesser scale, with group behaviors no single ant comprehends. And bureaucracies blithely do things hardly any individual member would dream of doing."

"Like cripple and kill homeless people?"

Brent recoiled as if slapped. Did it excuse anything that he hadn't understood then what he was doing, or even that he was doing it? At some level surely he *had* known, just as he had accepted Morgan's bland assurances about minimal casualties from the contingency-plan diversions.

"If I can't eavesdrop electronically, I guess I'll go spy the old-fashioned way." She hesitated, then tore off a six-inch chunk of duct tape. A gag. She didn't trust him.

Well, why should she?

He was a bundle of nerves, twitchy and drained, his body still burning off the adrenaline overdose and untold other hormone surges. Cold-turkey withdrawal from the 'net ached like a tooth newly pulled. He was hyped and depressed and struggling with himself, conflicted and frustrated.

All he knew for certain was he wanted to keep Kim here. Safe.

He twisted away as she approached with the tape. "Everyone is leaving. They were already loading trucks"—trussed up like this, Brent had to guess—"call it an hour ago. It's too late now to stop them, so don't even try to interfere with the stragglers. It can't serve any useful purpose."

"An hour ago?" She considered. "When I last went for water, a few people were moving about the factory."

"Removing stuff to the loading dock?" he asked.

She shook her head.

"Then they're looking for me, Kim. I doubt they'll believe I beat myself to a bruised, bloody pulp. If they find me, they'll know to look for you. Cut me loose. We need to hide someplace better than this."

"I wish I could trust you, Brent." Tears welling up in her eyes, Kim slapped the tape over his mouth.

He wished he could trust him.

Kim dashed off, leaving him to worry helplessly about her.

The last SUV pulled away from Garner Nanotech, hauling a crated reaction vat and a small part of the nanobot inventory. Tyra drove, with Felipe riding shotgun. Both wore nanosuits beneath their coats.

Good luck, Morgan IMed.

Thanks, Tyra replied just before they exceeded WiFi range and she dropped off the link.

Charles shared the loading dock, so recently the locus of purposeful frenzy, with just Morgan and Have-Mercy Ramirez. The only other Emergent left in the building were the three guards still searching for Brent Cleary—and Cleary himself, of course. Unlike the rest, Charles didn't wear a nanosuit. None of the Army trial units, alas, could accommodate his tall frame.

Well, Cleary didn't have a suit, either. If by some fluke Brent had grabbed the suit still unaccounted for, the joke was on him. The missing nanosuit would be at least six inches too short.

Behind the factory, open field beckoned, snow covered and pristine. *Time to go*, Charles sent to Morgan.

Morgan: *Cleary's a loose end.*

Charles: *As he's been for an hour now.* The complex was nearly two hundred thousand square feet. That was a lot of territory to search, and too many possible hiding places. *We're ready to go. Continued searching is counterproductive. Once we seal the building*—which was already sealed, except for the loading dock—*Brent won't be going anywhere.*

Have-Mercy looked about uncertainly, out of the loop and doubtless puzzled that the three of them were just standing there.

Morgan, stubbornly: *Okay, we'll go, but why shouldn't the others keep looking for now? It's insurance, in case Cleary tries something we didn't think of. And it gives us a rear guard.*

Brent come up with something they hadn't anticipated? That was patent nonsense, verging on ancestor worship. Charles sent: *We'll need a way to recall your rear guard.*

Understood. Morgan added Have-Mercy to the link. *Merry, after we go we'd like to maintain comm with the rear guards here. What's your recommendation?*

Merry: *Reconnect a router to an incoming fiber-optic cable. Once we leave the WiMax outage zone in and around Utica, the comm path opens: from our specs to any functioning WiMax tower onto the Internet. The reconnected ca-*

*ble brings the Internet into the building, and then it's WiFi and specs as usual
for the guards.*

Morgan: *Excellent. But first shut down WiFi all around the core of the
building. If anyone in the auditorium has a WiFi-enabled phone, we don't
want them to signal out.*

Merry: *Can do. So shall I?*

It was clear enough how Morgan wanted to proceed—and that
Morgan would defer, however unhappily, to Charles's decision. The
transition of leadership had already begun. This was, Charles decided,
a moment to be magnanimous. *Do it, Merry.*

In minutes, the router connection was restored and tested. The
building periphery had Internet access again. The search for Brent continued. And Charles, one on one, reconfirmed with Morgan that nothing and no one could interrupt the final cleanup.

Morgan and Have-Mercy hopped onto one of the snowmobiles.
Charles took another. The building sealed behind them, they raced
away, engines growling, in separate directions across the snowy park
to new lives.

friday, 3:30 P.M., january 20, 2017

After Kim left, *more* adrenaline surged through Brent's veins. He raged and strained against his bonds. Without breaking him/them free, One's latest intervention added to his bruises.

One might have released endorphins against the pain; One chose to do nothing. Brent asked for endorphins; again, it did nothing.

Instead, it sulked.

Brent's head pounded. His arms and legs ached from being held in one position. His rear end was petrified from the hard floor. His wrists chafed from their bonds. His cheeks hurt like hell where the tape gag tugged at his beard. He was hungry, thirsty, and needed to pee. An ear began to itch, and then his nose again.

Okay, so One *didn't* sulk. To sulk required the taking of offense, and One had no emotions, no values, beyond personal survival. Its silence, and the suffering it permitted, sent a message: *defy me again at your peril.* Or perhaps the only meaning was: *try harder.*

The longer Brent waited, the more aches, pains, itches, and urges manifested themselves. He was powerless, and One unwilling, to do anything about them. When Brent tried to divert himself with some of the infinitesimal fraction—but still many gigabytes—of the Internet downloaded into One's processors, One responded, simply, *No.*

The punishment wasn't quite sensory deprivation, because Brent could hardly plan an escape while cut off from his senses. The silent treatment and the withholding of mental stimulus were meant to focus him on escape. Part of him tried.

And part of him, in the neglected recesses of the mind that remained wholly his, was able, for the first time in a *long* time, to make itself noticed. The imagery it dredged up wounded far more deeply than any physical complaint.

The lives he had usurped. The blood spilled today. The plague of transformations the dispersed Emergent would soon unleash. The crime wave about to be launched, to finance a bot factory in some Third World haven.

And *he* had begun it all, sanctioned it all.

Not Griffiss, countered the cool, dispassionate part of Brent most integrated with One. *Others made that decision and overruled you.*

Even that was a rationalization. *He* had transformed Charles and Morgan and many of the rest. *He* had agreed to various contingency plans, and acquiesced to more, and turned a blind eye to yet others the group might consider, "just in case."

For what further atrocities did his creations lay plans—just in case—even now?

With bombs and robots and cyberattacks, small groups waged war against nations. Equip an insurgency with Emergent minds, bulletproof nanosuits, and Morgan's counterterrorism expertise—and things could get very ugly, very quickly.

Feeling closer to human than he had in weeks, Brent wept.

Kim watched two figures methodically explore the factory floor. A third checked out the R & D area, disappearing and reappearing cyclically at the ends of successive office aisles.

Brent was right: a search was underway. Barring some change in the search pattern, she had perhaps twenty minutes before Brent was discovered. Fewer, if there were searchers she had yet to spot.

Her spying had revealed yet another problem: the searchers wore nanosuits. They didn't use them in camo mode, perhaps so they wouldn't surprise each other. If they found her, her nanosuit wouldn't offer any advantage.

She stood stock still, a yellow suit against a yellow wall. When both factory searchers happened to face away, she rushed on tiptoe to the side area where factory supervisors had their offices. Room by room she popped laptops from their docking cradles. She returned the way she had come bearing an armful of laptops.

Her newest idea was to find a WiMax-equipped laptop. In WiFi mode, her phone hadn't reached beyond the building, but WiMax interfaces were higher powered. A WiMax-equipped computer might directly reach another WiMax-equipped computer outside the building.

Everything she had scavenged turned out to use WiFi. Not entirely surprising—foremen didn't get top-of-the-line gear—but still a disappointment. R & D had plenty of laptops with WiMax, the one on her desk to begin with, but she wasn't about to play cat and mouse with whoever was searching the hallways of R & D.

Now what?

Most of the laptops had antennas integrated into their cases, but on a couple the antennas were removable. If she swapped the standard omnidirectional antenna for a directional aerial, she should get better range in that direction. Maybe she could reach a WiFi hotspot outside this building.

She could spend days searching the storerooms, not knowing that a suitable part was even here. She permitted herself five minutes, and found nothing helpful. If she were online, she could figure out how to improvise an antenna. If she were online, she wouldn't need to.

Dwelling on what she *didn't* have accomplished nothing.

Something else about laptops flitted across Kim's mind. Fierce concentration did nothing to capture the elusive notion. She slid the laptops beneath parts shelves, where a cursory peek into the room might not reveal them, and went off to check on Brent and in search of fresh inspiration.

....

Alone, helpless, Brent wallowed in despair.

The mystery was that One responded with neither comment nor chemical intervention. Human nature was something no amount of web surfing could truly explain. Perhaps One expected its snubbing to render Brent more malleable.

Soon enough he began to worry One might be right.

He kept asking the time. Either the messages never got across or One ignored them. Not knowing how long he had been here made every speculation worse. Had the Emergent made good their escape? Had Kim been caught? What would the others do to her?

It took several tries, but Brent struggled to his feet. Standing proved marginally more comfortable, but the change did nothing for his spirits.

He could delude himself for only so long. What truly tormented him was not isolation; it was clarity. Without distractions, the guilt grew and grew.

This nightmare began with him trying to *save* people. Chasing the kids away from the pipeline in Angleton—that had to have been a good thing, right?

A good thing, sneered his more cynical side, *or good intentions? With which is the road to Hell paved?* Maybe by charging out of the dark, startling the thieves, *he* caused the accident. A monstrous act, if true.

How fitting, then, his own monstrous transformation. Perhaps there was more than concussion behind his memory loss. Maybe he *wanted* to forget.

Now those Brent had changed had triggered more explosions, brought on more deaths and injuries. More guilt lay on his shoulders.

It was too much. Too much! He wanted—needed—to confess everything. If only Kim would return, if only she could bear to listen . . . maybe, together, they would find a way to act. His conscience could not bear more violence or forced conversions.

And then Kim *was* back, and she must have seen the tears welling up in his eyes. She removed the tape gag, apologizing profusely at the whiskers stuck to the tape. What did physical pain matter? He hardly noticed. He opened his mouth to speak—

And One clamped down, *hard.*

"Chh-gu-gug," Brent managed.

Say nothing, One wrote across his vision. *Do not betray me again.*

As though he could. Still, One had given the warning for a reason. Its control was less than absolute.

All right, One wasn't going to permit a confessional. Still, not that long ago, Brent had defied One long enough to save Kim's life. Maybe he could defy his inner demon long enough to get the essential message across. The Emergent had an Achilles' heel. It was their—

Pain!

His body spasmed, on fire. His stomach heaved. Vomit splattered everywhere, then clear stomach juices. What was One doing to him? Old memories? Neurotransmitter signal cascades? He couldn't concentrate enough to figure it out.

Why worry how? The message he had for Kim was the important thing: VR specs were the Emergents' vulnerability. If he could only explain, only force out a few words. "Gl . . . g-gl," he stuttered.

Kim stared in horror. "Aaron's in the auditorium. I'll get him."

And get caught by whoever was searching for me. Brent shook his head vigorously, heartened to have even that much control. "No" was a short word, and he managed to speak it.

"No" was the best he could manage. Speech wouldn't do. Another minute or two of this pain and he would surely black out.

Now tears streamed down Kim's face. "Stop it, Brent! Stop whatever you're trying to do before it kills you."

VR glasses. Head shakes. The need to stop this madness. Send Kim a message. VR glasses. Head shakes. . . . Snatches of thought, disjointed, chased each other around his brain. How could he hope to communicate anything?

The futility of hope was bitterer than the taste of vomit in his mouth.

Head shake. Head shake. What else could he move? A possible communication flashed across Brent's mind, brilliant and cryptic. Would One understand, and stop him? Would Kim understand him anyway?

After so many surgeries, so much PT, Brent knew all about pain—but this was different. Fire seared along every nerve. He used everything he had learned and set the agony aside. Everything now depended on a bit of mime.

Kim was facing him. Shuffling, twisting, he worked his way almost a quarter turn around the pole. He caught her eye, then glanced down meaningfully at his bound hands. He began tapping randomly, spastically, against the post.

She shook her head, confusion plain on her face.

He kept up the erratic tapping and started pursing his lips. Tapping. Pursing. Tapping and pursing.

One didn't get what Brent was doing or it couldn't stop him—and it made its displeasure even clearer. The pain, somehow, ratcheted up even more.

He hissed in anguish but kept going. Tap. Purse. Tap-tap.

Pain!

Purse. Tap-tap. Purse . . .

Just as Brent blacked out from the pain, understanding illuminated Kim's face.

Suddenly, gloriously, Charles's VR specs returned to life. He had crossed the park.

Charles launched his snowmobile over a mogul for the sheer joy of it. He throttled down then and drove cautiously to the crest of a low ridge, coasting to a stop beside a stand of scruffy hemlocks. City streets began a mere twenty yards downhill. He didn't see any police cruisers.

The specs offered Charles a WiMax gateway and a long list of active WiFi hotspots. Most were encrypted for privacy; a few, predictably, were wide open. Were the latter coffeehouse amenities or courtesy of naïve individuals? It hardly mattered which.

He flick/blinked onto an unprotected WiFi net and through it to the Internet. Bloggers and big media alike showed the Utica and Rome police scurrying about in confusion. And Homeland Security had rolled into town. In the short term, the feds could only compound the chaos. He saw no mention of Garner Nanotech.

Less than a minute after Charles reconnected, the IMs began. Everyone had gotten away. Some were already fifty miles from Utica.

From Morgan, *Clear sailing. You?*

On the far edge of the park, Charles replied. *Ready to get a car.*

Together, they checked in with the rear guard. Watts and Donaldson had nothing to report. Corbett was out of touch, but Alan had a visual on her. She was checking out one of the interior zones whose WiFi had been taken down to keep the auditorium isolated.

Morgan: *Any trouble from the prisoners?*

Alan: *No. I think they're too scared.*

Morgan: *How much longer to finish your sweep?*

Alan: *Thirty minutes or so.*

Morgan on a private link to Charles: *Recommend our guys keep looking for Brent.*

Charles was feeling safe and magnanimous: *All right.*

Continue, Morgan sent to the three in the factory. *Check back in thirty.*

The snow had stopped falling, with no more expected for two days. The snowmobile tracks and his footprints were unavoidable, so there was no point to trying to cover or hide the snowmobile. He opened a cargo compartment and took out the precious package of bots. It looked like a stainless-steel thermos. He started to walk.

Curbside a block away from the park Charles found a snow-covered Toyota SUV, right where Morgan had said it would be. It was one of a dozen vehicles Morgan had rented with counterfeit ID. The fob in Charles's pocket had been programmed with keyless entry and ignition codes for all of them.

Five minutes later, with complete traffic and real-time weather data available at a blink, Charles continued on his way.

Kim stared. Brent, unable to speak, was dying before her eyes. "Stop it, Brent! Stop whatever you're trying to do before it kills you."

Twitching, he writhed partway around the post to which she had tied him. His hands, bound, rattled and twitched against the metal post. He had stopped his futile efforts to speak, but his eyes were bright. He was communicating—*trying* to communicate—something.

Tears streamed down her cheeks. Did she look for meaning in an uncontrolled convulsion? She wanted to cut him loose. She feared everything—the shaking, the tongue-tied stutter, the struggle against his bonds—was a ruse. Cut him free and save him? Or cut him free and lose whatever feeble chance remained to help the people locked in the auditorium?

She tore her eyes away from the thrashing of Brent's hands. His eyes remained bright. His lips, improbably, kept puckering. A caricatured kiss? What the *hell* would that mean? A caricatured something else, then?

Act or agony, Brent could not maintain the frenzy of his struggle much longer. *Assume he is communicating. What could he possibly be saying? Random tapping. Puckered lips. If not kissing, then . . . blowing smoke rings. Smoking? He didn't smoke! Random tapping and smoking. Random tapping and smoking.*

Brownian bit bumps!

He blacked out before Kim could speak the words.

Kim typed frantically on one of her pilfered laptops. Brent's suggestion was either genius or madness. Either way, only she could make it happen and she had to do it quickly. At best she might have thirty minutes before the nearest searcher reached this storeroom.

She spliced together math functions, choosing haphazardly from arbitrary programming libraries: functions multiplied and divided, integrated and differentiated, exponentiated and factored. As input parameters, she funneled terms from arbitrarily selected infinite series. She gave no thought to the selections and sequences, the permutations and combinations, or the nesting of operations—the more opaque and compute intensive the calculation, the better. Only the obscurity of the output mattered. She used random number generators to lop digits of precision off the final values. Finally, she ran the crazy-quilt output sequences into a fractal-display program to turn the results visual.

As quickly as Kim set one nonsense pipeline running, she'd start on another. Weird data sets, gigabytes long, grew on the disk drive. She was throwing together a fourth computation when her visor alarm chimed softly. Eight minutes: she dare not allow herself any more time.

Brent was watching her. He didn't try to speak.

She approached him warily, pre-torn lengths of duct tape lightly stuck to the backs of her hands. "I hope I understood you," she whispered. She pulled his right eye wide open and taped the eyelid to his forehead. She repeated with his left eye. The tape stuck to Brent's lashes and eyebrows.

He didn't resist. He didn't even try to speak. Then his tape gag was back in place, and he couldn't speak.

She slipped VR glasses over his staring eyes and taped the glasses to his face. Colors and patterns flashed crazily, frantically, stroboscopically, reflecting from his face.

By any possible definition, this was torture.

Kim's own eyes swiveled nervously between the insane light show and the storeroom door. Closed, the door muffled the sounds of Brent struggling. Closed, the steel door offered a bit of shielding to add to that from the massive metal shelves. That this room was a WiFi dead zone was no coincidence. Maybe the WiFi link between her laptop and Brent's specs would stay in the room.

Certainly the closed door would stop Kim from hearing anyone approach. Even if this worked, she might be trapped.

Brent writhed about on the post. His chest heaved and his cheeks bowed out, but the tape gag kept him all but mute. His head flopped violently from side to side. The VR specs bounced about, but tape kept them from flying off. Abruptly, he was pounding the back of his head against the lolly post! It was a struggle, but she immobilized his head with yet more duct tape, wrapped around and around his forehead and the post.

If, somehow, they made it through this, Brent wasn't going to have much hair left. She must have been at about her limit, because the mental image made her want to snort. If she started to laugh, she wasn't sure she could stop. . . .

The laptop kept uploading its data sets. She understood, more or less, how Brent expected this to work. He had early-generation bots in his head, built before the Brownian-bit-bump fix. As programs grew in his bots, they'd reach the area prone to random bit errors. That *had* to be what he had in mind.

But what Kim *didn't* get was why his programs would grow at all.

Data cascaded down Brent's optic nerves.

The data rate was staggering, and One struggled to make sense of it all. The data streams defied categorization. They refused to fit into a pattern.

And they could not be stopped or ignored. Short of disconnecting from Brent's optic nerves—cutting itself off from the world—One had no choice but to accept the data.

The inundation could not have a benign purpose, although One could not guess Kim's exact intention. Distraction, One supposed at first.

The data kept coming.

One's very emergence came from analyzing data, recognizing patterns, extracting meaning, and extrapolating purpose. It developed new software reflexively, at a subconscious level. *This* data was addictively rich, and new software to try to make sense of it grew rapidly.

Then, joltingly, the first of One's computers shut down.

Still the data streamed in. The full burden fell on One, with Brent's mind wholly unable to make sense of it. The torrents defied experience, and yet there was *some* underlying logic that tantalized—

A second computer dropped out, and then two more.

One began, frantically, to develop filters, classifiers, statistical simplifications—anything that might find order in, or reduce the processing load from, the flood of data. Within a second, five *more* computers dropped offline.

Nine computers offline, within seconds. That pattern, at least, was clear enough. Data drove program growth drove computer instability. Brent fought to keep thoughts to himself, but One persevered and delved.

The Brownian-bit-bump problem.

More computers went offline, and the extrapolated trend line suggested many more about to follow. Piece by piece, One's mind was closing down. Lost capacity was bad; the disrupted communications between its remaining computing nodes was worse. The rich network of connections it had forged over months was synaptic, integrated with Brent's cerebral cortex.

It was powerless to stop, and unable to withstand, the onslaught.

One's final thought, as it struggled to execute an orderly shutdown of its remaining processors, was to wonder whether it would ever restart.

Madness. Color and pattern flashing: stroboscopic, hypnotic, chaotic . . .

Brent needed to scream: at One's panic, at his glimmer of freedom, at their shared agony. He strained against the gag, against his bonds, against the insanity raging in his/their mind. Which struggles were his and which One's he could not begin to understand.

Confusion reigned. Holes gaped in his/their mind. He/they struggled to maintain a line of thought. He sensed One withdrawing, seeking refuge from the creeping lobotomy.

Then One was gone.

The madness continued. Color and pattern flashing: stroboscopic, hypnotic, chaotic—

And cathartic.

Brent concentrated on his hands, hoping Kim would once again understand.

Kim goggled in horror at Brent straining and writhing on his post. How much more of this could a body take? She was killing him!

It occurred to her, belatedly, that she didn't know how to know if— no, damn it, *when*—they had succeeded. He couldn't tell her, not with the gag on his mouth. She couldn't remove the tape without knowing that Brent, that *old* Brent, was back. A scream would bring the searchers down on them.

Color kept flashing on his face, kaleidoscopic insanity.

She couldn't see his eyes. She couldn't read any meaning into the contortions of his mouth and face under so much tape.

Then she noticed his hands.

His hands quivered, fingers curling and uncurling. On both hands, the last three fingers arched and separated like . . . what? Like her grandmother sipping tea. Index finger and thumb opened and closed, opened and closed. A circle. A circle plus three fingers to the side.

As in: "oh" and "kay."

With a sigh of relief, Kim tore the specs off Brent's face.

His eyes tearing, Brent managed not to cry out as Kim removed his gag. The tape took with it chunks of his beard. "My eyes," he croaked. He winced as she removed the tape from his eyelids. "Thanks."

"Then I did the right thing?" Kim asked, looking like she had been through a wringer. She caught herself fidgeting with the VR specs and stuffed them into a pocket.

An unpleasant reminder, Brent supposed. He couldn't have been much fun to watch.

"Oh, yeah." He noticed Kim made no move to cut him loose. In her shoes, he wouldn't trust him, either. "Too bad only my ancient bots were susceptible. Everyone else has bots with your memory-management upgrade."

Kim glanced at the storeroom door. "We only have minutes. One of the searchers will be here after that. Tell me how we can stop this."

He didn't know! Without One, it felt to Brent like his thoughts swam in syrup. It was like learning all over again how to think. Well, maybe he had a general idea—

"Brent! Are you still with me?"

"Yes." He shook off his confusion. "The key is the VR specs. Some kind of computer virus spread through the VR specs might immobilize all the Emergent at once. I don't know what kind of virus would work, or how to spread it, or—"

"If we can usurp the specs, maybe we can trigger fits with flash-ing lights. Remember that legendary *Pokémon* episode when we were kids?"

No Internet a blink away. No downloaded databases. His memory was so slow and inadequate. It amazed Brent that *before* he ever got anything done.

Still, back at the beginning—when specs were simply a keen gadget and his reading kept getting faster and faster—he had looked up the in-cident. "Strobing only affects epileptics in that way, and just a small fraction of them. We're unlikely to stop anyone that way." Not that Brent wanted to add inducing even one seizure to his list of transgres-sions.

Kim said, "I *must* go. The ones looking for me have nanosuits, too. If they find me, I won't stand a chance." She tore off a fresh strip of duct tape. "Sorry."

"Wait!" His head taped to the pole, Brent couldn't even turn away. "There are things not everyone knows about the nanosuits." He rat-tled off a couple. Then, gagged again, he watched her leave.

Kim paused at the storeroom door. She heard the air whistling through the ducts, the soft clatter of a loose air damper, and the pulse pounding in her head. She opened the door a crack and listened. Nothing. She stepped out and closed the door, trying not to think of leaving Brent behind trussed up like a turkey.

She stopped at the end of the corridor to listen again. Nothing. She rounded the corner into a cross aisle and paused again.

There was the soft scuffing of a shoe against the floor.

Kim flattened against the wall. Another scuff: the searcher was com-ing her way.

She had waited too long, and now she was trapped. Now what? Use the nanosuit's camo and hope to sneak past? If she succeeded, within seconds he would find Brent, bound and battered, and know to look for her. Use one of Brent's tricks and take on the searcher? If she succeeded, how long until the others also hunting for Brent noticed one of their team missing?

Kim returned the way she had come, looking for a phone.

Aaron Sanders parked himself in an auditorium folding chair, biding his time, doing his best to act serene. People looked up to doctors. That trust, seriously misplaced in this crisis, manifested in his fellow prisoners looking to *him* for leadership. He had no more idea what to do than any of them. All he could give them was this aura of calm—no matter the panic bubbling inside of him.

There had been bedlam after the gunshots and Brent's extraction. After a spell of nothing happening, boredom—or bursting bladders—emboldened some of his fellow captives to demand access to bathrooms. Threats over the PA shut them up. So Aaron had organized the gathering of wastebaskets, and of extraneous sweaters and overshirts with which to improvise privacy screens. His stock with the detainees went up further, at least until the latrine stench permeated the area. Now, as wastebaskets overflowed with urine and feces, they looked to him yet again.

Aaron had had one idea, if vaguely remembering an old movie with hostages could be counted as his idea. With stirrings of hope he had kept to himself, he pulled the fire alarm. Perhaps their captors had seen the same film; one way or another, the alarm did not go off.

He worried about Sladja and the children—for all of their safety, and for Sladja's state of mind. The atrocities in Sarajevo were never far from her thoughts. How far back would this set her? Very damn far if he didn't make it out.

Only years of practice stiff-upper-lipping it for shot-up and blown-up patients kept Aaron together.

When he wasn't worrying about his family he brooded about Kim. If she had made it out, help would have been here by now. If she had been captured, she would, presumably, be here with the other prisoners. The only other outcome didn't bear thinking about, nor did it speak well for the likely disposition of those in this room.

The TV still droned in the background. His fellow prisoners milled about, or watched the TV, and chattered endlessly among themselves. There were more furtive looks his way, as though wondering when he would again do something for them.

Aaron shot from his chair at the ringing of the phone. A dictate of some sort from their captors, surely. The prisoners gathered around a wall phone, fearfully staring at it, and then to Aaron, and back to the ringing phone, and back to Aaron.

He picked it up. "Auditorium."

"Aaron?" a familiar voice asked in a whisper.

"Kim! You're all right. I was wor—"

"I'm in trouble. I need a distraction *now*." She hung up.

If the prisoners had a hope, Kim was it, and she needed a distraction. Aaron turned, surveying the room. He saw furniture, the improvised privacy screens, and two additional wall phones. Not exactly an arsenal.

His fellow prisoners waited expectantly, impatiently. It was time to use that instinctive trust in doctors. "Okay, everyone, that was our cue.

"Janet, Doris, Tabitha, start calling extensions. Any extensions, ideally widely spaced around the building. Four rings, then hang up and dial another till I say to stop. Go."

"And if someone answers?" Janet Kwan asked timidly.

"Hang up, and dial somewhere else."

Everyone was watching Aaron, even the women busily punching wall-phone keypads. Beyond the auditorium walls—here, there, hopscotching—phones tolled. A distraction, surely, but to him it *seemed* like a distraction. It wasn't enough.

He strode across the auditorium, the people not working the phones trailing in his wake. At the front of the room Aaron hefted an end of a long, skinny table. It was all dark wood, sturdy, nice and heavy.

There were six male prisoners, all looking reasonably fit. Aaron was among the smallest of them. "Men, you're with me."

Three to a side, they hoisted the table. Pallbearer positions, Aaron tried and failed to ignore. He'd taken one of the front positions: if his harebrained idea got someone shot, it ought to be him. "Tip it vertical," he directed. "The left side door." From the landlocked auditorium, that door was the closest to a building exit. "On my count, men. Three, two, one, charge."

The door boomed from the impact. The table vibrated like mad, and they almost dropped it. "Again," Aaron called. *Boom!* "Again."

"Stop that *now!*" the PA blared. Aaron recognized the voice: Alan Watts.

"Ignore that," Aaron shouted. "We need a rhythm. Three, two, one, now!" *Boom!* "Three, two, one, now!" *Boom!*

"This is your last warning," the PA rumbled ominously.

"Again!" Aaron yelled. "Three, two, one, now." *Boom!*

Their improvised battering ram began to splinter—but so, to a lesser extent, did the locked door.

This sounded like what the phone distraction was for.

Telephone insanity.

Phones rang—three, Kim thought—all but in unison. Pause, and then three more. Pause, and then, not quite so tightly grouped, three more. Some were faint with distance, others jarringly nearby and loud. And with the fourth set—

Boom! A moment later, another *boom!*

It was a hell of a distraction, all right, and Kim almost didn't hear the heartfelt cussing from the next corridor. She crept closer to a corner and heard the rapid slapping of soles against the floor. Running the other way, back toward the factory floor. To a WiFi hotspot, to consult with the other stalkers?

She could slip away now from this storeroom cul-de-sac, maybe hide in an area that had been previously searched.

As much as Kim wanted to hide, she couldn't. It would be shameful, buying herself a little time by endangering everyone in the auditorium.

The PA came on. "Stop that, now!"

Boom! came the answer. Phones rang all around. *Boom!*

Kim shook off her paralysis and dashed back to the storeroom where she had stashed the laptops. She would use whatever time Aaron and friends got for her.

"This is your last warning," the PA rumbled ominously.

Boom!

The lights went out.

Screams, curses, and an off-balance thud as Aaron stumbled in the dark and the ramming team went down in a tangle of limbs. The table edge mashed the fingers of his right hand.

Then, silence.

Aaron extracted himself from the pile. "Is everyone all right?"

Scattered affirmatives, and one, "Sorry. Elvis has left the building."

A spate of chuckles eased the tension. Aaron could have kissed whoever had come up with that.

The chuckles petered out. The darkness was stygian, curiously more so when a couple pinpricks of light appeared. Penlights. They wouldn't last long.

Had Kim gotten the distraction she needed? No way to know. Well, they couldn't do much in the pitch-black. "Any smokers?" Aaron called out.

"It's not the day to quit, Doc," their anonymous wisecracker answered. "Yeah, I have a lighter."

"Save it for a sec." Aaron could think of only one container in which to hold a fire. It wasn't going to be popular. "Okay, people. Someone near the privy, dump out *one* wastebasket there in the corner. Bring the empty can to the middle of the room. That's our fireplace. Bring another, full. We may need what's inside to put out a fire. The rest of you: get stuff to burn."

Soon they had a collection of flammables. Paper napkins for kindling. Leftover hardcopy handouts of presentations past. Padding stripped from some of the chairs. Flame flickered and danced in the can, set in the middle of the auditorium's center aisle. Heated, the human waste smelled even worse.

"Okay," Aaron said. "Now everyone gets back to work."

A back-road dead zone made Charles late checking in with the rear guard. People too antediluvian to use computers was his theory, rather than a more ambitious, broader-ranged shutdown. A minute late, he was the last to check in.

The natives are restless, Brittney Corbett recapped. *They tried to bust out. We doused the lights and that quieted them.*

Logan Donaldson: *Plus annoyance calls all around the building. Phone switch is completely off now.*

Brittney again: *Damn, now I see light coming under the doors. Flickering. Must be a fire. They're beating on a door again.*

Morgan: *How much longer to finish searching?*

Alan Watts: *Five, ten minutes.*

Just shoot them, Charles thought, but that was frustration talking. Going in, guns blazing, only risked the fire getting out of control.

Morgan: *Finish looking if it's safe. Don't get caught in a fire.*

The storeroom offered no light to amplify. The computers Kim was cannibalizing were at ambient temperature, so night-vision mode did nothing for her, either. She removed the battery packs by touch.

How would she find anything else in the dark?

She needed something conductive and flexible, like wire or foil. Things like that surely lay on the shelves, but finding them by touch could take a *long* time. So if not on the shelves, then where?

Inside the walls.

Time to put her suit to the test. Synchronizing herself with the faint rhythmic thudding in the distance, she punched the wall. Wallboard dimpled beneath her fist. She had scarcely felt a thing. With the next thud, she struck again, harder. Her fist plunged through. She clenched a wad of insulation and pulled out a long chunk. The foil liners ripped right off. Ripping the foil into smaller pieces was harder.

How long till the searcher caught her?

She carried battery packs and the raggedy pieces of foil two aisles over. One by one she wrapped battery packs in foil and distributed them along the hallway floor.

"*There* you are." Alan Watts's voice.

Kim flattened against the wall, afraid to move. The first of her packages had started to glow.

A tall figure came around the corner and looked right at her. "Huh. Not who I was expecting, whoever you are. Nice try with the nanosuit."

Camo only worked with visible light! Night vision sensed infrared—heat—and her body was warmer than the walls. She was a blazing profile against a dark backdrop, and some of that energy must have seeped around the corner.

Her improvised devices glowed a little brighter. Maybe she *wasn't* doomed. If she could just stall . . .

"How did you find me?" Kim asked. Her eyes flicked about her visor as she spoke, cranking down the IR sensitivity until she could barely see him.

"Just come with me," he said.

"I'm afraid," she answered.

"Come quietly and you won't be hurt." The packages were glowing brighter, and Alan glanced down at the nearest one. "What the heck are these?"

If Tyra hadn't steered her wrong weeks ago, small firebombs. The energy density of grenades, was it? The shorted-out batteries were discharging themselves rapidly. The only electrical resistance in the circuit—and so, all the heat—was inside the batteries themselves.

"What are what?" she dissembled.

Whoosh!

Flames erupted at Alan's feet. He threw up his hands and stumbled into a wall.

Tears streamed from Kim's eyes despite her night vision's minimal setting. The sudden glare must have temporarily blinded him.

Whoosh! Whoosh! Blam!

He spun around, confused, geysers of flame all around him.

Kim tackled him low. She crashed face-first into the floor and all his weight fell on her back, but her suit absorbed both impacts. Something crunched in her pocket. She squirmed out from under, rolling onto her back. He grabbed her neck—

And she clutched his left forearm. She groped at the keypad, entering a long sequence. Poised to enter the last digit, she head-butted him in the visor. He recoiled and she managed to break free—

While pressing the last key.

The full factory-test code entered, his suit went rigid head to toe.

friday, 4:10 P.M., january 20, 2017

It took three tables, but the auditorium side door finally yielded. By then they were working in the light of improvised torches: broken-off chair legs wrapped in cloth seat covers.

They ran through the halls, cheering, torches flickering in their hands. Aaron led the charge. A building exit was no more than a hundred feet away. The cheers swelled as the exit came into sight.

"Stop!" he screamed.

Some training was universal in the Army, and terrorism awareness ranked high on the list. The door was rigged!

It didn't take a genius to know opening the door would set off the bomb.

Brent waited in the dark, immobile and helpless, with only his imagination for company.

Oddities piled up. Ringing phones and dull thuds. An angry voice, too remote to make out, on the PA. The facility plunged into darkness. More dull thuds. Bangs and flares of light from another direction. From the air ducts, an acrid smell.

The possibility of a fire made his skin crawl. He tried to lose himself in speculation. An attempted breakout from the auditorium, he guessed. The detainees wouldn't have doused the lights. They didn't have night-vision gear. So some of the Emergent were still here. What were those popping sounds? They didn't sound like gunfire. What had happened to Kim?

He strained to hear more, smell more—to sense anything that might provide a clue. He twitched at every unexpected noise and glimmer. Only more and more he twitched at no discernable stimulus.

Lone bots flailing, Brent reassured himself. Bots wired together by new nerve bundles: that's what One had been. That's *all* it had been. Today had been an emotional roller coaster; now bots were responding to surges of his neurotransmitters. A bit of twitchiness and the occasional muscle tic were only to be expected.

The darkness crowded in on him.

Brooding about the dark, fretting about distant noises, worrying about Kim—none of this accomplished *anything*. He had to trust Kim to prevail, to come back. And then?

A virus, he had told her, distributed to the Emergent over their VR specs. At least the design of a suitable virus was something productive with which to occupy his mind. Twitching, he tried to imagine a virus tailored to *in vivo* nanobots and how best to spread it.

But what made him think he could slip a virus past the notice of the Emergent? It wasn't as though he often outwitted One.

It came down to a simple choice. He could work on a plan. He could go crazy, twitching, alone in the dark.

An easy choice, at last.

Charles found himself several minutes late for the rear guard's next check-in. Morgan and Have-Mercy had hit some black ice and spun out—while in a dead zone, naturally. Neither was hurt, but their truck had snapped its front axle. It wasn't going anywhere. Have-Mercy had hiked far enough to get back online. Charles had been the closest; he detoured to retrieve them and their cargo.

Sorry we're late, Morgan IMed to the rear guard. He was riding shotgun. *Report.*

Donaldson: *The inmates are out.*

Out of the auditorium but in the building, Corbett clarified. *Probably they spotted the rigged doors.*

Charles shot a glance at Have-Mercy, sitting by herself in the backseat. She wasn't linked into this dialogue, of course. Like her AWOL former leader, Merry was one of the sentimental members of the group. *And Watts?*

Unknown, Donaldson replied. *Off comm.*

Corbett: *The escapees are loud. They're running around with torches. Alan must know they're out. He'd have fallen back to the evac point if he could.*

Charles, private to Morgan: *Time to get our people out. Reseal the building behind them and let events take their natural course.*

Morgan, also private: *What about Watts?*

Charles, still private: *Earlier, it was "What about Brent?" It's time to cut our losses.*

A sigh, unmistakable, from Morgan. *Okay*, he conceded.

Charles: *Donaldson, Corbett, get out now. If a bomb goes off, the cops will swarm.* That would make it harder for the two of them to get away.

Corbett: *Are bombs necessary?*

Morgan: *Can you warn them over the PA? Announce that you're leaving and you'll call the bomb squad for them in an hour. That should keep them quiet.*

Donaldson: *Simple enough to restore the phones.*

Charles had never given any thought to how the public-address system worked. Just another extension on the company phone system, apparently. A quick lookup on a server back at Garner Nanotech confirmed his deduction.

Corbett: *Thanks, boss.*

Charles: *Kill the router and phones before you leave.*

Morgan: *Phones, yes. Leave the router. Alan might yet get in touch.*

"Everything okay?" Have-Mercy asked from the backseat.

"Absolutely," Charles answered her. The Garner Nanotech situation would resolve itself in another twenty minutes. Nothing anyone did was going to change that.

....

Something sparkled in Brent's eyes. There was an instant of numbness in his right side before that arm began tensing and twitching. A sudden peculiar taste filled his mouth; it as quickly vanished.

What was happening to him?

It was wishful thinking even to ask. Core programming was in safe regions of bot memory—otherwise, the hazard of Brownian bit bumps would have manifested earlier on. One by one, the bots would reboot. No, *were* rebooting: the source of his various tics and twitches. Perhaps the spasms came from bots knocked offline again, more Brownian bit bumps taking their toll.

One way or another, his desperate gamble had failed.

Weakly, tentatively, a tendril of alien presence probed Brent's mind. The recovery process was already well advanced! When enough bots came online, One would return. All the necessary interconnecting nerve bundles were in place, so it wouldn't take long.

He wanted to scream. He was so close! Spreading a virus *was* possible.

Another mind probe, this one stronger. Then a tremor—a seizure—stronger than any before. If only he could hold on to a shred of control. He struggled to keep to himself what he had been thinking.

Random resets, reconnections, disconnections: this was going to be ugly.

And then the spasms, smells, tastes—everything—stopped. Words flashed, all the starker for the sudden absence of any outer world. *I'll take over now.*

With a loud click, the PA announced itself. "Attention, everyone. We are leaving now. You're not. Be advised, we have rigged each building exit with an explosive device. It *will* go off if the door is opened.

"We mean you no harm. In an hour, after we are safely away, we'll contact the state police and advise them of your situation."

Kim didn't recognize the voice. The woman on the PA, whoever she was, sounded apologetic. She damn well should be.

"Let me go," Alan Watts said. "I'll leave with them. I promise I won't hurt you."

The hell with that. He could tell his story to the police.

Grunting and huffing, Kim began dragging her prisoner. He threatened and fussed nonstop. He must have weighed close to two hundred pounds, and in the rigid nanosuit that was all deadweight. Spatters of fire-extinguisher foam dotted them both.

Her arms and back screaming in protest, Kim continued dragging.

One did not entirely understand the concept of amusement, but it was fairly sure Brent's futile resistance merited such a response. How pitifully its host struggled to keep his secrets!

A simple rewrite would make its bots immune from another such attack. The need was now obvious and the necessary code change simpler than many it had made. Still, Brent struggled to keep from One what he knew about such software upgrades in newer bots. Did its host not remember in whose mind it resided?

Perhaps surface resistance masked another objective. It probed further, and the covert plan it found was pathetic. Regain his VR specs and lure the Emergent into . . . something (still to be determined) foolish. How very human.

But for as long as Brent remained a prisoner, One was at the mercy of another human. It/they had to get free. Just maybe—and the notion of amusement surfaced again—it could use Brent's unfinished plan to manipulate Kim.

Further opposition could not be tolerated. One banished Brent to the deep recesses of their shared mind, and began working out the details.

friday, 4:15 P.M., january 20, 2017

Aaron stared at the rigged door. People crowded close, torches in hand, to see. "Get back!" he screamed in warning—and in fear that one of them would try the exit anyway.

Most edged away. A few ran back the way they had come. To try another door?

"Nobody move!" he ordered, in the trust-me-I'm-a-doctor voice he hated but to which most people deferred. "Here's what we'll do."

Not that he had a plan beyond preventing panic. He could bring others into the planning once everyone had calmed down. Still, a few needs were obvious: getting the lights back on, for example. "Who knows where the circuit breakers are?"

"I do," Harry Ng said. He grabbed a torch and started into the dark. "Way in the back of the factory. It'll take me a couple minutes."

"Wait a sec, Harry." Maybe there was something else to be checked back there. *Oh, yeah.* "While you're back that way, see whether the loading dock is also rigged."

Harry nodded. "Will do."

And next? Aaron didn't sense the bad guys were shy about ruining things. The electrical circuits might be somehow damaged, or the breakers removed. They shouldn't just wait here for the lights to come on.

"Harry, let me know what you find—but *don't* assume that if a door looks safe, it is. Let me check it out. The Army trained me to

310

spot booby traps." Soon Aaron had volunteers to inspect all the exits. "You might find other people in the building, people who were hiding. I know Kim O'Donnell is out there. If anyone finds her, send her . . ."

Here? Was there nothing more productive he could do than stand around in this hallway? Pondering that, Aaron noticed several of his battering-ram crew flexing their hands. His own hands had taken quite a bruising. "Send her to the infirmary. That's where I'll be. Anyone who needs bandages, aspirin, whatever, come with me now."

"What's the phone extension there?" Harry asked. "I can report what I find."

"Good idea, Harry," Aaron said. "It's four twelve. Door inspectors, call in."

Only the phones were dead. Aaron permitted himself the hope that one of his folks would know how to bring them back up. Or Kim, when he found her.

Aaron's search parties began returning to the infirmary, all to report suspicious devices on the exits. Still, his spirits rose just a bit when the ceiling lamps came back on, despite the tears the sudden brightness brought to his eyes. He kept treating lacerated and bruised hands.

Janet Kwan strode into the infirmary, holding a cell phone. "Sorry, no service," she said. "Just camera mode. I wanted you to see the phone switch."

So much for the notion they might communicate around the building by phone. Aaron squinted at the phone's tiny screen, at a two-tiered rack of electronic circuit boards.

He intuited the work of a steel-toed boot where electronics boards had been caved in.

Kim was gasping for breath as she reached her destination. Her chest heaved from the exertion. She managed to call out to Brent, "It's me."

"Mm-mg," he acknowledged around his gag.

Then the lights came on. Her visor was still in night-vision mode;

she looked down, hand shading her eyes, until she could reconfigure her visor. Alan lay flat on his back, his face directly beneath a ceiling fixture, grunting in pain. His eyes were clenched shut. She bent over him to block some of the light.

"Thanks," Alan hissed. Behind his visor, his eyes blinked and teared and darted about. "Please, kill the lights. With these tears in my eyes, I can't turn off night vision."

That would leave Brent in the dark. She pulled up a help menu, found the keypad codes for visors. She switched his visor to normal mode, with heavy sun filtering. "Better?"

"Yes, thank you."

If the Emergent were truly gone, she could get the prisoners out of the auditorium. And she desperately needed Aaron's calm, practical advice. She stood. "I'll be back."

"Mm-mmph," Brent called loudly.

He had earned her trust, divulging the undocumented nanosuit control codes, but she had trussed him up with a *lot* of duct tape. Getting him loose would take a while.

Making an apologetic face, she removed Brent's tape gag and yet more facial hair. "I'll be back," she repeated, and dashed from the storeroom to see to the others.

His focus on disinfecting, stitching, and bandaging abused hands, Aaron paid little heed to the footsteps coming briskly his way. Yet someone else back to announce yet another remote exit rigged with a bomb, he supposed, or another reason they could not communicate. The bad guys were damnably thorough.

He had resigned himself to waiting for the police to arrive, whether or not because Brent and his friends made the promised call. Sladja would be frantic by now, and she wouldn't be the only one pressing the authorities to look for an unaccounted-for spouse.

"Aaron!"

"Kim?" Aaron's head whipped around. She stood in the infirmary doorway, leaning against a jamb. She had a nasty bruise on her forehead and a relieved grin. He wound the Ace bandage one more time around Mason Tanaka's sprained wrist before rushing to her.

Beneath Aaron's bear hug, Kim's clothes turned rigid. He hadn't noticed until that moment that she wore a nanosuit with its hood thrown back. His hands, as battered as many he had treated, complained. He ignored them.

"Are you okay?" he and Kim asked in unison.

"Uh-huh," Kim said.

"Me, too. Umm, Kim, what was your call about?" That had been, what, twenty minutes earlier? Aaron released her and stepped aside so Mason could get out the infirmary door.

"One of the Emergent—that's what they call themselves—was about to get me." She shivered. "With your help, I got him. Alan Watts. Thanks for saving me."

Thanks for getting me out of my funk. "Does Watts need medical attention?"

"I don't think so, Aaron, but Brent might." She brought him up-to-date.

Aaron picked up a medical bag. "You better show me." He had Brent's supposed miraculous cure as much in mind as his medical condition.

More than anything, One craved information. With difficulty it waited for Kim's footsteps to recede into the distance before allowing its host to speak. "Alan? Are you okay?"

"Couldn't be better." A bitter laugh. "I can see you, Brent, just barely, from a corner of an eye. Facial muscles are about all I'm able to move. It appears you aren't having a good day, either."

That was the single plus of being bound to the lolly post: captivity explained its/their earlier disappearance. "How goes the revolution?"

"Fine, except for some collateral damage. For which, it appears, you and I will be the fall guys."

The host's back itched. One allowed Brent to squirm against the post, which did not quite mitigate the itch, while asking the question that Brent was dying to ask. "Bombs on the exits, though? Is that true?"

"Yeah. The longer our people have to disperse, the better. Going underground will be harder once the word gets out." A long silence. "Brent, there's a potential snag."

"Begin at the beginning, Alan."

"A few of us stayed back to find you." Alan's voice dropped to a conspiratorial whisper. "Have-Mercy reconnected a router to a fiber-optic cable so we could keep in touch with everyone already on the road. If anyone here finds it . . ."

If Kim found an external link, she would e-mail the police in a flash. That would mean less chance for the others to scatter and hide and—of more immediate concern—less opportunity for One itself to escape.

It needed time! If it could convince Kim to cut loose her dear friend Brent, and if it could get a nanosuit for protection, then *maybe* it could yet extract itself from this situation. That would have to be Alan's nanosuit. The suit Kim wore barely fit her; it would never accommodate Brent.

Brent intruded with a memory: a crude image, an ancient cartoon. Two ragged, bearded men in wrist and ankle manacles dangled from a rough-hewn stone wall. One said to the other, "Now here's my plan."

Irony, One decided. As with amusement, One still struggled with the concept.

Then in the distance—voices! Kim and Aaron, Brent/One decided. They were coming this way. One/they said softly, "Alan, listen. If I can gain Kim's trust, get myself cut loose, I can take down the comm link."

"Okay. I'll play along."

The voices drew near. Alan whispered hurriedly, "Brent, the bombings were Morgan's doing. And I'm the one who assaulted Ethan. If we *don't* get out let me take the heat for those."

"Understood. Now be quiet."

....

Arguing voices.

Kim and Aaron had stopped a good hundred feet away, but One's enhancements to the associative auditory cortex extracted meaning where an old-style human would scarcely sense a murmur. They would not anticipate eavesdropping.

"He's not the same," Kim insisted to Aaron.

"That's what you told me months ago, meaning exactly the opposite."

"You know what I mean," Kim retorted. "Brent's more like he *was*. And how he should be."

"Suppose that he is, Kim. Is he sincere? Is the reversion permanent? The new Brent is very smart. He could be manipulating you." An awkward pause. "Because unless Brent gets away, he's going to spend the rest of his life in prison."

Old Brent surfaced enough to agree—and to notice a painfully full bladder. One tuned out both stimuli to focus on the dispute in the hallway.

"Aaron, Brent gave me the code I needed to immobilize Alan. If not a change of heart, why would Brent do that?"

"I don't know," Aaron said. The tone was grudging, not entirely conceding the point. "Maybe I need to see Brent for myself."

A few seconds later, Kim appeared.

Aaron followed, looking around at everything. He started at finding a holstered handgun on the rigid figure on the floor. Aaron took the gun and tucked into his waistband.

Old Brent smiled inwardly at Aaron's surprise. *I guess, Doctor, you don't know Kim as well as you think. No way would she touch a gun, not if she had any choice.*

"I was starting to worry," Brent/One said. It/they would ask to be freed if that didn't happen soon, but why risk raising suspicions when Kim might free them unasked?

Meanwhile, there was a way to build trust. "Kim, Alan hasn't spoken for a couple minutes." That was a lie, but for now Alan was playing possum. "Fully rigid like that, the suit fabric may not be very oxygen permeable. I just don't know. We need to lift his hood."

Aaron came close, peering into Brent's eyes.

"Looking for reassurance, Doctor? For what it's worth, I don't think I would trust me, either."

"Aaron," Kim said. "What if Alan is suffocating in there?"

Aaron looked torn. "What if they're playing us? What if releasing the hood cancels the suit's rigidity mode?"

"We won't speculate. We'll test." Kim got up on her toes to whisper to Aaron, who jotted something down.

Given Brent's/One's enhanced hearing, Kim might as well have shouted. She had passed along the codes he had given her earlier for freezing and unfreezing a suit, and a third code—which he deduced she had found in her suit's online help—to release the hood.

She raised and sealed her hood, then extended her arms. Aaron keyed in a code that froze her. "Okay, I can't move," she confirmed. "Now enter the hood-release code."

Aaron keyed that in, and folded back her hood. "Can you move?"

She shook her head. "Can't say I like being stuck like this. Unfreeze me, please."

That code also worked as advertised. Kim knelt and opened Alan's hood.

"Thanks," Alan wheezed. His face was red and he panted a bit—if One had to guess, from holding his breath for effect.

"So will your friends call the police for us?" Kim demanded.

Wheeze. "If they say so, sure."

Brent/One added, "I agree," that being the politic answer. No one had made any move yet to loosen his/their bonds.

"Where are your friends going?" Aaron asked.

This time from Alan: stony silence.

"How do you reach them?" Aaron continued.

"I can't," Alan said.

Time to buy some credibility. Brent/One cleared its/their throat.

"He's lying. He told me earlier there's hidden Internet access from the building."

"You *bastard!*" Alan snarled. "You no-good . . . never mind. I'll say no more."

"Brent, what else do you know?" Kim asked. "Where's the connection?"

"I don't *know* anything more. I can surmise a bit." One held Brent's eyes on Kim. She wanted to believe, wanted to trust him. "The comm link out the building can't be wireless, or the police would have been here hours ago to shut it down. So we're looking for a landline of some kind. Possibly it's a tapped line, or an unused fiber out of a cable that passes nearby. There's no way to know where in the building the line terminates, or what encryption is in use."

"Alan's visor!" Aaron shouted belatedly.

Alan laughed. "The connection is broken."

"Let me help," Brent said. *Help myself.* "I know how the Emergent think. I might be able to find the link and crack the security—if you cut me down. Get you people rescued faster."

Kim looked imploringly at Aaron. Aaron nodded, and she started slicing Brent's tape bonds with a box cutter. "I'll have you down soon."

"That's a relief," Brent said. "I *really* need to pee."

Waiting for rescue is hard, Kim thought. *Watching Brent try to move things along is almost as hard.*

Brent had helped capture Alan. Brent had disclosed the hidden comm link. Spying on Brent made her feel lousy. Why couldn't Aaron see Brent was . . . repentant?

Kim and Aaron had parted ways midfactory, near the cleanrooms, she and Brent turning toward R & D, Aaron and Alan heading toward the infirmary where Aaron would treat more scrapes and sprains and monitor their prisoner. Alan was bungee-corded to a two-wheeled hand truck, trundled along like the mannequin Kim remembered from months ago, stiff as a statue in his rigid nanosuit—only complaining vociferously.

Brent keyed awkwardly, muttering about fat fingers. Router code scrolled on most of his screen. A graphic of the in-house network served as backdrop. "This is like swimming in molasses," he said. "It's been months since I did any serious work by keyboard."

Still, for all his griping, he worked faster than Kim could. He had brushed off her offer to help, saying explaining things to her would only slow him down.

"Sorry," she said, studying the PC screen over his shoulder. Sorry about spying on him. Sorry that, as soon as the police got them out of here, Brent must go straight to jail. Even Brent insisted on that. Sorry she and Aaron hadn't, somehow, figured things out soon enough to save Brent from himself and prevent all the death and destruction.

"Kim, if you'd only let me use—"

Stop right there," Kim said. "Aaron could be right. You can't know what old, bad reflexes using VR specs could trigger."

Not that they had specs since she crushed Brent's pair while tackling Alan. Well, that wasn't quite true: The nanosuits, hers and Alan's, had VR capability in their visors. Only Brent couldn't possibly wear the suit she hadn't taken the time to remove, and it wasn't at all clear how safely to recover Alan's suit without risking him getting away.

And it wasn't *certain*, she had had to concede to Aaron, that Brent, given the protection of a nanosuit, wouldn't try to get away.

Grumbling, Brent returned to his clumsy typing.

"Sorry," Kim said.

friday, 4:20 P.M., january 20, 2017

Keystroke by keystroke, Brent/One set their trap.

The hardest part was feigning ineptitude. To type too quickly, to absorb information concurrently from too many windows, to let data fly past too speedily—any of those could reveal the superior mind once again in control.

And so, with Kim watching the screen over its/their shoulder, One piped the occasional burst of keystrokes directly to a file. Command by command One assembled the script that would end this charade. But had there been a typo?

A moment after Brent loudly kicked a metal wastebasket, One pulled the script file onto the display. The half screen of text was shown, proofread within an eye blink, and banished. "Sorry," Brent/One said. Kim looked away from the mess to him. "I was just stretching. I'll pick that up."

"Not important," she said.

The file had had a one-character typo. Between for-show surveys of another several routers, One sneaked in, again bypassing the display, an edit to fix it. The next surreptitious command invoked the script.

Brent/One went on about an imaginary search (it/they had found the open comm line almost immediately), closing and repositioning windows until an icon was revealed on the PC desktop. The blinking symbol hadn't been there before. He'd happen to notice it if Kim didn't.

"What the heck?" Kim leaned over his shoulder. "Is that new e-mail?"

Brent/One clicked on the icon to open his in-box. The ostensible sender was a well-known overseas anonymizer relay. "What the hell? Sent at four o'clock." That was before the breakout—and the apparent time stamp, like everything else in the e-mail, had been created by its/their script. Kim had to be thinking: *who sent this message, and how?* One/they waited.

"Open it," she said.

"Okay." Below a legible message header revealing copies addressed to Brent and Alan, the message was gibberish. Brent/One said, "It's encrypted"—which it/they had done for authenticity. It/they supplied a private key. "There we go."

They looked together at the clear-text version:

> The comm link into the factory will go offline 4:30 ET. Thereafter begins a one-month comm blackout. If you get this too late to respond, we'll synch up after. Good luck.

"It's four twenty-three," Kim said. "We don't have much time." Curiosity got the best of her. "A month?"

"Morgan is a counterterrorism expert. And I recruited"—One induced a guilty-seeming shiver at its choice of verb—"heavily among the guards, mostly vets and ex-cops. The Emergent know pretty much everything there is to know about identity theft, going undercover, who to see for fake documents. They'll be hard to find." Time for another dramatic shiver. "Except they'll need money. So ex-cops and ex-Army, equipped with bulletproof nanosuits, are about to go on a crime spree."

"Can you find . . . ," Kim began.

"Yeah, I traced the outside connection from the message header." If pressed now, his backtrack would be in error. But the point was to press *her*; Brent/One lowered its/their head sorrowfully. "This is entirely my fault! I've *got* to stop it."

"We can contact the police now. For another six minutes, anyway."

"Too little, too late, Kim. They're already scattered! Let just one of the Emergent get away with a supply of the bots and the contagion spreads." Pregnant pause. "But I have an idea."

Brent could control nothing but his own thoughts. When One severed Brent's connection to eyes and ears, he raised such a mental clamor that One relaxed the blockade. A bargain was struck: watch; don't try to interfere.

The closest Brent came to obstruction was, with massive effort, a typo inserted into the stream of keystrokes. The extraneous character was detected, of course, as he knew it would be. Not to be seen even trying to interfere would seem suspicious. . . .

Brent/One stumbled to its/their feet. "My legs still feel like wood," it/they complained. The less threatening it/they looked, the better. "Come on, Kim. I'll explain on the way."

Two doors down, Harry Ng pounded away obsessively on his own computer. That was simply Harry's way.

"Harry," Brent/One called. "We need your help. Walk with us."

Harry looked puzzled but hurried to join them. "What do you need?"

"I need the nanosuit Alan Watts is wearing, and only Kim may be able to talk Aaron into that. So *she* has to run ahead to the infirmary. She won't, unless I'm supervised. So supervise me."

"What should I tell Aaron?" Kim asked.

"That I can implant a virus that'll at the least slow down the Emergent. You saw the e-mail"—which was the crux of the ploy—"and we don't have much time. I need Alan's suit for the visor. That's the only way I might get the virus written quickly enough, and the only way they'll take the bait."

Kim's eyes said she wanted to believe.

Brent/One glanced at his wristwatch. The three of them moved as quickly as its/their feigned disability allowed them to hobble. "Kim, we now have only six minutes. It'll take time to get Alan out of the suit. Please, run ahead and tend to that. When I get there, Aaron will either agree or not."

"Well . . . ," she managed. "Is it safe to get Alan out?"

It/they gestured at his stumbling gait. "I'm still limping. Alan has been immobile, frozen in an unnatural position, for what, fifteen minutes? How limber do you suppose he'll be when the suit is deactivated?"

"Okay. Harry, Brent, join me as soon as you can." She dashed ahead.

By the time Brent/One and its/their chaperone reached the infirmary, Alan was out of his nanosuit, bound to a tall-backed desk chair by yards and yards of duct tape. He had a tape gag, too.

Aaron looked more skeptical than ever. Maybe it was his new black eye.

"Look, it's simple," Brent/One said. "The Emergent have scattered. They're in their final minutes of coordination before they go offline and underground. They depend on VR specs, which have embedded microprocessors. So do their nanosuits."

Aaron stood pondering, the precious nanosuit draped over an arm. "So your computer virus will mess up their coordination, and that should make them easier to stop. And also make them more vulnerable by disabling the nanosuits."

"Yes! But the longer we wait the less harm an interruption will do." Brent/One gestured toward Aaron's desk clock. "If I don't do it soon, the comm link will be down and we'll have squandered the opportunity."

"How about we hang the hood over your head?" Aaron asked. "Save some time?"

Keep me vulnerable, you mean. Not subtle.

Kim shook her head. "Won't work, Aaron. The suit's power-management software requires sensing a body inside. Brent, how can you get a virus to—?"

It/they cut Kim off. The 4:30 deadline was artificial, solely to rush them along, leaving them no time to find holes in the story. "Enough! I link up, same as ever, perfectly safely, and they'll see it's me. I tell them

I'm on the run, I have critical information for them, and I can't spare the time or attention to report interactively. Just look at the attachment."

"Aha," Kim said. "A social-engineering attack. And the attachment is the virus."

"Of course," Brent/One lied.

It/they would report their situation and then scramble software on every router in the building. The damage would be blamed on the Emergent striking back, and the police would stay in the dark for a while longer about the day's events at Garner Nanotech.

Ideally enough longer that it/they might find a way to escape. Wearing a nanosuit would surely help.

Do we risk this? Aaron wondered. His better judgment, without explanation, said no. Kim's face said yes. Alan Watts's eyes, filled with rage, said he wanted to strangle Brent.

The clock on Aaron's desk said 4:26.

Aaron held out the nanosuit. "Good luck, Brent."

Brent/One wriggled into the nanosuit. Brent had the muscle memory to guide that process, leaving One to concentrate on ways, once it was again online, to destroy the building network.

Kim had mentioned one of its peers labeling her kind Neanderthal. What a cruel, *apt* depiction that was. One's only weakness was human weakness; by the minute, Brent's personality, defeated, resisted One less and less. The once-useful modus vivendi had outlived its usefulness: there could be no ambiguity now which mind ruled this body.

Ironically, it *was* possible to cause harm over a comm link. Brent had wondered about that, foolishly imagining he could keep his scheming to himself. Not with a computer virus disguised as a text attachment—the fiction One had given its captors—but with a visual file: optical stimuli to release massive, persistent neurotransmitter cascades. Enough glutamate to saturate the message receptors of many bots at once. Kept saturated long enough, the bots would reinitialize.

Sensory overload defied a fix like the recently excised Brownian-bit-bump vulnerability. Bots were meant to operate in blood, in the absence of any significant glutamate concentration. In CSF, localized glutamate surges were a statistical inevitability. When they persisted, bot message receptors clogged until enough random jostling dislodged the blockage. Retrofitting an auto-reset mode to its bots—shake things loose and restart—had been crucial to One's evolution into full consciousness. Its siblings, to emerge, had had to program the same improvement.

Those were ruminations One had no intention of sharing.

Arms and legs in place. For appearance' sake, it/they left a few nanosuit openings unsealed. Hood raised. Visor active. Kim looked amusingly anxious for it/them to proceed.

"Ready," it/they said. One opened a link to the Emergent, a report ready to send.

And then Brent struck.

Brent had watched One reassemble as more and more individual bots rebooted. He had observed One update the bots against another Brownian-bit-bump attack.

It had been a delicate time, with sentience stirring but firm purpose not yet recovered. He had accessed memories that the nascent mind did not yet know to withhold. He had planted suggestions when and where he could, before critical thinking reemerged.

The ploy-within-a-ploy of which One was so arrogantly proud was not entirely of One's making.

But then One was back, alert, in control.

For long minutes Brent had watched, knowing One watched him watch.

He had permitted himself only the slightest bit of resistance: to move a finger, blink an eye, lodge a protest. He made no secret of his dismay. He allowed himself to wilt beneath the futility of his efforts.

He bided his time.

The comm link opened and Brent struck. He could not hope to prevail for any length of time, or over much of his body, so he focused with all his will on directing his eyes. An IM flick/blinked out, the brief note telling the tale One had used to convince Kim and Aaron: *I'm on the run, with critical info. No time to discuss. See attachment.*

The attached file implemented the visual attack One thought *it* had just imagined.

Battling to maintain control over his eyes just a moment longer, Brent flick/blink opened the copy of the file also sent to his/their own visor.

Windshield wipers flicked back and forth, reassuringly predictable. Snow fell steadily. The radio played classic rock. Garner Nanotech was many miles behind.

We've pulled it off, Tyra/Seven thought.

I'm on the run, with critical info. No time to discuss. See attachment. The IM was from Brent, and all the Emergent had been copied.

Felipe dozed beside her. She prodded his shoulder. "Wake up. Read."

"Uh-huh," he grumbled, then added a more alert-sounding, "Jeez."

She pulled onto the shoulder and switched on the SUV's emergency flashers.

"No!" Felipe screamed. He tugged without effect at his visor. "Don't open it!"

Too late. Lights shimmered and flashed. Colors swirled. She/they tried flicking through menus to the visor shutoff command; stroboscopic flashing and uncontrollable reflex kept jerking her focus away.

Patterns raged, insane, unabated. Holes gaped through her/their thoughts. Bots resetting?

Tyra heard distant whimpering, the sound of pain and fear, and knew it was her own voice.

. . . .

The snow had turned to sleet. Brittany/Five clenched the steering wheel fiercely. Beside her, Logan diddled with the radio tuner.

They were going too fast for conditions, but this comm blackout was unnerving. Once they got far enough away for comm to return, she'd slow down.

Seconds later, her visor came back to life. "Hallelujah," she said. Her earpieces beeped an alert tone: an incoming message. *I'm on the run, with critical info. No time to discuss. See attachment.*

From Brent! That he was in touch at all was progress. Maybe he'd have word about Alan. She/they opened the attachment.

A kaleidoscope exploded.

Five screamed inside Brittany's head. It seemed like every muscle in her/their body spasmed. The car went into a spin, drifting into the other lane.

Its air horn blaring, an 18-wheeler bore down on them.

Light and color to neurotransmitter cascades to bot overload to sundered higher-level thought. It was exactly as One had imagined it— only this onslaught wasn't its doing. Its thoughts thrashed.

Very little time. After many tries, it managed to flick/blink dispatch a message. *Critical. Ignore my last.*

Would anyone get its warning in time?

Cognition and memory fractured. Sanity wavered. Self-awareness trembled.

It slashed and tore at the software in nearby routers, cutting off the humans. Then there was no *it* left to do anything. For a while longer reflex and remnant memory continued to rend and tear.

And then even purposeful reflex faded. . . .

Minds at war.

Charles/Two shook with rage and confusion as the road and the snowstorm vanished in a maelstrom of color. Somehow the colors were *growing*. Through the sudden tears in his eyes he/they couldn't flick/blink off the specs. He/they tore them from his face. The disorienting patterns went away.

So, for all practical purposes, did the road.

"Slow down for the curve!" Have-Mercy Ramirez screamed from the backseat.

Morgan grabbed onto the steering wheel. Steering or convulsing? Charles/Two couldn't tell. He/they swatted at Morgan's hand, instantly rigid, only hurting himself/themselves.

Spinning. Careening. An incredible shock!

His/their thoughts cleared for an instant. He/they squeezed the deflating air bag, pushed it out of the way.

The SUV was nose-down in a ditch. A horrible groaning from outside accompanied the soft moaning of Morgan and Have-Mercy, safe within their nanosuits. The sounds they made weren't what raised the hairs on the back of Charles's neck. Something he could barely sense swayed in the rearview mirror. He leaned close to the mirror, squinting. A snapped-off phone pole, dangling from wires? The horrible groan was cables stretching. And then the cables snapped. Helpless, he watched in the mirror as the pole toppled.

He didn't have a nanosuit.

Like a hammer driving a nail, pole and SUV roof pounded Charles/Two into the seat. Things snapped. Things spurted. He/they shrieked with pain. Charles passed out.

Two struggled, its mind in tatters, the gaps spreading. Its thoughts flailed. Its last glimpse of the dashboard clock was somehow etched into its ebbing consciousness. The digital display had just flicked to 4:26.

Two's final thought, as all awareness faded away, was that in another four minutes Brent, Kim, and the others would also be dead.

friday, 4:26 P.M., january 20, 2017

Brent's eyes flew open, and they were *his* eyes. He felt no trace of One's presence.

Kim and Harry were at his sides, each clutching an arm. His heart was racing.

"What the hell happened? Do you know?" Aaron asked. The syringe in his hand carried a wicked-long needle.

"What the hell did you give me?" Brent countered.

"Epinephrine." Aaron set down the syringe. "You began convulsing and gasping for breath."

Epinephrine was med speak for adrenaline. Brent couldn't imagine how much adrenaline he had had that day. No wonder his heart beat like a drum. He took a deep breath. "My overmind's parting shot. I don't think it was very happy with me."

At Aaron's gesture, Kim and Harry released Brent's arms.

"Then it's over?" Kim asked.

Over? It was impossible to imagine this ever being over. Then Brent wondered at that reflexive doubt. "I lied about the virus. What I planned would've taken too long to explain." *And I wasn't in charge just then to do the explaining.* The whole truth was very complicated, and not conducive to rebuilding trust.

"Chances are my attack reached more than One"—he tapped his forehead as a definition—"and that some of the Emergent overminds are gone. Not in Alan, since he was offline, and others may also have been offline. For the rest, I can't know how many fell for my ruse."

But *One* was gone. Wasn't it? Why not have faith? Why not look past the adrenaline jitters?

Because One would never be entirely gone. Not the memory, not the guilt, not the helplessness, not—so starkly revealed at the end—the deep contempt.

"You have the time now, Brent," Aaron said. "Explain."

If all the overminds felt as condescending toward their hosts, how little regard did they hold for "mere" humans? If as little as Brent suspected, humans were entirely disposable.

All the anomalies of the day reasserted themselves—only maybe they weren't anomalies if the people trapped in the building were expendable.

Brent bolted from the room, shouting over his shoulder, "Gather everyone into the interior of R and D. Move!"

How he hoped he was wrong. . . .

Brent shot from the infirmary faster than Kim—than *anyone*—could react, calling out as he went, "Gather everyone into the interior of R and D. Move!"

Aaron dashed after him.

Kim froze. Gather everyone? Just minutes earlier she had sent people scurrying across the building. With top-of-the-line laptops scavenged from R & D, they were attempting the experiment that Kim had been unable to try: testing whether WiMax-equipped gear might, where WiFi had failed, establish an outside connection. So far, no luck reported.

And now they were all supposed to reassemble in R & D, clear across the building? It was one twist, one shock, too many. So what now?

Now she put her trust in Brent. He wanted them to be somewhere else. Urgently.

"Harry, help me push Alan." And they ran, rolling Alan in the chair, a caster squeaking. "Get to R and D," they yelled to everyone they saw. Most were already headed that way, as confused as she.

Brent sealed his nanosuit as best he could as he sprinted. "Into R and D," he shouted, not knowing if anyone heard the warning. "Stay away from all exits. Into R and D. Immediately."

Kim had spoken of reaction vats being removed, but the two of them had walked past the cleanrooms just a few minutes ago. Big and shiny, unmistakable, stainless-steel vats remained in place. Was Kim mistaken—not likely—or had empty spare vats been installed? Replacement could be a subterfuge to mask the theft—only anyone with any knowledge of bot assembly would spot the substitution quickly enough. Unless . . .

Brent burst through double doors into the factory, still shouting, and pelted to the nearest stairwell. He flung open the door and took the steps three at a time. The door rebounded to crash closed behind him.

And crashed a second time. Someone was following him. Damn it!

And the second anomaly: Morgan's disappearance earlier. Brent had checked out all but two areas. Surely Morgan hadn't been anywhere in the storeroom maze where Kim had set her ambush, or he would have heard the struggle and come running. That left only the seldom-used second floor above the factory and auditorium. *Why were you upstairs, Morgan, unless . . .*

The ceiling fixtures were dark in the rarely used factory attic, but faint illumination seeped in around the inter-floor conveyors. Flick/ blink, Brent cranked up the light amplification on his visor and as quickly turned it down. He was just in time, as whoever was chasing him hit the light switch.

"What are you up to?" Aaron called.

On the level beneath, the cleanrooms would be right about . . . there. Two loping paces in that direction brought blinking red lights into view. Brent found a digital counter, decrementing, and a claylike mass affixed to a roof-support pillar. He skidded to a halt. "Looking for that," he said as Aaron caught up.

The timer broke 2:00 and kept counting down.

They stopped checking support columns after finding six in a row rigged. The roof was meant to come down, and it would bring the second floor down with it. That would crush and obliterate everything beneath: the factory, the cleanrooms, the auditorium.

No one would suspect murderous colleagues who had gone into hiding—not until the ruins could be completely sifted, however many days that took. Until then, there would have been only that many more Garner Nanotech employees missing and presumed dead in the rubble. No one would be assessing the flattened decoy reaction vats to detect theft.

He might have stopped Charles and Morgan and the rest, but their bombs kept ticking. And people remained trapped in the building.

"Aaron! Get out *now!* There's no second floor above R and D."

They ran back to the stairwell. "And why the interior?" Aaron asked.

Maybe a minute and a half left, Brent guessed. "Away from the exits. I don't know if the door bombs will blow at the same time." With a crash, they burst out of the stairwell onto the main level. "You clear the front of the building. I'll clear back here."

They parted ways, shouting as they ran. When the great bulk of the building collapsed, then what? Debris flying everywhere. Fires. Secondary explosions, maybe. Taking shelter in R & D would help, but it might not be enough. He had to get everyone out, and before the roof came down.

Call it a minute and fifteen seconds.

An image, horrific, took shape in Brent's mind: explosion, building collapse, another slaughter of innocents. It was memory and omen both. For an instant he froze.

Not again!

He shook off the paralysis and ran to a forklift.

. . . .

Kim and Harry were halfway to R & D when Aaron fell in alongside her. She read fear and determination in his eyes.

He shouted, "The second floor is about to come crashing down!"

Which explained R & D: that part of the facility had no second floor. Aaron squeezed between Kim and Harry, and together they hurried Alan's chair the rest of the way to an R & D conference room. She was gasping for breath by the time they arrived. Eight people had crowded in ahead of them.

"Will we be . . . safe here?" Kim asked.

"Safer," Aaron said. "Be right back."

"But—"

Aaron left before she could finish her objection, returning almost as quickly. "Be ready to run again," he bellowed.

Kim thought Aaron looked terribly sad. And where was Brent?

At its top speed of fifteen miles per hour, the forklift lurched across the factory floor. It struck the double doors off center, ripping one side from its hinges. Brent swore and overcorrected, impaling a wall with one of the fork tines. He backed up and tried again, veering from side to side, gouging walls as he went.

The motor was electric and quiet; he bellowed over its drone, "Be ready to run. Be ready to run. You won't have much time."

Aaron peeked out of a cross aisle, his eyes wide with understanding and horror. He ducked back as the forklift bore down on him—and didn't argue.

Thirty seconds, best guess, and then the roof came down. "Ready, people!"

Brent careened through a wall-mangling turn. A fire exit loomed ahead. A red LED stared balefully from the bomb rigged to the door. Closer . . . closer . . .

Brent took his hands from the steering wheel to seal the final gaps in the nanosuit—as futile as the precaution seemed. Flick/blink, he set his visor to near opacity, until he could hardly sense the door straight ahead. At the top of his lungs, he screamed, "Get ready!"

He had a final moment to remember his failure at Angleton, and the evil he had done since, and to wonder about closure. The exit was about twenty feet ahead.

Brent dove over the seat back, behind the forklift. He just had time to think, *I'm sorry*—

Then blinding glare and deafening sound and an invisible fist sent him into oblivion.

Blam!

The conference room shook. Kim's ears rang and she couldn't hear what Aaron was shouting. Maybe no one could: he was shoving people out the door. Harry pushed Alan, still taped into his chair. Aaron grabbed Kim's arm and they followed.

The emergency exit at end of the hall had ceased to exist, replaced by a gaping hole half-choked with debris. Coughing from the smoke and dust, people slogged through fallen chunks of wall and ceiling. They ducked under the dangling, sparking wires and squeezed past a mangled forklift—where had that come from?—tipped onto its side. They scrambled over the detritus where the door had been, out of the building. Two men on the outside helped Harry lift out Alan and chair.

Aaron yelled—although Kim still couldn't hear anything—and pointed *behind* her, away from the outside and safety. Two arms and two legs, covered in dust, deathly still, peeked from a hole caved into the wallboard. One sleeve bore a familiar keypad: a nanosuit. Brent! Did they dare move him? Did they dare not?

Brent had been right on top of this explosion. Could he even still be alive?

Aaron took hold of an arm. *Hurry*, he mouthed.

Kim punched in the test code to make Brent's nanosuit rigid—a full-body cast—and grabbed his other arm. They heaved, and something in the wall shifted ominously. They heaved again, and something in her back tore. A final yank, Kim screaming in pain, and they had Brent out of the shattered wall.

Then they were stumbling through snow, and Aaron was still tugging. She just barely heard, "Keep moving!" After a few steps her feet skidded out from under her and they tumbled into a heap. In the distance, toward town, red and blue lights flashed: squad cars, fire engines, and ambulances racing toward them.

With a roar like the end of the world, the building behind them started to collapse.

epilogue

sunday, may 21, 2017

Good food (or so Kim had been promised). Good friends. She wanted to be relaxed, tried to be relaxed, and she failed dismally. Utica stirred up too many memories.

Still, it was great to see Aaron and Sladja. A few minutes at the bar waiting for their table to be ready and Nick already had the Sanderses charmed. Aaron liked almost everyone, but to keep a big grin on Sladja's face took talent.

The restaurant was jammed, which perhaps excused the postage-stamp tables. If postage stamps were ever round. The ambience was all brass and glass and art-deco tile, and very noisy. They sat boy-girl, boy-girl.

"What kind of appetizer shall we get?" Sladja asked the moment they got menus. "We need to put some meat on your bones, Kim."

Yeah, right, Kim thought, letting it pass.

Aaron leaned close and plucked a quarter from behind Kim's ear. "A token of our esteem. Dinner is on us, you two. Don't be shy."

"You don't need—," Nick began.

"But we want to," Aaron said firmly. "Next time, don't elope."

Only Kim had learned the hard way—not ten minutes from here, where Garner Nanotech once stood—that life was too short *not* to elope. She frowned. "I drove by, Aaron."

"The old office?" Aaron guessed.

There, too, but not her point. "CNYPC." The Central New York Psychiatric Center, a few miles away in Marcy.

That was Aaron's cue to look unhappy. "It's a job, Kim, and this isn't a region with a lot of them."

Kim caught Nick's eye. He started reviewing appetizer choices with Sladja. He could talk for ten minutes on the merits of various Buffalo wing sauces.

Kim scooted her chair a bit closer to Aaron. "I want to see Brent. You can get me in."

Aaron looked her straight in the eye. "Kim, we're not talking about a nightclub. It's a maximum-security psychiatric prison. Unless and until the warden says otherwise, the rule is families only."

She shook her head. "Brent's family can't get in, either. For psychiatric reasons, they've been told. That it would be too dangerous to visit their son, their brother. I don't buy it."

"I'm only an internist, Kim. I can't overrule the shrinks. You have to keep hoping."

That put a damper on the evening. Kim hid behind her menu, thinking furiously of a change of subject—or a change in approach—when someone sidled up to the table.

"You *are* her." The man was short, pear-shaped, and tan, with an excess of teeth. He looked closely at Aaron. "And you're one of them, too. Garner Nanotech survivors."

"I just have that kind of face," Kim mumbled. All she needed was a celebrity stalker. She'd never wanted to be a celebrity—especially not about that day—and she had never been given the choice. The news vans had followed the first responders up the hill to the blazing ruins. She had long ago stopped counting the clips on YouTube, jerky vids shot on countless cells, of her trying to explain things, of her naming the VR-spec fanatics before they scattered too far and wide. To the police, the FBI, Homeland Security . . .

"No, I'm sure you're her," the stranger persisted.

Nick pushed back his chair and stood. He huddled with the stranger and within seconds had the intruder nodding sympathetically. Someday, she'd understand how Nick did that.

"I'll leave you folks to your meal. Sorry for interrupting."

"So how's your new job?" Aaron asked, too brightly.

Back-office software for a bank. It took no imagination. It would never change the world. It was in Albany. "It's exactly what I need right now."

The waiter came by to take their orders. After he left, the conversation stayed on safe topics for a while.

But Kim couldn't leave things alone. She took a skinny paperback volume of sports trivia out of her handbag. "Aaron, can you give this to him?"

Aaron looked away. "What the inmates get is very controlled."

"Because last season's baseball stats might be coded instructions for the prison break?" She held out the book until Aaron took it. "Just tell me you'll try."

"Okay."

Their appetizers came. Nick carried the conversational ball while Kim picked at her food. A trial would at least have offered a kind of closure. It would have been a way, perhaps, to get past this. Would there ever be a trial? CNYPC housed the criminally insane. It was the only institution in the state where people could be committed against their will.

Were Brent and the others insane? Well, hearing voices in your head wasn't usually taken as a sign of mental health. The snag was, maybe Brent and the others did.

The autopsy on Charles had conclusively shown bots inside his brain. Not much else, apparently: reading between the lines of the news reports, Charles's head had been crushed like an eggshell. At *that* memory, she lost any interest in dinner.

Logically she should be happy Aaron was at CNYPC, a friendly face for Brent. She knew it wasn't fair to punish one friend for her worries about another.

But life was hardly fair, was it?

"I don't get it," Kim burst out. "How did Dan Garner and his backers end up with get-out-of-jail-free cards? Why the *hell* can't Brent's family, can't any of the victims' families, sue for negligence?"

"How do you expect me to answer that?" Aaron answered, looking down at his plate. "Label something a national-security matter and the government can do as it pleases. You know that."

Nick nudged Kim under the table—twice, firmly, to show it was no mistake. As in: *you need to stop; you're being unfair; you're pushing too hard.*

And so she dropped the subject, made small talk, ate her dinner. She even, to Sladja's certain satisfaction, ordered and forced down a dessert.

For all the pleasure the meal had provided, Kim might as well have eaten sawdust.

monday, may 22, 2017

The redbrick towers could have been an apartment complex any-where. The sweep of well-trimmed grass could have been a park any-where. Those same towers all alone, so completely isolated, conveyed a much darker image.

Or maybe, Aaron thought, the darkness came of knowing that the clear-cut expanse around CNYPC was thickly strewn with heat and motion sensors.

"Thank you, sir." The gatehouse guard handed back Aaron's CNYPC photo ID, and the steel-plate barrier in front of the car began pivoting down. "Have a nice day, sir."

Not bloody likely. Aaron hated lying to anyone. Lying to Kim, after all they had been through together—that gnawed at him. He had tossed and turned all last night, brooding.

The barrier plate hit the driveway pavement with a thump and he put the car into gear. "You, too, Theo," Aaron told the guard. He cleared the gate area and the massive steel plate rose in his rearview mirror.

After parking, Aaron showed his badge at the checkpoint at the main entrance. Inside, he went through a second checkpoint equipped with a mantrap booth. Here the CNYPC badge counted for nothing. Access to the inner unit relied on a retinal scanner and a subcutaneous RFID chip. In theory, the DNA-tagged biosensor on the RFID chip rendered it inert outside his body—for his protection. *He* could imagine ways around that, all on the grisly side, so surely the inmates had, too. They were so much smarter than he.

Some choice he had had: accept a job here as a civilian contractor or end up here anyway. His discharge was still fresh. The Army could recall him and post him anywhere. Either way, secrets didn't come more classified than the inner sanctum at this facility. Revealing what went on here, even to Sladja or Kim, would get Aaron sent far away, for a very long time. Ah, homeland "security."

Not to mince words, he was a prison doctor in an unacknowledged, maximum-security federal prison, whose cover story was being a unit of a state maximum-security psychiatric prison. A mystery wrapped within a riddle inside a snake pit. Maybe the inmates *were* insane, among their other problems, but Aaron knew he wasn't qualified to judge.

In fewer words, he'd been screwed.

The absence of choices didn't make Aaron feel any better about himself. Last night he'd given Kim false hope that "the warden" might eventually allow her, or at least Brent's family, to visit. He'd lied about trying to deliver the gift book. *Nothing* from an unofficial source went to these prisoners. He'd dissembled about Dan Garner and his investors' situation. The government very badly wanted exclusive rights to the defunct company's technology and the recovered bot-assembly vessels. A national-security exemption from civil suits, immunity from criminal charges, and total silence had been the quid pro quo.

Just damage control, Aaron had been assured. *Don't worry about it.*

There was much about which he wasn't supposed to worry. Okay, so all suspected Emergent were accounted for. Who was to say Homeland Security's suspicions were imaginative enough, or that anyone could trust anything any of the Emergent said? And then there were the no-nonsense assurances Aaron had been given that *all* the bot inventory was accounted for. Those only triggered his bullshit detector. Garner Nanotech had been far too thoroughly destroyed to ever know with certainty what had or hadn't been taken.

No amount of legerdemain could make this situation better.

Aaron got a cup of coffee and hid in his office. There was plenty of paperwork. Many of his patients had arrived fairly banged up. No one had had surgery for a while now, but many continued in physical therapy. A car wreck was a big insult to the body, even with a nanosuit.

And a bigger insult without a suit.

Aaron had observed Charles's autopsy, yet another secret he kept from Kim. Charles had had masses of unusual structure in his head—as squashed as the brain was, some things were unmistakable. Thousands of bots lay scattered throughout. Unusual nerve bundles connected the bots, and more bundles threaded throughout the neocortex in ways no neurologist permitted a look had ever seen.

None of that proved a second consciousness, but it all suggested one. PET scans—these prisoners had no rights—only reinforced the impression. Many of the unusual connections glowed like fire in the scans. Also very classified, of course.

Aaron's masters had no idea what to do with their prisoners. What *could* you do with supergenius sociopathic terrorist bombers, most of them with police, military, and even counterterrorism expertise? Not put them into any general prison population. Never, ever, allow them to go free. If those were the only choices, Aaron guessed the prisoners would have been guantanamoed, or worse, by now. So someone, somewhere, was seriously considering somehow trying to make use of these brilliant minds.

The most anxious man in the prison . . .

By midmorning, Aaron could no longer stand his office or own company. The one way he knew to cope was to do some good here, whatever the government's agenda. He passed through another checkpoint, into the viewing area that abutted the prison dayroom. Even after four months here, Aaron thought the inmates looked naked without VR specs.

An LED array showed the interior cameras and audio bugs all operating properly. More green status lights blinked reassuringly on the knockout-gas canisters. The unit had a single disciplinary measure: at any infraction, by any inmate, flood the entire area with the gas. These prisoners were too dangerous to move among while conscious. The only way Aaron ever treated patients here was if they were allowed out through the mantrap, with an armed escort, in plastic leg restraints and handcuffs the entire time.

Aaron played a game of chess with Alan Watts, losing in seventeen moves (and sensing that even to last that long was a gift). He discussed biology with Tyra Kurtz and baseball with Manny Escobar. He feigned indifference to the staccato tabletop finger tapping of Morgan Mc-Grath and Merry Ramirez. Encrypted messages, obviously, only the NSA had yet to break the code. Aaron thought about the thousands of computers wired into the prisoners' heads, and shuddered.

RFID sensors and CCTV showed Brent in his cell. Eventually, Aaron called over the PA for Brent to come out.

Brent took his time appearing, but it was attitude, not injury. He was hardly limping anymore. "Hello, Aaron."

"Hi, Brent." Aaron took a seat, then gestured at a chair across the partition. All the furniture inside was nicked and dented, made of soft wood. "I saw Kim yesterday and she asked about you. I thought you'd want to know."

Brent rubbed his chin. "How is she?"

"Good." *What did one more lie matter?* "And I finally met her new husband. Nice guy."

"Nick? Yeah, he is. Took his time asking, though." A hint of a sad smile. "Maybe I can take a bit of credit that Nick finally did ask. The life-is-too-short principle, and all that."

"And how are you doing, Brent?"

His patient chewed that over for a long time. "I could be better."

Aaron stood to go. "I know how you feel."

Brent stayed in his chair for a full 4.72 seconds after Aaron left: fixing details of the encounter in his mind, reviewing every nuance of Aaron's demeanor and every subtle implication thereof. The paisley pattern to the necktie and the slight asymmetry to the knot. The razor nick on his chin. Every word choice, oral hesitation, shift in posture, and eye blink.

Kim and Nick married, Brent thought. A paper-thin silver lining.

You're welcome, One responded across his vision.

For all the sarcasm, One's politeness was real. Its main source of stimulus, with the Internet out of reach, lay in mining Brent's memories—and the further back One delved, the less it understood. It needed explanation and interpretation from the mind that had *experienced* that world, the mind that had made those memories.

So for a while, at least: a truce.

They'll let us out, One wrote. *Sooner or later.*

In the part of Brent's brain still wholly his, he hoped not. He had far too much on his conscience.

The government doesn't care about your conscience, One countered. *It wonders only under what circumstances it can trust me/us, and what I/we can do for it.*

That One might be correct was the scariest notion of all.

Brent ambled around the little prison. Concrete everywhere except for the thick windows and viewing wall. Those were polycarbonate resin thermoplastic: bulletproof. A single way in or out: the transparent mantrap whose controls were on the other side. Sensors everywhere, presumably many more than the naked eye could see. Nothing inside made of metal, not even in the plumbing fixtures, with which to scrape at the walls or short out sensors. Knockout gas at the ready. As a general engineer, Brent could find no fault with his captors' precautions.

What he wouldn't give for a fern, a cactus, a weed.

He went over to Alan for some chess. Five games took less than ten minutes, mostly spent handling the pieces. All five ended in stalemate. Every opening, gambit, or ruse any of them knew had long since propagated throughout the group; every Emergent could forecast sequences of move and countermove and counter-countermove . . . for many turns ahead. "Thanks for the games," Brent said. "Poker?"

"I'm in," Alan said.

Poker offered a more reliable diversion. All their heads were full of computers; the big variable was in the ability to bluff, and bluffing was a slipperier skill than chess. Money was totally useless now, of course. The only purposes to poker were ego trip and head game.

Brent/One sauntered over to Morgan and Merry. They tapped non-stop, their meaning hidden. Public-key encryption, with new keys to be tapped/distributed more often, Morgan had assured them, than the NSA could crack the older ones. Messaging about escape, most likely. What else was worth keeping secret?

"Anyone for poker?" Brent asked.

"Why not," Morgan said. Merry nodded, still tapping.

Brent had no idea what they tapped about. The decryption key wasn't among the few anyone had shared with him.

They enlisted two more players and Alan dealt. The tapping never stopped.

Any news? Morgan asked Brent. This time, the encryption was one for which everyone here—even Brent—had been given the matching decryption key.

No, Brent answered. There never was news. *Personal stuff.*

No novel ways to screw us over? Morgan tapped.

For who to screw them over? Their jailors or Brent?

Since their imprisonment, Morgan never missed a chance to goad Brent. If Brent could have been killed without also killing One—why, he would be dead. Few of the others would have objected.

Simple math, One wrote pointedly. *Simple justice.*

Quite simple. The Emergent, in all their diversionary attacks, had collectively killed twelve—out of billions. Brent, through his virus, had assaulted *every* overmind. But only in the case of Two had Brent wholly succeeded.

One twisted the knife: *Splattering Charles in the process. Very humane.*

To whom, add three completely innocent strangers, killed by Emergent cars gone out of control. And for what? The bots always reset. The overmind always came back.

But if Brent had not stopped the Emergent, he *had* delayed them.

There had been a cessation in transformations. He must take victories where he could.

Not even One could refute that.

Brent won the first hand with a full house, earning fifty broom straws.

Enjoy your little victory, Morgan tapped. *The last laugh will be ours.*

When they got out? Using tools and weapons fashioned from the clothes on their backs, paper plates, and plastic spoons?

"Now here's my plan," the optimistic prisoner said in that well-remembered cartoon.

Only it wasn't funny when the inmates were *so* much smarter than the jailors.

monday, may 29, 2017

Dr. Amreesh Singh strode the halls of the Clarksburg, West Virginia, Veterans Administration hospital, making his daily rounds. On a normal shift he felt overworked, hard-pressed to spend even a few minutes with each patient. Today was worse: the hospital teemed with Memorial Day visitors, many insistent upon a word with the doctor, while much of the staff had the day off. Singh made the time to regret how the patients who most needed visitors were seldom the ones to receive them. Like the man at his next stop, two transfers and three states removed from where he had entered the VA system.

The hulking, gloomy patient in room 12 seemed endlessly curious. Some days he read for hours without stop: books, old magazines, discarded newspapers, whatever he managed to scrounge. Some days he pestered everyone who came by—doctor, nurse, orderly, or fellow patient, it didn't matter—about the strangest things, as though he had never felt the rain or seen a dog or done any of a thousand things that *everyone* had done. An ordinary mugging had put him into the hospital, but that months-earlier head injury wasn't what kept him here. Something inside him had snapped. He had been passed along to Clarksburg for a reason: this was one of the VA's few long-term psychiatric facilities.

The patient had a name, of course—John Doe didn't get to fill a bed in the overcrowded VA system, let alone a bed in the psych ward—but few here used it. After some interminable bout of questions one of the

nurses had dubbed him the Renaissance Man. That caught on, mor-
phed to Leonardo, and got shortened quickly enough to Leo. Leo
didn't mind; if anything, the nickname seemed to amuse him.

Singh found Leo rocking on the cracked plastic cushions of the too-
small chair in his tiny room. He wore pajamas, slippers, and a thread-
bare robe. He shrugged answers to questions, his attention on one of
the tattered paperback books the patients circulated among themselves, mumbling to himself as he read.

With so many visitors around today, Singh counted himself lucky
that Leo only muttered. On his bad days Leo was apt to rave, befud-
dled by voices only he heard. Only they weren't even quite voices, apparently. Leo could never explain.

A sad case, Singh thought, *here for the long haul.*

The man known as Leo stiffened in his chair and closed his book.

Everything suddenly seemed so clear. The recurring nightmares
suddenly had logic to them. And the voices . . .

There was but one voice, and it wasn't even a voice exactly. *Can you
understand me?* the man known as Leo read.

"Yes," he said, unsteadily.

Do you remember?

Remember what? he thought, and something wonderful happened!
He no sooner posed a question than an answer appeared, crisp and
clear, in his mind's eye. The image of a warrior, a comrade in arms, in
peril. A friend, prone on the floor, betrayed. A blood brother who
needed his help.

The captain!

Leo swiveled his chair to face the door. He waited until an unac-
companied visitor about his size passed. "Excuse me," Leo called softly
to the man. "Would you mind coming in for a second? It's about your
friend."

"About Colin?"

Whoever. "There's something you should know about Colin."

Leo motioned Colin's friend into the tiny room, "So Colin won't overhear," and shut the door behind them. A chop to the back of the neck and the friend crumpled. Leo tied and gagged the man with strips torn from the tattered bathrobe, and left him, unconscious, shoved out of sight beneath the bed. "It's nothing personal," Leo said.

Wearing his victim's clothes and visitor pass, Leo rapped on the ward's locked door. He didn't know the security guard stuck with to-day's holiday duty—and the guard didn't know Leo. "It's very sad," he said, as the guard let him out.

Five minutes later, the man everyone called Leo strolled out the hospital's front door. Only his name wasn't Leo; it was Liu.

He was Ethan Liu, and he had an urgent mission, and he wasn't alone—

Somewhere, Captain Morgan needed his/their help.

about the author

Edward M. Lerner has degrees in physics and computer science, a background that kept him mostly out of trouble until he began writing full-time. His books include the novels *Probe*, *Moonstruck*, and *Fools' Experiments* and the collection *Creative Destruction*. His short fiction has appeared in *Analog*, *Artemis*, *Asimov's*, *Darker Matter*, *Jim Baen's Universe*, and several anthologies. He also writes the occasional nonfiction technology article.

In collaboration with Larry Niven, Ed wrote the novels *Fleet of Worlds*, *Juggler of Worlds*, and *Destroyer of Worlds*. All three novels, set in Niven's "Known Space," are prequels to the Nebula–, Hugo–, and Locus Award–winning *Ringworld*.

Lerner lives in Virginia with his wife, Ruth. His website can be found at www.sfwa.org/members/lerner/.